THE UNEXPECTED MR. HOPKINS

Book Six

Of

The Cassie Black Trilogy

TAMMIE PAINTER

Yes, book six, because trilogies (like undead witch hunters) refuse to be tamed.

The Unexpected Mr. Hopkins
Book Six of The Cassie Black Trilogy

Copyright © 2025 by Tammie Painter, All Rights Reserved

Daisy Dog Media supports copyright. Copyright fuels and encourages creativity, free speech, and legal commerce. Thank you for purchasing an authorized copy of this book and supporting the hard work of the author. To comply with copyright law you agree to not reproduce, scan, distribute, or upload any part of this work in any form without permission from the author.

This book is a work of fiction. Names, characters, places, and incidents either are the product of the author's imagination or are used fictitiously. Any resemblance to persons, living or dead, business establishments, events, or locales is entirely coincidental. This story was concocted entirely with human creativity; no generative AI was used in its creation.

You may contact the author by email at
Tammie@tammiepainter.com

Daisy Dog Media
Portland, Oregon 97222, USA

First Edition, February 2025
also available as an ebook

ALSO BY TAMMIE PAINTER

The Undead Mr Tenpenny: Cassie Black #1
The Uncanny Raven Winston: Cassie Black #2
The Untangled Cassie Black: Cassie Black #3
The Unusual Mayor Marheart, Cassie Black #4
The Unbearable Inspector Oberlin, Cassie Black #5
The Unexpected Mr Hopkins, Cassie Black #6
The Unwanted Inheritance of the Bookman Brothers
Hoard It All Before (A Circus of Unusual Creatures Mystery)
Tipping the Scales (A Circus of Unusual Creatures Mystery)
Fangs A Million (A Circus of Unusual Creatures Mystery)
Beast or Famine (A Circus of Unusual Creatures Mystery)
The Great Escape: 15 Tales of Humor, Myth, and Magic
Domna: A Serialized Novel of Osteria (Six-Part Series)
The Trials of Hercules: Book One of the Osteria Chronicles
The Voyage of Heroes: Book Two of the Osteria Chronicles
The Maze of Minos: Book Three of the Osteria Chronicles
The Bonds of Osteria: Book Four of the Osteria Chronicles
The Battle of Ares: Book Five of the Osteria Chronicles
The Return of Odysseus: Book Six of the Osteria Chronicles
13th Hour: Tales from Light to Midnight

WHAT READERS ARE SAYING...

ABOUT THE UNDEAD MR TENPENNY...

"...a clever, hilarious romp through a new magical universe..."

—Sarah Angleton, author of Gentleman of Misfortune

"Wow and wow again! I absolutely loved this book! You get such a feel for the characters and the story is so fast paced you don't want to put it down."

—Goodreads Reviewer

"Man oh man, did I love this book!"

—Jonathan Pongratz, author of Reaper

"...suffused with dark humor and witty dialogue, of the sort that Painter excels at..."

—Berthold Gambrel, author of Vespasian Moon's Fabulous Autumn Carnival

"...a fun and entertaining read. Great wit too."

—Carrie Rubin, author of The Bone Curse

ABOUT THE UNCANNY RAVEN WINSTON...

"More, please!"

—Goodreads Reviewer

"...quirky with a capital Q, and I mean that in the best way! ...I laughed out loud several times while reading this..."

—Bookbub Reviewer

"Magic, mayhem, mystery, it's all here."

—Bookbub Reviewer

ABOUT THE UNTANGLED CASSIE BLACK...

"...a great ending to a truly delightful ride."

—Bookbub Reviewer

"...super captivating! If you love magical hijinks, punny witticisms, and crazy adventure, then this is the series for you!"

—Bookbub Reviewer

"A truly satisfying end to a charming, funny, action-filled trilogy."

—Goodreads Reviewer

"The greatest secrets are always hidden in the most unlikely places."

—Roald Dahl

THE UNEXPECTED MR. HOPKINS

A FINAL NOTE BEFORE WE BEGIN

A little wasp-, math-, and alligator-filled warning…

This is the third book in The Cassie Black Trilogy 2.0. And since I find it's always good to start a book off with a dollop of mathematical confusion, that also makes it the sixth book in The Cassie Black Trilogy overall.

Now, if I haven't lost you already…

The Cassie Black Trilogy 2.0 is very much a traditional trilogy, meaning that the entire story takes place over the course of three books. So, if you haven't read Books Four and Five (*The Unusual Mayor Marheart* and *The Unbearable Inspector Oberlin*) before diving into this one, you're going to feel very, very, *very* lost.

Yes, I know getting lost can be a great way to discover new places and people, but it can also leave you stranded in a pit of ravenous alligators that you'll struggle to escape, only to find yourself smacking face first into a wasp nest occupied by wasps who have just won the Angriest Wasps of the Year Award.

So, unless you are both an alligator wrangler and a wasp whisperer, please spend some time with **The Unusual Mayor Marheart** and **The Unbearable Inspector Oberlin** before you start exploring the pages of this book.

And if you have already read those two tomes, **I'm so glad to see you back**, because it's finally time to wrap up Cassie's latest misadventure with *The Unexpected Mr Hopkins*.

PROLOGUE
ME AGAIN

Morelli here. Somehow I've gotten suckered, yet again, into starting out one of Black's books. Which really makes me wonder how that disaster of a tenant of mine can write hundreds upon hundreds of pages about her misadventures, but yet she has to fob the prologues off to me.

Normally, I'd chalk it up to laziness, but this time her fobbing off is due to the fact that she's landed herself in a pretty big dumpster fire. Namely, getting arrested. Now, while having her locked up and out of my sight is the stuff of my wildest dreams, in this case, I'm going to have to say it's a bit unfair.

I mean, all she was trying to do was warn Inspector Oberlin that these jewels she's been finding might be part of a plan to destroy the Magic world. But he interpreted Cassie's email as her throwing around a bunch of threats. So, now the jewels are locked away in one of the Academy's evidence boxes, and Cassie Black is locked away in one of the Academy's jail cells on the grounds that she's a danger to society.

As if.

I'm not saying she can't get up to a world of no good without even trying, but she can barely organize a cleaning schedule for her apartment, so how could anyone think her capable of arranging even a smidge of world domination?

But I digress. Busby Tenpenny's working on that side of things. Meanwhile, Lola's neighbor, Bunny, is missing; Cassie's former boss, Mr Wood, might be missing; and while many people think Cassie's parents are missing, they're actually on a mission for HQ and are uncovering some pretty interesting stuff — don't worry, last I checked, breaking the Confidentiality Spell to Norms like you ain't punishable.

On the up side, she's made buddy-buddy with the editor at the *Herald* after he spilled the beans about all those nasty opinion pieces about her (some of which were hilarious, by the way). And she and Alastair have finally gotten over their little spat. Although, that involved him revealing to her how he'd gotten all mopey over some silly prophecy that said Black might have to die to save the world. Which, I'll admit, maybe a few months ago I might've daydreamed about her being permanently out of my life, but these days that just doesn't sound so great.

Not great at all, if I'm telling the Great Troll's honest truth.

And, well, I probably shouldn't make this prologue about me, but Cassie gave me instructions to write whatever I wanted, so who's to stop me writing about what's new in my world, right? After all, I'm an integral part of the story too. I'm not just a doily-crocheting, bone-healing, TV-binging troll. I got depth. I got spin-off-character potential, if you ask me.

I also got a little bit of a broken heart because Matilda Marheart… well, I thought we was getting along pretty good. I even told her I don't mind she's a vampire so long as she don't mind that I'm half-troll. I made her that crochet version of her dragon Caliban, we had some dates, and I thought we was starting to become a thing. But now she's being all distant, and I don't know what that means. I'd like to believe she's not part of this supposed vampire uprising HQ's all worked up about, but her behavior lately…

Sorry, I'd love to go on more about Mattie, but Black said I had to keep this intro and catch-up under seven hundred words, and it's getting pretty darn close, so I best let you loose on this story of hers.

She just better have included all my witty quips and daring deeds.

CHAPTER ONE
THE COZINESS OF CONCRETE

"But you told me never to come back here," I said as Oberlin frog-marched me to the intake desk located on the ground floor of the Academy.

"To the school portion. I always knew I'd be seeing you in the law enforcement portion of this building one day. If you'd ever made it into the Academy's yearbook, I'd have put you down as Most Likely to be Arrested for a Future Offense."

"And that offense would be what, exactly?" I asked. Oberlin, by now, had grabbed some paperwork and started filling it out as the desk clerk gave me a sympathetic smile. Which I have to say was surprising given that most people in MagicLand lately greeted me with glares and glowers. And that was before I'd committed any arrestable offenses.

Not that I'd committed any in this instance, mind you. After Oberlin had kicked me out of the Academy, I'd been attempting to become a private detective. Things had started out well when Mayor Matilda Marheart had hired me to solve the case of the Missing Boncoeur Jewel. I'd also been on the hunt for several other missing objects, one of which was a massive and very problematic book, but several of which were small gems with personal meanings to their owners.

After much brain wrangling, historical education, and Crown Jewel viewing, I'd taken the wild guess that these smaller trinkets I'd already found (or had been sent, as was the case with a tiara that one of Morelli's contacts had swiped from a local museum), might somehow join together to create the larger, heart-shaped jewel the mayor was so desperate to get her hands on.

Which sounds pretty darn clever, right? The only trouble: there's a potential vampire uprising in the works, Mayor Matilda Marheart is a vampire, and this jewel, once assembled, could be used to defeat the vampires' worst enemy, which everyone assumes is us Magics because the discrimination laws we enacted against vampires turned out to do nothing but *increase* discrimination against them.

Anyway, in my attempt to warn my arch-enemy Inspector "Walrus Face" Oberlin about what the jewel could do, I wasn't terribly clear, and he read the email I'd sent him as me plotting against MagicLand. So, mere minutes after Alastair and I had made up after what felt like weeks of us not speaking, I ended up being hauled off to take up residence in one of the Academy's finest jail cells.

"That offense would be," Oberlin sniped as a pen began jotting his exact words onto an intake form, "the possession of objects which could be used to stage a coup against a magical community. Tenpenny, what's the statute number?"

"ROS 643.37."

The Tenpenny in this case would be Tobey Tenpenny, my cousin (to some degree or other) who was attending the Academy as a student and who had been assisting Oberlin on quite a few cases lately. As he cited that statute number, Tobey looked rather nauseous. And for good reason. His second attempt at the Exams (the test he had to pass to become an official police detective) was the following morning, and he was still suffering from an incurable case of test anxiety. He'd already failed his first stab at the Exams, but he'd somehow convinced himself that one more study session with me the hour before his second try would have him acing every question. But unless Oberlin suddenly got some sense into his head (highly unlikely) and let me go, that study session simply wasn't going to happen.

"Objects found at the business address of the accused," Oberlin went on as the enchanted pen continued its work, "include a book of troubling spells, a bag of marbles, a peacock brooch, and a pendant of the type formerly given to top performing agents at HQ. Her possession of them is highly suspicious."

"It's not highly suspicious," I complained. "They're all objects of clients I had."

"*Had* being the key word," Oberlin said dryly. As he and the pen finished up the form, Tobey passed me apologetic glances and mouthed words of encouragement, including how Mr Tenpenny, as a high-ranking member on the HQ team, would be on his way as soon as possible to sort all this out. Or, at least, I think that's what he meant. Lip reading isn't exactly my strong suit.

And if you're wondering where the tiara's jewel was, so was I. I knew it had a type of Concealment Charm on it, but for no one to have seen it in the safe, for it to not be part of Oberlin's haul? Well, that was either very worrying or some very clever magic.

Once Oberlin had signed the form and passed it to the clerk, the next event on the agenda for this outing to my friendly neighborhood cop shop was to have my fingertips coated in ink then pressed onto a record card. They then took what I'm sure was a lovely photo and read me a list of what I could and couldn't do. After this, I was handed off to a female warden whose name badge read *Gilly,* and whose lush and shiny auburn hair seemed too Golden-Age-Hollywood glamorous for a police officer.

I've never been in a Norm jail — which Morelli tells me comes as quite a surprise — but from everything I've learned from Professors Television and Movies, when the police book a perp they take all of the person's possessions and put them somewhere in storage. Then, when the hardened and now-aged criminal is released, some clerk — who is required to be either a gnarled, embittered old man or a scrawny, scruffy, and clueless young officer — sits behind a caged screen and counts back each item to the ex-con.

This didn't happen in Magic jail. Maybe they waited until Magic prison for that, or maybe Oberlin had been too gleeful over my arrest to remember proper procedure. As such, I'd been allowed to remain in my own clothes and to keep my phone, my Dollar Store notepad, and my pen.

Even so, as Gilly escorted me away from the intake desk, she asked what I had on me, then inspected the pen to ensure it hadn't been magicked to make it truly mightier than the sword. She then enchanted my phone so I couldn't make outgoing calls or texts. When I asked about this odd rule, she said it had been put in place after a prisoner had called every grocery store in MagicLand and placed daily orders for any fish or meat item from the close-out section.

"Someone let the deliveries pile up, and we couldn't get the smell out of here for months," she explained as we stopped in front of a cell that, with its floor-to-ceiling iron bars, reminded me of a jail cell from one of Morelli's 1950s sitcoms.

"The bars have been coated with protective magic, so I'd really recommend against trying anything," she told me as she pulled out the keys to my new digs. "And I mean *anything*. We had a guy in here who tried to perform an Amoeba Spell to slip through the bars. Instead, the cell turned it into an *Aretha* Spell, and he suddenly found himself in a sequined dress singing 'Respect' with a strong Motown voice."

"That actually doesn't sound too bad."

"It wouldn't have been, but the spell only seemed to know the chorus and wouldn't allow him to stop singing that chorus. The same lyrics over and over until Dr Dunwiddle came in and reset him. Now the mere mention of the word *respect* drives him to tears."

"Well, I don't plan on being in here long," I said confidently. I didn't mention that I wouldn't be able to magic anything anyway since my powers were on the fritz, and no one, not even Dr Dunwiddle, could figure out why. One spell could come out with more force behind it than a kick from a seriously perturbed mule, while the next might be as weak as a starving parakeet.

"That's what they all say," Gilly said, not without a hint of sympathy in her words. "And it's true. You'll likely spend a few days here, then there'll be the arraignment, then you'll be taken off to a higher security prison." Her face scrunched apologetically. "Sorry, that's not what you meant, was it?"

"Not really."

"Well, best of luck, regardless."

"What about visitors?" And yes, I was thinking about the picnic Alastair and I had been about to go on before Oberlin so rudely threw a spanner in the works. I mean, a cell in the Academy wasn't exactly a scenic landscape, but it'd be better than not getting any time together at all.

The guard shook her head. "Only people on official business, I'm afraid. HQ reps, your legal team, that sort of thing. And me," she added with an air of forced camaraderie. "Now, in you go. I'll be back up with some food soon."

The moment I stepped over the threshold, the barred door clanged behind me. I've never had claustrophobia, but the cramped quarters instantly had me imagining the walls closing in on me.

My new (and hopefully temporary) home was so tiny that if I stood in the center of it, I could reach my arms out and touch the two side walls and still have a slight bend in my elbows.

Inspecting my confines took all of ten seconds. The place had been made wonderfully cozy with the latest in trendsetting concrete and tres chic floor-to-ceiling grey paint. The furnishings consisted of a narrow bed and small desk with a stool, all of which were magically stuck to the floor. Well, I hope it was just magic gluing them in place. Other options didn't bear considering. A small, barred window near the ceiling of the back wall let in some light, but was too high for me to see anything but sky.

The place didn't appear to be ensuite, and I started fretting about The Facilities. Was there a shared bath? Did I just have to hold it until someone came along with a bedpan? Because let me tell you, with this whole situation putting my nerves on high alert, my gut was roiling and a place to go was becoming imminently necessary.

Again, as I said, the cell was small; even at a quick glance, it's not like I was going to miss one of its amenities. But as I paced across the limited space and stepped into the far corner, I tripped and nearly fell into a toilet.

I stepped back. No toilet. I stepped forward, and the toilet and a small sink appeared. When I turned around to take in the rest of my home away from home, things appeared as blurry as if looking through a fogged up window. I breathed a sigh of relief (and then tended to other forms of relief) as I thanked the Academy's designers for their privacy considerations.

Once done, I dropped onto the bed. And instantly regretted it. The mattress was about as thick as a worn-out sweater, and the frame that mattress was on was made of solid, unyielding concrete. The pain jarred up from my tailbone to the top of my head.

I cursed Oberlin. Could he really hold this much of a grudge against me just because I called him a dimwitted, pregnant walrus? He knew I had clients, who those clients were, and what they'd been after. One had been his own damn wife! And the book of troubling spells? That was Wordsworth's book. Well, his book minus two pages, which was why he'd refused to sign off on a job done and take the book back to his library at HQ.

My point being: I didn't steal any of those things to start a coup. In fact, I'd very much hoped to prevent one. Which brought to the forefront of my reeling mind that Oberlin had mentioned the Boncoeur Jewel when he'd arrested me — the very jewel that could give Matilda and the vampires power over their enemies. How had he known about that jewel? More importantly, *what* did he know about it?

I let out a grunt of defeat. There was nothing I could say that would convince Walrus Face of my innocence, or that my email had been an attempt to work with him, not against him. Luckily, I had plenty of people who would vouch for me. Mr Tenpenny, Olivia, Fiona, Dr Dunwiddle. They all knew about my client list. Even Morelli would stand up for me in a pinch. I had to wait until I could speak with them. Until then, I eased back onto the wafer thin mattress and stared up at the ceiling.

Which got pretty dull after about two minutes. And rather painful as my vertebrae and hip bones pressed into the unforgiving surface. I pulled out my phone, went into one of my half-dozen e-reader apps, and selected *The Count of Monte Cristo,* seeing it as a fitting choice for my situation and as something to take my mind off mysterious jewels, angry vampires, and power-abusing walruses.

CHAPTER TWO
A TENPENNY VISIT

About an hour after my incarceration, Gilly was true to her word and brought me a— well, I guess you'd call it a meal.

This 'meal' did not include a single treat from Spellbound Patisserie. Which, by all the laws known to man, should be deemed cruel and unusual punishment. Instead, I was handed a bowl of stale Cheerios that had the texture of rubber tires, and a cup of tea so weak I wondered how many times the tea bag had been reused.

It was late afternoon before I was able to speak to anyone I knew. The moment I saw him approaching, I ran up to the bars like a stray at the pound who's convinced this person will be their salvation.

"Mr Tenpenny, you've got to get me out of here," I pleaded.

"I'm still having trouble understanding why they put you in here in the first place."

"Yeah, you and me both. It's Oberlin. He's had it in for me since I was in his classes."

"No, that's not what I mean. Well, on a basic level it is. But if he suspected you of traitorous crimes against the Magic community, he should have had you sent directly to HQ, where we would have sorted it out the minute you showed up. But he's put you here," Mr T said irritably. The look on his face had me dropping heavily onto my concrete bed with dismay, frustration, and exasperation. And a fair amount of spinal pain. Take it from me: When you're trying to execute a perfectly sulky butt drop, concrete beds are best avoided.

"Tell me this isn't some Magic bureaucracy tangle," I said wearily.

"I'm afraid it is. Once you've been processed into a jail that isn't directly under HQ jurisdiction, it takes several rounds of paperwork to sort it out."

"You can't just...?" I waggled my fingers at the lock.

"Afraid not. I am sorry."

"So I'm really stuck in the hoosegow?"

"You should refrain from that word," Mr T said critically. "It doesn't suit you."

"The clink? The slammer? In the nick? The big house? Club Fed?" Even Gilly the Guard grinned at that one. "I mean, look at this place." I thumped the rock-hard bed. "It makes Morelli's building seem like a royal castle." I then wondered if Morelli might consider another remodel to turn the apartment building into an actual castle. After all, who ever heard of witches and wizards and trolls living in a two-story, brutalist-style home?

"It is rather spartan," commented Mr Tenpenny. "Even the Tower's holding cells offer more comfort than this. We figure if a person truly is innocent before proven guilty, they should be treated as such. Do you mind?" he asked the guard. She looked doubtful. "No one, unless they are inside the cell, will notice. And whenever Miss Black isn't in there, it will revert to being as dismal as before." After Gilly gave a shrug that was part acquiescence and part curiosity, Mr T dragged his fingers across the bars. As he made his way from left to right, the cell also transformed from left to right.

The barred front of the cell remained the same, but the two grey side walls brightened to a soothing shade of turquoise, and the window wall morphed into a mural featuring a vast savannah, complete with roaming elephants, zebras, and giraffes. And I do mean *roaming*. They migrated across the scene, occasionally stopping to nibble the vegetation.

A plush, deep magenta rug unfurled across the floor; the stool and desk transformed into two gorgeous pieces of ergonomic office furniture; and my bed, well, who would want to ever get out of a bed that fluffy and cozy? Unlike Pablo with his cat carrier conversion, Mr T did not provide me with hologram birds to chase. Which was regrettable since it might have helped in case I needed to try for an insanity plea.

I'll note here that Mr T also upgraded the loo, making it into a ridiculously vast space with that unattainable and over-the-top luxury of a bathroom straight out of a high-end interior design magazine. Seriously, though, how much room did he think I needed to pee?

"Thanks," I said, truly in wonder.

At Busby's invitation, Gilly stuck her face up to the bars and peered in. When she stepped back, she was smirking with approval, but merely said, "I see no difference."

"Now," Mr T said to me, "Olivia and I are sorting out the paperwork, but it will likely take time. A few days, a week at the most."

A few days? A week? I didn't have that much time. First, there was the due date for my detective's license application, which, even though Olivia had given me an extension, was still looming over me. Second, there was a vampire uprising that needed preventing. Third, and most concerning, were the missing people, namely Mr Wood.

"But I need your help with—"

"We're working on it, I promise. Olivia has your client list, and although your license application due date—"

"No, no, not that. I mean, yes, that, but Bunny, he's gone missing—"

"We have our best agents on that."

"Okay… Good to know, but Mr Wood is gone as well."

"Gone? How do you know?"

I explained Mr Wood's lack of texts, and what Daisy had seen with the Fairy Tags. These were small, magical gadgets (or possibly actual fairies, I still wasn't sure) that tracked the location of your luggage. Or in this case, your former boss, since Daisy had attached several dozen of them to Mr Wood before he'd left for the Cotswolds on a walking tour. And, as tense timing would have it, right before Oberlin premiered his Arrest Cassie Show, Daisy had informed me that every one of those tracking devices had stopped moving. Not disappeared. Not went offline. Just stopped moving. Which apparently wasn't normal.

"I never did trust anyone going to the Cotswolds," Busby muttered. Before I could say that Mr Wood may not have made it to his vacation destination, Mr T asked, "He was friendly with Morelli, wasn't he?"

"You can't suspect Morelli." Even I wouldn't stand for that. If anyone was going to accuse my landlord of high crimes, it would be me and me alone.

"No, of course not. It's just we have quite a few other items on our plates right now, so I might ask him to look into this. Although, Olivia does have him guarding Runa…"

"Trust me, Dr Dunwiddle will *not* mind a break from him."

Mr Tenpenny hesitated a moment before saying, "My apologies for sounding cruel, it's not how I intend this, but Nino Wood is a Norm, and the Magic community rarely looks into their disappearances." I understood, but I also felt distracted by a thought that wouldn't quite solidify. Then again, having to think about Morelli actually being useful does run the risk of breaking your brain. "In the meantime, chin up. I know you're of the opinion that we at HeadQuarters glibly allow things to slide past our limited attention spans, but we do know how to prioritize the problems of those who are special to us. Which is why we are diligently working on getting you out of here."

I probably should have gotten choked up about that, but all I could think about was Mr Wood. Well, and those rubbery Cheerios.

"Could you perhaps also prioritize sending in some fresh food for my meals? I think everything from the Academy's kitchens might have been on the shelf since the early eighties."

I gave Gilly an apologetic smile, to which she replied, "I assume you mean the 1880s?"

"I'll see what I can do," said Busby.

"And, Mr T?"

"Yes?"

"Could you let people know I can receive calls?"

"I would have thought you'd enjoy your time hidden away from everyone."

"I'm not the same anti-social person you met all those months ago."

"Indeed, you are not."

CHAPTER THREE
TRIGGER WORDS

I'd barely settled into my bed and book before Alastair called.

"I tried to come and see you," he said testily, "but they're saying no visitors are allowed unless on official business. They denied me entrance until I fill out a bunch of forms explaining my reason for visiting. Which they would then 'review'."

Alastair had apparently called the instant he stepped out of the Academy. He was so livid over being turned away from seeing me and was speaking with such vehemence that I could hear him through my sky-high window, which made for a weird and confusing sound duplication.

"Alastair," I said when he paused to catch his breath, "getting arrested for disturbing the peace is no way to hang out with me. So, please, calm down."

"Sorry, it's just the paperwork and bureaucracy and all of it," he growled. Literally growled, he was that riled up. "It's so frustrating."

"Really?" I snarked. "I have absolutely *no* experience with that sort of thing. You know, none of this would have happened if I'd been granted my detective's license when I'd solved Lola's Vanishing Vacuum case. If they'd just approved that stupid application, I'd be happily working away with HQ on the missing Magics stuff and be free and clear of all this jewel business."

Okay, maybe that wasn't true. Maybe Oberlin would have found some other way to haul me in on trumped-up charges, but at that moment, despite the cozy yet supportive bed Mr T had conjured, I really wanted to blame the bureaucratic thorn in my side for my predicament.

"Is there anything I can do?" Alastair asked.

"Besides figuring out some way to get me out of here?"

"Besides that, yes."

"You can make sure Leo publishes what he witnessed." Leo Flourish was the editor at the *Herald*, Rosaria's twice-daily newspaper. Through a video call, he'd seen my arrest in real time. He'd seen how Old Walrus Face had twisted the intention of my email about the jewels' potential danger against me. He'd also promised to make up for all the anti-Cassie articles his paper had been printing in recent weeks. If he was really my ally now, he wouldn't let a hot news item like this slip past him.

It was too late for his report to make it into the day's afternoon edition, but I wanted to be sure an eyewitness account to this injustice was front and center in tomorrow's morning paper. And, yes, I know, it's kind of weird that I now *wanted* my mishaps printed in the *Herald*, but this was a weird situation I never expected to find myself in. I explained all this to Alastair, and he agreed to contact Leo as soon as he was off the phone with me.

"Anything else?"

"Don't forget to feed Pablo. If you're afraid of him, then have Morelli put out food for him."

"I'm not afraid of him," Alastair said far too defensively.

"Kind of seemed like it," I teased.

"That attack of his just surprised me. I should have been more level-headed. I just… My mind's been elsewhere, I suppose."

"The commission?"

"Yeah, the commission," he said, his voice lifting. This was some mysterious project from some mysterious client that had been refusing to come together despite Alastair's talent with mechanical doodads. "That part I picked up from Uncommon Implements? I think it'll do the trick. Took them ages to get it in, but it's just what I needed. Sorry, I shouldn't be happy, but it'll be a relief to get that thing off my worktable."

"Then what?" I asked, since Penley Tremaine still hadn't reinstated Alastair's contract to make collectible timers for Tremaine's Toy Emporium. Tremaine had canceled the lucrative contract in a fit of misplaced petulance toward me after he'd gotten pulled in for questioning over the murder of Clive Coppersmith. Which meant, due to my troublesome clients, payment for this mystery commission was our only foreseeable source of income.

"Back to just working freelance, I suppose. I think enough people have gotten the bug for the timers that I can start some sort of home-based shop."

"You better check with Morelli first. He doesn't like changes to the building's usage codes unless he comes up with the idea first."

After a pause, Alastair said, "Sorry about the picnic. And about not talking to you about the prophecy."

"Yeah, you and me both."

It wasn't just that he hadn't spoken to me about the prophecy. He'd completely stopped talking to me for days on end except to snipe at me or complain about Pablo. Granted, the prophecy was worryingly spot-on about the jewels, the missing Magics, and my potential death, but he'd allowed his fear over what it said to drive a wedge between us. Of course, right when we'd finally made up and were about to head out for some much-needed time together, the Walrus had me locked up. Talk about your bad timing.

Alastair seemed about to say something more when a voice cut in across my phone. A tinny voice that sounded as if it had been recorded sometime in the early 1970s with the cheapest equipment on the market.

"This is the Academy's alert system. Your speech has included an excess of words that have triggered our alert system. Due to suspicions of escape attempts associated with these words, we will cut the connection in twenty seconds. This connection cannot be resumed until—" a blast of static covered up what I assumed to be a number "—hours have passed. Thank you for visiting the Academy's cells. Enjoy your stay."

"What words?" I asked irritably.

I hadn't really been expecting an answer, but the voice came back and stated, "Picnic, Pablo, worktable, and freelance. These are merely a few words that will trigger our system. Again, thank you for being a customer of the Academy's finest confinement lodgings."

"What the—?" I blustered. "How are those words in any way connected to a jailbreak attempt?"

"I can't believe they still have that system in place," Alastair commented. Then, speaking so quickly his words rushed over themselves, he added, "Look, Cass, I love you. I'll call as soon as I can get through ag—"

The line went abruptly silent, and for the first time in a long time, I felt truly alone.

I couldn't get back into my book after speaking with Alastair. First off, it was a bit difficult to focus on Edmond's nautical prowess on the *Pharaon* when I couldn't stop trying to figure out the exact scenario where *picnic*, *freelance*, and *worktable* had led to someone, perhaps named Pablo, staging a prison break.

My reading attention was again whisked away when Mr Tenpenny returned. Unfortunately, it was too soon for him to bring me any sort of updates on my release, but I suppose even HQ can't work miracles in less than an hour.

However, he did come bearing a box that set my mouth watering. A box that was quite hefty, I noted with some hope when he handed it to me. As soon as he left and Gilly went back to her other duties, I thoroughly checked the box's contents. To my dismay, no files had been baked into a baguette, and no skeleton keys had been slipped into the scones. Gwendolyn clearly needed to watch more prison break films.

Still, amongst the baguette and half a dozen treats (practically starvation rations, if you ask me) was a thick, roasted veggie sandwich. Gwendolyn had added a note saying she'd charmed the bread to not get soggy, so if the flavor was a little different from what I was used to, that was why.

Unless you count being able to determine the exact IBU of a beer from one sip, I don't exactly have the most refined palate. Even so, Gwendolyn's baking skills were so extraordinary that I doubt even the finest gourmand could have tasted the difference between her charmed and non-charmed sandwiches.

I wolfed down the veggie-stuffed bread, but decided not to dive into the pastries until I knew just how long I would need to ration my supplies. Or until I learned how often these survival boxes would be coming. I know… me showing self-control around sweets? What can I say? Jail does strange things to you.

Soon after I'd devoured the sandwich, a few more people rang, including Olivia, who reassured me that "this matter would be resolved, but it might take a little time." Rafi called soon after, wishing he could swap places with me because he'd been working on an Escape Hex and had yet to test it out in the field. This conversation set off the alert system, and he was cut off immediately. I'd assumed it had been the word *escape* that set it off, but the crackly and chipper voice informed me the trigger word this time had been *field*.

Runa called perhaps half an hour later and reminded me not to try to magic my way out of the jail cell, both because of my magical wonkiness and because she had no desire to fix whatever the hexes currently on the bars of my cell might do to me (apparently the cells shuffled between various retaliatory spells each week). She then complained that she was about to throw her own retaliatory hex on Morelli, who Olivia had recently made Runa's personal security troll. "He's like a shadow," she grumbled. "A shadow who insists on telling me better ways to do my job. I tell you, Cassie, if he ends up with his mouth permanently glued shut, I can't be held responsible."

Suddenly, from her end of the line, came sounds of a door opening, a bell dinging, someone crying, then Dr Dunwiddle asking what had happened this time. A brief, muffled conversation followed before Runa, sounding like she was at her wits' end, said she had to go to tend to Mrs Kawasara. Apparently, her latest gardening attempts had involved magically de-thorning her rose bushes, only to have the thorns sprout inside one of her heirloom apples right before she took a bite. Runa told Mrs Kawasara to get into the exam room, then muttered something about the woman looking like a poodle who'd been attacked by a porcupine.

Runa started to say she'd talk to Oberlin about continuing my sample collection, but the phone system had already been triggered. The combination of *apple* and *porcupine* were so concerning that my "calls would be monitored much more closely for the rest of my stay." Which the system hoped was meeting all my accommodation expectations.

CHAPTER FOUR
OH, SWEET SEABISCUITS!

Edmond Dantes was just about to wed Mercedes when my phone rang, startling me so hard the device fumbled right out of my hand. By the time I excavated the phone from the thick pile of Mr T's rug, the ringing was still going strong. And even though I didn't recognize the number, with little else to do, I accepted the call.

"Is this Miss Cassie Black?"

I groaned. Even in jail I couldn't escape a telemarketer trying to sell me something — probably an extended car warranty for the car I didn't even own. I didn't respond, but the caller continued on nonetheless. It was only then I noticed her bouncing British accent. "This is Jenny from Cotswolds Custom Tours."

"Um, hi," I said hesitantly, remembering it was already late afternoon in Portland. With the nine-hour time difference between the West Coast and the U.K., it would be well past Jenny's bedtime. I'd gotten used to HQ working at ungodly times, but a tour company calling in the wee hours? "Isn't it a little late for you to be working?"

"We at Cotswolds Custom Tours pride ourselves on being available at all times for the convenience of our clients."

I had no idea how to reply to this line that sounded like it came directly from a customer service training manual, so I merely said, "Uh-huh."

"We were wondering if you've heard from a Mr Nino Wood? He was meant to be on one of our tours. Records show he arrived at Heathrow, but we never managed to meet up with him at the airport. Of course, some people don't feel like waiting around for us and hop on the Tube or take a taxi to the hotel. And while it isn't uncommon for our guests and our greeters to miss each other, we usually find one another sometime over arrival day," she said cheerily. "I've been trying to call the number he gave us, but it only goes to his voice mail."

"You never met up with him? Ever?" I asked, feeling too much like I'd been sucker-punched in the gut to say anything else.

Mr Wood had arrived at Heathrow. That much I knew from the pictures he'd sent right after de-boarding. He hadn't gotten in touch since, and, before they stopped moving, no Fairy Tag blips had ever come from anywhere in the Cotswolds.

Because the Fairy Tags had only sent signals from London, I had told myself and reassured Daisy it was no big deal, that the first few days of the tour were spent sightseeing in London. I'd wanted to believe that Mr Wood hadn't been sending us photos of his retirement holiday because he'd forgotten his charger, didn't have a data plan for the U.K., or was simply too busy enjoying a wide variety of pig-based foodstuffs to keep us updated.

"Like I said," continued Jenny, "we do show a record of him having cleared passport control. After that, though, I'm afraid we've no sign of him. We're asking a few security people to examine the CCTV footage, but that could take a while. Since you were listed as his emergency contact, we thought it was time we get in touch."

Time to get in touch? He'd been absent from their little tour for three days. They were well overdue to get in touch!

Lately, I'd been debating the idea of whether Mr Wood —

who had somehow retained the magic Morelli had given him — was still a Norm, a Magic, or something halfway in between? Now, with this confirmation that he really was gone, my head swam with the fear that he'd been taken by whoever was kidnapping Magics. Which meant he could be anywhere.

Unfortunately, I was most definitely somewhere.

"I'm in a bit of bind right now, but—"

I hated what I was about to propose. Mr Wood had listed me (*me*!) as his emergency contact, the person he could count on, the person he knew would have his back if he got into trouble. But here I was, unable to help him. Grudgingly, I admitted to myself that there was someone else he trusted and who was equally concerned about him. And besides, it wouldn't be the first time she'd stolen my role in Mr Wood's life.

"Can I give you another number to call?" I asked. "The person is a friend of Mr Wood's, and she's in a better position to get the ball rolling. Would that be okay?"

"It would. We here at Cotswolds Custom Tours do pride ourselves on not losing our clients, and it would be in our best interest to locate him with any help you can provide."

Again, Jenny might have just read this directly from what her computer's Customer Service Perfect Prompt Program was displaying, but she did sound sincerely concerned. I gave her Daisy's number, feeling like an absolute heel for not being able to help Mr Wood myself after all he'd done for me.

Once Jenny confirmed the number, I told her to ring me with any questions or updates. I hung up but couldn't get back into Edmond's story. Mr Wood. He was actually missing. What was it with me and this serious issue of keeping the people close to me from vanishing?

* * *

The Unexpected Mr. Hopkins

Barely five minutes after I'd said goodbye to Jenny, my phone rang again. Who knew going to jail was the key to popularity? I took the call without glancing at the screen. I then cursed myself for not checking the number first.

Did I say I wanted calls? Why!? *Why* did I say I wanted calls?

"Oh my gosh, Cassie. Are you okay?" asked a voice that was brighter than a solar flare.

"I'm fine, Daisy. Why are you calling?"

Which I thought was a fair question. It's not like we were besties or anything. She worked for me because Mr Tenpenny had insisted I hire her after Mr Wood had announced his retirement. If not for that, we'd hardly ever speak.

"You're so funny, Cassie," Daisy tittered. "I'm calling because my friend is in jail. Duh. And I'm going to help get you out of there."

Oddly, I didn't scoff at this assertion, mainly because I could easily picture Daisy blinding the guards with her blazing white smile then bedazzling them with enough ditsy charm to Confound them, get their keys, then break me out of my cell right before their smile-stunned eyes.

"Don't trouble yourself. Mr T is working on it with HQ."

"Oh, fiddlesticks on that." Did she always speak this way or had her porous brain picked up Mr Wood's habit of cursing without curse words? "HQ'll take forever. And we need you out ASAP."

"Really? What? Like you miss me or something?" I asked, and for some reason I kind of hoped she did. It's always nice to be wanted, I guess. Even if it's being wanted by someone like Daisy.

"Of course, silly. And I was thinking about these classes I took a while ago, and how they might help—" There was a blip of silence on her end. "Hold that thought. I've got another call. Be back in a tick." The line went quiet for a few minutes, then Daisy burst back into the conversation with, "Oh my golly, Cassie! Mr Wood— That woman from the tour company, she said she called you, and now she called me, and— The Fairy Tags weren't wrong. Nino's gone. This is the worst thing to happen. Ever!"

"Worse than me being locked away for something I didn't do?" So much for our buddy-buddy moment.

"Oh, sweet Seabiscuits! It's all bad. Mr Wood is gone, you're in jail, and Tobey's going to fail his Exams tomorrow. It's like the worst week in the history of the world." I held my tongue about matters such as the Holocaust, a pair of world wars, me being made into an evil wizard's magic battery. Maybe the fumes from Daisy's nail polish had skewed her brain's sense of perspective. "What should we do? Where should I begin a search for him? I don't—"

"Daisy, stop," I said, cutting off her stream of panic before the Academy's Alert System cut her off for me. "The first priority is to get me out of here. You've been reading all those statute books. You must have come across something in them that might help."

"Well, sure. And then the classes I—"

"Look," I interrupted, because now was not the time to indulge Daisy's thoughts about how something like Beginning Watercolors from a continuing education group was going to be in any way helpful in this situation. She needed to focus her blonde brain on the task at hand. "If you remember anything from what you've read that might help with a wrongful arrest, let Busby or Olivia know. See what laws they can bend to get me out, then we can tackle Mr Wood's disappearance."

"Oh, my stars!" she enthused. "Are we going to solve a case together?"

I groaned, not thrilled about that 'together' part. Still, Mr

Wood needed us, and I needed all the help I could get. No matter how blonde or bubbly it was.

"We're going to try," I said through very tight lips as every piece of my being resisted the idea of partnering up with Daisy.

"I know just what to do, boss. Gosh, this is fun, isn't it?"

I let out a half-hearted noise of agreement. *Fun* was definitely not the F-word I'd been thinking of.

It was also not the F-word I blurted out an hour later when I saw who was standing outside my cell.

CHAPTER FIVE
THE PRINCELY PORTAL

"What are you doing here?" I asked at the sight of Morelli, not in a Gary-themed t-shirt, but in a three-piece suit that appeared to be cut just for him. I wondered if Mr T had done some sort of Expansion Hex on one of his own suits.

"Well," Morelli said in a very play-along-with-whatever-I-say manner, "as part of your legal team, I wanted to assess that our client was being treated properly."

"And am I?" I asked, wondering if he could see the work Busby had done to my cell.

"All looks on the up and up." Morelli then turned to Gilly and, using a polite tone I would never have thought him capable of, asked, "Could I have a private moment with Miss Black? Attorney-client stuff, and all that."

Gilly nodded, then stepped out of hearing distance as Morelli shifted his grip on the handle of the paper sack he'd brought in.

"Can't you harass Alastair for the rent?"

"Could, but it's nowhere near as fun."

"Did you really finagle your way in here just to pester me?"

"Nah, I mostly came to gloat about winning a bet on how long it would take you to get arrested."

"Who'd you make this wager with?" I asked indignantly.

"It was a betting pool. Had at least a dozen Magics in on it.

Most were from Rosaria, but a few wagers came in from HQ as well." He then explained that Rafi had joined in, but only to test out a Favorable Odds Charm he was working on.

Rather than elaborate, Morelli held out the paper grocery sack he'd been carrying. "For you. Thought it'd make the place more homey."

Gilly came over to peer in the bag. Once she nodded her approval, she passed it to me and stepped back to give us our privacy once more.

I reached into the bag and grabbed hold of something unbelievably soft to the touch. What I pulled out was a glittering purple pillow crocheted from, at a guess, Shimmer Sheep wool. Worked into the center on the front side was a cartoon likeness of Pablo.

"Thanks," I said awkwardly, truly appreciating the gesture. Then I came to my senses. "Hold on. You brought me home decor. Does that mean I'm not getting out anytime soon? What about this legal team you mentioned?"

"Let's just say, you have one, and I'm helping with a few technical matters."

"Why? What are you after?"

"Nothing. Does everyone who does something for you have to have an agenda?"

"Only half-trolls."

Morelli rolled his eyes. "So..." he began, as if hunting for small talk, which we did not normally do. "Good place to do some thinking, I imagine." I said it was. A long pause followed because, again, chit-chat is not our thing. "And what's been going through that head of yours? Or do I not want to know?"

I explained to him about the call from Cotswolds Custom Tours, about the Fairy Tags Daisy had put on Mr Wood, and about them going silent somewhere in London.

He considered this for a moment. Then, sounding pretty sure of his theory, said, "They could be inside a hidden portal."

"Hidden portal? In the middle of London?"

"Sure, that place is riddled with them. Hyde Park is especially tricky. And all the royal palaces are swarmed with 'em."

"Including the Tower of London?"

"Oh, yeah," Morelli confirmed emphatically. "Caused a bit of trouble with history, actually."

"Was this a portal you installed?" I asked, curiosity pushing my worries aside.

"Don't think so. That's not to say my team didn't build a few in our time. Served for good escape routes, and for getting in and out without the guards noticing." Then, as if realizing he was giving away information he shouldn't, he abruptly said, "They're all illegal, mind you, so don't go telling Olivia."

Portals, legal ones that is, all have to be registered with HQ to show where they start from and where they go to. Illegal portals, however, are not registered, and are often shoddily made, giving the user an uncomfortable ride. Still, they did the job in a pinch.

"I'll try not to bring it up," I told him. "So, this history?"

"You know the Princes in the Tower? Their disappearance?"

I nodded. These would be the two sons of Edward IV. When Edward died, the oldest of the two boys should have become king, but his Uncle Richard decided he wanted the job instead. Giving the impression he was only acting as regent, Uncle Richie put his nephews in the Tower of London, supposedly for their safekeeping, and swore to them that the oldest boy would be coronated 'any day now.'

Then, one night, the princes disappeared, were assumed dead, and Uncle Richie became King Richard III. All manner of speculation about who killed the princes has buzzed around the mystery ever since. Even at the time, questions were raised about whether they were killed at all when a boy named Perkin turned up in Somerset, claiming he was one of the princes. A claim that many people believed because the boy was apparently very convincing.

"Well," Morelli continued, darting a glance over his shoulder as if some nosy historian might be listening, "turns out, one of the Tower pixies left a hidden portal open one night when she was doing some maintenance. The portal went from the boys' room to a storage facility." Morelli then added sheepishly, "A storage facility somewhere in Somerset."

"So, the princes…?"

"For a while no one knew exactly where they'd gone. It was weeks before the pixie-portal connection was made, and that was only figured out when that Perkin kid started making his royal claims.

"Whole thing was a complete screw-up that shut down nearly all the Tower's hidden portals for a couple decades. Course, they were hidden, so it was a bit hard to account for all of them. Eventually, several were re-opened because monarchs liked to travel without the hassle of muddy roads. And the portals made it far easier for the randier kings to sneak out to… well, you know."

"Do you know anything about a portal in this particular location?" I asked, pointing to a screenshot of a Fairy Tag map Daisy had sent me that showed where the largest cluster of tags had been before they'd stopped moving.

"No," he said sarcastically, "that's why we call them *hidden* portals. Think about that one you lost Alastair and Tobey through. Couldn't see it, could you?" I shook my head. This would be the portal the Mauvais had vanished through right when I thought I'd gotten the upper hand. And he'd pulled Tobey and Alastair into it with him. "*Hidden*. That means they're also impossible to find unless you've been told right where they are."

"Or unless you've seen someone go through them," I said, thinking of how I'd been able to toss a stapler through the invisible, mid-air portal. To this day, I wonder where that stapler ended up.

"Precisely." An uncomfortable grimace on his face, he added, "One good thing about you being stuck in here is that I don't have to worry about you doing something stupid like stumbling into some random portal. Still, you won't be in here forever. Might be a good idea for me to go over my records and see what I've got for the Tower."

I wasn't sure why he'd need to check the Tower specifically, but before I could ask about this, Gilly announced that Morelli's visiting time was up. And I know this is going to sound really weird, but I wasn't ready for him to go.

"Thanks for this." I clutched the pillow, suddenly feeling a bit overwhelmed by everything.

"You'll figure things out soon enough, kid," Morelli said, his tone weirdly gentle. He then cleared his throat. "And, Black?"

"Yeah?"

"Rent really is due in six days and seventeen hours, so if you've got your credit card details on hand, send 'em my way."

"I'll keep that in mind. Do you take Monopoly money, by any chance?"

"Depends on the exchange rate," he quipped. Then, all joking aside, he whispered, "Just hold on tight, kid. Everyone's working on springing you outta here, okay?" I had to swallow back a small lump in my throat at the sincerity in his tone.

I then spent the next couple hours dwelling on why he hadn't told me they were working to clear my name. Only that they were working on 'springing' me out. For some reason, I had a feeling I wasn't going to like the answer.

CHAPTER SIX
WAITING, WORRYING, AND WANTON BRIBERY

Let me just say that, regardless of how cozy your jail cell is, it's still a jail cell, where there's little to do but wait and worry over when or if you'll ever get out. And my waiting was taking a worryingly long time, leaving me little to do but think as the afternoon crawled into evening with the speed of a geriatric tortoise trudging through molasses on a frigid day.

Because it was getting harder and harder to resist the pastries that were calling my name, my first bit of pondering was over how soon Mr T might be back with another box from Spellbound. But my mind soon wandered down a jewel-strewn path. What did I truly know about the jewels? All were red — possibly rubies, but I'm no gemologist — as was the Boncoeur Jewel Matilda claimed was a family heirloom. That couldn't just be a colorful coincidence.

I pulled out my notebook and flipped through the pages. Two words caught my eye: *friendship rings*. These were a set of rings with gemstones of roughly equal size, all cut from a single stone and intended to convey the ring bearers' equal importance to the monarch, whose ring held a larger piece of the gem.

It wasn't unreasonable to assume that if Queen Elizabeth had commissioned the split of one jewel to make the friendship rings I'd seen at the Tower of London, she could have done the same with any number of sparklies. Forget her moniker of the Virgin Queen; Lizzie might well have been England's premier Chop Shop Ruler.

But if the Boncoeur Jewel had been split in Elizabethan London, how had the pieces ended up in modern-day MagicLand? Did that even matter? A curiosity to be sure, but would it help tidy up this mess I'd gotten mixed up in? I doubted it.

I groaned with frustration. I'd merely been trying to launch my new detective business. Instead, I'd become tangled up in enemy-empowering jewels, problematic prophecies, and vampires vying to take over the magic world.

And they say marketing is the toughest part of running your own business.

My mind then wandered to earlier that day when I'd attempted to puzzle together Clive Coppersmith's marble with the jewels from the tiara, Winnifred's brooch, and my mom's pendant. (Holy hexes, had that really been only a few hours ago?) They had nearly formed a heart except for a gap in one quadrant. I still hoped that missing piece was one of the gems in the handle of Runa's stolen saw, but what if it wasn't?

My pessimistic stomach plummeted. What if it was some other gemstone? What if it took dozens of tiny pieces to fill that gap? It would be hard enough to find Runa's stolen saw, so how would I ever find an unknown number of itty-bitty jewel particles? Would I have to spend the rest of my days examining every ruby-filled bit of bling across the globe?

If I ever got out of my cell, that is.

I wrangled my mind back to a slightly more optimistic scenario: Assuming the Boncoeur Jewel was made up of only five pieces, and assuming I was able to find the fifth one, how did those pieces snap together?

Nothing on the edges of the jewels I'd found showed any indication of how they connected. There was no *'insert tab A into slot B'* for these things. So, how did they join to make a whole? Did I need to hammer them together? Did I need to go to Uncommon Implements and pick up some Supernatural Super Glue?

I bitterly reminded myself that it didn't matter, since I no longer had any gem pieces, anyway. Why had Oberlin been so adamant about seizing them and arresting me for what had essentially been his misconstruing the intention behind an email I'd sent him regarding the jewels?

I watched a herd of elephants traipse across the savanna and some gazelles bound past a stand of scrubby trees as I considered all I knew about Oberlin. Which wasn't much. I did know, from posters in his office and from the content of his lectures, that he was very anti-vampire. Was this just a general phobia of things that bite in the night, or did he fear the vampires might gain power unless he locked the jewels, and me, away?

The only other thing I knew about Old Walrus Face was that he had lost his bid for mayor to Matilda Marheart, a newcomer to Rosaria. She'd narrowly won the election, even though she'd been well liked at the start and had been a shoo-in for at least seventy-five percent of the votes. But then Oberlin began a smear campaign against her that included vague comments about her not being one of us and an enemy within, while also claiming he was the only candidate who truly cared about Rosaria.

Although Matilda did her best to maintain the high road, it turned into a vicious campaign, but once the votes were tallied, Matilda won with the slimmest of margins. In the time she'd been mayor, she'd seemed capable. As I've mentioned, despite so many Magic communities losing dozens of people to these mysterious disappearances, Rosaria had only lost two.

Trouble was, Matilda was at the center of a lot of suspicious incidents. She'd been seen at Clive's marble convention and — since Clive's neighbor reported seeing a slim, dark-haired person loitering near the apartment that day — may have been on the scene just before his death. Matilda had also been at a party with Winnifred Oberlin just before Mrs O's brooch went missing, and the pawnshop's intake receipt for that same brooch bore a false signature with Matilda's flourish.

Madame Mayor had also sported a bandaged hand and had been coming from the direction of Runa's the morning of the clinic's first break-in. Matilda had been right there hovering over me after I'd been attacked at my parents' place, then had the very pendant I'd lost during that attack hanging from her hallway mirror a few days later. And then there was Sebastian's footage of someone who resembled Mayor Marheart entering Bookman's Bookshop right before the return of Wordsworth's book. A book that had gone missing after an annual gathering of Bookworms that Matilda had attended as part of her mayoral duties.

Seriously, a ton of bricks hitting me in the head would be more subtle than all these clues pointing a very large finger to Matilda's double-dealing.

I settled back into the comfort of my bed, letting my mind roam and my eyes drift shut as the mural's creatures sauntered across the African plain.

A strange bird call suddenly broke the peace of the savannah. Wait no, the birdsong was coming from under my pillow. I dove my hand under, accepted the call, then fumbled out a hello.

"Oh, I'm sorry, Cassie. Were you sleeping?" Fiona asked.

"No, not sleeping." Okay, I was. Soothing savannah scenes are very relaxing regardless of how many clues you need to unravel. "Just thinking."

"About anything in particular?"

Ugh, where to begin to answer that? My suspicions about Matilda? My concerns for Mr Wood? My worry about getting my detective's license? My struggle with not scarfing down the box of pastries mere inches from me?

"The jewels," I said, settling on my biggest conundrum. "They just keep nagging at me. I mean, don't you find it weird how so many of these jewel bits have all been in Rosaria or Real Portland? Do you know anything about that?"

"I'm afraid not. It is curious, though, and not something I've considered. I could look into it if you like."

"If you have time," I said, feeling instantly guilty that Fiona, who had to deal with both HQ research requests *and* sophomores, would offer up any of her spare time to look into my problems.

"I'll see what I can do. Tell me, what else were you pondering? I can't imagine jail is anyone's idea of a mindfulness retreat, but it must be giving you time to consider your cases, yes?"

"In a manner of speaking. I've been trying to wrap my head around how the jewel pieces stick together. Is there any chance they could be placed next to each other for them to snap into place like magical magnets?"

"Oh, no, that never works," Fiona said without hesitation. Rather than explain her certainty, she paused a moment, then said, "It could require some form of reuniting spell."

This ignited the proverbial light bulb over my head.

During my arrest, Oberlin had noted that Wordsworth's book contained banned spells. I already knew this, but the Inspector wasn't exactly a bibliophile, so his knowing what that particular book contained struck me as odd even then. He'd also been pretty critical of me trying to locate the other copies of the book. Could the missing pages contain a spell to bring the jewels together?

I shook my head. That was quite the leap even for my overactive imagination.

"Trouble with that is," Fiona continued, "unless you're very careful with the pieces you want to unite, you end up pulling in all kinds of unwanted stuff. As you can imagine, something like cat hairs infiltrating a Weapon of Magic Destruction can really make a muddle of things."

"So, hypothetically, how would you put together a Weapon of Magic Destruction?"

"If it were up to me, I'd use some sort of frame or vise that's enchanted to hold the gems together. It'd be challenging to build. In fact, I've never heard of such a project or tried anything like it myself."

"No desire to take over the world with an enemy-defeating jewel?"

"I can barely manage some of my students, so no. Speaking of, it's nearly time for class, but is there anything you need before I go?"

A thought struck me before she'd even finished her offer.

"Could you ask Professor Dodding to call me?"

"Of course," Fiona readily agreed, then surprised me by not questioning why I wanted to speak with him. "Anything else?"

"An *Escape From Jail for Dummies* book would be nice."

"I'll see what I can dig—"

"Many apologies for interrupting a valued customer's conversation," said the familiar mechanical voice, "but you have mentioned dummies, vise, and professor in this conversation. Due to security concerns, your call will be terminated immediately."

The line went silent. Shaking my head over why the word *escape* hadn't triggered the alert system, I leafed mindlessly through my notebook as thoughts flicked in and out of my skull.

Matilda wanted the Boncoeur Jewel. A jewel that could defeat her worst enemies.

She was a vampire. The vampires were getting restless, according to HQ.

Matilda had my mom's pendant. She was on the scene where other jewel pieces had gone missing.

Matilda had shown interest in the security around Wordsworth's book. She had obtained the book, then got rid of the book that was now missing pages that might or might not contain a jewel-binding spell.

You can understand why I was a little suspicious of the mayor's true motives. Okay, super suspicious.

Still, all of these facts were spinning around like a record on repeat without gaining me any true insight. Paying more attention this time, I read what I'd written in my notebook.

On one page I'd been making a tally of missing Magics. I'd also jotted down a note about Norms being found dead in their homes. Killed in a ritualistic manner without much blood being left on the scene was all the articles provided. Could that mean the vampires were once again attacking Norms and disregarding the rules the Magics had put upon them? Why had I put these on the same page? Did I think they were related? I honestly couldn't remember.

But why were Magics going missing in the first place?

HQ was convinced that the staggering number of Magics who'd gone missing recently were tied directly to a possible vampire uprising.

I'd have been inclined to agree, but here's the strange thing that my little pea brain couldn't reconcile: if Mayor Marheart was the Wicked Vampire of the Pacific Northwest and in charge of getting a jewel that could be an important weapon in a vampiric coup, why had only two Magics gone missing from Rosaria — Bunny the Bad Drummer and Mel Faegan?

The trouble with that line of reasoning was why, when Mel had been returned to Rosaria, did he nearly have a heart attack when he saw Matilda in Dr Dunwiddle's exam room?

And why had Mr Faegan been returned without his power? Were the vampires, who were naturally strong absorbers, pulling power from us to boost their strength for the upcoming uprising? Or was it to weaken as many Magics as possible to make the uprising that much easier? Could it be both? A kill-two-birds-with-one-stone sort of thing. Or would it be a buy-one-get-one-free situation? Did vampires use coupons? Did they have blood bank loyalty cards? A free pint after ten purchases? Ad campaigns that touted, *Good to the last drop*?

Clearly, my line of reasoning had gone way off course, but trying to get back on that course only made my head run in very annoying circles.

Dusk was settling both outside my window and on the savannah (where I noticed some lions starting to prowl), and boredom had my eyes drooping by the time Gilly the Guard approached the bars of my cell to announce it was time for dinner.

Which was stretching the definition of the word as she passed me a tray on which was a cup of broth of what looked like dishwater garnished with a tablespoon of frozen peas and carrots. This was accompanied by three crinkled packets of broken soda crackers, a slice of plastic-wrapped American cheese, and a bottle of water. My gaze drifted from the tray to her face, which did look apologetic at the dining options.

"It's not much better in the employee cafeteria," she admitted. "You want it?"

"Just the water, thanks." I then pointed to the Spellbound box on the desk. This might come as a shock, but there were still several pastries left. "You want one?"

"As long as you're not bribing me," she said, her stomach audibly growling.

I held the box out for her, and she selected an apricot tartlet. Despite its lack of chocolate, it was one of my favorites, mainly because it was seasonal and — as Gwendolyn had proudly assured me — only on offer at Spellbound a few weeks a year. I mentally grumbled over Gilly's choice, but I let her take it with an encouraging smile. As I've noted, Professors Television and Movies have taught me well, so I knew better than to argue with a prison guard if I wanted any amount of fair treatment.

And I don't know if this counts as a teaser to get you to turn the page or if it's foreshadowing, but that sweet pastry sacrifice was soon to pay off.

CHAPTER SEVEN
WOODCUT CURIOSITIES

No rescue came for me that first night. However, after many *many* tries, Alastair did discover that the waiting period after being cut off by the Academy's system was four hours. And, every time the waiting period ran out, he immediately called me. Which I'd like to say interrupted my sleep, but even in the most comfortable bed I've ever stretched out in, my head was jackrabbiting around too much to allow me any amount of deep rest.

The next morning, my in-and-out dozing was interrupted by the cursing, bustling, and grumbling of a police station getting its work day underway. As my eyes drifted shut once more, my ringing phone obliterated any chance of returning to sleep. It took my groggy eyes a moment to recognize the number.

"Dr Torres?" I mumbled in that way of trying to sound wide awake when you are far from it.

"Hello, Cassie. How are you?"

"Um… confined?"

"Yes, I heard about the arrest." Because, again, the speed with which gossip spreads amongst Magics — and apparently anyone associated with Magics — is a phenomenon that needs to be studied by physicists. "I'm sure it'll all be cleared up in no time."

"I don't think you understand the nature of my relationship

with Inspector Oberlin. I'm sure the only reason I'm in this cell is because he's out scouting for the dankest dungeon with free space available. Anyway... what's up?"

"Well, I've been thinking about our visit with Professor Dodding." No surprise there. Pascal Torres was the curator of the Oregon Historical Society's museum as well as being one of the rare Norms who'd been granted a deep insight into the Magic world. He also happened to be a huge fanboy of the wizened and wise Professor Dodding of the Museum of London. We'd gone to see Dodding a few days ago, and I could easily imagine Torres spending the time since our meeting dwelling on, analyzing, and transcribing every scrap of the conversation.

"And this thinking entails...?" I asked, as I pulled myself to sitting and plucked a cupcake from my Spellbound box. On the cell's rear wall, a giraffe was nibbling at an acacia tree, and the blazing African sunrise behind him made for a gorgeous scene.

"His brief mention of Matthew Hopkins. The name wasn't unfamiliar to me. It caught my attention and wouldn't let go, so yesterday evening I began digging around for his connection to... well, anything, really."

Fiona had also mentioned this Hopkins character in passing at dinner the other day, but for the life of me I couldn't recall what she'd said. In my defense, I had just learned that Matilda Marheart was a vampire, and that I might be on the hunt for a jewel that could destroy all Magics, so maybe cut me some slack for my memory lapse. I asked Dr Torres what he'd found out.

"Hopkins was a witch hunter. This was in the 1600s during the time of James I. Supposedly, Hopkins was the greatest of witch hunters, killing hundreds of your kind in the name of religion. Stood quite firmly on that religious high ground from what I've read. A fervent zealot who claimed his cruelty and bloodlust to be god's wishes. And to achieve those wishes, he wasn't above using witchcraft. In god's name, of course."

"Of course," I agreed. This was interesting, if rather disturbing, but I didn't see how it tied to anything I'd been working on. The jewel had been last seen in Elizabeth I's hands; and although James I inherited the English throne from her, nothing so far had indicated he'd ever possessed the jewel.

"And the connections? Did you find any?"

"Indeed I did. A pair of woodcuts of James and Hopkins. Not very memorable pieces and easy to skim past, unless something in them grabs your interest."

"I assume they do?"

"Exactly. In one, James is handing Hopkins what looks like a heart. It could all be symbolic, of course. People back then loved sneaking hidden meanings into their art. But we know that James, despite a great fear of Magics, was very curious about the magic world. If he had the jewel, he may have had some inkling of what it could do."

"But if the jewel was split during Elizabeth's reign and given to her courtiers, how would James have it?"

"A smart line of thinking, but here's the intriguing bit: soon after the start of his reign, James issued a decree demanding the courtiers of Elizabeth return any jewel-bearing gifts she had given them. He claimed it was the Crown's property, not theirs. This courtier business has really sparked my curiosity, and as soon as I get a few things written up, I'm super eager to look into it." I'm not exaggerating when I say you could light up a city with this guy's enthusiastic energy. "But back to King James for now. As I said, James, well, he may or may not have dabbled in magic, but he definitely had people around him who did. And when I went down that rabbit hole, I found another familiar name."

"Who? Wait, sorry, how did you find all this so fast?" Because this did seem like an intense bit of research to have conducted in the three days since we'd visited Professor Dodding.

"Well," Dr Torres began, and I could practically hear the blush in his voice, "after we visited Professor Dodding, I emailed him to ask if I might submit a paper related to what we'd discussed. He said he'd be glad to read it, and if he liked it, he would submit it for an award he judged. So I, well, I sort of dove in headfirst and really haven't come up for air since. It's going to be quite the paper, if I do say so. Now, as to the familiar name... It was William Boncoeur. This craftsman of yours seems to have lived an incredibly long life."

Magics had long lives, but that could hardly explain such longevity.

"There was more to the woodcut," Dr Torres continued before I could ask what he'd found out about William Boncoeur. "In James's other hand was a box. It's hard to tell, but it looks like a jewel box with a small, I guess 'cage' is the best word for it, at the center. A similar jewel box is seen in a second woodcut of James from the same folio, but it doesn't have that cage."

This all seemed curious and something perfect for a trivia night, but I still couldn't see how it had much bearing on things. Although, I had been awake for over five minutes without any tea, so that could account for my slow thought processes.

"So, could the box have been from Elizabethan times, then James altered the lid to have the cage added?" I asked.

"It wouldn't be the worst guess, but we really can't say definitively. However, the titles of the woodcuts are very intriguing. Are you ready for this?" I said I was. "The one without the cage is inscribed with *Vulnerable*. The other is called *Empowered*. Hold on, let me send them to you."

A few seconds later, my phone pinged twice with the incoming photo files. I didn't look at them just then because a number of thoughts started whirring through my head all at once, none of which I could put into words.

Dr Torres must have misinterpreted my silence as doubt or boredom, because after a moment of silence he said, "Well, I find it interesting, at any rate."

"Sorry, it is interesting; I just don't know exactly *why* it's interesting. But I'm inclined to believe it's going to be more the troubling kind of interesting rather than the did-you-know-octopuses-have-three-hearts kind of interesting." After assuring Pascal that this animal fact really was true, I asked, "How's everything else, then?"

"Oh, quite good. Still haven't convinced them to move the *Hart of the Fores*t to my office, but that's not for lack of trying."

This was a painting in the lobby of the Historical Society that featured a stag standing in a sunlit forest. The canvas took up nearly the entire entry wall and was so big I doubted it would fit in a freight elevator, let alone Pascal's office.

Just as I was about to ask Dr Torres about his paper for Professor Dodding, the Academy's alert monitor system cut in. This time the woman didn't speak in her usual calm and mechanically measured manner, but in a tone of utter alarm. "Forest, office, and convinced? All in the same sentence? That is clear and damning evidence of plotting. Your attempt has been noted in the database. This call is terminated immediately. No more calls from this caller will be allowed. Ever!"

Ever? Could the system possibly program my phone to block Pascal from ever phoning me again? I wouldn't be surprised. Also, who had been at the center of all these prison breaks from the Academy? A bunch of Scrabble champions?

When the line went silent, I pulled up the images Pascal had sent. While King James resembled the portraits I'd seen of him, Hopkins looked as generic as any other person in a woodcut. Even so, he didn't appear at all threatening. Looked a bit wimpy, if I'm being honest. Which likely hid his true nature.

I scanned the first woodcut, especially the heart James was holding. It was an anatomically correct heart. Not a stylized one like you'd seen in a Valentine's Day card, but an actual mammalian heart. Clutched in James's other hand was a small box with a flat lid. No indentation for a jewel. No wire mesh to hold the jewel in place.

In the second image, James was again holding the box. This time it had a small indentation in the center. However, what truly caught my eye, and what Pascal had failed to mention, were the items surrounding James's head. To be honest, if you didn't have a mind full of jewels, you'd have mistaken them for flies. Perhaps a political commentary on James's bathing habits. But if you *did* have jewels on the mind, the five specks floating around James's noggin looked very much like little diamonds.

I went back to the first image. The five specks were absent. Five diamond-shaped specks. Was this confirmation that the Boncoeur Jewel really was made up of only five gems? If so, that meant I only had to find one more missing piece. Which was a huge relief since I'd probably have crawled into a corner and curled into a ball of despair if I had to locate another dozen or so bits of gem.

Still, this knowledge, while good, was of little use since it provided no clue where that final piece might be.

My phone pinged again with a message from Fiona that she'd forwarded from Pascal saying, "This always makes me calm and content." Attached to it was a snapshot of the *Hart of the Forest*.

I lay back in my bed and stared at the painting. It was calming, but my mind was racing too much to fully fall into its serenity. Still, were stags anything to be calm about? I mean, I've seen the YouTube videos. Bambi can definitely do some serious damage with his antlers if you catch him in the wrong mood. And how do you defend yourself against that sort of attack? Marshmallow Charm on the tines? When hiking, always carry bear spray and a hacksaw—?

I bolted up from my pillow. Runa's saw. The client had been Somebody Stagman. If *stag* and *hart* referred to the same thing, and if Matilda's ancestors had kept up this heart-naming convention over the centuries (William Boncoeur and Matilda Marheart being two examples), then could *Stag*man actually mean *Hart*man? Did this confirm that the saw once owned by What's-His-Name Stagman contained the final piece of the jewel? A prospect that seemed even more tantalizing since Runa had a reputation for working with vampires.

But did that make sense? None of the other jewels had been owned by Heart-named people. None had any connection to vampires that I knew about. But it seemed like too much of an obvious lead not to want out of my cell right that very instant to go hunt down a damn saw I'd stupidly kept neglecting to look for.

Before I could chastise myself further, my phone blared with an incoming call, the screen somehow flashing an announcement that it was from a person I'd requested to speak to, and I should answer immediately.

I really needed to talk to Daisy about whatever she'd done to my phone. And how she'd done so without ever touching it.

CHAPTER EIGHT
CHOCOLATE: PURE MAGIC

"I hear you miss me," Professor Dodding said with a raspy chuckle.

"Right now, I miss everyone," I told him.

"Yes, Busby told me you're in a bit of a scrape, but I'm sure he'll get it sorted. And Fiona mentioned you wanted to chat with me."

"Well, not so much *chat* as get some more information from you, if you have time."

"For you, my dear, always. Now, what did you want to know?"

"I'm not sure exactly."

"Well, that should make for a wonderfully exploratory phone call. Were you looking for more about the Boncoeur Jewel? Because I'm afraid, at this point, that Dr Torres of yours knows more than I do. He's very enthusiastic, isn't he?"

"That he is." Professor Dodding might be out of new details about the jewel, but might he know anything about Wordsworth's book? I asked him if he'd ever heard of it.

"Ah yes," he replied, the usual jovial tone in his voice taking on a tone of distaste, like a prize-winning dog breeder having to discuss the merits of mutts and mongrels. "It contains some very troubling spells. And I have been concerned ever since hearing the news that Mr Wordsworth's copy went missing. But you found it, didn't you?"

"Minus two pages, yes."

"Ah, then my worries can't fully be alleviated, can they? Some spells in there are quite vexatious."

"But that book is huge. How would anyone know which spell to look for?" Because I was assuming that, like prophecies, spells were worded as vaguely as possible.

"Because, as per the Magic Morality Code from 1215, we Magics are required to clearly title our more complicated spells. This was right around the time we also helped the Norms draft that Magna Carta of theirs, and we were on quite a roll of churning out decrees and demanding clarity.

"Of course, it made perfect sense, since it would be a spot of bother to start in on a spell that you thought made your home invisible to unwanted aunts coming to visit for an indeterminate time, only to discover you're actually doing a spell to attract a fire-breathing dragon to your doorstep. Although, I suppose that would take care of the visiting-aunt problem, wouldn't it? Anyway, the spell would likely be titled something so obvious that even Chester would be able to guess what it might do."

Suddenly, a question popped into my head I hadn't considered before. It's amazing how inquisitive the mind gets when it's got nothing better to do. "You don't happen to know why there were three copies of the book, do you?" It was a long shot that Dodding would know, but if he didn't, Fiona might. And if worse came to worst, I supposed I could ask Wordsworth, who would likely yammer on about how his copy had been the best one, and how I'd ruined everything by not finding it in time to save it from irreparable damage.

"It was common practice back then," replied the professor. "Just as with the Magna Carta, several copies were made for other communities to study or to simply add to their collections.

It's actually quite rare that only three copies were made, but I suppose that might have to do with it being such a monstrosity of a tome."

"Is Wordsworth's the original?"

"I couldn't say for sure, but most likely it is. He only allows the best specimens into his collection. Did you know he wouldn't take, even as a gift, a copy of my book *Chocolate: Pure Magic* because it wasn't the first one off the presses?"

I momentarily pictured Dodding heaving against the levers of a Gutenberg-style printing press, even though I was sure Dodding wasn't *that* old. Okay, fairly sure.

"But it contains dangerous spells," I said. "Doesn't it run the risk of someone using those spells if you have a bunch of copies floating around?"

"It does, but with only three, I suppose that lessens the chance of evildoing. Also, each copy would have its own protective spell on it."

"What sort of protective spells get put on books?" I asked, even though I'd learned firsthand about one of them.

"Well, you might enchant a book to catch on fire if someone with bad intentions was flipping through it. That's what I think happened to the copy at the British Library. You heard about that one, didn't you?"

"Just a tidbit here or there."

"Ah, you should really follow my Faebook account. I keep it up-to-date with regular videos about breaking news, historic whatnots, and of course, chocolate reviews. I don't like to brag, but I have nearly thirty thousand followers."

Yes, this hundred-and-something-year-old academic was more social media savvy and popular than me. Why was I not surprised?

"But other spells, less flame-based spells, are also used to protect books. The flame one was quite popular around the English Civil War, but it really has no subtlety."

"And the more subtle spells…?" I prodded before he started on about magic styles through the ages.

"Let's see… Well, of course you've got the disappearing page trick. Not a very clever protection, if I'm being honest. There are also shifting books. Those are quite special if you can find one. But my favorite books are those protected by ink-shifting magic. Makes the words go blurry unless you know the counter spell.

"Oh," he exclaimed as if just remembering another favorite, "I nearly forgot about the one that causes the pages to always appear upside-down no matter how many times you turn the book. With the swishy handwriting those old copyists used, you can barely read them right side up to begin with. Really, there's no limit to how you could protect a book. But most people stick with the basics unless they're feeling especially creative."

I wasn't feeling especially creative, and I was now feeling dismayed. If there were all these spells to protect the book, it could quite literally be anywhere. Hell, by this logic, one of the statute books Daisy seemed to be enjoying so much could be hiding *The British Wizard's Guide to Magical Creatures, Untoward Spells, and Enchanted Objects of the Tudor and Stuart Eras*.

"Go on," encouraged Professor Dodding, "ask me another question. This is such fun."

I wasn't sure how I felt about my career crisis and my need to stop a vampire coup being his entertainment, but since I had him on the phone, I said, "You told me before that the Boncoeur Jewel, if reassembled, could give someone power over their enemy. Any idea how that works?"

"As with any magic, it all depends on what the person's intentions are. But in general terms, the jewel would know the heart of its holder. It would sense who was the biggest threat and, if you wanted that threat to go away — which I imagine you would — the jewel would give you the power to vanquish that threat. You'll think me cheeky for saying this," he added, a twinkle in his voice, "but I could talk to you all day. Your inquisitiveness is such a delightful diversion."

"Glad to be of service. But how does the jewel give that power? Does it make you stronger? Give you really good luck? Weaken your opponent?"

"That I'm not sure of. The newfound ability could be physical, magical, or just a big surge of brilliance. Again, it would all depend on intentions, needs, desires. Speaking of desire, should I send you some chocolate bars?"

"I'm okay for now, thanks. Can I ask one other thing?"

"By all means."

"If you had the pieces of the Boncoeur Jewel, how would you join them together?" Because I figured if I kept asking, someone was bound to know the answer to this problem.

"Oh, now that is a challenging query. An interesting one as well," he said in a way that implied he didn't know but could spend hours guessing. "The pieces themselves wouldn't stay together without help. Would you glue them together before the spell? I suppose a Binding Hex, but then you risk layering spell on top of spell, and if you want to work a nice chunk of sinister power into something, it's important to keep your dastardly charms as pure as possible. I'm sorry I don't know for certain, but if you discover the answer, do let me know."

I told him I would, not bothering to mention the fact that, according to the prophecy, if I did figure out how to join the jewel together, I'd be setting into motion my own death.

Which is a rather morose thought before you've even had your first cup of tea for the day.

CHAPTER NINE
LEGALLY BLONDE

Since that pair of phone calls had left my brain racing with even more befuddling thoughts, I was wide awake when Gilly showed up for her morning shift. When she passed a steaming mug through the bars, I began to refuse, unable to bear another cup of ten-time-recycled oolong.

"I brought a little something from home," she assured me. "Fortnum's Breakfast Blend work for you?"

I glanced into the cup to see, not something that looked like diluted dishwater, but a mahogany-brown liquid that smelled rich, caffeinated, and amazing. I thanked her with a cheese scone.

Two hours later, I'd worked my way through my remaining pastries (my confinement finally having gotten the better of my self-control), I'd paced my cell at least fifty times, and I'd found myself too bored to read, so I'd ended up doing nothing but staring at the wall. At least I was finally learning how to meditate.

Unfortunately, that meditation was interrupted by a bubbly bright voice coming from down the corridor.

Great Galadriel, were they resorting to torture now?

"She's just here, ma'am," I heard a male guard say. *Ma'am?* Who in their right mind referred to Daisy as *ma'am*? "Just down there. You'll see Gilly, the guard on duty. You have a wonderful day," he said soppily.

Daisy thanked the man with as much warmth as if he'd just donated a thousand dollars to the Flying Cat Rescue Society. When she reached my cell, she greeted Gilly like an old friend, then beamed a smile at me. I did my best not to flinch away from the bedazzling brightness, but what in all the sulfurous stink of Hades was going on? Mr T had told me not even twenty-four hours ago that I couldn't have visitors unless they were here on official duty. Did that rule only apply on the first day? And if I was allowed visitors now, why did the Bubbly Blonde Beacon have to be my first? I returned to the certainty that this had to be some form of torture.

Although she had brought a Spellbound box, so maybe torture with a side of strudel?

Daisy, her ponytail swishing, blasted a smile at Gilly. "If I could have a moment alone with my client, that'd be super of you."

Client? First Morelli, now Daisy? Either the Academy's receptionist was easily fooled, or I was having auditory hallucinations.

"Sorry, can't do that," Gilly asserted.

"Oh, well, that's okay, then," Daisy said, completely unfazed by the rebuff as Gilly stepped a polite distance away. "And how are you, Cassie? Are they treating you well?"

"What's going on? Why are you here?"

"I'm your attorney. Duh."

"You are?" I could feel Gilly's skeptical eyes slide our way. "I mean, that's right. You most definitely are. Silly me," I gave a self-deprecating chuckle, "I must be suffering from a bit of jail brain."

"This is such a hoot," said Daisy, glancing innocently between me and my guard, who still looked dubious about this whole thing. Can't blame her for that. I mean, Daisy comes across as the sort who couldn't even spell *law*, let alone practice it. "Anyway, I just wanted to come by and make sure all was okay, and to let you know that me and my partner are working hard on getting you out of here."

"Partner?"

"You know. Mr Eugene," Daisy said in an oh-my-god-everyone-knows-that way. "He gave a good report on your conditions here, and we've evaluated what needs to be done. He's really proven to be quite the asset when it comes to figuring out how to get you out from behind those poopy bars." As she said this, she shifted the Spellbound box she'd been holding.

"And all charges dropped?" I asked.

"Well, that too, if we have time," she said offhandedly. "But mostly on getting you your freedom back. Won't that be super?" She smiled broadly and looked back and forth between me and Gilly as if we were all getting ready for a girls' day out. Gilly at least looked more amused than wary now. She was also hungrily eyeing up the Spellbound box, and I could see there'd be more bribery in my near future. "Anyway, I just wanted to let you know we're on your side, and Mr Eugene wanted me to bring you these."

Daisy was about to hand over the box when Gilly stepped forward.

"I'll need to check those first."

"No problem," Daisy said cheerily and lifted the lid.

Inside were the usual array of Spellbound pastries, another couple of sandwiches, and at least two dozen cookies. But there was also a small round loaf that appeared to be pumpernickel, or some other dark bread. Gilly, after a twitch of a grin, gave a nod then stepped back. I wondered if she'd already set her sights on something she might like.

Daisy passed me the box, but when she and her ponytail made to swish away, I called after her, "Has Tobey gone to his test yet?"

Gilly was already halfway down the corridor to escort Daisy out, but she remained where she stood when Daisy returned to my cell. Her ponytail sagging slightly, Daisy gave a weak nod and said, "He wasn't too happy about it. Nerves, I suppose. But I told him if I could pass the Magic bar exam after only a week of classes, he could pass those silly old Academy Exams."

"Wait," I whispered, "you really are a lawyer?"

"Well, technically, sure. Remember? When I called yesterday, I told you I took some classes."

"But...? Since when?"

"Dunno. Since I was like maybe fourteen. Just one of those silly teenage whims, you know?"

"But why aren't you—?" By now Gilly was heading back toward my cell, likely eager for Daisy to leave so she could select something from the Spellbound box. I didn't want her to overhear that Daisy wasn't actually my lawyer, that Daisy was, as far as I knew, nothing but my assistant at a floundering detective agency, so I merely said, "—practicing full time?"

"I just couldn't bear those power suits. I mean, they're so dull, am I right? So I just do *pro bono* stuff when the mood strikes me. Okay then, I should get going. Too-da-loo!" She waggled her fingers at me and Gilly before bounding off like a pink-clad Tigger.

"She's..." Gilly began, before hunting for the right word. "Energetic."

"She most certainly is. Cookie?" I offered.

"Don't mind if I do," she said as she selected a chocolate

biscotti from the box. "And, just a bit of advice, but that pumpernickel might not last long. Now," she said pointedly, "if you wanted to sample that bread ASAP, I'm just going to make sure your 'lawyer' is able to find her way out."

"But…" I began, completely confused. Did she have a weird thing for pumpernickel?

Gilly started to head out, but stopped after about three paces and came back to my cell. I wondered if she was going to pass on more pumpernickel advice. Instead, she stepped close to my bars, a look of utter sincerity in her dark eyes. "My parents, my grandparents, my aunts and uncles were all killed by the Mauvais's people when I was little." She blushed slightly. "You're kind of my hero."

"Could you repeat that so I can record it?" I asked, thinking of all the times over the past few weeks when I could really have used a bit of buoying up.

She gave an encouraging smile, thanked me for the treats, and headed in the direction Daisy had gone.

I placed the box on the cell's desk and opened it again. The round loaf really did look like nothing more than bread. Certainly not bread of Gwendolyn's usual quality, but bread nonetheless. It took another several moments of staring at it before I recalled another round, dark object that had been sent to me. A perfect sphere that, once I touched it, pulled me into an illegal portal that had whisked me out of HQ and back to Portland.

At the time, I'd assumed that illegal portal had been built by Morelli, who, thanks to his less-than-on-the-up-and-up past, knew exactly how to make a portal that couldn't be tracked by HQ. So, had Daisy asked him to make this one? Or had it been Morelli's idea? How had Gilly recognized it after just a glance? Where would it take me? And more importantly, would it work in an enchanted cell, or would I be ripped in two if I tried to use it?

There were so many questions, but I could already hear the sound of Gilly's supportive shoes striding back down the corridor. If I wanted my one ally in the Academy to maintain her plausible deniability, now was not the time to ponder the deeper, and possibly painful, mysteries of life.

I shoved my phone in my back pocket, grabbed as many cookies from the box as I could, then touched my free hand to the pumpernickel.

CHAPTER TEN
FINGERNAILS & PONYTAILS

You know how I've complained endlessly about Corrine's courier portal giving a bumpy ride? Believe me, compared to traveling by illegal pumpernickel portal, Corrine's mail slot is a top-of-the-line Mercedes cruising over a freshly paved road after having been outfitted with the best shock absorbers on the market.

I was shaken. I was rattled. I was twisted, twirled, then spit out like a watermelon pip at the finals of a world championship seed-spitting competition. I then crashed down hard on a stony floor. However, because I have priorities, none of my cookies ended up broken despite the hard landing.

The space I was in was dark except for dim and flickering torchlight, dank with the smell of stone that has never known a dry day, and vaguely familiar. Heavy footsteps closed in, then I heard a stomp, a crunch, and a squeak before a pair of meaty hands were hoisting me up to standing.

"Mr Cassie!" cheered Chester. "You're not broken." Which was a fair point since I do have a strong track record of showing up places with shattered body parts.

"How did you—?" I stammered.

"Sir Morelli told me you'd be coming." Chester was already

leading me down the corridor and up some stairs, my feet and legs following along since my brain was too baffled to understand what was happening. Why would Morelli and Daisy spring me from jail only to send me to the Tower of London, aka 'royal fortress, castle, and *prison*'? "I like him, that Sir Morelli, even if he's not very good at rat hunting."

Chester continued to prattle on about Morelli, who had apparently promised Chester a hand-knit pair of woolen gloves with a matching hat for the winter. Meanwhile, my gut churned with worry. My being here didn't bode well. Although they hadn't used the exact word at the time, I'd essentially been HQ's prisoner once before. And I'd been hoping that was a once in a lifetime thing. My mind was so occupied with worry over what kind of cell I'd end up in that we reached Olivia's office before I knew it.

"Sir Olivia, Mr Cassie has made it. And she's in one piece."

"First time for everything. Come in, Miss Black." Olivia emphasized my name, perhaps trying to impart a lesson about proper titles and forms of address on Chester. A lesson which I was sure wouldn't stick, since trolls are very much creatures of habit. Olivia then dismissed Chester, and when I stepped forward, she arched an eyebrow at the stack of cookies I was clutching like a lifeline to the outside world. "I see you've brought provisions."

"Cassie, please, have a seat," said Mr T. I'd been in such a stunned state that I hadn't even noticed he was in the room with us. As such, I did a double take before stumbling toward the chair in front of Olivia's desk that Busby had indicated.

"What just happened?" I asked, setting my cookies on the desk and gesturing for Olivia and Busby to take one. I mean, just because my brain had moved at least fifty miles beyond bewildered, didn't mean I had to be rude.

"It seems you accidentally fell through a portal the Academy wasn't aware of," said Olivia, her tone filled to the brim with mock innocence and wonder. "Of course, we have no idea where you might have ended up."

"Another missing Magic," Mr T said with feigned regret. "Such a shame."

"Is that how everyone's going missing? Are they here?"

"If only it were that easy," replied Olivia. "No, you are here because you were wrongly arrested, and it would have taken far too much paperwork and time to get you out the legal way." I nodded, as if I had a clue of what was going on. "Now, this isn't a vacation," Olivia barreled on, paying no heed to my confusion and need for a few moments to fully grasp the situation. "Your first order of business will be to retrieve your belongings from the Academy. Runa, Busby, and Fiona have filled me in on your thoughts regarding the jewels, and I believe you're correct. Or at least on the right track."

"I have to go back to the Academy?" I asked, now reaching record-setting levels of bewilderment. I know sometimes Magics, especially HQ Magics, have some seriously harebrained ideas, but sending me back to the jail they'd just sprung me from? That seemed incredibly illogical, even for them.

"To get your items," Olivia said slowly, as if I was the one who was making no sense whatsoever.

"They don't have the tiara, though." Seriously, even at the time I knew I sounded idiotically slow, but my brain was doing the mental equivalent of highly advanced gymnastic stunts that should not be attempted without a team of paramedics nearby.

"That's been taken care of," said Mr T, who then produced a small metal tin from his jacket's inner pocket. I recognized it as the mint tin he'd crafted to expand into a safe and had given me as an agency-warming gift. The safe itself had been raided and emptied by Oberlin when he'd come to arrest me. At the time, the tiara had been mysteriously absent from the safe.

"Daisy was kind enough to send me my favorite mints," Mr T said cheekily as he expanded the tin back into a safe and gestured for me to do the honors. I unlocked it, then grasped the handle to open it.

To this day, I can't say what put the dread in my belly. Perhaps it was just my ever-present pessimism, but somehow I knew I'd be disappointed when I looked inside.

That pessimism turned out to be spot-on.

"The tiara..." I couldn't finish the statement. Could I just not get a break once in a while?

"Yes," said Busby, beaming a proud smile. "It's an unintended feature of the safe. The Replacement Hex Morelli's contact used on the tiara, combined with the protections I'd already put on the safe, somehow has allowed the tiara to hide itself. Rafi's beside himself with excitement trying to figure out how to make a reliable, intentional spell out of that combination."

A fuzzy blanket of relief wrapped around me. Silly old pessimism.

"So how do you undo whatever spell's got the tiara still hidden?" I asked. Then, with a chuckle, I added, "Because it's going to be kind of hard to rip the ruby out of it if I can't see it."

Mr Tenpenny's proud smile instantly fell. I just hate it when I break him.

"What are you talking about?" he asked. "I checked the moment Daisy sent over the tin. The tiara was in there. A half-blind cave fish wouldn't miss that gaudy thing." Busby squatted down next to the safe and peered inside, staring dumbfoundedly at the empty interior. "I don't understand," he muttered.

"I don't either," Olivia said tersely after confirming the safe was indeed completely void of tiaras. "But this makes it even more urgent for you and Cassie to return to the Academy and collect the other jewels before they fall into the wrong hands."

"But I can't go back to the Academy," I said, slowly coming back to myself. "Oberlin would just throw me back in a cell."

"Not if you're in disguise."

"Look, I don't rate Oberlin's intelligence as much higher than that of a particularly dimwitted fruit fly, but I think even he would see past a floppy hat and pair of sunglasses."

"That's not exactly what we had in mind," said Olivia, who then opened a folder in front of her, glanced inside, and closed it again. "Now, please stand. We can do this seated, but it's more efficient and comfortable if you're vertical."

Too befuddled to question or deny this odd request, I stood beside the desk. Olivia then gave me what was probably supposed to be a reassuring smile before moving her hand, palm facing me, in a circular motion like someone wiping down a fogged up mirror.

My face tingled. Not in a bad way. Like in the way of putting on a high-end, super refreshing, skin-rejuvenating facial mask. I then felt my hair tug straight back and away from my face. And, wait, was it growing? After this strange sensation, the tingly feeling shifted to my hands, where the skin became smoother and my fingernails lengthened from the short nubs I usually maintained. The newly even and tidy nails then turned from bare to bright pink.

There were odd, shifty sensations along a few other areas of my body as well. My feet definitely became smaller as they slid about in my size nine knock-off Keds. But all the while I kept looking at those fingernails. The perfect shape of them. The color. My head whirled. I'd seen that shade of varnish before.

My gut twisted. They couldn't have. They *wouldn't* have.

Once all the slippery skin sensations and corporeal weirdness came to a stop, Olivia pushed the Tea-lephone toward me. I stepped back, nearly tripping out of my now-oversized shoes and shaking my head like a child who thinks that if they don't look at the booboo on their knee, it doesn't really exist.

"Go on, Cassie," Mr Tenpenny encouraged. "Take a look. You'll have to eventually."

"No, I won't," I said petulantly.

"Cassie," Olivia warned, a commanding steel in her eyes.

I stepped up to the Tea-lephone's shiny surface.

"You need to open your eyes," Olivia said. I hadn't even realized I'd been squeezing them shut as tightly as possible. I dared to open one eye, then the other. And only because I feared Olivia's wrath did I not throw up right there all over her desk.

The Tea-lephone wasn't a perfect mirror, but it served the purpose as I gazed down at it. My eyes— Sorry, *someone else's* eyes widened with unadulterated shock. My worst guess of what all the shifting had meant had been one hundred percent correct. I glared at the nail varnish again before looking back up at Olivia, who had the audacity to smile over a job well done.

"What have you done to me!?" I blurted.

CHAPTER ELEVEN
THE DISGUISE

"Now, Cassie," said Olivia after I'd spent several minutes bemoaning and cursing what had been inflicted upon me, "please stop complaining. It's a very good disguise, and it required a lot of quick work from Rafi."

"Rafi did this to me?" I shouted. "It's not even legal to do this to someone, is it? I mean, you've made me… blonde!"

"Being blonde is not illegal," Mr Tenpenny stated.

"But Morphing is. You told me that Morphing oneself to look like a living person was very, *very* illegal."

"This isn't a Morphing Spell," Busby explained calmly. "It's merely a disguise."

"A *Daisy* disguise!"

"And it was very kind of her to allow us to make you over in her image. She even lent us some clothes to complete your makeover," Olivia said as she held up an overstuffed, designer brand handbag that I assumed contained various pieces of Daisy-ware. "It'll make it possible for you to return to Rosaria without being questioned, and you can enter the Academy without risk of being arrested. It really is the best solution."

"I'd hate to see your worst." I leaned forward again and stared into the teapot's reflective surface, then poked at my new face with its weirdly smooth skin. Did Daisy sleep in a vat of moisturizer to get her skin to glow like this? I wrinkled my perky new nose. Then I recalled the other areas of shifting and pulled at the neck of my shirt. Looking down, I saw no change to my slim frame, then gave Olivia a questioning, and somewhat disappointed, glance.

"We've adjusted your height and shoe size a bit. However, for, shall we say, privacy's sake, anything normally under clothing remains all yours."

"But my voice?" Which sounded normal to my ears.

"Will sound like Daisy to other people. The Disguise Spell puts some sort of Voice Modulation Charm on your throat. You'd have to ask Rafi for the particulars, but not now. As I said, your first order of business is to get back to the Academy as quickly as possible." Olivia said this as if it were the most logical plan of all logical plans.

"Okay, first off, do I work for you now? Because last I heard, you said I couldn't be involved with HQ stuff until I got my license. Secondly, are you insane? I just escaped from the Academy, and I didn't even use the words forest, field, or freelance." Olivia, rather than look annoyed that I'd called her insane, looked confused over the string of words. I told her about the Academy's phone monitoring system.

She shook her head. "I can't believe they're still using that outdated system. A creation of an overambitious M.A.G.E. team member. And, no, it is not insanity that has me wanting you to return to the Academy. They still have your belongings, and we need those gemstones you found. Which is why you and Busby will be returning with this—" She flicked her hand and a sheet appeared between her fingers. When she slid it toward me, I leaned forward to see it was a Property Requisition form with the HQ stamp. "You'll then bring the gems back here where we can keep things safe—"

"Safe? You already lost the tiara," I snapped.

"Once we have them," Olivia continued, her glare being the only response I got to my critical outburst, "we can hopefully get to the bottom of what all this means."

"But why do I have to go? Especially like this?" I'm not proud of how whiny those two questions came out of my, or rather, Daisy's mouth, but I really resented having to go back to Oberlin's realm after having just pumpernickled my way to freedom. And to do so as Daisy seemed like rubbing salt into very raw wounds.

"Because you need to get there and get your belongings before they discover your cell is empty. And, yes, especially like that, because, as you are aware, Miss Honeysuckle is your legal representative in this matter. And according to this," Olivia tapped a line on the form that said Daisy had the right to transfer the objects from the Academy to HQ on my behalf, "she has certain attorney-client privileges."

"Then why can't she do it?"

"Besides the fact that the paperwork is a complete bluff?" Mr T queried. I arched an eyebrow, surprised that HQ would dive into the realms of forgery just to help me. "These are *your* cases. Not Miss Honeysuckle's. Therefore, as I taught you in your mentorship, *you* must take responsibility for the items involved in those cases. Also," Busby said, looking slightly uncomfortable, "as illogical as it may seem, over the course of my career, I have always told myself not to ignore hunches, and my hunches lately have been telling me that you might have a connection with these jewels. And while I trust Daisy," he added gravely, "I worry about the jewels getting into anyone's hands but your own."

There was a ton to unpack in that statement, but I left the suitcase shut, and instead asked incredulously, "Is her name really Daisy Honeysuckle? Was she grown from a botanical experiment gone awry or something?"

Olivia chastised me with a glance. I dropped the subject, although not the image of a blonde head growing from a well-tended bed of soil.

"It will also help us see how well Rafi's Disguise Charm works," noted Mr Tenpenny.

"Wait. You don't know how well this thing works? Like, I could accidentally Morph back into myself with half a dozen cops standing around? You do realize that if I get thrown back behind bars, they're not going to be allowing any more boxes of pastries or 'pumpernickel'—" I put air quotes around the word "—anywhere near me."

Olivia gave a shrug. "I'm sure it'll all work out."

Because Magics were, if nothing else, weirdly self-assured about even the vaguest of plans.

Before I could ask about extraction contingencies in case Rafi's spell went kaput, my phone rang. Yes, I realize it's incredibly rude to stop mid-conversation to take a call, but the ring tone was not what I'd set it to. Rather than the gentle chimes of my normal setting, it was letting out the warbling wail of a European ambulance. I checked the caller ID and groaned to see it was Daisy. Even worse? She wanted a video call. On the third ring, the urgency level thingie she'd somehow put on my phone shot to its highest level.

What? Had she run out of mascara?

"Yes?" I answered with about sixty pounds of impatience.

"Cassie—" Her fretful expression suddenly widened with glee. "Oh. My. Pixies! You look amazing!"

"I look like you." Except for the scowling, we were mirror images of each other. Which was more than disturbing to see on my screen.

"I know. Ooh, did Olivia get the outfit I picked for you? You're going to look fabulous in it."

"Again. I'm going to look like you in it."

"Exactly! It's my favorite Gigantio Armani skirt suit. Gigantio himself selected the fabric to best match my coloring, and the style is so—"

"Did you call for anything other than fashion commentary?"

Daisy, clearly remembering the true reason for her call, instantly turned to fretful again. Seriously, her face changed more quickly than the Oregon weather.

"Yes, the dots stopped moving."

"Great," I said, having no idea what she was talking about.

"The *dots*, Cassie," she urged. "Mr Wood's dots. The Fairy Tags. They stopped moving."

"You've told me this, remember?" And I think it shows a great deal of character growth that I refrained from throwing a joke about air-headed blondes at her.

"I know, but they *all* stopped moving. And now I've just noticed six have started up again. Like, they're just sort of circling."

"Maybe their batteries were on the fritz?" I asked, having no idea how the fairies on the Fairy Tags stayed fueled up. I also had no desire to continue seeing a double dose of Daisy on my phone's screen. "Hold on. I can't handle this. I'm switching to voice only."

"No, these are top-end Fairy Tags," Daisy replied once I'd clicked the appropriate button and brought the phone to my ear. "Not those cheap knock-off Sprite Tags. They're guaranteed to stay energized as long as you need them to." Again, I needed to find out exactly how these things worked and what fairy labor laws were being violated, but now was not the time.

"Okay," I said, feeling Olivia's impatient stare burning through me. "You've got the Fairy Tags app. So maybe you should look up where the signals are coming from," I suggested in the tone of someone explaining the alphabet to a football player who's suffered far too many blows to the head.

"Yes, I did that. That's why I called. At first they weren't sending out their exact location. I don't know, maybe after being still for so long, they need a bit to get going again?" Okay, that had me convinced these tags were real fairies. Ones who had to do calisthenics before jumping into a day's work. "But then, like I said, they just sort of started circling, and that's why I called you."

"I'm not sure I'm in a position to do anything right now," I said as Olivia began testily tapping her nails against her desk.

"But you are," Daisy insisted as brightly as a motivational speaker. "The six tags— Okay, sometimes they don't send out a signal at all, which is weird. But when they do bleep, they're bleeping from somewhere in the Tower of London." I would have again protested that I couldn't do anything about this, but my jaw had dropped so far that I was temporarily incapable of speech. Possibly taking my silence for reluctance, Daisy added, "I'm just so worried about Mr Wood. It's making me feel very poopy."

"Maybe you should come to London and check on those last signal locations," I said, since, from the visual daggers she was shooting, I doubted Olivia would let me pop off to wander about the Tower for a bit to look for my former boss.

"Well, and I hope this doesn't affect my performance review." Performance review? Wait. Could the universe really smile down on me so much that it would allow me to tell Daisy exactly what I thought of her? Oh, the fun I could have. "But I can't travel anywhere," she added meekly.

"What? Are you sick?"

"No, but thank you for asking."

She didn't explain, so I prodded, "So why can't you travel? Did you get a kitten? A puppy? A particularly needy houseplant?" Forget how to work the doorknob, I did not say. See, *so* much character growth.

"No, none of that. It's just, I tried to go through a portal, and it wouldn't let me go anywhere. All I can figure is that HQ traced my portal usage, and they noticed I was in London when we had that little problem at the British Library." This little problem being a rare and valuable book bursting into flames. "I think they've banned me from traveling to London. Or maybe to anywhere. I'm afraid to try again. I haven't even told Tobey. He'll be so upset if we can't go somewhere tropical for our honeymoon, but I hear the Rosaria Grand Hotel is very nice. Their gnomes—"

"Daisy, please press pause on your mouth. Did anyone specifically say you were barred from travel?" I looked questioningly to Olivia and Mr Tenpenny, but they both shook their heads no.

"Well, not really. I thought about asking, but then they might question me about why I'd gone to a certain library with you, and you're already having enough trouble with your magic and the license deadline, that I didn't want to heap more strikes against you."

Which was weirdly nice and made me feel kind of bad for all the ideas I'd just had of what I could put in her performance review.

"Thanks for that. But if a travel ban came from HQ, it would involve paperwork."

"That's true. They do love their paperwork."

"Maybe it's something else," I said, trying to be helpful.

"Like what?"

I was very tempted to say her healthy diet might not be providing enough of the sugar that was vital fuel for all Magics, but what was more at the forefront of my mind was that my magic problem might be contagious. After all, as disturbing as the realization was, the person I'd spent more time with than anyone else over the past several days had been Daisy (yes, typing that did make me shudder a bit). And while I'd love to lay claim as the person who broke Daisy Honeysuckle, it had the same ick factor as kicking an overly perky guinea pig.

"I'm not sure," I said. "Maybe go see Runa, though. I'll see what I can do. Is there a way for me to check the last location of the Fairy Tags that went offline? Even just a screenshot or something of where—?" An incoming image pinged through before I'd finished speaking. "K, thanks for that. Also, is there a way for me to track where these six Fairy Tags have been? A report or—"

And before I'd finished *that* sentence, my phone pinged again. I looked at the screen to see the Fairy Tag app downloading onto my device, along with a detailed listing, complete with GPS coordinates of all the Fairy Tags' previous locations with what I assumed were the six live ones highlighted in pink. If nothing else, Daisy was preternaturally efficient.

"You'll really do what you can?" Daisy asked.

"I'll try," I said, noting and shrinking from Olivia's ever deepening scowl. "I'm not sure if HQ will listen, though."

"But Nino's sort of one of us. He's Magic. In so many ways," she added, and I could practically hear the twinkle in her eyes.

Still, I had to agree.

CHAPTER TWELVE
IN THE CHANGING ROOM

Once I ended the call with Daisy — and before Olivia or Busby could get a word in — I told them, "I need to see if I can find Mr Wood."

"I'm afraid I can't let you go after him," said Olivia.

"Yes, you can. You have to," I told her. Busby stiffened and shook his head. He had a point. Olivia wasn't the kind of person who was used to being contradicted. Also, with her drop of banshee blood, even a tiny shout from her could kill me, making it even more crucial that I watch my tongue around her.

"Look, Cassie, I'm sorry to say this, but your Mr Wood is not a priority. That sounds harsh, but we have much broader concerns at the moment. I'll put a couple people on the lookout for him, but your time needs to be used far more effectively."

"By going back to the Academy?" I criticized. "Mr Tenpenny could take that little form just as well as I could."

"Cassie, as Busby just explained, you are very much involved in this on many levels, and I don't want you bumbling around trying to find one Norm. It is vital that you return to the Academy and get your belongings. In fact, with this tiara mystery, it's now imperative you get those jewels back before the vampires lay their hands on them. I don't know exactly what kind of power the Boncoeur Jewel might give them, but it's becoming painfully clear that we must keep them from getting it if we're to have any chance against them in an uprising. An uprising that will lead to the subjugation and deaths of many, *many* more people than just one Norm. Do you understand?"

"Couldn't we just *avada kadavra* them?" I asked, which stirred a grumbling noise of complaint from Mr T.

"This isn't Harry Potter, Cassie," Olivia said witheringly. "This is real magic. Now, please, go change, or I will use a BrainSweeping Charm to force you to do so." More softly she said, "This really is for the best, and I do promise to put some people on the search for Mr Wood. Okay?"

Seeing my stubbornness wasn't going to get me anywhere but in deeper trouble, I nodded.

Olivia held out Daisy's bag that cost more than my monthly rent. "Feel free to use the room behind that tapestry to change."

I slipped behind the tapestry to find the most luxurious of executive restroom facilities. Seriously, the space was bigger than my first apartment. It also seemed to be soundproofed as I could hear no voices or other noises coming from beyond the door.

I checked the Fairy Tag app that had appeared on my screen. Again I wondered how Daisy was doing these things to my phone, but there was no movement, no live signal showing on my screen. Figuring the fairies were taking a coffee break, I hurriedly scanned the information Daisy had sent. From what I could tell at a glance, none of the tags had ever left London, meaning Mr Wood really hadn't made it to the Cotswolds unless he'd gone on a wild shopping spree to replace every scrap of clothing and luggage he'd brought.

As I kicked off my shoes, my heart nearly jumped out of my chest when six dots on the app's map began blipping a steady signal where there'd been none before. I was trying to zoom in to see if I could determine their exact location when an all caps text from Daisy chimed through with the message: *THEY'RE BACK!!!* Which, if not for the string of happy-face emojis that followed the words, would have come across as threatening. Once the message cleared, I finished zooming in.

Daisy hadn't been wrong. All six Fairy Tags really were clustered within the Tower itself, circling a single location like tiny vultures honing in on a bit of roadkill.

I ran the risk of Olivia and Busby thinking I didn't know how to dress myself, but I couldn't take the chance of the tags moving or going offline again. I texted Rafi, asking him if he had Nigel's number. Rather than text back, he called me mere seconds after the text had gone through.

"So, Nigel does have a number — all the Yeoman Warders get a mobile for emergencies — but it might not do you any good."

"Why?"

"I don't think he quite understands how mobiles work. He's sort of missed out on that technology. Why, what's up?"

"I need someone to see what's happening at a certain location."

"Ooh, like an underground party?"

"No, not like an underground party. Look, I'm pretty sure after haunting the place for a couple decades, that Nigel probably knows the ins and outs of the Tower better than any of us." I then explained the Fairy Tags, how they'd all stopped moving, but that now a handful were circling somewhere in the Tower of London complex. "And he might just be able to help me with sorting out where they are."

"Smart thinking. I'll give you a call back when I find him."

For an agonizing few minutes I watched Mr Wood's Fairy Tags circling a single spot. My only thought was that Winston's gang of kleptomaniac ravens had stolen the tags from Mr Wood and were now flying around with them. Which I suppose could have happened. Mr Wood could very well have gone with his tour group to the Tower, the ravens spotted the gleam of the tags, and then picked them off one by one like chimps picking nits off a fellow troupe member. I was just relaxing into this theory when, barely five minutes after I'd hung up, my phone rang, startling me out of my reverie.

"I've got him," Rafi told me.

"How does this—?" Nigel said, his voice sounding far away from the device. "Oh, I see. But then you just press the whole thing against your face? Not very hygienic for the skin, is it? Oh, right. Hello? Hello, Cassie, can you hear me?"

I could hear him. Likely half of London could hear him because he was shouting into the phone.

"Nigel, yes, I can hear you. You don't need to speak quite so loudly."

"Really? I can't imagine why not. This thing doesn't even reach my mouth."

"Trust me. Now, Nigel, listen close. I need you to go to the raven enclosure where you're going to look for something."

The *click click* of Nigel's shoes came through the phone, and I could hear tourists chattering in the background. Along the way, Nigel told me (and Rafi, I assumed) how his latest ghost tour had cackled and hooted over the number of tourists who'd twisted their ankles after being foolish enough to wear high heels to the cobblestoned grounds of the Tower that day.

"You don't tell them about the history of the Tower?" I asked.

"Some enjoy that, but most have lived so much history, or, well, *haunted* so much history that they far prefer getting a chuckle over the mishaps and foibles of the living. Okay, I'm here. What am I looking for?"

"Take about five steps forward and a couple steps to the left."

"Is this some silly dance you're capturing on video? Am I

going to go *viral*?" he asked, sounding enthusiastic about the prospect… and like he'd just recently learned the modern meaning of the word 'viral'.

"It's more of a treasure hunt. Now, what do you see? You're looking for small devices, round with white and silver on the casing. And they'd be about—" I tried to recall what Daisy had told me about the tags "—a centimeter in diameter. There should be several of them."

"I'm looking, but I don't see anything. Hold on. No, sorry, just a piece of gum wrapper."

The signal from the remaining tags kept circling.

"Look up. Anything hovering above your head?"

"No, just a walkway. I'm under the Bowyer Tower."

"Okay, two more places. First, go to the raven enclosure itself."

Nigel did so, telling me along the way that he'd been training Winston to come to the sound of a whistle. "His arriving out of nowhere absolutely delights my tour groups. Both the living ones and the ghostly ones."

This did sound like something tourists would enjoy, but when Nigel checked inside the ravens' enclosure, he found nothing that matched my description. Although he did scoldingly ask Winston how they'd managed to get a child's toy shield and sword into the enclosure. He also mumbled to himself that this would explain the wailing seven-year-old he'd had to console earlier in the day.

"Okay," I directed, "now go up to the walkway above you and see if you find anything."

"The walkway? Will this thing be able to do that?" he asked, and from the decrease in volume, I assumed he was asking Rafi. "Really? The signal can go all the way up there? What marvels! Alright," he said after a few moments, "I'm on the walkway, and I see nothing except tourists. It's quite crowded today, in fact. The good weather, you know."

"Have Rafi work up a way to block that area off for just a moment. Tell him a Patio Charm might work."

This spell, one of Rafi's inventions, created a private oasis which tourists would, without even noticing, skirt around, allowing the people inside to carry on without disturbance.

Nigel relayed the message, then in a tone of absolute wonder, said, "That is very clever, young man. I'm looking around, Cassie, but there's nothing." Before I could ask, he said, "Looking up, scanning the walls, the sky above, and nothing that seems out of the ordinary."

I cursed inwardly, but thanked Nigel for his time, exchanged a few pleasantries, then we said our goodbyes. This was followed by a fair amount of confusion over how to hang up and what sounded like Rafi trying to grab his phone back. Suddenly, there was a loud *clack* and the call went dead. I had a feeling Rafi would either be spending the next hour doing his best with a Repair Charm or heading off to the store to buy a new phone.

It only took a few moments to change out of my off-the-rack, mostly secondhand clothes and into Daisy's bespoke blazer, blouse, and skirt and a pair of stylish sneakers from an overpriced, eco-conscious brand. It took another five minutes for me to get over how much I resented how well everything fit and felt on.

When I stepped out nearly half an hour after going in, Busby shot up from his chair. "If you're ready," he said, sounding somewhat worried as he bustled toward me. He shot a look back at Olivia, her face creased with irritation. Seriously, if she were a cartoon, she would have had steam coming out of her ears. Mr Tenpenny grabbed me by the elbow and shuttled me toward the door, muttering, "We really ought to go."

CHAPTER THIRTEEN
LESS SCOWLING, MORE SMILING

Mr T and I emerged on Lola's street in Rosaria. The scent of spicy breakfasts being fried up made my stomach rumble despite the three cookies I'd gobbled down before leaving HQ. Other than a few kids playing and a pair of neighbors chatting, the colorful neighborhood was quiet.

"Any luck with Bunny?" I asked. This was one of Lola's neighbors. A special needs fellow who filled the street with the noise of his attempts to play drums.

Mr T's thin lips tightened. "I'm afraid there's no trace of him. Just like the other missing Magics."

"And Mr Wood? You heard Olivia. No one seems to care that there's been no sign of him for days." My feet suddenly felt weighed down despite the lofty footbed of Daisy's shoes.

"You know I like Nino as well," Busby said, sympathy filling his voice. "Which is why, while you were changing, I argued with Olivia about including him in our list of missing people, but she's being rather stubborn about turning our resources to finding any one individual. She says it's better to tackle the whole problem, not just one aspect of it." I was about to protest that Mr Wood wasn't just a cog in a machine that wasn't acting up to snuff, but

Busby cut me off. "I have asked around, but even I don't know exactly what we can do. As a Norm who has never been registered as having magic, he's out of our jurisdiction. But I do, as I've said before, have a few people scouting around."

I can't say why, but until HQ were firmly committed to looking for Mr Wood, I decided not to mention the Fairy Tags' activity. Besides, with their on-and-off signaling, the devices could simply be defective. "Are there any ham- or bacon-themed restaurants in London?" I asked.

"There is, of course, the Pret á Manger franchise. They have quite a selection of breakfast and lunch sandwiches that contain ham and bacon. Sausage rolls as well, although they pale in comparison to what the Tower's pixies can whip up. Why do you ask?"

"I still have this hopeful image in my head of Mr Wood having found one of them and just whiling away his entire vacation sampling the many things you can do to a pig." After several steps of silence, I asked, "You really don't think his disappearance is related to our missing people?"

"I don't think so. I know Nino has some magic in him, but Rafi's gone over the lists of the missing, and they're nearly all strong Magics. Not a single Untrained has been taken, so I doubt these villains would be interested in Mr Wood's meager amount of power."

"But Mr Wood has several Magic friends. What if they were interested in him to get to you, me, or Daisy?" Mr T stopped and glanced at me with what I think was a look of pride. "What?" I asked cautiously.

"That's a very smart line of thinking. We do, of course, have Norm friends, but not many who know what we are. Dr Torres and your Mr Wood are the rare exceptions. I will try to bring this up with Olivia after we get your things."

"What do you think they're doing with all those Magics?"

"I honestly hate to think of what's being done to them. To have so many disappearing without any sort of ransom or ultimatum or anything of that sort is rather disturbing."

"It has to be to steal their power. You heard about Mel Faegan being returned without any magic juice left in his system, right?"

"I did," Mr Tenpenny managed to say through tight lips. "I keep asking myself how he escaped or, if he didn't escape, why his captors sent him back. Runa says he still can't speak about it. She's worried that might affect his ability to fully recover. I don't think she'll need to send him to HQ's medical ward, but she's leaving the possibility open."

A thought struck me just then.

"Is Winnifred still there?" Winnifred (the poor woman) was the wife of Inspector Oberlin and had been a client of mine. I'd solved her case, but as bad luck would have it, she'd been violently attacked before I could deliver her brooch to her and get her signature on my detective's license application. It had been touch and go for the first twenty-four hours, after which the medics at HQ placed her in a medically induced coma to ease her healing.

"She is. Still not up to par, but she is awake, and they say she's progressing. Whatever that means," he added critically.

Once we turned onto Magical Main Street, I realized how much nicer it was to be Daisy than myself. People smiled at me, said hello, and just seemed genuinely pleased to see me. Then, for some reason, they would don expressions of confusion, upset, and hurt feelings.

"Less scowling and more smiling," Mr T hiss-whispered. "Daisy smiles. A lot."

He was right. I was so used to being greeted by angry stares and downright contempt that I couldn't help but glower at most of my fellow Rosarians. I threw on my best attempt at a beaming smile. After the next few passersby gave us a wide berth, Mr Tenpenny passed me a side glance.

"Dear Merlin, you look demented," he said. "Smile like you've just discovered Spellbound is giving you free pastries for life." I did my best. Mr T sighed. "It'll do. Just, maybe, practice a bit."

"What if I think dumb? Witless? Like an eager-to-please puppy who doesn't know any better?" I tried it, even though the broadness of the grin made me feel like a circus clown and the widening of my eyes made me worry they might just fall out of my head.

"That actually seems to be working," Busby said approvingly.

Just then, Tobey came striding toward us. I instinctively ducked my head, expecting him to be mad at me or, at the very least, disappointed for not being able to make our study session that morning. Which is why, at first, I couldn't understand why his eyes lit up when he saw me, nor why, when he reached us and before I could avoid it, he'd wrapped me in a warm embrace and was lowering his lips to mine.

Suddenly remembering what and who I looked like, I jerked back.

"If you kiss me, I have a knee that would very much like to meet certain delicate parts of your body."

Tobey staggered back, looking for all the world like a man whose world has just been shattered.

"What did I—?" He tilted his head, a look on his face like he was replaying what had just happened in his head. "Cassie?" I glowered at him, and he took several steps back. "I'm pretty sure I'm going to need therapy for this at some point in my near future."

"Yeah, you and me both."

Tobey then chuckled, possibly in the denial stage of his

mental crisis. "I've got to get a picture," he said as he reached his hand to his back pocket.

"Do it, and the only way you'll be able to retrieve that phone will be via a very thorough internal prostate exam."

Tobey gave a resolute nod and eased his phone back into his pocket. "What's going on?"

"I've been liberated from my jail cell, and I'm in disguise. Duh."

Did I just say *Duh*? Holy hexes, was I becoming Daisy-fied? Was this disguise causing permanent damage?

"And now we're on our way to the Academy to collect Cassie's things," said Mr T. "It might look good if you went with us. Hold hands, you two." Like a pair of choreographed dancers, Tobey and I stepped away from each other. "Look, you both want to be detectives in your own right. Part of detective work sometimes requires going undercover, playing a part. So, hold hands when we walk in or, Tobey, I will tell Daisy you aren't vegan; and, Cassie, I will tell Alastair about that torn page in his most valuable comic book."

This had been a little accident when I'd been reading Alastair's premier issue of *Batman*. I was supposed to clean the apartment that day, so, as I read, I'd been absent-mindedly tidying up dust particles with a Shoving Spell. I'd gotten a little distracted by Bruce Wayne's derring-do, and the dust cluster had drifted over to me, sending me into a fit of such violent sneezing that I nearly dropped the book. Stupidly, rather than let it go, I'd held on, and now page sixteen had a three-inch rip down the middle. I'd told no one, I'd slipped it back into its plastic sleeve, and, as far as I knew, the book hadn't been taken out since.

"How did you—?" Mr T merely lifted his eyebrows. "Right. Magic."

I took hold of Tobey's hand.

CHAPTER FOURTEEN
HUMAN AFTER ALL

"Your Exams are this morning, correct?" Mr Tenpenny asked, in a really awful attempt to sound like he was making casual conversation.

"Supposed to be, but Oberlin had some unexpected business to tend to, so they're trying to find someone else to proctor the test. We're supposed to wait in the exam room in the meantime. Gives me time to meditate, go into a real Zen state before the test starts, right?" Tobey added, in his own very poor attempt at sounding casually unconcerned.

"Well, use it wisely."

To keep up our ruse as the perfect couple, Tobey placed a grudging peck on my cheek before lumbering toward the stairs that would take him from the lobby to the Academy's testing room. Mentally, I wished him luck, but I didn't think his mindfulness mumbo jumbo was going to clear away the doubt that was screaming from his pores.

As we neared the door to the police station part of the Academy, Mr Tenpenny stopped me and said, "When we get in there, I'll do most of the talking. But you're going to need to hold your head high and act as confident as Daisy would in such a situation. Ready?"

I could go into the details of the extraordinary levels of

anxiety my nerves reached as we approached the screened-off intake desk, of Mr T explaining HQ's requisition demands to the young clerk, of the clerk's lack of resistance once the form with Olivia's signature was shown to him, of the bedazzled look in his eyes when I gave him my best Daisy smile, and of the interminable wait while he went to fetch my stuff. But let me just boil it down to what I said when the clerk came back.

"What do you mean, *they're gone*?"

"This locker noted on the intake form—" His voice cracked as he pointed a shaky finger at the sheet he'd pulled from a filing cabinet before heading off to the storage area. "It's empty. This," he gingerly pushed Wordsworth's book toward me like offering a hunk of raw steak to appease a snarling Rottweiler, "was on top of the locker, but inside—" His voice broke off with a squeak, and he looked like a puppy who fears being scolded by the person he most wants to please. "There's nothing inside."

I was about to rail against the poor guy, but Mr T stepped forward, shooting me a look to stand down since it wasn't the clerk's fault. I had my doubts on that count. I mean, I still wasn't used to my whitener-powered dental weaponry. What if I'd smiled too broadly? What if the sparkly nature of Daisy's teeth had short-circuited something in the guy's brain?

"Are there other lockers you could check?" Busby asked.

The clerk, a true beanpole who was probably six foot four and weighed all of a hundred and sixty pounds, swallowed hard, his Adam's apple rising and falling.

"I did, sir. That's what took so long. I thought maybe someone noted the number wrong. But none of the three lockers that have items in them have *these* items in them." Again, he pointed to the intake form.

"May we speak to Inspector Oberlin?" asked Mr T, as if he hoped Oberlin might be free for a spot of tea and crumpets.

"He's out, sir. Had to run an errand."

"Yes, so I heard," Busby said tersely, and I don't know if the irritation was over Oberlin's absence or the reminder of Tobey's test. After a contemplative moment, Mr T said, "This is rather concerning. When will the Inspector be returning?"

"I don't know, sir," the clerk croaked. "I'm really sorry, sir."

"It's not your fault, I'm sure. But those objects," Busby said, as if choosing his words very carefully, "might be quite dangerous. I'd like to hope this is just a clerical error and that whoever took them doesn't know about their potential power. I don't want to jump to conclusions. After all, it could just be coincidental, but it is vital we find Miss Black's belongings."

"And find Mr Wood while we're at it?" I threw in, figuring squeaky wheel and all that.

"Ca— Daisy," Mr T began, barely catching himself, "if the person who took your client's belongings knows what they can do if they're joined together, your Mr Wood will be the least of our worries. Are we agreed to work on this first?"

I reluctantly agreed, and we were about to turn away when the clerk said, "There's one more item of Miss Black's. As her lawyer," he said to me, his eyes begging for approval, "maybe you should look at it?"

The clerk slipped a piece of paper toward me. *Cassie* was written on the front in a familiar, flourishing hand.

"Why is this here?" I asked incredulously, then remembered to throw a bit of Daisy's ditzy-ness into my tone. "I mean, like, why wasn't it delivered, like, super directly to my client?" I then tilted my head to give a buoyant swish of my ponytail, truly feeling like I was channeling my inner Daisy to a T.

"I started to, but the guard on duty, Gilly, said Miss Black was sleeping." Only then did I notice the clerk had a half-eaten cinnamon roll sitting on top of a Spellbound napkin. I'm telling you, pastry bribery is a rampant and dangerous problem in MagicLand.

I took the note and gave it a quick glance.

"Mayor Marheart, like, *totally* wants to see my client," I said to Mr T's curious look.

"Thank you for everything," Mr T told the clerk before we headed back out to the lobby where Busby put a Shrinky Dink Charm on Wordsworth's book to make it the size of a small notepad.

"What next?" I asked.

Slipping the miniaturized tome into his jacket's inner pocket, Mr T replied, "I believe we should go see Mayor Marheart. I'm quite curious to know what it is she wanted."

"Wait. What if she's the person who took my stuff?"

"A fair thought, but how would she have gotten past the sergeant's desk, made it to the storage area, and known the combination to get into the locker where your things were?"

"Well…" I began, struggling for something to counter his annoyingly logical statement. "She could have glamoured the clerk."

"Glamoured him? As in, made him more attractive?"

"No. Vampires, they influence people to bend them to their will. Glamouring. That's how they can lure victims to them to suck their blood."

"Cassie, these are real-life vampires. Not fictional ones. They retain some magic, but nothing different from what you or I could do."

"So… a BrainSweeping Charm?"

"That mesh screen in front of the clerk?" asked Mr T. "It's an Anti-Hex Screen. Top of the line, I believe. Any spell to influence, coerce, or bribe the desk attendant absorbs into the mesh and dissipates."

"One of Rafi's creations?"

"No, Alastair's, actually. How are things on that front?"

"Better. Although, this—" I indicated my current state of appearance "—is going to make things very awkward. I mean, what if he likes this better?"

"I doubt that he would. And if he truly loves you, he'll see past it. Love, in this case, is most definitely not blind."

We'd been speaking in the lobby area of the Academy, and, even though he knew the Exams hadn't even started yet, I wondered if Mr T was lingering around in the hopes of seeing Tobey bounding down from the Exam room with a smile on his face and a detective's badge pinned to his shirt.

I was just about to tell him sticking around wouldn't change Tobey's test results when Busby glanced down at one of the end tables in the lobby. On it was a two-day-old, thoroughly thumbed through copy of the *Herald*. Busby, despite his insistence that he thought the *Herald* barely good enough to line a bird cage, seized it.

"What in the—?" he practically shouted as he shook the paper at me. "Have you seen this?"

"If you'd stop flapping the thing at me, I might be able to see it. What is it?" I asked as he slapped the paper into my hands.

"It's an absolute disgrace. Slander— No, maybe not. Invasion of privacy. Yes, that's it. Using my likeness without permission."

Now, you've read quite a number of words about Mr Busby Tenpenny. He's the poster child for that stereotypical stiff British upper lip. He's cool and collected, handling problems and emotions with grace, sangfroid, and perfect posture. So to have him blustering, nearly shouting his disgust in a public place, well, it was kind of a relief to discover he really was human.

"There." He jabbed his finger into the folded-back page. "See that? *That* should not be allowed. Never mind Matilda for now, we are going to the *Herald's* offices this instant to complain."

I bit back a smile at his indignant attitude. After all, I'd nearly grown immune to the things the *Herald* had been printing about me in its opinion section over the past several weeks. That's not to say I wasn't relieved when Leo Flourish, the paper's editor, swore he'd do everything in his power to turn the paper in a less anti-Cassie direction. But to see the normally unflappable Busby Tenpenny well and duly flapped and ready to unleash some harsh words on Leo was almost amusing.

An amusement I knew to keep to myself as I raced after the Tenpenny Tornado that had just stormed out of the lobby.

CHAPTER FIFTEEN
A TENPENNY TELLING OFF

What had Mr T so upset was a photo of him taken when we'd recently come back from HQ. At the time, he'd been thoroughly sozzled by banshee booze, and when the photo was snapped, he'd been drunkenly draped over me as I lugged him home.

"This issue is from two days ago," I said as I chased Mr T down the Academy's broad entry stairs. "How are you only just seeing it?"

"I've told you before, I do not take that paper. And for good reason," he huffed. "This is an outrage."

Mr T's determination had him double-timing it down the street, and I had to jog to keep up with him. Once at the *Herald*'s offices, Mr Tenpenny politely but tersely asked the receptionist to get us in to see Leo Flourish on urgent HQ business. Perhaps it was the steely fire in his eyes, perhaps it was the rigid determination in his stance, but the receptionist didn't try a single delaying tactic to get rid of us. Instead, she attempted a Dial the Boss Spell on her desk phone. Nothing happened.

With a look of irritation on her round face, she said, "Been doing that all day. Leo's gotta get this system checked out. Just go on up. Third floor, biggest office. I'd have someone show you up, but half the staff is out with some cold or something. Probably just taking advantage of the nice weather," she grumbled in a way that left no doubt she'd be calling in 'sick' herself the following day.

Busby insisted it would be best if I kept my identity secret until we returned to HQ, so once we were in Leo's office, I maintained my Daisy disguise with a bright smile on my face and a glittering twinkle in my eye. Meanwhile, Mr Tenpenny let loose. He never truly raised his voice, but he did speak in a manner that carried the full force of Magic HQ behind it.

I felt bad for Leo, but I knew to stay well out of Mr T's warpath. As I lingered back, I caught sight of that morning's edition. A broad headline on the front page asked: *Is Inspector Oberlin Playing Fair?* A photo showed the Walrus standing next to my open safe, looking grim and gruff as he glared at me. Leo's paper had caused me no end of trouble, but from the quick snippets I could read, he seemed to be making good on his promise to clear my name. The thought produced a genuine smile, knowing I had to accept my allies wherever I could find them.

Leo was earnestly assuring Mr T that the *Herald* had turned in a new direction after Leo's mistake of leaving the paper in the hands of someone more bent on vengeance against me than journalistic integrity, but Busby — his pride truly wounded — wasn't ready to back down.

"Regardless of how you intend to run the *Herald* in the future," Mr T said as he slapped the offending paper down on Leo's desk, "I would very much like to complain directly to the photographer who took this picture. He should know very well that this sort of thing goes against all the rules of proper journalism. Unless you no longer consider your paper proper journalism, Mr Flourish. Perhaps it's humorous fiction you're aiming for?"

"This is a serious paper, Busby, and you know it."

"Not for the past several weeks. In fact, your quality has been sliding for months. Now, the photographer," Busby asserted. "I have a right to speak with him."

"You have the right," agreed the editor, who did indeed look shamefaced at Mr T's evaluation of his paper. "Unfortunately, the guy quit yesterday. Asked for his last paycheck and took off."

"I suppose that's a relief, then."

"It's not," said Leo irritably. "I've got who-knows-what-percentage of my staff out sick, including most of the photography people. I don't know if it's truly something going around, or if they're staging some sort of protest against me for defending the RetroHex Vaccine — something we've been taking since we were kids without any controversy — but it's making it rather difficult to run this paper properly. I'm already behind on the afternoon edition."

"I'm sure it will all blow over," said Busby, his voice still judgmentally imperious. "But I would encourage you to do better, Mr Flourish. Less opinion, fewer made-up facts, and more actual news. There are people going missing all around us, and yet you've dedicated your time and newsprint to this drivel."

On the last word, Mr Tenpenny thumped the photograph that had so displeased him. Even I thought he was being a bit unfair. The *Herald* had been giving over large amounts of front-page space to lists naming all the missing Magics, reporting the staggering numbers, and providing insight into the lives of some of those who had disappeared.

"You're right," Leo conceded. "I was an idiot. Speaking of missing Magics, word has been trickling in from other communities that a few of the missing have been coming back without their magic intact, much as we saw with Mel Faegan."

"Have you heard if any of them recall what happened?" Mr T

asked, speaking less like an egregiously offended member of the public and more like a professional HQ agent keen for facts. "It would greatly help our inquiries into the matter."

Leo shook his head. "Unfortunately, this is all rather new. It's been tough to tell if they simply can't remember, or if they aren't ready to. But I plan to keep on it regardless of my staff shortage."

"Do that," said Mr T. "And anything you find, please relay it to HQ as soon as possible. This has moved far beyond the realm of worrisome. If I may ask, what else are you working on?"

"Is this HQ trying to thwart the right to a free press?" Leo asked, but in a way that was more banter than challenge.

"We haven't the time nor the desire to do any such thing."

"Then I think you might be interested in some *proper journalism* I've been working on," said the editor wryly.

"And what would that be?" asked Mr T, his voice still cool, but with a hint of curiosity in it.

"Inspector Wesley Oberlin. His twenty-fifth year at the Academy is coming up, and he thinks it would be good if we did some sort of biographical piece about him." Leo's tone indicated that he had his own thoughts on the matter, and that Oberlin might not like those thoughts. "After his unfair arrest of Cassie Black," he gestured toward the copy of that day's *Herald* in front of him, "I'm not sure I really want to do the expected thing. So I've been researching, doing some digging."

"And you've come up with what, exactly?"

"I looked back, searching for any articles about Oberlin, looking for some juicy gossip that might clue me into something more interesting than just the usual. But there really isn't much other than his anti-vampire stance, his work as an officer, and one case in particular where he'd questioned some bruises on a young Magic."

"Oberlin? A good guy?" I couldn't help but ask.

"Perhaps," Leo said with a dismissive shrug. "I'll include that part, of course, but I'm wrapped up right now in his politics. His whole issue with Matilda Marheart. We all know about his campaign against her, and one could understand the bad feelings against an opponent, but even now his politics are clearly anti-Matilda, which makes me wonder why. Does he just hate the idea of women in power, or is there something more?

"I was thumbing through *An Enchanted History of the Portland Community* to see what I could find on Oberlin and came across an entry soon after he'd joined the Academy's force. The entry showed him in full uniform with a bunch of other cops standing up against what looked to me like a bunch of hippies with signs touting *Equality for Everyone,* and *They Don't Suck, You Suck.*

"The caption noted this was a rally for vampires to be treated equally, and that Oberlin had been especially zealous in dispersing the crowd. It's all making me eager to dig into this anti-vampire angle of his, how it relates to his distaste for Matilda Marheart, and what it might lead to."

"Unless your article is full of praise, Oberlin isn't going to be happy about what you come up with," Busby commented.

"No, but like I said, the *Herald* is turning in a new direction. Part of that direction means not becoming a tool for politicians' games. Journalism, Busby," he said with a confident grin, "that's the name of the game. And, look, sorry about the photo. If it makes you feel any better, it did give plenty of people a much-needed chuckle."

"It most certainly does not."

"Then I'll print a statement on the front page of the afternoon edition that the photo was staged as part of a stunt for charity. Your reputation will remain intact. And it'll give me something to fill column inches since so few of my staff have gotten their articles in."

"Thank you for that," Mr T said, sounding truly touched by the offer. "Now, we really ought to be going. I thank you for your time, Mr Flourish. And please remember to maintain the integrity of your profession in the future."

As soon as we began walking away from the *Herald*'s offices, Busby said, "I do wish I hadn't sent your parents on that mission. We could probably use their help at the moment."

"You can't call them back?"

"They're somewhat embedded. Any call would risk exposing them."

"Sorry, what? You said they were only scouting around. You never said anything about being *embedded*."

"Don't worry." Which, as everyone knows, is the first thing you say when someone should very much worry. "They have a Rapid Recall Charm on them. If they're in any danger, or if we truly need them back, they'll be alerted and will hopefully be in a situation to return via the temporary portal they've been assigned."

This mostly reassured me. Although they were as uncomfortable a mode of travel as Morelli's illegal portals, temporary portals had a trace on them, meaning HQ could track my parents' approximate location, if need be.

"But how do they carry a portal around without it being noticed by this mystery group they're with?" I asked.

"It's on a pendant your mother is wearing."

"A pendant," I said, thinking of my mom's necklace I'd found, lost, then found again. And thinking of where I'd found it that second time.

"We need to talk to Matilda Marheart," I asserted.

"No," Busby said sternly, "I know you want to follow up on that note of hers, but I think we should get back to HQ to inform them of what's happened at the Academy and discuss what steps to take next."

"Look, Matilda has been pretty adamant and pushy about me finding her jewel, even though she knew all along it would be a difficult case."

"As you would say, and this has to do with what, exactly?"

I explained to him about the various connections between Matilda being seen at places where pieces of the jewel had been, as well as her being at Wordsworth's convention from where his book had gone missing, and her presence at Bookman's right before that book reappeared.

"Plus, she had my mom's pendant dangling from a mirror in her entry hall. Tobey saw it and told me about it. That's how I was able to, um… retrieve it."

"Retrieve it how?" Busby asked, one eyebrow arched.

"I didn't break in, if that's what you're thinking. And speaking of break-ins, there's Runa's clinic as well."

"Runa's clinic?"

"The broken glass? Matilda had a bandaged hand that very morning. And the saw that was stolen? It contains the final piece of the Boncoeur Jewel. Or, I think it does. Anyway… we now know she was at the Academy—" I held up the note "—right around the time my items went missing. That's way too many incidents to be coincidence."

"You make a valid point." Mr T paused a moment as if considering something. "I believe we can spare a few minutes to go see the mayor, but after that we really must get back to HQ."

"Can't you just text Olivia with the news?" Mr T's cheeks blossomed with warmth as he kept his eyes rigidly forward. "Do you not know how to text?" I prodded.

"Of course I know how to text," he blustered. "Only…" He pulled out his phone. "I've forgotten my passcode. Olivia insisted on resetting it for security reasons, and with all that's been going on, I've forgotten what she changed it to."

I looked at Mr T's phone. It was the newest model, and I had a feeling I knew exactly how to get into it. I told him to hand it over. I then waved my hand over the device as if performing a spell.

"I've tried various charms and none of them work," he protested. "Should you be doing that? Your magic might not exactly play nicely with technol—" I held up a finger, indicating for him to remain silent while Cassie the Great worked her wonky magic. I mumbled some words about revealing, opening, submitting to our wishes.

"Are you sure you know what you're doing?" Mr T asked, like someone losing all confidence in their tech guru. "I can take it to the—"

"Speak your name," I said in my best Mystical Magician voice as I turned the phone toward Mr T.

The front camera was on, allowing him to see his face as he said, "Busby Tenpenny."

The phone gave a little chime, then I turned it back around to check I'd gotten to the home screen.

"Never doubt my skills," I said as I handed his phone back to him

"How did you—? You didn't even try a code."

"Mr T, it's a new model. You get in by face and voice recognition."

He stared at the phone in amazement. "I wondered why Olivia took my photo when she returned it to me."

Delighted to have proven myself useful for once, Mr T and I continued on to Matilda's house. Unfortunately, we weren't the first ones to the party.

CHAPTER SIXTEEN
STUNNING THE WALRUS

On Matilda's tidy front lawn were four Rosarian police officers, their hands held ready to fire off a round of Stunning Spells. As Oberlin led Matilda out of her home, her eyes caught sight of me, then lasered in on Mr Tenpenny, begging him for help. I didn't know what he should or could do.

"We need to talk to her first," I told him. "Before Oberlin does."

"What do you expect me to do?"

"Throw some HQ weight around, obviously."

After adjusting his tie and pocket square (both emerald green and dotted with tiny strawberries), Mr Tenpenny stepped forward. "Inspector Oberlin, thank you for your assistance in apprehending our suspect."

Oberlin, who, in my opinion, already looked rather stupid, looked even more idiotic as he stared dumbly at Mr T for several seconds before finally puffing up his barrel chest and stating, "This is our prisoner, Tenpenny, not yours. As you can see, we were here first."

"Finders keepers does not apply to people, I'm afraid."

"I was thinking it was more a first-come-first-served situation," said Oberlin, as if truly seeking clarification in the matter.

"Either way, HQ has sent me to collect Mayor Marheart for questioning regarding certain matters having to do with her activities in this community and beyond." Which I have to admit was wonderfully vague and, also, not a lie. "She will be processed by us and detained by us, if need be. No sense cluttering up your jail with riffraff, correct?"

"True. There's already one hunk of riffraff I'm dealing with. But, as I always say, the more the merrier, especially if they're behind bars." He chortled over his own quip, then his eyes darted to me. Although he seemed about to question why Daisy Honeysuckle would be roaming around Rosaria with Busby Tenpenny, he did little more than give a nod of greeting. As for me, I was very tempted to stamp on his toes. After all, he wouldn't dare arrest Daisy, would he?

"Need I remind you that I outrank you, Inspector?" said Mr T, sounding very imperious, very willing-to-pull-rank.

"No, but Matilda Marheart is a dangerous individual. I'm afraid you don't know what you're dealing with."

"As a cooperation between our agencies, I would appreciate it if you enlightened me as to the exact nature of what you think this danger might be."

"Matilda Marheart is a vampire. Or is it vampress?" He mumbled to himself. "Either way, very dangerous, and very much not someone we want in our community. Especially not in such a high position in that community."

I considered what Leo had just told us. While I had my own worries about Matilda Marheart, Oberlin bore a pretty vile grudge against her. Was this arrest merely because she was a vampire, or was there something more? Had Oberlin actually been doing his job and found crimes to charge the mayor with? Or was this arrest for more personal, more vengeful reasons? If so, he couldn't exactly admit that to an HQ representative, could he? Still, Oberlin didn't seem ready to back down from taking Matilda into his custody.

"I'm well aware of what Ms Marheart's lineage is," Busby said, "and I have no fear of her, nor do I question her motives—" Wait. He didn't? Why not? She was a glamourer and jewel thief and she might be sucking the power from missing Magics. Did I miss the memo where we decided she wasn't something to be panicking over? "—and neither should you. This wouldn't be a spot of pettiness on your part because you lost to her, would it? Or are you going to claim she wasn't voted in by a majority of the people of Rosaria?"

"They didn't know her true nature," Oberlin insisted. "She's done very well at hiding what she is."

Through all of this, Matilda remained silent and maintained a calm façade, but I didn't miss the anxious attention in her eyes as she watched the verbal tennis match.

"Yes, well, thank you for alerting me to the danger this woman presents," said Busby. "I will see she's handled with extreme caution. We'll be on our way now."

Matilda already had her hands bound by a Handcuff Hex, so Mr T simply turned her away from Oberlin's men and guided her back toward her front door.

"You can't take her back in—" Oberlin began, his thick mustache bristling with indignation.

"Never fear, Inspector. We have a temporary portal ready to take her back to HQ." Busby touched his tie pin, a rose gold piece that was inset with a small black stone. "As I said, we came prepared for this arrest." Oberlin again looked at me, clearly ready to ask why Daisy would be assisting HQ with this, but Mr T barreled on, giving Oberlin no chance to speak. "I thank you and your team for doing the hard work for us. Very commendable."

Mr T instructed me to open the door, which had thankfully been left unlocked. Just as Matilda crossed her threshold, Mr T turned back to Oberlin as if he'd just remembered something. "And, Inspector?"

"Yes?" growled Oberlin.

"HQ have also taken Miss Black into our custody. If you could explain why your station was unable to relinquish her items to us, I would appreciate it."

And with that, Mr T closed the door on Oberlin, who looked like he'd just taken a direct hit from his officers' Stunning Spells.

"I didn't do anything wrong," insisted Matilda as soon as Mr T undid the Handcuff Hex.

"You didn't divulge who you were when you ran for office," Mr T replied coolly.

"That's not a crime. I didn't change my name. Anyone could have looked up who I am. In truth, I half-expected the *Herald* to run an exposé on it. I suppose they might have if they hadn't been so focused on insulting Cassie Black."

"Glad to do my part," I said, without thinking. Matilda narrowed her eyes at me, not in a scary way, but like a myopic trying to hone in on text that's too small.

"Cassie? What's—?"

"HQ gave me a makeover," I said bitterly.

"It really is for the best," Mr T stated, as if that was to be the last word on the subject. "Now, Mayor Marheart, why was Inspector Oberlin arresting you?"

"I have no idea," she said, a bit too quickly to seem entirely believable.

"It's nothing to do with your people?"

Matilda shook her head. "Until very recently I've barely been in contact with any vampires beyond my own family and the ones in Rosaria."

"*Ones*?" I blurted. "As in multiple?" Just how many bloodsuckers were there in MagicLand?

"We like to keep a low profile. What you just witnessed out there is only one reason. Any crime that occurs gets blamed on us. I'm also well aware that HQ believes we're responsible for the missing Magics and that we're planning an uprising, but that's simply not true."

"That remains to be seen," said Mr Tenpenny. I've only observed Busby in his official capacity on a few occasions. However, whenever I have, the stern features I'd grown used to in our day-to-day interactions turned truly formidable when he leveled his gaze on a suspect. I wasn't even the focus of that gaze just then, and I still felt a chill run down my legs. "You said you'd been out of contact with your people until very recently. Is that to do with the jewel you want found?"

"It does," replied Matilda, "but I'm afraid anything I say would be rather incriminating."

"Which is a very good reason to tell us what you know. This is not the time for secrets, Madame Mayor. In fact, I think you better explain yourself, since Cassie informs me you had what's possibly part of that very jewel here in your home." Busby tipped his head toward the mirror at the end of the entry hall. "Care to explain that?"

I didn't think it was possible, but Matilda's face went even paler than normal. Mr T fixed that you-better-tell-me-now stare on her once more. Did they teach him that during his HQ training? Could I learn it? I hardened my expression and narrowed my eyes at Matilda. But damn it, it was like Daisy's face had a default Smile Mode, and I ended up beaming a cheery grin at my adversary.

"What is she doing?" Matilda asked Busby, who looked at me with an expression of utter bafflement.

"I fear the day we figure out the motives behind anything Miss Black does may never come."

"I was being tough, steely, getting my suspect to submit to my will," I explained.

"By smiling at them like you're barking mad?" asked Mr T.

"Do not question my methods."

Matilda and Mr T exchanged rueful glances, then Busby stated, "The pendant, Ms Marheart. It was here. How did you obtain it? And what is your reason behind wanting the Boncoeur Jewel?"

"I think I would prefer to continue this interview at HQ," Matilda stated flatly. "There are things you need to be made aware of."

"Hold on," I interrupted. "Since when do prisoners get to make demands like, '*I'm not going to talk until you whisk me away to London?*' Because if you keep up that sort of thing, you're going to get a lot of people wanting to be arrested."

While keeping his eyes locked on Matilda as if trying to suss out her deepest secrets, Mr T said, "In this case, I believe it's a valid request. We just need to figure out how to get to HQ without going past Oberlin."

"I thought you had a temporary portal." I pointed to his tie pin.

"No, that was just a ruse to get Oberlin to back off. Fiona picked this up for me a couple years ago from an estate sale. Although, as I recall, the person who had died was quite adept at crafting portals, so I suppose I ought to be more careful when handling it before I end up somewhere in Newfoundland. Your home, Matilda…" Mr Tenpenny pondered. "The Real Portland side is quite near where Cassie lives, isn't it?"

"It is?" I asked, completely stupefied. I mean, you've heard the description of my neighborhood. It's not the kind of place mayors who are also vampires reside. Then again, Portland did have the strangest of setups, where an upper middle class street could be only two blocks away from a downtrodden one. Matilda's home, it turned out, was located on just such a street.

"Yes, about seven blocks to the south, I believe."

"That will work. We can walk from here to Cassie's building, then use Eugene's portal to get you to HQ."

"Wait. Morelli has a portal direct to HQ?" I asked.

"Of course he does," Mr T said, seeming to feel no need for explanation as he gestured for Matilda to show us the way to her doorway to Real Portland.

CHAPTER SEVENTEEN
LEGAL BLAH BLAH BLAH

"I don't like leaving Rosaria like this," said Matilda once we'd stepped through a pantry door and onto a tree-lined sidewalk in Real Portland. "Something's going on there that doesn't sit well with me."

"And this something is…?" asked Mr T.

"Someone in the community is working against the Magics, and I don't mean to brag, but I believe my presence has kept it from going too far. Still, for the life of me, I can't figure out who it is."

Just then, my phone blared out a notification. It was Daisy. On a video call. Again. Grudgingly, I accepted.

"Oh my golly!" she said by way of greeting. "I knew that Gigantio suit would look perfect on you."

"That would be because it's custom-made for you," I said, as if explaining to a particularly dimwitted gerbil how to un-shell a peanut. "I assume you've seen it on yourself before now."

"Sure have," she tittered with a blinding smile. The smile quickly dropped and she leaned closer to the phone. "I only called to warn you that someone at the Academy informed Oberlin that your cell is empty. The Inspector just phoned the agency asking what I knew about this, and you wouldn't believe what a good job I did at playing dumb."

I had so many comments on the tip of my tongue, but she had sort of sprung me from jail, so I held back. "I'm pretty sure I'd believe it." Okay, I *mostly* held back. "What did he say? And what did you tell him?"

"I said very sternly that, as your lawyer, I should have been informed immediately of your absence, and that it was super poopy of the Academy not to contact me directly. He seemed kind of confused by this, and asked why I'd been at the Academy trying to collect your stuff if I thought you were there, and I said it's the agency's property, and that I was responsible for agency stuff. Plus, some legal blah blah that really had him at a loss for words."

"Did he buy that?"

"Seemed to. I'm very persuasive."

"Daisy," Mr T cut in, "as soon as Tobey finishes his test, I think it best for you two to come to HQ. I'd prefer you and Tobey away from Rosaria for now."

Which, in hindsight, Rosaria turned out to be a far safer place than anywhere near HQ, but we'll get to that soon enough.

"Um, okay," Daisy said tentatively, looking anywhere but directly into her phone's camera. She then forced a smile. "It sure is good he's already done. Wouldn't want to keep you waiting, right?"

"He's already finished?" Mr Tenpenny asked, a touch of hopeful pride in the question. Daisy nodded, her smile wavering. "And he did...?"

"Not so good. He did get his name and the date right this time, though. I told him that's improvement."

"And the rest of the questions?"

"He got ninety-eight percent of them wrong."

"He only scored two percent?" I asked incredulously. Mr T gave me a withering sidelong glare, and I wondered what

Matilda was making of all this as she gave no indication she was even listening. "I'm just saying that level of failure takes real talent."

"And," said Daisy, "he's pretty sure the ones he got right were only because, halfway through, he was running out of time and started randomly marking answers on the test sheet just to fill it in."

"At least he has one more try," conceded Mr T.

"Exactly," beamed Daisy. "And he'll pass without a hitch, I'm sure."

Mr Tenpenny handed me back my phone. Looking very concerned, Daisy whispered, "He will, won't he?"

I shrugged and ended the call.

"You can't blame me this time," I protested. "This was all Oberlin's fault. If Tobey and I had had that study session this morning—"

"Yes. I mean, no, I don't blame you. But ninety-eight percent of the questions wrong? That has to be a record. And not one I thought any Tenpenny would ever set."

It took until we'd turned onto my street before I realized what might be in store for me.

"I'm just going to take a wild stab in the dark and guess that I'm to become one of the Tower of London's 'welcome guests' again," I said as we crossed the parking lot of the shuttered business next to my apartment building.

"You'll have much more freedom of movement this time," replied Mr T. "But, yes, for now, I believe it's safer for you, and more convenient for us, if you remained at HQ."

"Then I hope the Tower's pet policy includes cats, because I'm not going back there without Pablo."

"I was planning to suggest the same," Busby said, which made me wonder just how long they were going to keep me at HQ. And if I'd have to spend that entire time looking like Daisy.

Once I entered the front door's security code and we'd stepped into the building, I was faced with an obstacle. Or, rather, two obstacles. Both staring at me and both barring the stairway to my apartment. Although, one was looking at me with very lovey-dovey eyes. This had to be the one who'd wanted me to put in a good word for him to Daisy after she'd dropped off the invitation to Mr Wood's retirement party.

"It's me, not her," I told him, and something in my voice and non-twinkling eyes must have rung through to his love-struck ears, because his soppy expression fell in an instant. It then rose again just as quickly.

"Then there's still hope for me with her?" he asked optimistically.

"I doubt it."

"Please, Guildenstern," said Mr T, "if you wouldn't mind letting us through, we are rather in a hurry."

"Only because it be you asking, Busby," the gnome said. Then, after shooting a snide scowl at me, Guildenstern stepped aside.

"How do you tell them apart?" I whispered once we'd reached my welcome mat.

"It's quite simple," Mr T said. He then explained his system for telling gnomes apart. A system that sounded anything but simple to me.

I froze the minute we entered the apartment. Alastair was in the kitchen, eating straight out of the cereal box. Something he always got on my case about. The hypocrite. Still, I couldn't help but dash over to him and reach out for a hug, forgetting my disguise.

Alastair backed away until he bumped into the counter, then looked directly into my eyes. His entire face opened into a broad and welcoming grin as he set the box of granola down and grabbed hold of me.

"I can't believe you're here. *How* are you here?"

"I do hope you recognize me and that we don't have to have a discussion about your lack of boundaries with other women."

Alastair held me out at arm's length, his eyes filled with warm sincerity. "Cassie Black, I would know you anywhere."

So, I guess Mr T had been right. Love really wasn't blind.

Just as Alastair moved in to give what I had a feeling was going to be a long and knee-weakening kiss, there came a sound of throat clearing from the doorway. Alastair and I both turned to look at our forgotten guests. And we both blushed. We then stepped back from each other, and Alastair greeted Matilda and Mr T.

It was only then I noticed an envelope on the counter, open with a fair number of twenty-dollar bills sticking out of it. To my questioning look, Alastair said, "I forgot to tell you when I called last. The part from Uncommon Implements worked. I delivered the commission this morning. And got paid. Obviously."

"Morelli will be relieved." I was about to give him a congratulatory kiss when the throat clearing came again.

"I hate to break up this reunion," said Busby, "but it is rather urgent we get back to HQ."

"I really only came up to get Pablo," I told Alastair. I then turned to Mr T. "He can come too, right?"

"Yes, we've already established that you can bring Pablo."

"No, I mean Alastair."

"Actually, yes, that's a good idea, but not just yet. Alastair, we're going to need to convene at the Tower, and I believe it would be best if all of us were there. Do me a favor and call Runa. Tell her to use her portal to get to HQ as soon as she can. If Morelli's there, have her bring him along as well. Let them know it's not optional. Then go next door and tell Fiona the same. Both of you will want to bring your research notes. Understood?"

Alastair gave a curt nod, and I swear I felt his arm twitch as if fighting back a salute to Busby's command. Once I'd grabbed Pablo, I stole a quick kiss from Alastair, then gave him the briefest of explanations of what was going on and a bare-essentials packing list before hurrying back down the stairs after Busby and Matilda.

The two were waiting at the end of the hallway, not far from Morelli's door. Set in the wall was a black, glass orb that I'd always assumed was a security camera. Its installation at shoulder height seemed a bit odd, but I'd assumed Morelli had simply been too lazy to get out a stepladder to put the camera in its proper, ceiling-high location. Mr T took Pablo's carrier from me. I thought he was just being gentlemanly until he said, "Matilda, it'll be a tight squeeze with this portal, but you'll need to take Cassie's hand so she doesn't end up in Morocco."

I was about to say that I wouldn't mind a trip to Morocco when Matilda gently grasped my hand. Her skin was marble smooth and just as cool, and as she and Busby reached toward the portal with their free hands, I fought the urge to shout, "Holy hexes on high! I'm holding hands with a vampire!"

CHAPTER EIGHTEEN
MAGIC BOOGEYMEN

For a portal Morelli installed and likely helped construct, this one's ride wasn't too bad. The only problem was that the thing had clearly been designed to be used by one person at a time. With me, Matilda, Busby, and Pablo all squishing through together, it was an extraordinarily slow and painfully tight journey, and I was left gasping for breath when we finally stumbled into Olivia's office.

Matilda brushed down her pant suit, Mr T adjusted his pocket square, and I, well, since I was in Daisy disguise, I didn't have a single hair out of place. What sort of spells did she work on herself each morning?

"This is unexpected," said Olivia in a rather calm tone for someone who's just had three people and a pet carrier snap into existence in her office. Although, maybe she'd gotten used to it, since Runa, Tobey, Daisy, Alastair, Morelli, and Fiona were already there. All adjusting their clothes or smoothing down their hair. All except Daisy, of course. "Busby, care to explain?"

"We have some concerns about Mayor Marheart. When we began questioning her, she requested she be brought here."

All eyes fixed on Matilda.

"I've really done nothing wrong," she insisted, a warbling note of uncharacteristic anxiety in the words.

"Nothing?" I asked pointedly. "You've been trying to destroy MagicLand—"

"MagicLand?" she asked.

"Her name for Rosaria," explained Tobey.

"You really are bad at naming things, aren't you?" she noted, as if that was the main issue.

"Not the point," said Olivia, her eyes burning into the mayor with a dark intensity. "You're a vampire. You've been working with the other vampires to stage a coup against Magics."

"And I've defended you," seethed Runa, the hurt in her voice as clear as cling wrap. "All along I've stood up for you and your kind, believing Magics and vampires could work and live together, telling everyone they were wrong to think terribly of your people."

"And I appreciate that."

"So then why are you doing this?" I asked.

"Doing what exactly, Miss Black?" the mayor asked coolly.

This threw me for a moment. Hadn't Olivia just mentioned the coup-staging thing? But I suppose if Matilda needed details…

"Well, for one, you have been very keen on finding a jewel that supposedly provides the owner power over their worst enemies."

"And are you my worst enemy?"

"Maybe not me specifically," I replied, "but Magics in general." When Matilda gave no response to this, I continued, "Two, you've been— and by *you* I mean vampires, so don't go all nit-picky on me —killing Norms."

"Something you've sworn not to do," interjected Runa. "And something that goes against everything the Vampire Tolerance Act stands for. I marched with your kind to fight for that. What a waste of shoe leather."

"Runa, that's not really fair," said Morelli, but even he was looking at Matilda with less fondness in his eyes.

"Three," I went on before anyone else interrupted my reveal-the-killer's-motive moment. "You stole Wordsworth's book that has some spell in it that… Well, it can do something bad. I think. And four…" I paused. "Oh, fairy farts, now I've forgotten what four was."

"Missing Magics," whispered Daisy, who was at Olivia's desk, absent-mindedly fiddling with the corner of a page in *An Enchanted History of the Portland Community*. At a quick glance, I saw it was the page with the photo of my parents receiving their award. Devin Kilbride stood between them, his arms draped over them as they all smiled for the camera.

"Why did you bring that?" I asked.

"I'm still working on my entry," Daisy replied. This would be her recording her marriage to Tobey. Which had yet to take place since Tobey hadn't even proposed to her yet. And I know Daisy was showing all this Smart Girl stuff with the lawyer thing and the reading-Dickens-at-three-years-old thing, but I couldn't help but wonder if she was stuck on writing out the entry because she'd forgotten how to uncap her poof-topped pen.

But before I could say anything, something caught my eye.

In front of Daisy I now saw, or thought I saw, a page with a short bit of text and what looked like a numbered list. Had she turned the page without my noticing? Should I book an eye exam with Dr Dunwiddle? Blinking to clear my vision, I looked at the book again. The photo of my parents and Kilbride was just as clear as it had been a moment ago.

I shook my head. If I was already starting to hallucinate, I really needed to work on some stress management techniques.

"I'm sorry," blurted Morelli. "I know Black's got some big

speech thing going on, but this whole—" he waggled a finger between me and Daisy "—is really throwing me off. Does Black have to keep that disguise up?"

Which may have been one of the nicest things Morelli had ever done for me. Olivia quickly agreed that the disguise was no longer necessary. Moving her hand in the opposite direction she had earlier, she wiped away the spell, returning me to my non-blonde normalcy. When I asked if I could change into my own clothes, Olivia reluctantly agreed, making it very clear she would not be pleased if I dawdled this time.

"Where was I?" I asked after I emerged from the dressing room five minutes later.

"Missing Magics," Daisy whispered again.

"Yeah, that. You," I pointed to Matilda, "have been kidnapping Magics, stealing their power to weaken them, using it to bolster yourselves, then who knows what you're doing to them afterwards, but it's pretty telling that hardly any have escaped."

"Such as Mr Faegan?" asked Matilda.

"Exactly. I saw how he looked at you when he woke up. He was scared. Now why would that be?"

"I was given a report about that. I get daily briefings, but this was an emergency report—"

"Report? Briefings?" Morelli stammered, like someone just realizing they know nothing about their supposed love interest. "What reports would these be?"

"Reports of a..." Matilda seemed unwilling to use the word she needed. "You've served in the forces, Genie. You should know reports are sent to higher-ups on a regular basis."

"Merlin's beard!" I exclaimed. "Are you like the Captain of the Vampire Army?" Which, yes, would be the first number one hit from the band Vampire Playbook.

"I'm actually the queen of the vampires of the Western United States, but I like captain better. Sounds a little less campy."

Daisy had gotten up and was starting to curtsey. She stopped when I nudged her with my elbow. "Sorry," she said, "just manners."

"So, you're queen or captain or whatever," I said. "Which means you could call up your people at any moment. So why shouldn't we be arresting you right this very second?"

"Because it'd be pretty stupid to lock up the strongest ally you have."

"Only I get to call Black stupid," asserted Morelli.

"Plenty of people call her stupid," Runa reminded him.

"Yeah, but only I get to do it to her face."

"Could we please focus on the matter at hand?" interjected Mr Tenpenny. "You must be honest with us, Matilda. Are the vampires responsible for the missing Magics?"

Matilda shook her head. "We've been trying to stop it."

Which sent everyone asking a hundred questions all at once. Olivia cut them off with a shrill whistle.

"For the next several minutes," Olivia commanded, "Mayor Marheart is the only one allowed to speak in response to the questions Cassie will be asking. Miss Black, please continue."

"Um, okay, so... Mel Faegan," I said hesitantly, my cheeks burning at being thrust into the center of attention. "He recognized you. It scared the daylights out of him. If you're not guilty of something, how do you explain that?"

"It wasn't me he recognized, but my twin brother, Martin. We're not identical twins, obviously, but we do look very much alike. Martin discovered and went to where Mr Faegan and a few other Magics were being held by a small group of Norms.

"Martin had brought along four or five members of his team.

They'd really only planned a rescue attempt, but a fight broke out. A fight to the death. And I will admit that, while we do not have violent tendencies these days, when we are pushed, we fight viciously. Mel Faegan likely saw some disturbing things during what ensued. My best guess is, due to the similarity between me and my brother, the sight of my face likely brought back the raw memories of what he'd witnessed."

"And you didn't report this to HQ?"

"Do you think anyone would believe a vampire? Especially considering HQ's suspicions lately?"

"Does this mean you know where the missing Magics are?" I asked hopefully.

"No. Unfortunately, where they had Mel was merely a holding area. We only recovered about six Magics, and I doubt they'll ever use the place again, considering."

"Considering…"

"Considering that my brother left no survivors."

"And your brother and his team have done this more than once? Are these the ritualistic Norm deaths that have been in the news?"

"Exactly," Matilda said in a way that made it seem like she was ready to close the subject.

Runa raised her hand, looking between me and Olivia as if asking whether questions might be allowed. I shrugged, and Olivia gestured for her to go ahead.

"If these were Norms holding Mel and the others, how were they able to extract Mel without him losing his wits?"

A good point. Mel had no detectable magic on him when I'd seen him, and that extreme level of power removal normally leaves its victim a babbling, incoherent mess.

"That I don't know," replied Matilda. "It would make an excellent topic for study if we make it through this."

"Through what, exactly?" asked Olivia.

Matilda took a deep breath, as if fortifying herself for what she had to say. Or as if delaying while she made something up.

"Through a well-coordinated insurgency of witch hunters."

Daisy yelped, then slapped a hand over her mouth.

"Witch hunters?" I scoffed. "What? Is this like a Magic version of the boogeyman?"

"No, they're people who hunt witches," said Daisy, presumably meaning to be helpful.

"Yes, I gathered that, but this is the twenty-first century. Witch hunting sounds a bit far-fetched. I mean, Alastair and Fiona's research. HQ's reports. All evidence points to the vampires being up to something, right?" I asked Olivia. She nodded, passing Runa an apologetic look.

"But it really never added up," Alastair insisted. "I've said several times that the research wasn't conclusive."

"I'm inclined to agree," said Fiona. "What we have doesn't definitively exonerate the vampires, but the witch hunter angle does make more sense when you look at the evidence in that light."

"Look," said Olivia, taking charge of a room that seemed on the verge of speaking over one another once again, "I am trying to keep an open mind, but the information I've been given all points to vampire involvement in some concerning matters. Can you, Ms Marheart, provide concrete evidence to the contrary?"

"No," Matilda replied. Morelli's face fell. "Sorry, I could tell you everything, but I would like someone here who can corroborate what I'm saying. Since you want concrete evidence, that is," she said sharply, like someone who knows their word might not be trusted.

"And you have someone in mind?" asked Mr Tenpenny.

"Yes, and from the last report they sent me, I believe they will be available tomorrow morning. If you could grant me that much time, I will continue answering all your questions."

There was a fair bit of grumbling and doubt, and I could only imagine a flock of vampires (name of Vampire Playbook's debut album, obviously) swooping through the office's arrow slit windows, rescuing their queen, and taking us all as their prisoners.

Eventually, Olivia broke through the din, saying, "Clearly, we have matters to address. Matters that *need* addressed, but I have a feeling there will be new information that might upend many of my own plans and assumptions. I myself need time to re-evaluate matters. Then we can proceed. Is anyone worried about the world ending before daybreak tomorrow?"

"Well, a bit," I admitted.

"Then you might want to enjoy a good meal before then. Mayor Marheart, Chester will show you to your room, where I would ask you to remain until called back down. Is that agreeable?"

Matilda gave a graceful nod of acquiescence. Moments later, Chester escorted her out of the office.

CHAPTER NINETEEN
THE MEANING OF LETTERS

The following morning, at a far earlier hour than I would have preferred, Alastair was called down to Olivia's office. I assumed this meant for me to go as well. I mean, all this had come about because of my cases and my clients, and it would involve my life being put on the line (supposedly... I still didn't put much faith in prophecies). But when we got to Olivia's office — and despite Runa and Fiona already being there — Olivia gave me a look that implied this wasn't a 'plus one' kind of event.

Saying she wanted to go over everything they'd uncovered in their research before meeting again with Matilda, Olivia insisted Alastair and Fiona take a seat. I expected Runa to take the chance to wander up to the medical ward on the Tower's top floor, but Olivia asked her to stay put, clearly not ready to let Runa roam around unguarded.

I was left standing, feeling like an overstuffed and battered sofa that someone had dumped in an IKEA showroom. Olivia glanced up and looked at me like, well, like I was an overstuffed and battered sofa that someone had dumped in an IKEA showroom.

"Sorry, Cassie, I forgot to say that Rafi wanted to see you whenever you had a chance. Now would be a good time, yes?

You remember how to get to his office?" Olivia asked in that way of a higher-up dismissing someone. The perplexed look on my face must have spoken volumes. "At the moment, it's at the end of this hallway. Two flights up, then four doors down. You'll probably be able to identify it from the mess spilling out the door."

I followed Olivia's directions to the letter, but somehow emerged onto the uppermost floor of the White Tower, just outside of the Magics' medical ward.

I don't know if it was my attempt to kill time, or if I hoped I'd find another door that would lead me straight to Rafi's office, but rather than turn around and go back the way I came, I went in and, after a couple turns, ended up outside the room my parents had been kept during their recuperation. And yes, the pessimistic side of me half-expected to see them in there once again, in full catatonic state with Jake the Nurse calmly spooning mashed potatoes into my mom's mouth.

In a think-of-the-devil moment, as I continued down the corridor I ran into Jake the Nurse, his mismatched eyes greeting me warmly.

"You're a bit too healthy to be here, aren't you? Simon and Chloe doing well?"

"That's the question of the month, isn't it?" To his confused expression, I said, "They returned to work, despite not being back to full power."

"Ah well, that's perhaps a good sign," he said doubtfully. "Still, it really was amazing to see them up and about and able to walk out of here on their own after, well, you know."

"Yeah, I just wish that up and about didn't involve them zipping off on HQ missions."

"It's certainly nothing I'd have recommended, but no one asked me. You know your way out?"

"Heading there now, thanks."

Jake turned to get back to his duties, but just as I approached the door that would take me back to the stairwell (I think) a familiar voice called from the room I was passing by.

"Cassie?"

I peered in and was surprised to see the woman inside. She was sitting up, a book in hand but resting face down like her eyes had grown too weary to read another word.

"Mrs Oberlin? I thought you were—" I cut off my words. Following her attack, and after seeing her prone body hauled away by the Rosarian medics, I'd thought she was dead. Tobey had quickly corrected that assumption, telling me she'd merely been placed in a medically induced coma.

"Out for the count?" Winnifred said, finishing my sentence as I stepped into the room.

"That's one way of putting it. So, stupid question, but how are you?" She didn't look great. Her eyes had dark circles under them, her nail polish and several of the nails themselves were chipped, and let's face it, no one looks their best in a hospital gown. Still, she had a spark in her eyes that showed she had plenty of fight in her.

"Well, I'm hardly ready to dance the night away at a policeman's ball, but I'm alive, alert, and getting rather bored. They tell me that's a good sign. How's the detective agency?" I made an uncomfortable noise. "That good, huh? My brooch never turned up?"

"No, it did," I said, feeling eager to share some good news. Until I remembered it wasn't all good. "Then it didn't." I explained how I'd found her brooch at a pawnshop, how I'd been about to return it to her the day she'd been attacked, and then how it had gone missing from police custody. At this, her brow furrowed and she snapped the book shut. From the look on her face, I thought she might throw it at me. "Sorry," I said warily.

"No, don't be sorry. Like I said, I hated that gaudy thing. It's certainly caused quite a mess, hasn't it?"

I shrugged a response. "Do you remember anything from your attack? When I found you, you were writing in the dirt. Does that sound familiar?"

"Of course it does. I was blacking out a bit, but for some reason I thought I could write the name of my attacker." Her face darkened and the blips on her heart rate monitor started coming more quickly. If they ratcheted up too much, I knew I'd be asked to leave. "Then, as things started spinning, I realized spelling out the full name would take too long, would require too much brain power, so I tried to get the initials out. Did I?"

"There was only a single letter. An M. Was that for Matilda?"

"Matilda?" she scoffed. "Hardly. Besides, Stunning Spells of that ferocity are never used by vampires. Why would they when they can glamour their victims into submission?" I *knew* vampires glamoured! Where was Mr Tenpenny to hear this? "The police, however..." she said, and now the blood pressure numbers jumped.

"Wait," I said slowly as I pictured the cops on Matilda's front lawn, the Stunning Spells they'd been prepared to cast. "Police?"

"That letter wasn't an M. It was a W. For *Wesley* Oberlin. He took me by surprise, but I know my defense spells. Walloped him good, too. That pacemaker of his is the only reason he's not the one bored to death in a hospital bed. He hit back hard, though, and that's just something I won't stand for. The minute I'm out of here, he's going to be slapped with divorce papers so hard he's going to think they were carved from stone."

"Why would your husband attack you?"

"*That* is a question I would very much like answered, Miss Black. Perhaps I could hire you to find out?" she said with mocking sweetness even as the monitors began beeping an alert.

"Why haven't you told anyone?"

"Who would I report to? The police?"

I could see her point and was about to tell her to file something with HQ when Jake rushed in, the look in his eyes no longer warm.

"You're upsetting this patient. There was supposed to be a gnome on duty to guard her. I'm sorry, Mrs Oberlin. Security here is usually much better. Miss Black," he said curtly, "could you please leave so I can stabilize my patient?"

I muttered several apologies that Jake gave no response to as Mrs Oberlin assured him she'd only gotten worked up over thoughts of her 'rat bastard of a husband,' not over anything I'd done. Still, I thought it best to slip out the door while Jake was busy.

CHAPTER TWENTY
SIGN LANGUAGE

Could Winnifred be right? I wondered as I counted steps and checked hallways, trying to find Rafi's office. Had Old Walrus Face attacked her, or had the attack spell scrambled something in her head? I mean, I'll be the first person to list Oberlin's faults, but he'd never come across as anything but doting toward Winnifred. So why would he ambush his own wife?

After climbing and descending enough stairs to give my legs flashbacks of my previous weeks in the Tower, I finally peered down a hallway that had a jumble of overstuffed boxes piled outside a familiar door.

When I entered Rafi's office, he was seated next to a jar that was big enough to contain an entire human head. But rather than holding the remnants of a productive day at the guillotine, the jar had a dozen or so flies buzzing around inside. Rafi glanced up at me, gave a brief wave hello, then, seeing my scowl, did the best example of a double take I've ever encountered.

"What?"

"You made me blonde!" I shouted. "You Daisy-fied me, you cursed elf!"

Rather than look affronted, Rafi burst out laughing.

"They actually went through with it?" he said as he gasped to catch his breath. "Oh sweet Galadriel, I only crafted the spell as a joke. I didn't think—" And here he had to stop speaking to avoid hyperventilating with laughter.

"Are you done now?" I asked once he'd gotten a modicum of control over his giggling.

He snort-laughed, then pulled as serious a face as he could muster. "Yes, quite done." Another snort. "Sorry, it's just. You. As a perky blonde. It really is the perfect disguise. If only I could be as clever with this lot."

He turned his attention back to the jar, scrunched up his nose, and did an overbite thing with his front teeth.

"*Rattus*," he said emphatically, as if urging the flies to do his bidding. Whatever that was.

Other than one fly getting slightly bigger and springing a naked, wormy tail out its backside, nothing happened.

Rafi slumped back with a sigh.

"I can create a private bubble so Magics can have a picnic right in front of a Norm and not be seen. I can turn you into a happy-faced blonde. I can charm a door to serve as a butler — thanks for the name, by the way. So why is this so bloody buggery... *bloody* hard?"

"What exactly are you doing?" I asked as the be-tailed fly swerved and swayed into his companions, the tail making for an awkward rudder he wasn't used to.

"Working on a rat charm. I want to turn these damn flies into rats. Tell me, should that be so hard? No, it shouldn't."

"Stupid question, but why?"

"I don't know why it's so hard. I'm the best spell crafter at HQ. I mean, look what I got them to do to you," he added as he bit back a laugh. Then he sighed and said with derisive scorn, " '*Clever Rafi, just give him a task, and he'll craft a spell for it.*' " Then, more somberly, he asked, "Is it the flies, do you think?

Could they be resistant to my charms?"

He then fixed his attention on me, and I did not like the mad-scientist look in his eyes.

"No way." I held up my hands as if warding him off. "I am not going to be your guinea pig. Or your experimental rat. And that's not what I meant. Why would you want to make anything into a rat? I'm no fan of flies, but at least they have short life spans."

"Because Chester has squashed all the rats in the Tower."

"*All* of them?"

"As far as we can tell. The gnomes have been scouting around for me, but haven't turned up a single one."

"And that's not a good thing, because…?"

"Because Chester's bored. He's getting up to all sorts of trouble. Harassing tourists who don't look like they're having the time of their lives, pestering the Yeoman Warders if there's even a hint of lint on their uniforms. He's even dressed down the ravens for squawking in the wrong key. We need some rats to keep him occupied. So I thought, well, we've got plenty of bugs around here. Maybe if I just craft a simple transforming charm to turn them into rodents, Chester can get back to his favorite pastime, and things can go back to normal." Yes, because if there was one thing the Magic side of the Tower was, it was normal. Said no one, ever. "But I can't figure out how to do it."

"Hence the ratty face?"

"Thought it might give them the idea."

I watched the flies for a moment. The tail on Rafi's test subject gradually shrank. Although, by then, he had gotten somewhat used to it and ended up bashing straight into the side of the jar when he took off. You could almost hear his buddies laughing at him.

"But most spells aren't spoken," I said. Along with the lack of cauldrons when making potions, this had been a big disappointment. I'd been hoping to get to spout some cool Latin phrases, even an *abracadabra* or two, but it turned out that most magic only required intention and the proper hand motion. Well, and control over your power, which I always seemed to have in short supply.

"Have you tried hand motions instead of words and weird facial expressions?" I asked.

"Didn't work," he replied, sounding rather annoyed.

"How do you make a spell, anyway?"

"Mostly start from basic sign language. Shoving Spell, you push your hands out, that sort of thing. It gets more complicated with the more advanced spells, where you need a strong dose of visualization, but basic transforming charms shouldn't be this tough. I mean, if I was trying to change the flies into airplanes, sure. But animal to animal isn't that hard. Or shouldn't be," he sighed.

"What hand gesture were you using?"

Rafi crossed his index and middle fingers, then swept them rapidly across his nostril two times. "It's not a glamorous gesture, but once I get it to work, I can hone it into something that looks a little less like I'm trying to fling snot from my nose."

It seemed too obvious. I mean, who was I? I didn't know how to make spells, and here was Rafi, an elf with who knows how many centuries of experience with this sort of stuff. But I'd had a very frightening childhood, and my only escape had been the local library where I'd dive into any arcane topic that would take my mind off the terrors of whichever home I'd been tossed into.

"So," I began hesitantly, "that's American Sign Language for rat."

"Well, I don't think the flies speak French."

"Don't be bitchy. What I mean is, these are British flies, so maybe…"

Yeah, it did sound as stupid out loud as it had in my head.

"Wait, there's other types of sign language?" asked Rafi, truly bewildered.

"You're how old and you didn't know that?"

"Don't be bitchy."

"Touché. But yeah, there's loads of other sign languages. In British Sign Language—"

"I make that sign, then offer them a cup of tea?"

"You could try that. Or you could do this." I stuck my index finger near my nostril and did a twisting motion.

"Gads, that's really no better than the previous one. How do you know this?"

"Spring break, fifth grade. The library had a deaf librarian on staff. From Manchester, I think. I hated talking to people, but with her, I didn't have to talk, so we chatted quite a lot."

"You're very weird, Cassie Black. But also very clever. Should I give it a whirl?"

"Just be sure to think ratty thoughts."

"I always do."

Rafi focused on the jar, his eyes darting around as if following one of the flies. I really hoped it wasn't the one who'd just had a tail. He'd already had a rough enough day. Rafi took a deep breath, focused on one of the flies, and made the sign.

There was a brief pause, then the fly fell straight to the bottom of the jar.

"Oops," we both said.

"Or not," said Rafi, as the fly elongated. Then, with a *snap*, changed into a small, bedraggled black rat. The other flies stayed well clear of their new roommate. Rafi whooped with triumph. "You are a genius! One more time." He made the sign again, and another fly turned into a rat. "Chester is going to love this!"

I wasn't sure how I felt about that. Turning flies into rodents that would be smashed under Chester's boot seemed really wrong. I explained my misgivings to Rafi.

"Don't worry. You don't change the underlying nature of the creature. It looks like a rat, but it's still all fly inside. Which means it's likely going to die within a day or two anyway."

"Still, the smashing…"

"So now you're Buddha and have never whacked a fly with a newspaper?"

I grudgingly saw his point, but it definitely wasn't a bit of spell crafting I would be putting on my resume. If I actually had a magic resume, that is.

Rafi tested the spell on another couple flies, quickly working out how to make the hand motion less nose-picking and more smooth-magicking. He was about to try the modified action on another victim when someone knocked on the door. I tensed, certain it was someone coming to escort me back to Olivia's office to face whatever Matilda Marheart had in store for us.

"You'll get that while I return these guys to their former glory?" Rafi said distractedly.

When I started toward the door, I noticed giggling coming from behind it. At first I thought it was Daisy and Tobey come to announce their engagement (gag). But apparently I'm one of the world's few giggle connoisseurs, and I noted that the woman's giggle didn't have the tinkling quality Daisy's did.

Still, the giggle, despite not hearing it for most of my life, was innately familiar.

My heart leapt in my chest. It couldn't be.

CHAPTER TWENTY-ONE
WONKY MAGIC FOR ALL

The knock sounded again, and I practically stumbled over my own feet to get to the door. Okay, who am I kidding? I *did* stumble over my own feet because they're very long and I'm very clumsy.

I pulled open the door, and there they were. My parents. I don't know what was wrong with me — temporary insanity, perhaps — but the moment they stepped in, I wrapped them both in a hug. Then I hurriedly let them go when sanity returned.

"You two are never allowed to do that ever again," I scolded.

"Come visit you?" my dad asked.

"No. Leave without telling me. I was really worried."

"We brought snacks," my mom said and held up a bag with the Spellbound Patisserie logo on it.

"I don't want them." I was lying. I *so* wanted them. "I want you to say you'll keep me in the loop from now on. What were you thinking? Your magic isn't stable—"

Just then, I paused. I could smell nothing on them. Clean clothes, my mom's rose soap, but no hint of my dad's cinnamon scent, or my mom's fresh-mown grass fragrance.

"Where's your magic?" I asked, the question brimming with cautious criticism.

"It faded," said my dad, almost offhandedly like this was no big deal. "It's why we were perfect for the work HQ needed done. Even though it wasn't what they'd planned on us doing, it worked out really well in the end."

"We might even get another medal," said my mom as she plucked out what smelled like a rosemary-and-black-pepper scone from the Spellbound bag and handed it to me. Despite my worry, my relief, and my wanting to slap them to see sense, my stomach growled. "Should we dash over to Olivia's office, then?"

"We'd be a bit early, but no harm in that," my dad replied as he reached into the bag and pulled out a ribbon-wrapped stack of gingersnaps. Peering over my shoulder, he asked, "Want one, Rafi?"

"Don't mind if—"

"Oh my blessed dragon balls!" I cried. "You cannot seriously be standing here acting like everything is perfectly normal. Like you've just returned from an afternoon of shopping. You've been gone for I-don't-even-know-how-many days. Gone on a mission you shouldn't have been assigned to in the first place and have lost, what, all of your magic?"

Although, I did have to admit they appeared healthier than they had the last time I'd seen them. In the entire time since we'd been reunited, to tell the truth. My mom's cheeks had filled in, and my dad had lost much of that perpetually hungry look he'd had. Except in his eyes, which were greedily sizing up the scone my mom was still holding out.

"We should really get to Olivia's," said my mom, after I'd accepted her buttery offering. "She can call up some tea to have with these."

"So, your magic?" I prodded after Rafi had bid goodbye to his flies and we'd all stepped into the hallway.

"We're fine," assured my dad. Then, around a corner, and

barely ten paces from Rafi's office, he stopped at the massive oak door to Olivia's office. Ten paces? Ten bloody paces! All those stairs I'd climbed? All those hallways I'd checked? My loathing for the whims of the White Tower's floor plans skyrocketed.

"Of course, there's a risk of danger in any mission," continued my dad, after quickly greeting Busby, Fiona, Runa, Chester, Tobey, Daisy, and Olivia. I took a seat in the chair he pulled out for me, but remained on the very edge of it, ready to get up and rant if need be. "But we really were perfectly suited for it. And, in truth, it ended up being a very safe assignment that garnered a lot of information."

"You shouldn't have been sent on any mission," I complained again.

"They didn't send us," said my mom. "We volunteered."

"Oh, well, that's better," I said, the sarcasm adding a piquant bite to my scone. I glanced worriedly at the Spellbound bag, then at the number of people in the room. Was I expected to share?

Thankfully, that question was answered when Olivia snapped her fingers and various sweet treats and hot drinks appeared on a side table.

Runa ignored the snacks and went over to my parents, checking their eyes, their pulses, their scent. The first two earned her approval. The final one earned her scorn.

"All the hard work I put in to get your levels up," she grumbled. "I don't know how long it's going to take to restore you this time, or if I even *can* restore you."

"Wait," I said. "You might not be able to restore their magic?"

This was like a punch to the gut. Only Magics could live in MagicLand. Norms weren't even allowed to visit, otherwise the place would be overrun by influencers snapping selfies and getting in everyone's way. Tobey had been the rare exception before I'd filled him up with Cassie power, but that had only been because Mr Tenpenny could pull all the right strings for his grandson.

My parents had served HQ well, but would it be enough to keep them in MagicLand? It's not that I couldn't go visit them in whatever Norm home they ended up in, but it wouldn't have the convenience of being just a few, traffic-free blocks away. Plus, if they didn't live within MagicLand, how were they going to bring me treats from Spellbound, or let me add my pastry purchases to their tab?

"Tough to say," replied Runa. "Magic levels as low as these two have plummeted to are never easy to rejuvenate, especially considering their previous near extraction. We'll work on it as soon as possible, but for now, best put down the scones and start in on the cookies. They have a higher sugar content. Think of it as priming the pump."

Rather than the cookies, my dad grabbed one of the thick and gooey cinnamon rolls that had just appeared. Runa nodded approvingly.

"I'm afraid the Starlings aren't the only ones with low magic levels," said Fiona. "I've been feeling rather off lately, as well."

"For how long?" Runa asked. Perhaps realizing her tone carried a hint of accusation, she added, "Sorry, it's just I've heard the same from a few other people. And then there's this…"

Judging from her hand motion, Runa was attempting a Shoving Spell on one of the pens on Olivia's desk. It barely moved. Runa narrowed her eyes at the pen and tried once more. Again, the pen shifted no more than if a gentle breeze had whisked through the room.

"Interesting," Olivia said, then performed her own Shoving Spell. The pen moved without hesitation. A perplexed expression on her face, she looked to Busby who was standing with Daisy and Alastair. "You lot, could you try that?"

Mr Tenpenny stepped forward and tried a Shoving Charm on the pen. It skittered away like a frightened beetle. Alastair, too, had no trouble shifting the pen across the desk. He then raised his eyebrows to Daisy in a go-ahead-and-give-it-a-try kind of way.

"My magic's been a big poopy head too. But," Daisy added, sounding tentatively hopeful, "maybe it's just poopy with portals."

When she tried a Shoving Spell, though, the pen barely moved a millimeter.

"That should have gone across the room," she said, visibly shaken by the possibility of what she might become.

"Rafi, if you will." Rafi accepted Olivia's invitation, and the pen rolled obediently to the left. Of course, being Rafi, he put a little spin on the spell that then turned the pen into a sunflower which he handed to Daisy.

"Now is not the time to show off," Olivia scolded. Her brow was furrowed, like a student who's just been asked to explain quantum computing on the first day of Physics 101. "Cassie, it's probably safest for us all if you don't try. I'd hate for my desk to go flying out the window. Fiona, Chester, Tobey, your turn to give it a go."

"What are you thinking?" asked Runa, but I had an inkling as Chester and Tobey had no trouble moving a pencil without touching it, whereas Fiona's spell did little more than make the pencil shudder.

"Non-human Magics still have their power?" I asked, looking to Olivia for confirmation.

She nodded, but Tobey protested, "Last I checked, I'm human."

"That's a matter for debate," I said. But he was right. Why would some Magics have power while others didn't?

Olivia drummed her fingernails on her desk several times, then immediately stopped. "Cassie, your magic."

"Is still off-kilter," I said. "But it's been that way for quite a while now. This," I gestured to Fiona and Daisy and Runa, "is very new, I take it?" They each nodded.

"No, not your magic *now*. Although, that's still a matter we need to address. But your magic in the past. As in, a few months ago when you gave your magic to Tobey, Busby, and Alastair. I have a feeling that's why whatever is happening to other Magics isn't affecting them."

"But how? Especially when Cassie's magic is a complete mess?" asked Runa.

"That's a question I'll leave for you to solve," said Olivia while giving Runa's hand a gentle squeeze.

"Great, another medical mystery," Runa complained. "Black, I swear your magic is going to be the death of me."

"Maybe not the best time to use that turn of phrase," I suggested as Chester was sent to collect Matilda, and the rest of us turned our attention to the mounds of sugary snacks.

CHAPTER TWENTY-TWO
A LITTLE LEEWAY

The pile of food my parents managed to stack onto their plates was an engineering marvel, and the way they could extract just what they wanted from anywhere in that pile would have put a Jenga champion to shame.

"Now," said Olivia once Chester had delivered Matilda to the office and everyone had settled into their snacks, "should we discuss your findings, Simon and Chloe? And then we'll evaluate how they relate to Ms Marheart's information she has yet to share."

My dad conceded the floor to my mom, since he likely found it hard to talk with his lips coated in cream cheese frosting.

"Well, HQ was worried about the missing Magics being a sign that the vampires were rising once more, so we were sent to spy on them, to see if we could get an indication of when and where things would begin. Since our magic signature was already so low, and would get even lower without infusions from Runa, we were perfect for the job. They wouldn't detect us as being anything other than Norms."

"One of the updates you sent reported that you stopped following the vampires, though," noted Mr T.

"We knew that it would be going against orders," said my

dad, "but we figured moving in closer was warranted when we saw them attacking Norms."

"So, hold on," I cut in. "You two were posing as Norms, *moving in closer* as Norms, in the very place where vampires were going around killing Norms? Because that's what we're talking about, right? Not attacking, but killing."

"We were perfectly fine," said my mom. "I mean, we were a little nervous when we approached the vampires after an, um, *attack*—"

"You. Approached. The vampires. The Norm-killing vampires!?"

My parents looked at each other as if confirming something. "No, I don't think the one we approached had killed anyone, but she did introduce us to Martin—" my mom tipped her head to Matilda "—who had."

Did you hear that? That was me banging my head on the desk. I was starting to wonder if the Mauvais didn't so much *capture* my parents as they simply walked up to him and handed themselves over.

"Cassie," said Olivia, "I realize this is causing you distress, but your parents are obviously fine. They have no puncture wounds in their necks, and they are giving no indication that they are ghosts wandering amongst us. So, please refrain from your commentary unless you'd like me to put a Silencing Spell on your mouth."

"That's an option?" quipped Runa.

I picked up a cranberry scone and nibbled as my mom continued.

"We'd been watching the vampires, and I'll admit we were quite shocked when we saw the first attack. Simon wanted to call it quits right then and go back to HQ to let you know that the vampires were up to their old tricks again. But I said to wait."

"And why is that?" asked Olivia.

"It struck me as odd that they would target just one person. Three of them had gone into the victim's house, so the killing was hardly done to make a filling meal. And when they left, there was little sign of… well, feeding. No blood on their lips, no telltale dribbles on their shirts, showing it was methodical, not fueled by bloodlust."

"Then, before I could stop her," said my dad, "she was going into the house to inspect."

I groaned and threw up my hands in exasperation at this.

"That was quite risky," said Mr T, and I nodded emphatically. "Norm police could have picked up forensic evidence that would point them to you."

"Busby," said my mom, "if you don't think we know how to cover our tracks, then you didn't train us very well, did you? When I examined the victim, he had only one set of puncture wounds on his neck. And while they did consume the blood, I'm sure it was only to prevent it from spilling on the very lovely floors. Parquet," she clarified, sounding truly impressed, as if now was the time to delight in the interior design features of a murder house.

"So then you approached the vampires?" asked Mr T.

"No, I had a look around the house while Simon stood guard outside. I didn't like what I saw. Leaflets about evil being amongst us, about 'others' being the reason for the downfall of society, about how certain people were trying to brainwash children."

"That seems like the usual rhetoric these days for the nut jobs," Runa scoffed.

"Yes, but it was the message at the bottom of the leaflet that was different: *Witches and wizards need to die. We know how to protect what's important to YOU. Join the hunt today.*"

"And then a vampire—" My mom looked to Matilda. "Claudette, I believe?" Matilda nodded. "She caught us looking at the leaflet, and it certainly gave me a start, but Simon still had just enough magic in him and she smiled upon recognizing what we were. We told her what we were up to, and she took us to Martin."

"Unfortunately," my dad said, "he was the one who'd taken care of the homeowner, and his teeth were still— How do I put this... Stained?

"Regardless," my mom continued despite my grimace, "Martin was glad to explain what they'd been up to. He got us in touch with Matilda. She thought we should lie low, but we argued we really were the best for the job. So, we went over a few tactical things and then we infiltrated the witch hunters."

Again, I groaned. Both at the situation and at the way my mom said this. It was as if they'd just decided to join the local art committee. Seriously, you give your parents a little leeway, and what do they do? They go and join a band of witch hunters.

"That was not a wise move," criticized Busby. "You should have come straight to HQ with your findings." I was never more in agreement with Mr T than at that moment.

"Chloe's magic was undetectable, and mine had faded to the point that I doubt any Norm, even if they knew how, would be able to sense it on me. Once we'd consulted with Matilda, and knew Martin was in place if we needed him and his team, we went to the address on the leaflet."

Okay, I'm not exaggerating when I say I was literally on the edge of my seat, straining forward with both impatience to hear more and with incredulity over their rash behavior. Unfortunately, I stretched so far forward I fell out of the chair. Which really had me wondering if all furniture had something against me.

"Sorry, sorry," I said, picking myself up off the floor. "You were saying... A group? Bad guys...?"

"Exactly," my mom replied brightly. "And the woman who answered the door took us in immediately."

"They just let you in?" asked Olivia skeptically.

"Oh, yes. We're apparently very believable as righteous busybodies who want to control what other people do," my mom said as she primly adjusted her cardigan. "Plus, they want as many recruits as possible. There's supposedly a leader, but we never saw him."

"Or her," corrected my dad. "Don't be so sexist, Chloe."

"My apologies. You tell the rest. I need one of those slices of molasses cake."

"We didn't want to be too obvious," my dad began as my mom went over to the treat table, "but we did glean some information. We're pretty sure they're responsible for the missing Magics. To what purpose, we couldn't figure out, because as far as I understood it, they aren't killing them. They did go on about how the leader was about to return and would have an untold power he'd — because it was a he, after all — never had before and would easily be able to defeat their worst enemy. After that, the witch hunters were certain they'd have no trouble taking down the rest of the Magic world."

My stomach dropped. I caught Mr T's eye, but if he was concerned, he gave nothing away.

"That's a bit over the top," said Runa.

"We thought so too, but they fully believe it. And from various snide comments some of them made, I got the impression that they have a spy in our midst. Perhaps more than one."

My dad looked to Matilda for confirmation, but Olivia spoke up before the mayor could add her two cents.

"When you say 'our midst'," asked Olivia, "do you mean within HQ? Because I could really do without another enemy amongst our ranks."

"No," replied my dad. "I can't say exactly why, nothing was said outright, but I do believe they were referring to Rosaria. We wanted to learn more. We could tell the home we were in was only a meeting point. It was a three-bedroom, single-level house, so I doubt they were hiding a crowd of Magics in the basement. Chloe did ask at one point if we could meet their leader, trying to act all starry-eyed and cult-follower-ish, but with us being newcomers, they weren't exactly forthcoming with much information in that regard."

"Simon and I would have stayed longer with them. The woman whose home the meetings were in offered us the use of her spare room, but Martin had told us another team was on patrol in the neighborhood and he couldn't guarantee they wouldn't target that house. And, well, you know how vampires can get when their thirst is up." My mom tipped an apologetic nod to Matilda. "So, since we didn't think we'd be able to convince a group of hungry vampires that we were merely stopping by on behalf of their queen before—" she mimicked biting, her teeth clicking together "—we decided to call it a night."

"And we were smart to do so. The woman was found dead two days later, and the death was reported the same as the one we'd inspected earlier. Their papers described it as a 'ritualistic killing.' Very euphemistic, those Norms."

"And do you know where these witch hunters are now?" asked Busby.

"Not exactly," said my dad. "There appear to be pockets of them near most magical communities. That's how they've been able to take Magics. They merely wait until one of our kind needs to run an errand on the Norm side of the world, and then… Anyway, until recently, they were pretty much scattered all over the place."

"And now?" I asked, concerned about the uncomfortable look that had crossed his face.

"They seem to be concentrating," replied my dad.

"Well, sure," I said, "I imagine it takes a great deal of thought to throw over an entire world of people."

"No, I mean concentrating, as in gathering, congregating in one place."

"And that place would be?" Busby asked.

"London. We believe not far from the Tower."

"From HQ, you mean?" Olivia asked worriedly. My mom nodded. "So what we have are vampires killing off witch hunters, witch hunters gaining strength, possibly with our own magic, and gathering together; a spy in Rosaria; and still no idea where the missing Magics are."

"We could go back—" began my mom.

"No, you've done enough," asserted Olivia, just as I was about to say the same thing. "And if I hear of you trying to embed yourselves with witch hunters again, I will Extract you myself to ensure you are too brain-dead to do anything so foolish ever again."

CHAPTER TWENTY-THREE
REVERSAL TRICKS

"We need to figure out what this all means," continued Olivia. "I could have sworn the vampires were at it again. I do apologize, Matilda."

Matilda bowed her head rather graciously for someone whose entire race has just been accused of wanting to kill every Magic in existence.

"I wonder what the witch hunters meant by this leader of theirs returning," said Mr T. "And what I mean is, where has he been? Why now? Any indication of that, Simon? Chloe?"

"Possibly both," my dad replied. "There was mention of a jewel, or rather, pieces of one. They said the pieces were to be delivered to their contact soon, and a rumor was swirling around that they were closing in on the final piece. Not sure what any of that means, and, unfortunately, no one ever mentioned any names."

"I'm afraid we know what the final piece business might mean," said Mr T, then quickly explained our jewel theory.

"And how do you fit in with all this?" Olivia asked Matilda. "You and your kind?"

"We've been keeping an eye out for any witch hunter activity for centuries. It's been a couple hundred years since we've seen any real trouble from them, but my family… we've never been the bad kind of vampires. Even our oldest ancestors survived on animal blood, or the blood of people already dying. We were always on the side of Magics, watching out for you, so to say. Guardians, regardless of how you treated us.

"My family has seen the rise of witch hunters several times. And we've knocked them back quite handily, if I may say so. We know the signs, and although we couldn't prove anything until the Starlings' infiltration, we were certain they were regrouping, likely through social media, where they've been spreading lies about Magics being the cause for all the problems in the world: disease, war, high gas prices. It doesn't take much for them to spin a conspiracy theory. If they put their time toward writing fiction, it would be too ridiculous to believe. This time, however, we got wind of it a little too late. Several Magics had already been taken by the time we stepped in."

"Do you have any information about the missing Magics?" Mr Tenpenny asked. "Where they're being held? What's being done with them? Why we've received no ransom requests or anything of that nature?"

"Given the state of Mel Faegan and a few others we've rescued, we're convinced the witch hunters are taking power from Magics to become strong enough to fight you."

"Hold on," I interrupted. "Witch hunters, the people who hate magic so much they would kill people who practice it, are using witchy magic to fight witches?"

"I doubt they see the irony in it," said Matilda. "After all, it wouldn't be the first time evil people have twisted their own morals to achieve their goals."

"I have a question," I said, and damn it if there wasn't a hint of Daisy perkiness in my voice. Dear Merlin, had that disguise scarred me for life? Matilda raised an eyebrow, indicating for me to go ahead. "The book, Wordsworth's book. You took it, didn't you?"

"Yes," Matilda replied, being absolutely no help. I really should know better than to ask closed-ended questions.

"Okay... Why? And how did you get it out of a crate that Corrine had protected with tons of spells? And did you take the pages? And if so, what did they contain?"

"Am I supposed to remember all those questions?"

"Do your best."

"I was at the Bookworm conference, and I was rather taken aback when I saw that particular book there. I couldn't believe Wordsworth would be so careless as to put that book on display. When I asked him about why he'd brought it, he'd said it had been a request. He'd assumed it had been the event organizer, but couldn't quite recall if the man had ever given his name. On hearing that, I did my best to keep as close an eye on it as possible.

"Nothing untoward happened, but when the crates were being packed up at the end of the event, I asked Corrine about the protections on her shipments. She'd gone above and beyond with her spells, everything seemed professional, and I know Corrine runs one of the most reliable delivery services, but I just couldn't risk someone being careless with that book. So, I broke through the protections and took it."

"But what sense does that make?" I asked. "You took the book, then you dumped it at Bookman's Bookshop?"

"I did that because I knew Wordsworth had hired you. I wanted you to find it so you could get your license. I truly did. I figured some good should come of my thievery, since I was too late to prevent what I'd been worried about."

"Which was...?"

"That the pages containing a certain spell had been taken. Sometime during the conference, someone got to that book and managed to steal the pages. For a talented Magic, it would only

The Unexpected Mr. Hopkins

take the right spell and a tap of his or her fingers against the cover while casually passing by the display."

"And the spell on these pages…?" prompted Mr T.

"Will raise the dead," Matilda replied. "My great- great-whatever wrote it to bring back her dead husband." To my confused expression, Matilda said, "Vampires aren't immortal. It takes a pretty strong illness to kill us off, but we can die. Nevertheless, the spell works."

"Wait, wait, wait." Despite all the sugar, my brain was simply not keeping up with all this. "We're raising the dead again?" I looked to Mr Tenpenny, aka 'formerly dead guy' whose return to life got me tangled up with the Mauvais. "Is this going to involve me fighting an evil wizard again?"

"Not an evil wizard, no," said Matilda. "But you might have to fight Matthew Hopkins."

"Matthew Hopkins," Fiona declared with sudden realization. "That's what has been bothering me about all this jewel business."

"Did I miss something?" I asked.

"In one of Banna's old records, she notes— Hold on, it's here somewhere."

Fiona unzipped a slim handbag that barely looked big enough to hold an empty file folder. I'd always assumed she'd be tidy and organized with her paperwork, but when she asked Busby to perform a Reveal Spell on her handbag, my assumption was proved wrong. The action transformed the open purse into a table top and the loop handles into legs. The table, about the size of a nightstand, was covered in chaotic stacks of papers, books, notepads, and various colors of pens and pencils.

"What's that you're always saying about *me* needing to tidy up?" I asked Mr Tenpenny. Then, with a *tsk-tsk* tone in my voice, I added, "And you living with someone who's carting around something like this."

157

"Apparently I didn't know my wife was hiding things from me," Busby said good-naturedly.

"Only my messy paperwork, dear. Now," said Fiona once she'd found the folder she'd been after, "according to Banna, the greatest witch hunter was a Matthew Hopkins."

"Dr Torres mentioned him," I said, recalling my conversation with him— Good goblins, had it only been the previous morning? "Said he hated witches, but gladly used witchcraft to kill hundreds of them."

"Exactly. And with such a zeal for his chosen profession, he didn't want his own death to stand in the way of continuing his work. So— and again, this is according to Banna, so I assume it's true. She may have been no friend of ours, but she was meticulous in the accuracy of her historical records. Anyway, before Hopkins died, he allowed for certain rituals to take place to bring him back should a time come when he was needed once again."

"So what happened after he died?" I asked. "Obviously witches didn't stop being persecuted."

"A few people carried on. The mess in Salem, Massachusetts, was all at their instigation. But without Hopkins lashing the whip, so to speak, the 'fad' dwindled. Still, as new witch hunters came and went, one or two people would always be charged with the task of carrying on the knowledge of where the ritual was located and how to perform it. The unearthing of the jewel pieces may have been what they were waiting for, because I fear whoever has inherited the title today believes now is the time to act."

"Act? How do you mean?" asked Olivia, even though I had a troll-sized feeling I already knew the answer.

"I mean," Fiona replied, "that they will soon raise Mathew Hopkins, if they haven't already. And once he's back, he'll use the Boncoeur Jewel to defeat his worst enemies."

The absence of the jewels and my lack of diligence in finding Runa's saw struck me more keenly than ever.

"If we only had a copy of that book for ourselves," noted Mr T. "We would be able to undo all of this."

"You're thinking of the reversal trick?" Fiona asked him.

"Reversal trick?" I asked.

"No spell is written that can't be reversed," explained Fiona. "Usually it requires nothing more than reading the spell backwards. After all, performing magic isn't like cooking eggs, where there's no going back once it's done.

"Of course, it takes a strong Magic to undo the work of another, but that matters neither here nor there since Wordsworth's copy is incomplete, the copy in the British Library is useless—" I worked very hard at not glancing away guiltily when she mentioned this "—and we've no idea where the third copy is. If it even exists."

"That fire at the British Library is seeming more ominous than before," muttered Busby. "What if it was someone preventing us from gaining access to that copy?"

"Let's just be glad they don't have the final piece of the jewel," Olivia said. "Is there any way to trace where it went? If the pieces were given to court favorites, surely we should be able to trace the lineage down to today."

"I don't know if we have time for that," worried Mr T. "Still, it wouldn't hurt to put someone on it." I volunteered Dr Torres for the job, figuring he'd love adding it to his Boncoeur Jewel knowledge to impress Professor Dodding.

"If he agrees, that would be quite helpful. Just tell him to keep in mind that it could have been lost, stolen, given to a servant, or even pawned for ready cash within a mere decade after it was received."

I was glad to see I wasn't the only pessimist in the room.

CHAPTER TWENTY-FOUR
SENTIENT JEWELS

As if needing to collect our thoughts, we all tucked in to a pile of sandwiches the pixies had sent up. All except for Daisy, who went over to a side table, pulled a flower-topped pen out of her handbag, then opened up *An Enchanted History of the Portland Community.* From the look of determined concentration on her face, I figured she had finished with the engagement plans she had already made for her and Tobey, and was now was adding every detail she had in store for their future life together.

I'd like to say the respite gave me time to come up with all kinds of brilliant deductions, but all I could think about was getting every scrap of food off my plate to see what type of sandwich might appear next.

After I'd made my way through a Caprese on ciabatta, a portobello-and-Swiss on a brioche bun, and a peanut butter and honey on whole wheat, Matilda said, almost dismissively. "Your conclusions about an uprising weren't wrong, Olivia. You just had the wrong culprit. I haven't been trying to destroy Rosaria, I've been trying to protect it. You see, there's a prophecy tied to the jewel—"

"Well aware of that one," I said. I was about to give Alastair a scolding stare, when Morelli's phone distracted me by bleating out an alert message. Mumbling an apology, he snagged a turkey-bacon wrap and dashed out of the office. Perhaps a marathon of *Black Adder* reruns had just started.

After arching an eyebrow at Morelli's odd behavior, Busby got the conversation rolling again. "I believe this prophecy says something about the jewel helping the possessor defeat his or her worst enemy. So, if whoever you've been protecting us from has the jewel…?"

"They will destroy Cassie," Matilda responded. "And the rest of us will fall quite soon after. I'm not saying we won't put up a fight, but if that jewel gets in the hands of the wrong person, it won't take long to break our defenses."

"Well, that's a cheery thought for a Tuesday afternoon," I said.

"It's Thursday, Cassie," said Runa.

I glanced at the calendar on Olivia's desk. Indeed, it was.

"But how can I be their worst enemy? I mean, I know I have a talent for annoying people, but I don't even know these people. How could I have ruffled their feathers so badly?"

"It's well known across the Magic world that you defeated the Mauvais," explained Matilda, "and that you're one of the strongest Magics we've seen in decades. They're convinced that if you have the jewel, you will defeat them. That makes you their worst enemy."

Talk about a bitter bite of cupcake to swallow. You think you're doing the right thing, you think you're saving your parents and most of the world from an evil wizard, and all you get are jewel-crazed lunatics coming after you.

"I hired Cassie truly believing the Boncoeur Jewel was a single, intact gem," Matilda continued, "but very recently my brother dug up some information implying it had been split centuries ago. Since then, I've been doing my best to get the pieces into your hands."

"I would very much like to hear more about that," said Mr T, "especially considering that all the pieces Cassie did find have now been stolen."

"Stolen?"

"Afraid so."

"That's not good."

"I never found the final piece, so it could be worse," I said, surprised to find myself being a glass-is-half-full kind of gal.

"Olivia told me about the missing tiara," said Runa. "If they were able to snag that right from under our noses, we have to assume they already have the final piece."

Well, that certainly shattered my glassy optimism.

Matilda nodded solemnly, then said, "As to your question, Busby, I'd already planned to come to Rosaria. I've been well aware of the prophecy for years, and I'd followed various pieces of legend that pointed to the Boncoeur Jewel being somewhere in the Portland community. But when I learned Cassie had become a citizen of Rosaria, I was even more keen to keep an eye on things. I suppose I could have just gotten a job at the Wandering Wizard, but it was election time, and I couldn't bear to see that blowhard Oberlin take the mayoral spot."

"And the original jewel?" asked Fiona. "Do you know much about that?"

"I only know it dates back centuries in my family, and that somehow it ended up in the hands of Queen Elizabeth. She had a lot of enemies. Girl power wasn't exactly a thing back then."

"Barely is now," I mumbled. Matilda, Runa, and Fiona all nodded in agreement.

"Elizabeth kept the jewel as a protection from all the enemies that kept popping up early in her reign, but once she settled into a comfortable role as leader of England, she decided she wanted to share the protection with the rare few people she trusted. The jewel was split who-knows-how-many ways, but she never let the pieces stray too far from her, just in case her worst enemy came knocking."

"So who was the worst enemy?"

Matilda shrugged. "Doesn't really matter, does it? She had so many. But she lived out her reign without needing to reunite the jewels. There are rumors another charm was put on the pieces to never be too far apart, to somehow always be in close proximity to one another, to be at hand when needed. Does that sound like something that's possible?"

Through a mouthful of B.L.T., Fiona said it was.

"As I said, Martin only just discovered the Boncoeur Jewel had been divided. I didn't know how many pieces there were or how they came together, but I figured getting as many pieces as possible into Cassie's hands couldn't hurt. Why do you think I left the pendant out so obviously?" she asked, but gave me no chance to respond. "Because you're a strong Magic, and I'm pretty sure you're the one who's meant to bring them together. I was a bit slow on the draw with Winnifred's brooch, but I did return to the pawnshop to try to buy it back. The clerk showed me the sales receipt, and when I saw your name… well, it's not often a vampire has chills run up her spine." Matilda gave a gracious smile. "It just proves the jewel wants to come together. That it's time for it to come together."

"The tiara," noted Mr Tenpenny. "It wasn't amongst the jewels Inspector Oberlin took as evidence, but it also was no longer in the safe when Cassie opened it yesterday. Could it have somehow lost itself to rejoin the others?"

"Did you have any Concealment type spells on it?" asked Rafi. Busby nodded. "That could explain why, as you say, it 'lost' itself."

"How do you mean?" asked Mr T.

"While it was hidden, while it was in whatever dimension

things go to when we Conceal them, it may have sensed the other jewel pieces. If these things really want to get the band back together, it could have chosen to reappear wherever its friends are."

"So our hiding it sent it right to them?" I asked, completely exasperated. You just couldn't win with magical objects, could you? Rafi said it likely had. "Well, that was certainly nice of us. I still don't understand," I said to Matilda, "if you wanted me to have the jewel pieces, why did you attack me and steal my mom's pendant? That hex really hurt, you know."

Matilda looked thoroughly confused. "I didn't take it. I found it."

"Yeah, when you ripped it out of my hands after blinding me and scorching my face."

"That wasn't me, Cassie. I swear. I had just turned onto your parents' street as part of my daily walk. When I was about four houses down from the Starlings' place, I saw someone racing away — a tall, lanky fellow, but I didn't get a good look at him before he worked a Cloaking Hex on himself. There was no point chasing him, but the air was buzzing with whatever strong magic had been done.

"Then I found you barely conscious. I helped you up, saw the damage to your face, and wanted to get you to Runa ASAP. As we were leaving, I saw a necklace had been left on the walkway of your parents' front garden." I suddenly recalled Matilda bending down to fetch something as she'd led me away. "This was just after Martin confirmed the jewel had been split, and the idea came to me that you might be destined to bring the pieces together. That's why I insisted Wesley bring Tobey to dinner. I put the necklace and pendant in plain sight, hoping Tobey would tell you he'd seen it. And he did."

"Couldn't you have just slipped it through the agency's mail slot?" I asked.

"I wanted to make sure that you got it and no one else. Which you'll have to admit was good thinking, given the break-in at your agency."

I hate it when people insist on making such good points when I really want to blast their reasoning full of holes.

"I only wish I'd been as clever with the brooch. Still, that one also got to you, albeit in a more roundabout manner."

"I don't understand why you took the brooch to the pawnshop," I said. Then, to give credit where bubbly credit was due, I added, "Daisy noticed your signature on the intake receipt."

"Again, I only had the tiniest of inklings that the jewel might have been split at that time. When I saw the ruby in Winnifred's brooch, knowing what I did about Oberlin's ancestry, I thought it might possibly be one of the pieces. So, when I was with the Oberlins one evening, I took it. Once I got it home, though, I sensed no special magic on it."

"If you didn't like Oberlin, why would you spend any time with him?" I asked, but what I should have been asking was what she'd meant about Oberlin's ancestry. Hindsight. Twenty-twenty. Et cetera.

"As a vampire, I've lived with the reality that it's best to keep your enemies close. I wanted the Inspector to think I was little more than a glad-handing politician, schmoozing and boozing the higher-ups of Rosaria. Anyway, Winnifred, let me tell you, that woman cannot hold her wine. As I was handing her her coat, it was easy to slip the brooch off the lapel."

"But she said she lost it in Australia, during a police thingie in Canberra."

"We'd been *discussing* Australia. It was a party at the Academy. The Canberra community had just gotten a dog who can sniff out magic artifacts, and Wesley had set up one of those photo prop things with an Australian theme to celebrate, even hired that photographer from the *Herald*." I darted a glance to Mr T, whose lip had curled at the mention of his camera-wielding nemesis. "I swear Wesley must have gone on half the evening about getting a police dog for Rosaria.

"Winnifred, meanwhile, well…" Matilda made the drinky-drinky hand tilt. "She went on and on about how she hoped they could keep the dog at her house so she could dress it up and make it a Faebook sensation.

"Anyway, when the brooch didn't give off any sort of 'magical' signature, I felt silly and was going to return it to Winnifred. But by then, she'd hired you, and I couldn't very well be found with it, so I got rid of it at the pawnshop. That clerk is very susceptible to the Confounding Charm."

"I noticed. But why not just sneak it back into Winnifred's house?"

"I suppose I panicked. I thought Winnifred might have reported it missing to the Academy. With Wesley already looking for something against me, if he found out I'd taken it, well, I'm sure he would have paraded the thieving vampire through the streets of Rosaria. I had planned on sending Winnifred an anonymous email after I'd visited the pawnshop, pretending I was an employee and asking her if she recognized the brooch. But, before I could, you came along and the jewel found where it needed to go. It's like the Boncoeur Jewel wants to reunite, and it knows just who can do that."

I slumped back in my chair. Like I didn't have enough to deal with without throwing sentient jewels into the mix. Then I recalled another source of Matilda Suspicion.

"The morning of Runa's first break-in," I began, channeling my inner Hercule Poirot, "your hand was bandaged. Like someone might have done if they broke through a glass window."

Matilda looked stumped, like I'd finally caught her out. Then, the light of realization dawned on her. "I was coming from my workout at The Yeti's Yoga Studio. Tried to do a handstand for the first time, and took a pretty hard tumble. I was just heading to your place to see if Genie could patch it up."

"And I suppose you weren't involved in Mr Coppersmith's marbles," I sighed, feeling defeated as I tried to wrap my head around all the clues I'd missed and conclusions I'd pole-vaulted to.

"No, that was all you. Again, it's like the pieces want to be rejoined. By you."

"That's all interesting," said Runa, "but it doesn't explain why Clive is now dead and Winnifred was violently attacked."

"And why," I added, "have they been willing to hurt others, but they haven't tried to kill me?" A happy thought if there ever was one.

"They may have seen you as useful," replied Matilda. "Think about it. In a remarkably short time, you found three of the jewel pieces. They may have kept you around, hoping you'd find more. Or they may have wanted to avoid attracting attention to themselves. The death of Mr Coppersmith and the attack on Winnifred may have happened before they realized those two no longer had the items they were after."

I was just about to tell them what Winnifred had told me about Inspector Oberlin attacking her, when Morelli stormed in and demanded to speak to me.

CHAPTER TWENTY-FIVE
CAUGHT ON CAMERA

There's something you should see," Morelli said under his breath after he'd pulled me into the hallway.

"I really don't have time for show and tell," I began, but cut off the attitude when I saw the urgency on his face. "Will it be quick?"

"Well, it's pretty short, but I don't know if the aftermath will be quick."

"Are you being vague just to make me curious?" Morelli shrugged, then pulled out his phone and entered the passcode. Standing next to me so our shoulders were side by side, he then held the phone so I could see as he opened up a private messaging app whose logo I didn't recognize. "What is this?"

"Trollegram. One of my contacts built it. She's got her own server. Keeps our messages entirely safe from prying eyes."

I arched an eyebrow at him. "Exactly what level of troll espionage are you working at?"

"I'm not an active agent anymore, but that doesn't mean I don't stay in touch. Especially given how I've got a tenant who has an unbelievable talent for getting tangled up in bigger messes than I ever saw while on duty." He tapped on a message that included a video. He then pushed the play icon and turned the phone to landscape mode to make it easier to watch what had been recorded.

I knew what I was seeing, but also couldn't believe what I was seeing. That couldn't possibly be—

"Play it again," I said. Morelli complied. I don't throw around the word gobsmacked lightly, but in this instance, I was well and truly gobsmacked.

On the screen was a tubby man who, although he'd pulled a knit balaclava over his eyes, hadn't gotten one long enough to hide his entire face. As such, I had no trouble identifying the very distinctive walrus mustache of Inspector Oberlin.

It took a third time through before I determined the video had been shot across the street from the Academy's rear employee entrance. If not for his poor attempt at concealment, Oberlin would have appeared to be leaving work for the day. The balaclava was an idiotic accessory that screamed, *Foul deed underway!* But I suppose some people need to dress the part when committing crimes. And this was indeed a crime I was watching, because tucked under Oberlin's left arm was an evidence box.

"Pause there," I said when Oberlin came waddling out for the fourth time. "Can you zoom in on the box?"

"You're not going to be surprised."

"I didn't think I would be."

Morelli zoomed in. The video quality was insanely good, and on the side of the box I could read the very number of the box listed on the clerk's form from when Mr T and I had tried to retrieve my stuff. Morelli returned the video to its regular size and let it play through. Once the door had closed behind him, Oberlin clutched the box under his arm while darting glances up and down the side street as he scurried off into the shadows.

"Your contact didn't follow him?" I asked.

"Not exactly. This was taken from a camera they'd set up. If they'd been in the field, they would have, but instead—"

"So Oberlin could have gone anywhere with my stuff? With

stuff that could very likely mean the end of our world as we know it."

"World's always changing," Morelli said stoically.

"Oh, great. You've gone philosophical. We need to know what Oberlin did with that box, and all we have is this—"

"If you'd stop talking for five seconds," Morelli growled. He then softened the chastisement with a grin that said he knew way more than he was letting on. Trolls can be so annoying. "It's not all we have. From things Mattie's told me, I've had some suspicions about Oberlin, and I've had one of my scouts on his tail for a while now. Just happens my scout's school schedule coordinates nicely with Oberlin's work schedule. Means I can have my contact inside the Academy keep an eye on him during the day, and my other scout can start in as soon as school's out."

"I'm sorry… You have—? Scouts? Contacts?" I sputtered. I mean, this was the guy whose biggest organizational task — I'd always assumed — was sorting out which classic reruns to watch when. So to find out he had a team of spies across MagicLand, and who knew where else, was a little tough to wrap my head around. All I managed to say was, "You have been very busy."

"I'm good at time management. Anyway, a system's in place. My contact sent over the footage straight away, and my scout was on Oberlin's tail just a few minutes after the video ended."

Then, because the universe loves to get cheeky with its timing, Morelli's phone began ringing. Apparently, I'm not the only one startled by that sort of thing, because the noise made Morelli fumble with and nearly drop the device. I caught it before it hit the ground, then handed the blaring thing to my landlord, aka "Morelli 007".

"It's my scout," Morelli said as he answered. "Yeah? No, that was a stupid move. You had direct orders not to try to seize him — He didn't— It did? I'll tell you how. He had a temporary portal. Damn it— No, you did fine. Keep on him, we're coming straight away."

Morelli stabbed at the phone to end the call. "Come on, Black, we gotta go."

"What just happened?" I asked, but didn't hesitate to follow after him.

"That walrus-human hybrid just handed off the stuff."

"How?"

"Must have had a temporary portal."

"And where might he have gotten that?" I asked, knowing Morelli built them.

"Don't ask me. Been years since he's seized one of mine. They must have someone on their side who can build them. Which, obviously, isn't good. My scout— that idiot, putting himself in danger like that —has Oberlin held with a Freeze Hex. It won't last long, though."

"And we're not alerting Olivia because…?"

"Look, we can either catch Oberlin in the act, or we can sit around filling out paperwork for HQ, who will then organize a committee, who will then decide how best to assemble a team to haul him in. It might tick Olivia off, but better to ask forgiveness and all that."

"Good point," I said, gasping for breath to keep up with Morelli's surprisingly quick pace. "Although, these bad guys taking the stuff but leaving Oberlin behind does prove one thing."

"What's that?" Morelli asked as he whipped open what I thought was a closet door and grabbed my hand. Suddenly, we were racing along the streets of MagicLand, the quick change and the long-distance portal travel making my head swim a bit as Morelli, not releasing my hand, dragged me along.

"It proves I'm not the only one who doesn't want to be around him."

"He's not going to want to be around me if he's doing anything against Rosaria."

"That's very patriotic of you," I teased as we barreled around a corner. "Where are we headed, anyway?"

"To meet up with my scout. He'll—" Just then Morelli and a teenage boy collided. "Watch where you're going—" Morelli growled, before seeing who he'd run into. "Cicero! You've still got him?"

"This is your scout?" I asked. "Aren't you the troublemaker from Fiona's class?"

"I just get bored," the kid said as he flicked part of his dark mop out of his eyes. "Besides, helping out this guy is punishment enough for anything I might do in class."

"Not sure if Fiona would feel the same way."

"She's the one who hired me out to him. Community service, she called it."

"No, you had it right the first time. It's punishment," I said.

"I don't need to deal with two smart mouths right now," Morelli barked. "Cicero, where'd you leave the target? You never leave the target!"

"Just there," the kid said with a grin and pointed to a medium-sized, overweight mutt with quite a lot of fur around his upper lip. The dog, leashed to a bike rack, wore the dejected look of a canine who's already tried and failed to escape his collar.

"You should not—" Morelli blustered, while I tried not to laugh. "This is not protocol!"

"I got an A on my Transformation Charm test. Figured it was good use of my skill set."

"Undo it," said Morelli. "We need to talk to him. But put a Handcuff Hex on him the instant you change him back to human form."

Cicero complied, as Morelli and I both held our hands ready

for a Stunning Spell. But when Oberlin resumed his normal shape and species, he looked too shellshocked to put up much of a fight.

"Think we might have a word with you, Inspector?" asked Morelli, and if I thought he'd been surly when he'd demanded rent from me over the years, it was nothing to the threateningly low rumble behind his words as he loomed over Oberlin like a predator. Wait. Do walruses have predators?

"I could have you arrested, Morelli. You had someone attack me, you're holding me under duress, and I still have a few charges I never brought against you. Should I bring them up to HQ, perhaps?"

I kind of wanted him to bring them up now. They sounded juicy.

"Since we're chatting about crimes, Inspector," Morelli spoke the title with absolutely zero respect behind it, "we should discuss your role in shifting some stolen property this evening." Oberlin made a derisive huffing sound, but didn't say a word. "You didn't answer my question, Inspector."

"You didn't ask one."

"Okay, then." Morelli stepped in closer, every ounce of his large frame radiating menace. "Where are Cassie Black's items that you stole from the Academy's storage area?"

"They aren't *her* items," Oberlin said belligerently.

"I think HQ would like to have a word with you about that," Morelli said sweetly. "Care for a little trip?"

"You have no authority to arrest me."

"Who said anything about arresting? We're just two people going on a little trip together." Morelli began tugging Oberlin toward a phone booth. How many portals did Morelli have set up around Rosaria? "Cicero, you did good work. Cassie, grab hold of my arm. This is going to be a tight squeeze."

CHAPTER TWENTY-SIX
AN OVER-VERMOUTHED MARTINI

We tumbled out inside one of the round towers of the Tower of London's curtain wall. Within seconds, a trio of Yeoman Warders had surrounded Oberlin. They then assisted us in escorting him to Olivia's office, where they left us with friendly nods, as if we'd just come off one of their tours.

"You do seem to understand the meaning of good timing, Mr Morelli," said Olivia, as casually as if complimenting someone on their choice of shirt. "Inspector Oberlin, take a seat."

Oberlin did as requested. The moment he sat down, a strange clamping noise came from the chair's seat. Oberlin shifted, struggled, but the charmed chair held him firmly in place, and even though he wiggled about trying to free himself, the legs didn't shift or scoot across the stone flooring.

"I try my best," said Morelli. "Not sure what you mean, though. About good timing, that is."

"While you and Cassie were absent, Matilda's brother Martin sent over a photo. Seems one of his team came across a few things of interest. So, Inspector, perhaps you could tell us why you're consorting with witch hunters?"

"I am not consorting with witch hunters," blustered the

Walrus. "The very idea goes against everything I stand—"

"Is this the person you have been in contact with recently?" Olivia asked, producing a photo and showing it to Oberlin.

"I— That is—"

"Is this person familiar to you or not?" asked Olivia, her Rs rolling with ferocious Scottish intensity.

"He said he was working to rid us of the vampires," Oberlin explained belligerently. "Why else would he—?"

"Why else would he want the collection of gems that Miss Black has retrieved?" The cutting nature of Olivia's words made Oberlin wince. "Tell us your reasoning behind this, Inspector Oberlin. And I suggest you be *very* honest."

"You act as if I've committed some heinous crime, but all I was doing was protecting my fellow Magics. You've been shaking in your boots about the vampires, while I've been actively doing something. The person I gave the jewels to is going to use them to fight those bloodsuckers. They're filthy creatures who shouldn't be allowed to live amongst Magics. You've done nothing to stop them except send me a report saying they're plotting an uprising." He shot a scornful glare at Matilda, who remained calm and poised. Although I did notice a smidge of smug satisfaction in her eyes.

"We may have been wrong on that account." Morelli arched an eyebrow at Olivia's understatement. "Okay, we *were* wrong on that account."

"It's not wrong," Oberlin protested. He then jut his index finger at Matilda. "*She's* been planning something."

"It's you who've been planning something, Inspector," Olivia stated coolly. "And I have the feeling you are so witless you don't even know it."

Oh, how I wanted to shout, *In your walrus face!* But I'm mature (sometimes), so I merely thought it. Repeatedly.

Olivia pointed again at the photo. "We have every reason to

believe that this person is part of a group of witch hunters. He asked you to obtain the items Cassie found, yes?" Oberlin grudgingly nodded. "Items you falsely arrested Miss Black for possessing."

"And you had the gall to accuse her of being a cheat," admonished Busby, and I beamed with pleasure at the chastised look on Oberlin's face.

"So, let's get this straight," said Morelli. "You stole from Cassie— No, hold on. Since you took the items from evidence, that means you stole from the Academy itself. And then you did what exactly?"

"I don't need to answer to you," Oberlin said, and I swear his mustache bristled with stubborn indignity.

"Then answer to me," demanded Olivia, her tone gravely serious. Sometimes HQ drove me bonkers and treated me like I wasn't even in the room, but at other times it was really satisfying to have them on my side.

"I gave them to someone who wanted them."

"That's not an answer," I said. "I mean, it is, but it's not a great one."

"Wesley, I suggest you answer whatever we ask you as clearly and thoroughly as possible," Olivia told him. "We do still have dungeons here at the Tower, and you'll be a guest of one unless you tell us what you know. Starting with whether there was talk of a man called Matthew Hopkins."

"Hopkins? Yeah, he was mentioned. A lot, in fact. And why wouldn't he be? He's the greatest vampire hunter in history."

Olivia pinched the bridge of her nose and shook her head, the beads at the ends of her braids clicking against each other as she did so. Finally, she looked up, her gaze leveled on Oberlin.

"That's *Helsing*. As in Von Helsing. Not Hopkins. Are you truly an example of the best the Academy has to offer?" She held up a hand when he opened his mouth. "Never mind. Don't answer that."

"You say you went along with all this because you assumed they were on your side against the vampires," Runa said. "But you're not as stupid as Cassie thinks you are. You had to suspect something wasn't right, so why did you keep going along with it?"

Under his soup strainer, Oberlin pinched his lips and looked like he was going to refuse to reply. Then something happened that I would not have believed if I hadn't been standing right there witnessing it: Tears came to his walrus-y eyes.

"Wesley?" prodded Olivia gently.

"I only did it for Winnifred," Oberlin pleaded.

"For Winnifred?" I blurted. "You attacked her. You attacked your own wife. Sorry," I said to Olivia's shocked expression, "I meant to tell you, but Morelli whisked me away before I got a chance."

"Did you attack your own wife?" asked Olivia, fury darkening her cheeks.

"Only to protect her. They'd been threatening her. Said if I didn't comply, they'd hurt her. Bad. And then I found out they were coming for her because I'd taken too long to get them what they wanted. They thought I was going against them. I figured if I got ahead of their game, if I did something that would have her safe in the Tower's medical ward, she'd be out of harm's way. I couldn't ask you to hide her, because then you'd start asking questions. I only hurt her because I love her."

"You have a very strange way of showing it, Walrus Face," I said, and as a show of how off-kilter he was feeling, he didn't even scowl at the nickname.

"They would have done worse," he muttered, true pain in his eyes. "So, yeah, I attacked Winnie, then arrested Cassie soon after. And, first chance I got, I gave them the jewels she'd found. They said it would be for the greater good."

"Why would you think these people were up to any sort of

good after they'd threatened Winnifred like that?" asked Morelli.

"Because he wanted to believe they were fighting against his enemy," I said. "He hates vampires, so he would do anything to help out anyone else who was against them. No matter how vile they were, no matter how immoral they seemed, he sided with them for his own agenda."

"That's very astute, Cassie," observed Olivia. "Have you been studying criminal psychology in your spare time?"

"No, I'm just overly familiar with American politics."

"Anything to say to that, Inspector Oberlin?"

"I may have let a little prejudice cloud my judgement, but it's too late. They have what they need."

"And I'm afraid they've already made use of it," said Mr T.

"How do you mean?" asked Olivia.

"The gems, if possessed by someone who knows how to use them, who wants to use them for evil purposes, will weaken Magics. I believe that might explain why so many Magics are experiencing trouble with their power."

I recalled the receptionist at the *Herald* complaining about her co-workers being off sick, and of Daisy wondering why she couldn't travel via portal — something that requires reliable magic.

"But he handed over the jewels less than an hour ago," I said.

"Not if that temporary portal was also a time dilation portal," said Morelli, his tone that of someone just realizing how stupid they'd been.

A time dilation portal, like the one in Dr Torres's office, made it so you arrived at your destination at the same time as when you left your starting point, no matter the time difference. For example, if you traveled by normal portal from Portland at noon, you'd arrive in London at nine p.m. But with a time dilation portal, due to some trickery with physics, you could leave Portland at noon and arrive in London at noon.

"So if the witch hunter was in, say, Japan at the time of the transfer...?" I began. It made a sort of sense, but something nagged at me about it. Namely, why my magic had been wonky for weeks. Long before I'd ever encountered a single piece of the Boncoeur Jewel. But now wasn't the time to figure out that conundrum.

"With the international date line, they would have had a day, possibly a few hours more than that, to use the jewel against us."

"Wesley, you've been so focused on your prejudice that you've failed to see the real threat going on," Runa jeered. "You should have known better."

"None of you knew," he snapped back.

"We're not police inspectors, are we?" Morelli said sarcastically, but with absolutely no malice in his voice. It clearly unnerved Oberlin. "You've had access to information we haven't. You've had direct communications with them. You could have looked up information on the people you were dealing with to see if they were legit. But you did none of those things because you thought they hated the same people you do."

"And now several pieces of the Boncoeur Jewel, possibly all of them, are in the witch hunters' hands," noted Olivia. "Do we still have no idea how they join together? Because my only hope is that they don't know either." Olivia looked to Oberlin, who shook his head, ignorant on the matter. Probably on a lot of other matters too, now that I come to think of it.

"I think it's a cage sort of thing." I explained the woodcut images Dr Torres had sent me. "Fiona told me these jewel pieces aren't just going to snap together on their own. You probably need to put them in something that can hold them in place. Tighten it down, then magic should take over from there, right?" Everyone was looking at me like I'd just made some sort of leap in quantum computing. "It's just a guess. Alastair, you know about mechanical things. What do you think—?"

Beads of sweat dotted Alastair's face, and I wondered if he was getting sick. He hadn't slept much recently, and likely hadn't been eating right either. All because he was so fixated on—

"Alastair," I scolded, "did you build another item that could destroy the world?"

"Oh, come on," said Morelli, "you can't go accusing him of helping the bad guys again."

"She might not be wrong this time," Alastair admitted.

"If I survive this without getting obliterated by a witch hunter," I said, "we seriously need to have a discussion about your work choices."

"Care to explain yourself, Alastair?" Busby asked flatly.

"An order came in for something that could be adjusted to hold small items of various sizes and shapes until they could be joined together. Sort of like a vise, but they said it had to be very precise. I assumed it was for a woodworking project, for making tiny items for dollhouses or something like that. It was detailed work, but it should have been fairly straightforward except I kept having trouble getting the tension and torque just right. Cassie and Morelli can confirm that. But once I got the final part I needed, it came together no problem. I dropped it off just the other day to the person who commissioned it."

"And that was—?" prodded Olivia.

"I don't know exactly. They did everything through the *Herald's* offices."

"And you never took a name? Never saw the person," Morelli asked. "And how did I miss this happening right under my nose?"

"Because you were too busy making crochet dragons for a certain someone," I commented.

"And perhaps because I had him occupied with guarding Runa," admitted Olivia. "Do you have anything to say for yourself, Inspector? Anything you'd like to tell us?

"I know I'll never partner up with a civilian again."

"I think you have more to be concerned about than who your future colleagues might be," said Mr Tenpenny. "It's your future cellmates you ought to be considering, because even the most hardened Magic criminal will not take kindly to treason of this level."

"Regardless, the damage has clearly been done," said Olivia wearily. "It's now time for you to help us repair that damage. Can you tell us anything about where the witch hunters are? What their aims might be? How long before they act? Anything?"

Oberlin shook his jowly head. "I only know they were taking Magics for some sort of experiment. Testing out how they could use them against us. I didn't quite understand it all."

"Hold on," said Runa, as if just realizing something, "these colleagues of yours asked you to steal my saw, didn't they?"

Oberlin nodded. "There's a piece of the jewel in the handle."

I knew it! Although being right in this case didn't feel that great.

"Inspector Wesley Oberlin," said Olivia in very official tones as the chair released its hold on the Walrus, "you've been cooperative, so no dungeon for you yet, but your room will be heavily guarded, and you will be expected to assist HQ in anything we request from you. *Anything*." To the rest of us, she said with grim determination. "We must assume the witch hunters could start something at any moment. It will come down to a fight, and we *all* need to be ready."

"Where do you think you're going?" Runa snapped, and we all looked to where she was glaring.

Oberlin had backed his way toward the door.

"You weren't thinking of weaseling out of your punishment, were you?" asked Busby, in a menacing tone I'd never heard from him before.

"I— No. I wouldn't do that. It's just I can't—"

"Wesley…" Busby put an incoming-nuclear-bomb amount of threat behind the single word.

"B-b-but—" Oberlin's panicked eyes pleaded with anyone who might be willing to help him out.

"You're not a walrus," I said. "You're nothing but a chicken."

"Call me whatever you like, but if by *anything* you mean for me to fight them alongside you, that's just not going to happen. They'd kill me the instant they saw me on your side. I can't, I won't, and you can't make me," he insisted petulantly.

Oberlin couldn't fight, but he sure could try to flee. Until, that is, he ran smack dab into Chester's torso, bounced off the hard surface, and stumbled back onto his butt.

Her words as dry as an over-vermouthed martini, Olivia told Oberlin, "Chester here is very good at persuading people to obey orders."

"As I'm sure is Mr Morelli," said Mr Tenpenny. "Eugene, would you mind going as well?"

Morelli gave a sharp nod. "I'll need to make a statement of what my scout witnessed, anyway."

"Keep very precise records of that, will you?" said Olivia. "My trust levels for the Inspector are about as slim as a fairy wing."

"I've been trying to tell you all along he was no good," I said.

"Hard to believe someone with your social skills can be such a good judge of character," quipped Runa.

"Hidden talent, I suppose."

Olivia grinned at that, then said to Oberlin and his two very large guards, "You three go have a chat about duty and honor and sworn oaths to protect, okay?"

"Yes, sir, Sir Olivia. Come on, then." Chester pulled Oberlin to his feet by the scruff of his collar. "Hey, has anyone told you you look like a walrus?"

CHAPTER TWENTY-SEVEN
IN PLAIN SIGHT

After Chester and Morelli hauled Oberlin off, I celebrated a successful walrus hunt with a trio of cupcakes from the stack the pixies had conjured onto the side table. I then wandered over to see what Daisy was up to. Okay, no, I didn't suddenly develop some sort of interest in Daisy, but she was idly looking through *An Enchanted History of the Portland Community,* and I was curious to see if I was still having stress-induced hallucinations.

Daisy didn't seem to mind as I watched over her shoulder, and after seeing a dozen or so pages behaving as they should, I shrugged off yesterday's weirdness to the strain of being in jail, of traveling by pumpernickel, of becoming Daisy-fied, and of making far more discoveries about vampires and witch hunters than my brain was ready to handle.

Daisy stopped on a page that featured a candid shot of a group of kids, like the ones you see in a high school yearbook. They all wore looks of surprise, and all had cameras either around their necks or in their hands.

"Who is this?" I asked, noticing a picture of a gangly fellow with dark hair. Something about him struck me as familiar.

Fiona was nearby and glanced over at the photo. "Ah, that's Gibson Todd."

"Oh, yeah, Gibson," said Daisy reminiscently. "We were in

photography club together. I was the one who took this picture. Surprised them just before club time started."

"You were in photography club?" I asked. Not that I didn't think Daisy could snap a photo, but I just pictured her extracurricular activities as involving more pompoms than flashbulbs.

"Yep, won loads of first prizes. But I did in most of the clubs I joined," she said, not in a bragging way, but in the way of someone who assumes winning unlimited numbers of prizes is everyone's normal. "It's so fun getting awards, don't you think?" See what I mean?

As Daisy prattled on about the various honors she'd received simply for knowing how to press a button on a camera, I looked at the guy in the photo more closely. And then it dawned on me. This was the photographer for the *Herald*. It had to be him I'd seen. The dark-haired, lanky person who'd been there catching nearly every one of my awkward moments over the past several weeks and supplying images to go with Calder Hackett's anti-Cassie opinion pieces.

The desire for petty revenge bubbled in me. I may not have the clout to get this guy's camera license revoked (or whatever photojournalists had), but Mr T? An HQ bigwig? He'd be able to run this guy through the wringer.

"Mr T," I called over to him, "if you wanted to file a complaint with Leo, this is the guy who took your picture without your permission."

"I would, but if you'll recall, that photographer recently left the *Herald*'s employment."

"Oh, that's a shame to hear," said Daisy. "But I'm sure he can get plenty of freelance work. Funny how you don't think of photographers, do you? You just show up somewhere, and then there's pictures of it."

If you've ever been right near an old church with a big bell tower, and if you've been there at the wrong time, you'll have been subjected to the bone-rattling sensation of bells cling-clanging and ding-donging with a frightening amount of gusto. That captures exactly how I felt at Daisy's words.

Photographers did blend into the background. Photographers can go into any situation, any scenario, and be perfectly accepted because they're reporting the news, capturing the moment, whatever. They move around events without much notice, and they can get close to people and objects without it seeming odd. Or even noticeable in some cases.

Photos had kept cropping up in all these cases of mine.

The photo of Clive at his marble conference. The photo of Winnifred with her brooch. The photo of Wordsworth at the Bookworm convention. And I was pretty sure this Gibson Todd had been there snapping away at the scene of Runa's break-in.

My attack at my parents' place. Had that flash been from a camera or from the attack spell? Or, who knows, a camera enchanted to cast an attack spell at the click of a button? Regardless, someone tall, slim, and dark-haired had been following me around, taking pics of every pratfall. I had thought it was Matilda, but what if...? And what if that person had been watching out for how I was proceeding on my cases?

"What do you know of this Gibson?" I asked. I'd been so lost in my own thoughts, though, I hadn't realized the others had continued chatting and were already on an entirely new topic of conversation.

"He was always a little strange," said Daisy.

"Strange how?"

Fiona took up the question. "Seemed to feel a sense of guilt about being Magic. He has a Norm mother, Magic father. The father left the picture soon after Gibson was born, and his mother was, well, rather devout. She allowed his magic training since letting his power run amok would be problematic, but I heard she shamed him whenever he returned from classes."

"There were bruises," whispered Daisy. "I remember Inspector Oberlin trying to help Gibson out, but Gibson refused. Got pretty heated about it too."

I recalled what Leo had told us in his office, about Oberlin raising questions about bruises on a young Magic. I guess maybe he did have a good side. Albeit, a very tiny one. I then explained to them the rambling thoughts about Gibson that had been flicking through my brain.

"When Gibson was my student," said Fiona, "he often had essays full of rhetoric against magic and how it was akin to evil. I don't doubt that has carried on through adulthood."

"So if a witch hunter was looking for an insider to do his dirty work..." I began.

"They couldn't ask for a better candidate," continued Fiona.

"It's obvious he's involved, isn't it? And then — like you said, Mr T — he quit the *Herald* the very morning the jewel pieces went missing. It's like a billboard with a big, flashing arrow pointing to a picture of him and announcing, *This is our guy.*"

"The trouble is that he has left the *Herald*," said Mr T. "We don't know where he is. I can put out an alert for him, but for now, we need to focus on the person we do have in custody."

Before I could argue, Olivia cut me off, saying, "Of course, we will ask Inspector Oberlin if he is in league with Todd, but I doubt their relationship has improved over the intervening years."

"And what you have is only speculation, Cassie," Busby said. "I do agree his presence at these events is intriguing, but it may only be coincidence. Please, try to put Gibson Todd from your mind and concentrate on more pressing matters."

I didn't appreciate my brilliant deductions being put on the back burner, but I knew better than to press the point.

CHAPTER TWENTY-EIGHT
FAVORABLE ODDS CHARM

As Olivia and Busby discussed the possible implications of what Oberlin had done and what punishments to recommend to the council, something that had been pushed to the back of my brain came skipping right back in.

"Mr Wood," I said, which, given that I was just standing in the middle of the room with a fresh cupcake in my hand, may have seemed a bit random.

Olivia let out an irritable sigh. Busby quickly cut in before she could tell me off. "I know he's important to you, but as a Norm, Nino is not our priority," he insisted.

"No, it kind of is. Promise you won't get upset."

"What have you done?"

"It wasn't me, it was Morelli. So, if you're going to get mad at someone, he's your troll. Anyway, remember when Mr Wood got beat up, when he nearly died?"

Mr T turned to Olivia and said, "We asked Eugene to help Nino Wood recover."

"Yes, I recall," commented Olivia. "But I thought this Mr Wood's recuperation went well."

"It did. But Mr Wood has this appetite for sandwiches, and he also needed fairly regular doses of painkillers."

"Please get to the point, Cassie," Olivia said wearily. "There's quite a bit going on at the moment."

"Morelli gave Mr Wood some magic to help speed the healing process. It also made it so Mr Wood could get his own meals and medicine by magically summoning things to himself."

"I don't see the problem," said Olivia. "Magic doesn't stick to Norms. He should have been free and clear of it within a couple hours of Mr Morelli's assistance."

"Well, it stuck this time. Mr Wood doesn't really know how to do much with it other than to levitate sandwich fixings from his fridge, but he is most definitely holding on to the magic he was given."

"I've never heard of such a thing."

"Doesn't matter," I said, earning a look of taken-aback surprise from Olivia. "What matters is that, technically speaking, Mr Wood is a Magic. And he's missing. He never met up with his tour group, and he never sent Daisy nor me a single sausage roll photo."

"Please tell me that's not a euphemism for something."

"No, I do mean actual sausages in pastry. My point is, before he left, Daisy loaded Mr Wood up with Fairy Tags. They stopped moving when he was in London… except for a few near the Tower that came back online. If you consider Mr Wood as a missing Magic, other Magics might be wherever he is. So, if we go after him, it'd be a two-birds-one-stone kind of thing."

"I'm all for it," said my dad, although he looked completely done in, and my mom's eyelids were drooping.

"No," Olivia said firmly. "Runa would kill me if she heard I sent you out again. And Cassie, as I said earlier, I will put some people on this. As soon as I organize a team to start the search, you will give them what information you have regarding these Fairy Tags."

"If there's going to be a team going after Mr Wood, I should be the one leading it," I stated, and wondered where this bold attitude had come from. I mean, a few months ago, I would have cowered before any of Olivia's orders.

Olivia, mustering her patience, had the grace to don an apologetic expression. "It's not that I don't think you're competent, but the missing Magics case — which now might include your Mr Wood — is still an official HQ matter. Without your license, I'm afraid it would be dangerous for us both if I were to give you any detailed information about it."

"This is ridiculous," I said, and Alastair winced at my harsh tone toward Olivia. Which, fair point, since it's usually good life advice to never anger a woman with banshee blood.

"What exactly is ridiculous, Miss Black?" Olivia asked tersely.

"This whole can't-tell-Cassie-anything-about-anything thing."

"Very eloquent," quipped Mr T.

"You know what I mean," I said, pacing the office since I was too frustrated to stand still. "We've got loads of missing Magics. And we now know the missing Magics are tied to this whole jewel-witch-hunter problem, but yet you can't tell me what you know or let me do anything with their cases because of this stupid license thing."

I was referring to an HQ restriction on anyone sharing information with me regarding the missing Magics case because I was still an unlicensed detective. It involved a form of Confidentiality Spell, meaning whoever *did* tell me anything official risked being immediately extracted. Makes Norm bureaucracy not seem so bad, right?

"You know from experience," I continued, "that I'm good at finding people. But you're wasting that resource. How are you going to feel if those Magics are killed before the application due date goes zipping by in—" I glanced at Olivia's desk calendar and honestly couldn't remember what day it was "—in a bit."

Without hesitation, Morelli rattled off my limited time frame, down to the minute.

"Why do you know that?" asked Olivia, looking truly mystified. "And know it with such accuracy?"

"I've got a sort of thing with calendaring. Bit O.C.D. about it, actually. Developed it while in the M.A.G.E."

"Cassie, this has been explained to you," interjected Mr Tenpenny. "We can't tell you anything about the missing Magics case due to the way the license application works. It's not an ideal arrangement, but we have no way around it."

"Actually, I've been working on that," said Rafi.

"You have?" I asked. "And you didn't bother to tell me this?"

"I didn't want to get your hopes up, but I did tell you I'd make up for that little incident that I should have been more aware of before sending you in."

I barely refrained from saying, "*You mean sending me into the British Library before you'd verified that the book I was after wouldn't burst into flames?*" But since I was still trying to keep that destructive outing under wraps, I bit back the words and merely said, "Thanks. I think. Does it work?"

"Pretty sure. So," he said, addressing the room like some sort of Victorian-era magician pulling his audience into his next trick, "we have Cassie Black, who has a license due date. She's actually solved several of her cases that, under normal circumstances, would have earned her the signatures she needs for the application. This proves she can do her job, and so, by the laws of probability, she'll get her license, right?"

"Unless we've all been destroyed by this Hopkins character," noted Morelli.

"Already calculated into the probability, because if we are destroyed, then the license would be a moot point, so it negates a few things in the equations. Anyway, so this all works into what I'm calling the Favorable Odds Charm. It's based on probability and can be applied to the bureaucratic do-hicky that makes it so you can't tell Cassie about official cases."

"I think my brain just broke," I said.

"So, this does what, exactly?" asked Alastair, his face showing true interest.

"I believe putting a probability spin on the license requirement should make any charm regarding it assume the application has been completed and approved. I'd like to get rid of the license spell altogether, but it's been so long that I can't remember how to reverse it. Apologies for that. I had a lot of anger issues in my younger years."

"Wait," I said, "what exactly are you saying?"

"That I crafted the license spell. It was when I first started working for HQ. This was before Olivia was our fearless leader. I was in a rebellious mood over the limitations put on elves and other non-human Magics, so I made sure that every bureaucratic step I was asked to create was as baffling as possible. Drove a few Magics mad."

And let me be clear that Rafi didn't sound one bit contrite about that last sentence. Rather, he seemed proud of his mentally destructive handiwork.

"You've certainly mellowed over time," said Mr T.

"Having a boss who recognizes my talents has helped," Rafi said with a wink to Olivia. "Anyway, with the freer reins I've been given, I've been trying to loosen up a few of the tangles as they crop up, but this one proved to be a real bugger."

"Yes, well," said Olivia, "do note, that free rein doesn't mean I'm in any way comfortable with training Chester to be a secretary."

"He doesn't even really want to do it," I said, recalling what Chester had confessed to me and Mr T.

"Ah, well, then maybe I should ease back on that. Now, as for this spell, should we give it a whirl?"

"What will happen if it goes wrong?" I asked.

"Not quite sure. Death, dismemberment, permanent bad hair day? All part of the spell crafting fun, isn't it?" he replied with reckless cheer. "Now, the extension was set by you, yes?" he asked Olivia. She nodded. "Which means I should be able to enchant the calendar with this Favorable Odds Charm to make it believe the application requirements have been met..." Rafi snapped his fingers over the calendar. A red checkmark appeared next to the words *CB License Due*. "Um, yeah," he said uncertainly, "someone want to go ahead and try to tell Cassie something about the missing Magics case? Oh, and, Cassie, this only delays the requirement to get your license. It doesn't erase it. If the due date goes by and you haven't completed your paperwork... Well, we'll see, won't we?"

"I'm not sure I like your version of helping," I said. Then, looking between Olivia and Mr T, I asked, "So, anyone willing to test it out?"

Busby shrugged with reluctant acceptance. "I've been dead before. It's inconvenient, but seems to only be temporary." He took a deep breath, grit his teeth, then related one of the facts they'd uncovered about the missing Magics from Seattle.

We all waited a moment. Mr T didn't start having any sort of fit, his eyes didn't take on the dull vacancy of someone who's been extracted, and he didn't drop over dead. In fact, he didn't seem affected in any way by the revelation.

"Seems to have worked," Rafi said after letting out a lengthy exhale that was full of relief. "Just let me know if you have any side effects later."

"Such as?" Mr Tenpenny asked worriedly.

Rafi considered this a moment, then said, "Seizures, I think.

Pretty violent ones. You might want to keep pillows on hand. Wear a helmet, perhaps."

"So, where do we begin?" Alastair asked after several moments of awkward silence.

A question to which I had no clue how to answer.

But before I had to, a man in a red-and-black jacket, ruffed collar, and jaunty black hat burst into Olivia's office.

Nearly everyone in the room spun around, their hands ready to throw a Stunning Spell, if not something worse, at the intruder.

CHAPTER TWENTY-NINE
NOT THOSE KIND OF PIPES

"Stop!" I yelled. "It's just Nigel. Wait," I said, turning to him. "You're not planning to overthrow HQ, are you?"

"The to-do list is already brimming over for the week, so, no."

"What are you doing here, Nigel?" Olivia asked, brusquely but not unkindly. "You know you need to make an appointment if you have matters to be addressed."

"Right, yes. I just thought it might be urgent."

"What might be?"

"Are you still looking for a secret room?" Nigel asked me. "Because it's just... well, I heard a knocking sound in the pool area."

The White Tower, in a room far below where tourists were allowed to explore, had an enormous swimming pool that was like something straight out of a movie centered on the extravagances of a Roman emperor. If you can imagine trompe-l'oeil columns on the side walls, a back wall with Roman mosaics depicting Neptune cavorting with dolphins and mermaids, and in-pool lights that made the water sparkle, you'll have a fair idea of what the Tower's pool is like.

"Likely just the pipes," said Olivia.

"No," Nigel mused, "sounded nothing like bagpipes. Not even like a pan flute. It was definitely a knocking sort of sound."

"I didn't mean that kind of— Never mind. I'll let the maintenance pixies—"

"No, sorry, I misspoke. Not a knocking, a drumming." Nigel then tapped his fingers on his thigh, and something about the rhythm, or lack of rhythm, seemed familiar.

"Was that what you heard?" I asked. Nigel nodded. "Do it again."

Nigel did, and a flash of a vacuum came to mind before I realized why the sound was beating away at my memory banks.

"Bunny," I said.

"No, that would be thumping," said Nigel, who thumped his boot against the ground.

"Not the animal. A man. Seems to be doing his best to drive his neighbors bananas with percussion instruments. Mr T, remember that woman in Lola's neighborhood? She told us that whenever they've put a Silencing Spell around Bunny's house, it doesn't stick. What if it's not Bunny's house, but Bunny himself? So, if the kidnappers put a Silencing Spell on wherever Bunny and other missing Magics are being kept, it might not work."

I'm proud to say there were plenty of shocked agreements to my deductive reasoning. Sadly, no one applauded my genius, but maybe next time.

"We need to get down there," I urged. "Since I'm now allowed to help you look for missing Magics, that is," I added wryly.

Because we'd have to move quickly through one of the more popular exhibitions in the White Tower, Olivia insisted everyone except herself, me, and Mr Tenpenny stay behind, but that they should be ready if needed. With Nigel taking the lead, we dashed off to the pool. Well, as much of a dash as you can get when four people need to surreptitiously slip through a maintenance door (aka 'pool entrance') while going unnoticed by gaggles of tourists.

Once down the steep stairs to the pool, we waited. And waited. And waited. Nigel's face grew more and more sheepish as the minutes passed.

"Are you sure it was our pool? You didn't go for a swim anywhere else?" asked Olivia. And the question was fair. Nigel didn't have the best track record of keeping his facts straight.

"Quite sure." Nigel then wavered. "Mostly sure. Maybe it was just pipes. But what I heard sounded nothing like 'Scotland the Brave'."

"Again, Nigel, not those kind of—"

Olivia stopped speaking and cocked her head like a cat who's just heard the treat bag being shaken. I didn't catch anything at first, but then, very faintly, I heard a discordant *tap tap tap* followed by a series of beats that seemed to have abandoned all the laws of rhythm.

"That's it!" exclaimed Nigel right when Olivia and I started to follow the sound. We shushed him, but the sound had stopped.

Olivia looked about to scold Nigel, but I stopped her. "Trust me, Bunny'll be back at it soon enough."

And he was. This time, we moved more quickly and ended up at one of the towel lockers at the far end of the pool. After giving each other a questioning glance, I said, "I'll open it. You two stand guard with spells ready to go."

Surprisingly, the head of HQ actually took my orders.

I flipped open the lid to the locker and saw…

"Towels?"

"It has to be a portal, but you can usually see something of what's beyond," said Olivia as she began pulling out stacks of white, fluffy towels and dropping them on the floor. The pixies were not going to be happy about that. "Runa knows portals. We should—"

"No," I interrupted, and Olivia arched an eyebrow at me. "I mean, she does, but she knows the legal type of portals."

"And your suggestion is…?" asked Olivia.

"Promise me you won't hold anything I say against him. Or me."

"I don't like promises of that nature, but as this is an emergency, I'll allow it."

"Morelli. He knows illegal portals, and I'm going to bet the portal in this locker isn't registered with HQ. We need his sort of expert help."

"Tell him to finish processing Oberlin and get here as soon as possible."

I texted Morelli, telling him to come to the pool area straight away. I also mentioned to be sure to bring Runa. If there were missing Magics on the other side, I didn't know what state they might be in, but I doubted a single half-troll's healing abilities would be enough to handle the triage.

Once Morelli arrived with Runa huffing behind him, we explained the situation, what we'd heard, and what we didn't find.

Morelli inspected the towel locker, seeming to focus on something at the back of the second shelf before asking, "Anyone got a pencil or pen, something pokey."

"*Something pokey*? Is that a technical term?" I asked.

"You're skinny enough. How about I experiment with you?"

"Please give him a pen," sighed Mr T. "I've seen how long this banter can go on."

Morelli took the fountain pen Olivia handed him and prodded at the upper back corner of the shelf.

"Looks like nice work. It's hard to hide these types of portals, but whoever did this knows their stuff." To our looks of growing impatience, he added, "It's a closed system portal."

"What's that mean exactly?"

"It means that this building, house, room, whatever's on the other side of this thing is currently on its own— I dunno, *plane*, I guess you'd call it. The only way out of that plane is through another portal within it. Basically, the people on the other side of this thing aren't *somewhere*. They're not, say, in a studio over on Camden Street; they're literally living within a portal itself. That's why it's been so hard to find them."

"And the connector portal? The way out you mentioned?" asked Busby. "Where might that lead to?"

Morelli shrugged. "Anywhere, really. But I imagine not too far, possibly even within the Tower."

"Seems a bit risky."

"It is, but with these types of portals, you gotta keep the other doorway relatively close, otherwise things get sorta *stretchy*."

"But why would they build the portal in the Tower?" asked Olivia.

Again Morelli shrugged. "It wouldn't be the first. Like I was telling Black recently, the Tower's riddled with hidden portals. This might be one of those, but if it's newly built, it could just be them showing off, flaunting their cleverness in your face. Just count yourselves lucky you found this one." He received more than one questioning look in response to this. "These types of portals… How do I put it? They're kind of *floaty*. This one's here now, but it could wander off to some other location any second. Tower Green, your office, anywhere within a couple-mile radius."

"We have to go through," I said after swallowing back the uncomfortable thought of this Matthew Hopkins portal-ing into my room in the middle of the night. "We know Bunny is on the other side. Others might be as well. And if this thing can move willy-nilly, we need to go now."

"You risk being trapped," said Morelli. "If the maker of the portal detects you and has time to lock down the other end, you're stuck. Forever. Although, it's you, so maybe that wouldn't be too bad."

"Would that mean the people inside are stuck forever?" asked Busby before I could comment.

"Theoretically. Like I said, I ain't come across many of these. Most were just used for an hour or so for secret M.A.G.E. meetings, then closed off immediately afterward."

"We have much to discuss, Mr Morelli," said Olivia, not threateningly, but in an I-might-have-to-add-you-to-the-payroll kind of way.

"So, how do we do this?" I asked, keen to find out if anyone besides Bunny was inside.

We did this by volunteering me for the job. I was the skinniest and the most limber, which meant once we got the shelving out of the locker, I was the best candidate for squeezing inside the thing.

"Try sticking your hand through first," suggested Morelli. "If we don't hear an immediate snap, it means they aren't guarding the portal."

"Snap? What kind of snap?"

"*Snap*, as in the portal closing and crushing your hand."

"That's what I figured."

"Don't worry, kid. You're used to it by now."

After making some remark about that not being helpful, I grit my teeth and pushed my shaking fingers slowly through. Nothing happened other than a sensation of my fingers feeling a little too long. Then, with one quick motion, I pushed my hand through up to my wrist. Again, nothing happened, but Morelli told me to hold it for a count of ten, just to be sure.

"You know, you could have done this part," I complained.

"Yeah, but that squirmy look you got on your face right now is priceless."

I'd reached nine when something brushed against my fingertips. I screamed and yanked my hand out. The sudden switch in dimensions, or whatever it was, sent icy prickles throughout my hand and up my arm. I started shivering.

"Her hand!" cried Runa.

Oh dear Glinda, I knew it. It had been crushed to bits just like every other time I attempted a magical rescue mission. The icy sensation must have dulled the pain, but I was sure I'd make up for that later.

"Come on, Cassie," insisted Runa. "What's it say?"

I dared to open my eyes. My hand looked normal. Not swollen, not mangled, not missing any digits. Between my first two fingers, though, I held a small scrap of paper. Paper that looked very much like a piece of Pret á Manger wrapper.

Morelli plucked the paper from my fingers and read, "Help us." And when I glanced over at it, I recognized Mr Wood's handwriting.

It was a successful rescue mission. The most graceful rescue mission? No. But it was successful. Since, according to Morelli, these types of portal could be temperamental and disappear entirely if disturbed, we were afraid to break down any of the locker's walls for easier access. Nevertheless, with much grunting and tugging, we managed to get out over three hundred missing Magics, including Bunny and Mr Wood.

Although Runa determined that nearly all of their magic was gone, our newfound friends appeared to be in good health. Nevertheless, she called down the Tower's medics to give each person a more thorough exam.

Bunny showed no sign of anything wrong, and preferred tapping away at the pool room's walls with a pair of chopsticks he'd found somewhere to being poked and prodded by someone in a white lab coat. As for Mr Wood, he was as robust as ever. After many thanks and awkward hugs, I sent an order to the kitchen pixies, and he settled onto one of the pool's side benches to tuck into the tallest B.L.T. I'd ever seen.

Once the medics had gotten to work, Busby suggested inspecting the space the captives had been in. And I'll give you one guess as to who got volunteered again. You'd think being the person who's supposedly meant to save the world would get me out of things like that, wouldn't you?

Forming a sort of chain with everyone holding hands so I could be yanked out if needed, I went in. It was a good-sized space that Mr T later agreed had likely been treated with some sort of Expansion Hex to accommodate the numbers of people we'd found. It reminded me of a high school gym when it needs to temporarily be made into a shelter during a natural disaster.

There were cots, there were blankets, there was a table stocked with some basic packaged food and drinks, but what struck me most were the number of absorbing capsules on small side tables next to each cot. The second thing that struck me was, despite the number of Magics we'd pulled out, the confined space had no scent of magic in the air.

The capsules next to the cots were all empty, as indicated by their color, but a locked, wall-mounted cabinet at the far end of the room held a liter-sized glass jar brimming with capsules that pulsed with a purple glow, showing they were full of magic. On hearing this, Olivia went in herself and magicked the thing off the wall and handed it out to us. She then worked a Replacement Hex so whoever came in wouldn't immediately be aware of their missing goodies.

We debated whether a team should stay inside the room to ambush the deviants, but Morelli worried the portal might close at any moment, so Olivia deemed that attempting any heroics was too risky.

"Better to be proactive," Morelli told Olivia as he began to seal off the Tower side of the portal as best he could. "Regardless of why or when this one was built, we can at least shut down one route of entry to them. Of course, there's no telling how many more hidden portals there might be, but this one makes it pretty clear they have full access to the Tower. When they're ready to attack, there's really nothing we can do to stop them."

"Thank you for ruining my appetite for dinner, Mr Morelli," Olivia said before marching away, the *click click* of her heels echoing throughout the pool room as she left.

CHAPTER THIRTY
PRESSING NEEDS

Sometime in the far too early hours of the morning, I woke from a weird dream that went from witch hunters plugging me into the Mauvais's magic battery contraption to Tobey tiptoeing around my room and rifling through my things. When I sat up and glanced around in the semi-darkness, I was relieved to see I was, one, not strapped to a modified dentist chair and, two, that my room was empty of cousins-of-some-degree-or-other.

I quickly dropped back to sleep.

Until my phone jarred me out of that sleep. I really needed to properly set up the Do Not Disturb function on that thing.

My immediate instinct was to hurl the noisome device across the room and go back to DreamLand, but when I saw the number, I groggily took the call.

"Hello?" I said. Okay, *tried* to say. My muscles don't tend to work first thing upon waking, and that includes my facial muscles.

"Sorry, were you napping?"

"It's barely five a.m. here, Dr Torres."

"Should I let you go?" he asked in that way that clearly implies your caller doesn't want to be set aside.

"No, s'alright. You didn't know I was here."

"Here?"

"HQ. Sorry," I mumbled, getting out of bed to not disturb Alastair any more than I already— Actually, when I looked over, he was still fully asleep and snoring gently. Which seemed really unfair. "You know about HQ, right?"

"Oh, yes. My husband and I have been to the evening festivities there several times. We've never had more fun."

This would be a bit of after-hours entertainment Magics like to have in the armory display within the White Tower. Using a few flicks of the wrist, they bring the suits of armor to life and cross their fingers that the historic attractions don't wander off before the tourists start pouring in the next morning.

"Is that what you're calling for? To tell me about what historians get up to for fun?" I asked as goosebumps prickled my arms. The rooms at the White Tower might look like modern hotel rooms, but it's still a castle, so even in late summer, the mornings are chilly.

Luckily, I'd considered this and had had Alastair bring my favorite black hoodie. But when I reached for it, it wasn't in the center of the dresser where I remembered leaving it. I patted around in the dark until my fingers found it on the right-hand side of the dresser, then I shrugged my way into its warmth.

"Not today," replied Dr Torres with a chuckle, "perhaps some other time. No, it's to do with what Busby Tenpenny wanted me to look into. There really are some interesting connections between your jewels, including the tiara," he added with about six tons of hint behind the comment.

"How do you know about the tiara?" It was a far stretch to think Dr Torres could have swiped the glittering headpiece from my safe, but my head had been so full of suspicion lately it was hard to stop the idea from flashing through my skull.

"I didn't know a thing about the tiara until recently when the local curators' newsletter I receive had a fluff piece about it and its supposed disappearance. It included a photo, and my eye was instantly drawn to that ruby centerpiece. The circumstances of the disappearance sounded rather familiar, so I took a wild guess that it has to do with the Boncoeur Jewel. Or am I jumping to conclusions?"

"No, you're spot on. But what do you mean by this being a familiar circumstance? Has someone pulled this sort of thing at your museum?"

"No, no, nothing like that. But there was a weekend seminar Olivia had me attend about how to spot magical fakes and trickery. It was very educational and has come in handy a few times, especially considering Portland's close history with the Magic world, but this was the first time I'd ever seen a Replacement Hex in the flesh. Or rather, not in the flesh, as I witnessed when I went to check it out."

"You went to the Portland Art Museum?" I asked worriedly.

"Don't panic. I asked no questions. I merely went to the tiara's display, and let me tell you, the Replacement Hex is impressive. Had I not known, I wouldn't have suspected a thing. Anyway, that's neither here nor there. Busby asked me to look into some things. Of course, I'd already discovered a fair bit in the short time since we last spoke. What I've added, though, it's pretty good stuff, and I might send it over to Professor Dodding once I type it up into something less jumbled. Or do you think that would be too bold?"

"No, not at all. And this new stuff has to do with the Boncoeur Jewel?"

"Yes. Look, I know this is a big request, especially since I've just woken you up, but once you glance it over, could you give me your honest opinion of whether it's worth bothering the Professor with? I know it doesn't answer every question regarding the jewel pieces' whereabouts, but it is quite interesting."

My curiosity now about as pressing as my need to pee, I told him I'd be glad to give my opinion. To which he thanked me profusely and went on for a few minutes about how he hoped to impress Professor Dodding, but also worried about the professor's opinion. At some point, I had to cut him off and tell him it would be fine, that Dodding would love any new information, and that I really needed to get going — in more ways than one.

I'd barely ended the call before an image pinged through of a lined piece of notebook paper filled with messy handwriting. Below what looked like random notes jotted down while doing research was this...

> **Brooch** - Winnifred Oberlin, but formerly owned by Nadine Oberlin, mother-in-law - Nadine direct descendant of Elizabethan courtier, Thomas Wyatt
>
> **Marble** - Clive Coppersmith, supposedly in family for years - Clive's great-grandfather from side branch of R. Devereux, Elizabethan courtier.
>
> **Pendant** - Chloe Starling, gift from HQ - pendants began being handed out at time of Elizabethan era. From paintings, it's possibile this one once owned by F. Drake or W. Cecil, both favorites of Eliz I. Known to be passed down to grandmother(?) of Chloe Starling. Grandmother returned pendant to HQ to be given to Chloe during honors ceremony.

Below this, in a note to himself, Torres had written:

> This is a bit of a stretch, but the paintings of Drake and Cecil show both men wearing a similar piece of jewelry. Also, in his painting, Cecil is shown wearing a

ring with a ruby inset. Coincidence? Looking too hard for connections? Why would he have two pieces of Boncoeur Jewel?

Saw *- Runa Dunwiddle, previous owner Stagman, no obvious connection to Eliz. Court. More research needed.*

Tiara *- "Borrowed" from Ptld. Art Museum. More research needed but portrait of Elizabeth found in which she's wearing a filigree tiara with ruby centerpiece. Again, trying too hard to make connections, or actual piece of jewel? Also, line drawing found in Brit.Natl. Portrait Archive of Queen Anne wearing very similar tiara. Anne known to have strong connection to Rosarian Magics. Coincidence, or exciting possibility?*

Conclusion for write-up: Clear evidence of five (six?) pieces of jewel. All, except tiara, found within Rosaria and with ties to Elizabethan court. Queen Anne (tiara wearer) also known to have played part in Rosaria, so…?? Consider who in Rosaria related to Eliz. Court. Continue research at…

After that, Torres had listed several sources whose names I could barely read. I just hoped he could when he got back to them later.

What he'd found was beyond interesting, and the connection to the royal court stirred up plenty of intrigue. Still, how had all these Elizabethan jewels ended up in Portland, with most being found within the boundaries of MagicLand itself? And if Torres's research was right, if there really might be six pieces… well, that was annoying. I was having a hard enough time finding and keeping five pieces, let alone throwing a sixth one into the mix.

I sent a text back to Dr Torres, telling him to definitely go ahead with compiling what he'd found into something for Professor Dodding, to which he replied with a string of starry-eyed emojis. I then sent a note to both him and myself to look into any connections between Old Lizzie, Queen Anne, and the citizenry of MagicLand. Mr Tenpenny might know, and if not him, then Dodding might be able to come up with something.

My fingers had grown cold from holding the phone, so, as I ducked into the ensuite loo, I shoved my hand into the hoodie's pouch. And was nearly stabbed by whatever was inside. I hadn't remembered putting anything in there the last time I wore it, but after Portland's blazing hot summer, that time had likely been in the spring when I was still working in the cold confines of the funeral home's prep room, so who knows what I might have stashed away. Slipping my hand back in, I felt a slim and smooth length of something. I just hoped it wasn't a finger bone.

Hey, don't judge. You'd be surprised what ends up in your pockets when you work at a funeral home.

What I pulled out was not a finger bone — small favors, right? It was a thin, metal tube tapered and flat at one end with a slit near the tapered end. Attached to it with a thin piece of string was a tag, similar to a specimen tag you'd see in a museum. On it, in handwriting that matched what was on the sheet of notes I'd just been sent, was written, *'Keep with you at all times.'*

It all felt very Alice in Wonderland, but at least Dr Torres hadn't written *'Eat me'* or *'Drink me'* on it. I wiped the tapered end, then blew gently into it and produced a raspy call that didn't carry beyond the bathroom's walls. I shrugged inwardly, removed the tag, and, not wanting to tempt fate, tucked it into my skirt pocket when I got dressed later that morning. I just had to hope Pascal Torres hadn't been coerced by an evil wizard to send me an object that could spell my doom.

Which is something I still can't believe I have to worry about.

The second time my phone rang, it did wake Alastair. Barely. Like a grunting, lumbering zombie, he staggered from the bed and into the loo, paying me no heed as I took the call.

"Cassie, Leo here. You're at HQ, right?" I wasn't entirely sure how he knew this, but I told him I was. "Look, I don't expect you to divulge any state secrets, but I'm wondering if you've got any info for me about something."

"I doubt it," I said. "I mean, unless you want to know down to the minute which flavor of scone will be coming out of the Spellbound ovens."

"I agree that's very important information, but the thing is, my magic. It's not right. I can barely get the presses to cooperate. They keep splattering ink all over page six, and since so many of my staff are out with some mysterious illness, I've got no one here who knows how to fix it. They say they feel fine, but their magic is off, not working. Other Rosarians are having the same complaint, and the Anti-RetroHex Vaxxers are saying they told us all along that the shot would do nothing but weaken us. They're having a field day with it."

"Well, you can tell them it's affecting nearly every human Magic." Every human Magic except those who'd been given my power at some point in the past — a curiosity that was still bugging me. "It's not the vaccine."

"That's relief. I was—"

"It's witch hunters."

"Witch hunters? In this day and age?"

"Yep, apparently alive and well. And it sounds like their leader, Matthew Hopkins, is on his way back from the grave just to throw a little zealous terror into the mix."

"Great Gandalf's ghost! I did a historical piece on him a couple years ago. But how?"

"You're going to print this? Like an official scoop?"

"Of course, this is just the kind of reporting the *Herald* needs to get itself back on track."

"Well, then, probably best not to mention my name. Just say a resource from within HQ, okay?"

"Got it."

And so I told him what I'd learned from Matilda, my parents, and Morelli's contact. So much juicy info that, even without an enchanted pen, Leo Flourish would have no trouble spinning it into a gripping, two-thousand-word article.

"If I can get the presses to behave for half a minute, I'll get it out in the next edition."

"You realize people might not believe you."

"I'll jump off that bridge when I come to it."

Leo did write up a bold article about what we'd discussed. Confident without striking fear, and matter-of-fact while still grabbing your attention. The only problem was, by the time that morning edition came out, a whole lot of breaking news had taken place, including a pitched battle within the Tower of London and me getting into a heap of trouble.

And, unlike my heap of trouble with the Mauvais, when I'd purposely walked into his trap, this time, I managed to tumble into a mess of danger without even trying.

CHAPTER THIRTY-ONE
THE VAGUEST OF PLANS

Alastair and I had barely gotten dressed before Olivia's voice came through the bedside clock, telling us to meet her in her office as soon as possible to figure out our next steps. Several of the others were already there when we showed up. As were a random assortment of scones, jams, turnovers, croissants, and wonderfully strong breakfast teas.

"Leo Flourish called me," I said as I mounded my plate with one of each type of pastry. "He's going to get the word out about what the witch hunters are doing, especially in regard to our magic and how it's not the vaccine causing the problem."

"I'm not sure what good that will do," said Runa. "People will believe what they want to believe, regardless of the hard evidence right in front of their faces."

Before anyone could comment on this, and before I had a chance to bring up Dr Torres's notes, Rafi rushed into the office and straight to Olivia's desk.

"This just arrived," he said without any preamble or greeting as he shoved a folded sheet of paper toward Olivia. From what I could see, it had been sealed with wax and bore Olivia's name on it.

"Who delivered this?"

"A missing Magic, and not one of the ones we retrieved

yesterday. I was in the mail room, looking for my shipment of newt saliva and—"

"Thank you, Rafi," snapped Olivia, who then instantly seemed to regret her tone. She tapped the edge of the letter on her desk as she said, "This proves one theory. They have access to the Tower, and not just through the pool room. Mr Morelli," Olivia tried to maintain a calm façade, but the muscles in her jaw flicked with tension, "have you any idea how many of these hidden portals there might be within the Tower?"

Morelli thought a moment, then replied, "Sorry, that'd be impossible to say. And before you ask, the portals could be scattered anywhere across the grounds. Turn a corner and you could step into one. A certain stone in a wall might be a gateway that'd let them in. And there's the mid-air ones that could open up—"

"Yes, Mr Morelli, I get the idea," Olivia said bitingly. "We are vulnerable to invasion. The most secure complex in London that has never been breached is open for attack. How could this have happened?"

"You mean besides all the portals Magics might have installed for convenience, or royals might have had put in for late night rendezvous?" Olivia gave a conciliatory nod. "Best guess is that over time, witch hunters have been within these walls. I'm not talking the past few weeks," Morelli clarified in response to Olivia's scowl. "I'm talking about over the centuries. A witch hunter pops by to visit the monarch, they install a couple portals. One gets imprisoned, they sneak in a portal. A group arrives as tourists, and you get portals dotted around as they stroll. It's a security matter I've always wanted to address, but I haven't worked out how you'd detect an illegal portal being smuggled in."

After a moment's grim silence except for the *tap-tap-tap* of the envelope's crisp edge against Olivia's desk, Mr Tenpenny said to her, "You have to realize this means they could come in at any time. From the interviews I conducted last night and this morning with a few of the recovered Magics, during their captivity, they overheard talk of storming the Tower and taking us by surprise. Perhaps we should look at that letter Rafi has delivered? After he explains a bit more about how he got it, of course."

"Like I said," began Rafi after Olivia gestured for him to continue, "I was in the mail room, and a woman was in there. Seemed terribly confused. Had no scent of magic. Healthy, though. When I asked her if she needed help, she merely said they'd sent her back to deliver that." He pointed to the message. "She wouldn't clarify who *they* were and seemed pretty dazed, so I got her to the medical ward, then I came here straight away."

Olivia cracked the seal on the letter and began to read. She couldn't have gotten through more than half of the cramped text before she sighed heavily and stopped reading.

"Busby, it appears your interviewees are not misinformed." Olivia's voice cracked, but she swallowed hard and went on, her voice shaking only slightly. "They don't give a time, but they make it clear there will be an invasion by the witch hunters quite soon." She glanced at the letter again, her face bitter with rage. "They have used magic taken from our own people to return Matthew Hopkins to 'full vitality.' He has all the jewel pieces and will reunite them to put an end to Cassie Black.

"An army of witch hunters has also been supplied with magic via the absorbing capsules. It will be their job to take down HQ, and then—" Again, she bit back her emotion. "It's signed *Gibson Todd*." She placed the letter, face down, on her desk. "We need to close down the Tower, get the tourists out. Chester, could you see to that?" Chester agreed, looking proud to have such a responsibility.

"But—" began Morelli. "And don't take this the wrong way, Black, but even if they kill Cassie and take over HQ, there's thousands of other Magics across the world to fight back."

Rather than respond, Olivia glowered again at the sheet before her. "It seems they have already put that aspect of their plans into place." She held the letter out to Runa. "Can they really do that?"

Runa scanned the letter, then, more to herself than anyone else, she muttered, "You know very well they already have." As if to prove her point, Runa attempted a Shoving Spell on one of the tapestries. It barely fluttered.

"So they really did steal our magic?" murmured Fiona. Olivia nodded. "But how? I'd say that's impossible if I wasn't seeing it for myself."

Olivia gestured to the note. "The absorbing capsules. The power taken from the missing Magics will give them the strength not only to fight us, but also to use certain hexes to drain our power. These are ancient hexes, ones I haven't heard of being used in over two hundred years. Normally, you need to be near your victim to make them work, but perhaps the Boncoeur Jewel has provided them a new layer of power. Basically, they can now absorb our magic from near or far. If they keep it up, our magic will diminish entirely. Or, at least that of human Magics. Who's to say if they're already figuring out how to use it against non-human Magics."

"So, if it's an extraction, will it leave every Magic a babbling idiot?" I asked.

"From what we've seen so far, likely not," said Runa. "We seem to retain our wits, just not our magic. We will essentially become Norms."

"The letter says in this day and age," Olivia noted wryly, "it's far easier to get away with remote extraction via ancient hex than burning people at the stake."

"Something about that doesn't line up, though," said Mr Tenpenny. "Cassie, your magic has been off for, what, a couple weeks now? When did that start? Think of an exact timeline with your cases."

"After I'd found Clive's marbles, I think. Wait, no," I interjected, cutting off whatever Busby had been about to say. "Sorry, but I just remembered I couldn't do a Heating Charm on some noodles the very evening Matilda hired me. That was at least a day or two before finding the marbles."

"But the jewels," said Fiona, "several of them, at any rate, were in Rosaria. Considering the prophecy—" Alastair grimaced, but Fiona continued "—the jewels could have been affecting her magic long before she ever discovered them. And no, please don't ask me to figure out why they hadn't affected her prior to all this. My only theory would be that one was nearer to her than in the past, but it's a rather weak theory and we have enough to contend with right now without losing ourselves in guesswork."

"Still, there is the prophecy," Olivia said, a touch of determined hope in her voice. "I'm more than certain that if we can get the Boncoeur Jewel into Cassie's hands, it will be exactly what she needs to defeat Hopkins."

"Yeah, trouble is, a walrus gave away my only weapon. If not for that, I'd—"

"No," Alastair cut in. "You can't let her go after Hopkins. You've seen the prophecy," he said to Olivia, his tone nearing belligerence. "Even if she succeeds, she'll die if she goes against him."

"We'll all be ruined if she doesn't fight him," said Olivia.

"We can't allow her to do it on her own," said Mr T emphatically. "Especially if Hopkins has an untold number of magic-fueled witch hunters at his back."

Olivia started to argue, but I waved my hands. "Hello, I am

still here, you know. Don't you think you might want to consult the person you're planning to send into the fray? Or is this like some sort of magic conscription?"

"You can't back away from this," insisted Olivia. "It's too important."

"I don't plan to," I said. Which kind of surprised me because it was one of those situations where you totally intend to say, *Um no, I'd rather not die fighting a zombie witch hunter who seems to have some serious muscle behind him*, but then you end up going all heroic when you open your mouth. I'm sure you can relate.

"Cass," pleaded Alastair, and the pain in his voice made my heart ache, "please. You can't do this."

"I can. Well, I can take a fair stab at it, at any rate." Okay, it wasn't exactly as inspiring as the pre-battle speech in *Braveheart*, but at least it was succinct.

"But the prophecy—"

"It's just words. It's not written in stone. Wait, it wasn't written in stone, was it? Because in that case—"

"This isn't the time for jokes, Cass."

"Believe me, facing my imminent death is the best time for jokes. Otherwise, I might rethink this."

"You won't have to do this alone," said Tobey.

"No offense, but considering the results of your Exams, you're not proving the best at trials and tribulations." I punctuated this with a grin to show I was only teasing.

"Tobey's right," said Rafi. "If we can get our own little army together, she'll at least stand a chance against Hopkins."

"An army of what?"

"Dunno," Rafi said with a shrug. "I suppose whatever we can muster."

Because when going into battle, it's always good to have the absolute vaguest of plans.

CHAPTER THIRTY-TWO
THE CRASHIEST OF CRASH COURSES

"We're going to need to figure out who can be called up to fight in a pinch," said Morelli. "I'm more than willing, but that's not going to get us far."

"I can call in a favor to the elves," said Rafi. "My cousins were just complaining about how bored they'd been lately."

"Rafi, this isn't an entertaining day out," chastised Busby.

"Oh, I'm well aware of that. But we can fight. We look all lithe and lovely, but we're mad accurate with a bow and arrow, we can throw a fighting spell with fierce precision, and if it comes down to hand-to-hand combat, that calming-aura thing we've got going on can really disarm an opponent."

"Call up the elves, then," said Olivia, some relief in her voice.

"The vampires will stand behind me," said Matilda. "And I have an idea for how Caliban could help."

"Please, just don't let him burn the place down," said Olivia. "Historic Royal Palaces gets so grumpy about that sort of thing."

"The missing Magics," said Runa, "if there's going to be a fight here, we should get them out. Plus, there's going to be injuries, and the medical ward, even with several more Expansion Hexes, won't be able to handle so many patients at once. Anyone who can go home should be sent back to their own communities."

"Agreed," said Olivia. "I'd like to address them first, though."

While Tobey and Rafi went with Fiona to begin inventorying what weapons were on hand, Alastair and I followed Runa, Mr Tenpenny, Daisy, Morelli, and Olivia up to the Tower's medical ward.

"So many," said Alastair upon seeing the majority of the recovered Magics gathered together. "If they've all had their power taken from them, can you imagine how strong the witch hunters are?"

"Probably best not to think of that," I said and slipped my hand into his. I decided not to bring up that those we'd recovered might only be a portion of everyone who'd gone missing.

A handsome, chisel-chinned medic who looked more like he belonged in a hospital-themed soap opera than a real-world medical setting, explained that once a system had been put into place, processing the swarm of patients hadn't taken terribly long. Unlike Mel Faegan who'd been traumatized by the vicious vampire-witch hunter fight he'd witnessed, our batch of Magics seemed none the worse for wear other than being shaken up by their lack of magic and feeling desperate for some fresh food.

They also seemed to have found a certain camaraderie in each other. Some of which I'd like to attribute to Mr Wood, who was standing at the window of a very Expanded hospital room and regaling a rapt audience with the story of discovering Mrs Escobar — his dead client and Pablo's former owner — turning out to not be quite as dead as expected. He worked some pretty good quips into his tale and had the no-longer-missing Magics giggling in all the right places.

"The loss of their power..." mused Mr T. "They should be utterly depressed. He really is quite the character, isn't he?"

Before I could agree, Olivia stood in the doorway to the room and called for everyone's attention. The cocktail-party buzz quieted as all eyes turned to her.

"I am sorry for what has happened to you. For many of you, while it will be a long road to recovery, we will do our best to restore your magic. In the meantime, I promise that we are preparing to take down the people who did this to you. Rest assured that we will do our best to keep this from happening to anyone else. Once you have been given the all-clear by one of our medics, portal stations have been set up based on your home locations. Proceed to your station, and we'll soon have someone escort you home where you can recuperate."

"I'm not going back," insisted a woman with a soft Dublin accent. "If there's vengeance to be had against these people, count me in."

This was met by several shouts of agreement.

"This will be dangerous," Olivia stated, "and you've already been through too much."

"Exactly," said the woman. "We want to kick their magic-stealing arses."

Olivia raised a questioning eyebrow to the handsome medic standing beside her.

"Should be fine. They're healthy, but," he said, raising his voice above the noise of cheering, "you will have to fight like Norms. No magic, no spells, no hexes."

"If you still want to join us," said Olivia over the murmuring this had stirred up, "we are procuring some weapons from the Tower's storage areas. But before you commit, you need to truly absorb what you've just been told: You will have no special powers, neither for protection nor for attack."

"We'll have the power of Magics standing up for themselves!" called out a stout American.

Olivia had to bring the room back to order after the hooting and whooping this sentiment had stirred up. "Do any of you have any experience in fighting like Norms?"

"I've seen a lot of Arnold Schwarzenegger movies," volunteered a pudgy fellow whose blonde hair was sticking up every which way. Bedhead or intentional styling, I couldn't say.

"Ooh, I did like him in that *Kindergarten Cop*," said the Irish woman.

"It was a little off-brand at the time, but—"

"This is not the time for a critique of Mr Schwarzenegger's film career," Olivia seethed. Struggling to restore her patience, she said, "Morelli, take this lot to the practice room where you will give them the crashiest of crash courses in hand-to-hand combat. Chester will bring you what weapons he can muster, and then you both can see if any of your recruits can handle a broadsword or halberd."

"Will do, boss," said Morelli. "You lot, come on, we've got some stairs to descend and some moves to teach you. Alastair, Daisy, I could use your help too."

Like ducklings after their mother, the Magics trailed after them with Olivia pulling up the rear as the medics bustled around doing what they could for the few patients who hadn't fared as well as the others.

"Should I go with them?" Mr Wood asked me. "I'm not sure how well I'd do in a fight, but I'm willing to try."

"You will do no such thing," I protested. "You need to go home."

Like the others, Mr Wood no longer had enough magic to get himself through a long-distance portal without an escort, but I needed him back in Portland where he'd be safe. I spotted Nigel and called him over.

"Would you like a tour?" offered Nigel, who I later learned

had gone to the medical ward first thing that morning to visit 'his' Magics and see how they were doing.

"Nigel," I grumbled, "I don't think now is the time for sightseeing."

"Of course, not. Just a little Beefeater humor. Now, what can I do for you?" I explained that I needed him to get Mr Wood to one of the Rosarian portals. "Not a problem. And on the way, if we happen to see some interesting sights—"

"Nigel," I said warningly, but Mr Wood touched my arm to quiet me.

"I'll be fine. And I have a feeling me and... Nigel, is it?"

"Pleased to meet you," said Nigel, sticking out his hand to shake.

"As I was saying, me and Nigel are going to get along splendidly as he shows me around." To my worried look, he said, "Believe me, I'm not one for violence. I promise I'll pop into one of these portals as soon as Nigel gets me to the right one."

After I bid him a reluctant goodbye, Nigel and Mr Wood walked off. Before they were out the ward's door, I heard Mr Wood ask his newfound friend, "Do you like B.L.T.s, by any chance?"

CHAPTER THIRTY-THREE
BLOOD SAUSAGE & PTERODACTYLS

The next few hours were just a whole lot of waiting for the invasion, collecting weapons, hasty training, and planning without any idea of how to plan for what was to come or *when* it would come.

I wanted to fight just to burn off the three million gigawatts of nervous energy coursing through me, but it was decided (not by me) that my main role would be to focus solely on Matthew Hopkins. Apparently, getting myself injured right before he came for me wasn't how HQ saw me winning the war. Which is ridiculous. If you've read about any of my fights with the Mauvais, you'll know I do my best work with broken bones and bruised kidneys.

So, my belly roiling, I roamed the walls and the grounds watching for any sign of Matthew Hopkins. How I'd recognize him, I wasn't sure, but I had a feeling the old-timey guy brandishing a caged jewel and calling all the curses known to man down on me might stand out in a crowd.

As I made my rounds, I spotted Morelli. He'd been working with his troops of formerly missing Magics in the open space of the Tower's grassy moat. Some bore true weapons such as swords and maces, but I noticed quite a lot of them were twirling cricket bats. Did HQ have a cricket team? Again, one of those mysteries of the universe to ponder another time.

Just as I approached Morelli, who stood on a low, wooden dais to address and observe everyone, Runa strode up with about fifty men and women. All were preternaturally beautiful with an air of calm. One of her group, a man full of confidence and timeless grace and who bore an uncanny resemblance to Matilda Marheart, strode up to Morelli and held out his hand to shake.

Morelli hesitated just a moment, then reached out his hand in a gesture of welcome. From Morelli's ranks stepped forward a big brute of a man in a red baseball cap. Once he reached Morelli, he shouted with the twang of a southern accent, "We're not siding with them!"

"And why not?" demanded Runa.

"Because they're all blood sucking monsters. Shouldn't even be allowed amongst us."

"Tell me, when exactly was the last time a vampire did you harm? Caused you trouble? Threatened your way of life?"

The man shot his head back and forth as if looking for someone to back him up, to provide him an answer. "Well, they haven't." He then puffed out his chest and boldly proclaimed, "Not yet, anyway."

"And have any of you been harmed physically, emotionally, or financially by a vampire?" Runa persisted.

Morelli's fighting force murmured and shuffled about shamefacedly until an elderly man said, "One took the last piece of blood sausage off the breakfast buffet one time I was in a hotel in Birmingham." He then added, "Apologized, though, and offered to split it with me."

"Yes, quite the horrible people, aren't they?" sneered Runa.

"You have a choice: You can keep up with your ridiculous prejudices, or we can have the vampires by our side in what's to come."

"And what is to come?" asked a mousey looking woman in a pale pink dress.

"That I do not know. These are witch hunters. *They* are who you should be fearing. *They* are who you should be prejudiced against and see as a danger, not the vampires. Because let me tell you, there's nothing more dangerous than a group of people who ignores logic, who insists they're right, and who is willing to throw all caution to the wind to defend what they've convinced themselves is true regardless of all evidence to the contrary."

"And how're the vamps going to help with that?"

"In any way we can," said the vampire who I assumed was Martin, Matilda's twin brother. "We have been fighting for you prior to this battle, and we will continue to fight for you even if you don't join us."

This brought about another round of shamefaced shuffling.

"Like Runa said," growled Morelli, "you have a choice: be complete stubborn asses like these witch hunters, or fight together with the people who have come to your aid despite how you've treated them over the years."

I thought to mention Rafi's assemblage of hundreds of elves, but figured Morelli was making a really rousing speech that I shouldn't interfere with.

"Well?" Runa snapped. "Join or be jerks?"

A few people, looking unsure of themselves, muttered *join*, but slowly, the momentum built and soon enough even Mr Red Hat was enthusiastically chanting, "Join! Join! Join!" loud enough to make the stones under my feet rumble.

I then realized it wasn't their shouts causing the vibrations.

The Unexpected Mr. Hopkins

"What's that?" asked the mousey woman as she stared up into the sky.

Silhouetted overhead was a bat-winged creature, pinkish crimson in color and with a body larger than a double-decker bus. Unable to believe what I was seeing, my brain stubbornly insisted: *pterodactyl*.

And no, I don't know why it seemed more logical to think a long extinct animal from the age of the dinosaurs was flying over my head, but get in touch with me when you see *your* first dragon in the flesh, and tell me how rationally your brain handled that moment.

The creature let out a piercing call, then a low rumble that again shook the stones under my feet. Matilda waved her hands and called out, "Cally, you came. Good boy!"

"Is that Caliban?" I asked Morelli, who I'll be honest, had eyes nearly as wide as mine as he gaped up at the flying lizard.

"I guess so. Honestly, I thought that picture of hers was some computer-generated thing. I never believed it might be real."

"Mr Morelli," Matilda's brother said with pure upper-crust politeness, "we have Magics brandishing weapons, we have vampires thirsty for a hunt, and it would appear we now have a dragon who I know for a fact loves showing off his flame-throwing skills. Shall we do this?"

"We shall," said Morelli awkwardly. As Martin led the troops off, Morelli turned to me, worry (and perhaps brimstone fumes) moistening his eyes. "Guess it's time to save the world."

"It would appear so," I said through the lump in my throat.

"You watch yourself, kid."

"You too." Then, because it was all getting far too sappy, I teasingly added, "Genie."

Morelli, a watery grin on his face, swooped his arms around me and wrapped me in a hug I didn't pull away from. "I'll still be expecting rent when this is over, so don't you dare think dying is going to get you out of it," he said, his voice choking. He then let me go, turned away, and marched off.

Morelli as captain, or general, or whatever you call the person who sorts out where fighters go, turned out to be surprisingly skilled. First, he arranged people into battalions made up of around thirty fighters that he dispersed across the Tower's grounds. A smart move since, even though it's a sizable bit of land, within the walls of the Tower, fighting space gets pretty tight. Too many fighters in one spot, and it would turn into nothing more than a jam-packed mess.

Secondly, he organized the battalions in a way that ensured Magic solidarity. With only a little grumbling from the overly proud elves, Morelli assigned each of his units equal numbers of vampires, elves, human Magics, and Yeoman Warders (proving they really will do anything to protect the Tower). It meant no one type of Magic being could claim they'd done more to save our world than another. It also provided a balance of Magics who had to fight like Norms, elves who could fight with magic, and vampires who could whip out the fangs if needed.

Once sorted, the units arrived at their posts.

The witch hunters showed up barely twenty minutes later.

CHAPTER THIRTY-FOUR
WHAT GHOSTS CAN DO

The first witch hunters, around twenty of them, popped into existence at the northern edge of the moat's lawn.

Caliban had been soaring overhead, keeping an eye out for just this sort of thing. I honestly never expected a reptile to have such excellent eyesight and reaction times, but he spotted the newcomers within mere seconds of their arrival, swooped down, and delivered a stream of flame right at them. The lawn will recover. That first batch of witch hunters will not.

Caliban was able to maintain this for the next five or six appearances. Although the elves cast Dousing Charms over any fires that popped up where they shouldn't, some stonework still shows scorch marks where the blazes got a bit out of hand.

After the seventh group was turned to ash, there was a pause in witch hunter arrivals. Stupidly, hope swirled around the grounds that the battle would be that easily won. That all the witch hunters had been defeated without any loss of Magic life.

But, like I keep telling people, optimism is the stupidest thing you can ever let sneak into your life.

The pause must have been nothing more than a re-evaluation of tactics, because suddenly, across the grounds, hundreds of witch hunters pop, pop, popped into existence. Caliban managed to get a few, but it was a losing game of Witch Hunter Whack-a-

Mole in the Tower of London as they began pouring in too quickly and in too many places for him to keep up. Not to mention, a dragon's firebox doesn't contain a bottomless pit of flame and needs recharged after a while.

Caliban out of commission to re-stoke his fire, the fighting truly began.

And all I was allowed to do was roam the walls, waiting to meet my fate with Matthew Hopkins.

I was just passing through the Bloody Tower for the third time when Nigel and Mr Wood came jogging up to me. Well, okay, Mr Wood was doing a sort of tubby man trot as Nigel chummily goaded him along. Still, they were approaching at more than a walking pace.

"What are you doing here?" I asked Mr Wood. Then, to Nigel, I said, "I thought you were taking him to a portal to send him back to Portland."

"Oh, I did. Knew right where one was, actually. But… well, the portal remained solid when he tried to step through."

"Learned that one the hard way," Mr Wood chuckled as he pointed to a small lump on his forehead.

"But, Nigel, you could have taken him through, then come right back."

Nigel shook his head. "I'm not Magic. Recovered quite nicely from being a ghost, yes, but that didn't fill me with any of your kind's superpowers."

"But you could have found someone," I said, grasping at straws.

"Well, yes, I know," said Mr Wood, "but everyone was so busy, and I didn't want to bother anyone, so I just joined in the party—"

"This isn't a party, Mr Wood. This is a battle scene. You could get hurt."

"Ah, yes, I see that now. Kind of gathered that it wasn't a tea party when a vampire ripped the throats out of a couple people. Rather disturbing, but all for a good cause, I'm sure," he added in far too chipper a voice. "And really, it's okay; I'm part of a team."

I couldn't help it. I pinched the bridge of my nose and shook my head, completely understanding everyone's continual frustration with my own stubborn behavior.

"Mr Wood, despite the prevalence of cricket bats—" where were they getting those things, anyway? "—this is not a 'team'. This is a fight to the finish."

"Sorry, shouldn't have said *team*. A troop. A squadron. A fighting force. And here is my commander." Mr Wood spread his hands as if introducing Nigel to a captive audience.

Nigel, wearing a broad and mischievous grin, handed Mr Wood what looked like a helmet from World War I. He caught me staring at it. "I took it from the war museum. Don't tell anyone. Although, I'm sure Historic Royal Palaces will understand. Unusual circumstances and all that."

"You can't take him into battle with you," I argued. "His fitness regime is walking three blocks to the butcher's to get his favorite type of bacon."

"Nothing to worry about," Nigel said, blithely ignoring that there was *everything* to worry about. "We have plenty of backup. They'll be doing most of the fighting. We're really just commander and second-in-commander."

"You can't send him into battle," I insisted.

"I'm not. We're sending them in," said Nigel, grinning delightedly as he spotted something over my shoulder.

I turned around to see something shimmery down below, like the silvery mirage you sometimes see on hot pavement. It then disappeared.

To my unspoken question, Nigel waggled his eyebrows then nudged Mr Wood.

"Undo Incognito Mode," my former boss called out, looking quite pleased with himself.

There, hovering in the air behind the two most unlikely war commanders, was a troop of ghosts. At a guess, I'd say there were a hundred of them, but it's kind of tough to guess numbers when you can see straight through the people you're trying to count. Some looked like they'd just stepped off the set of a historical drama, others looked very modern-day. Some appeared to have died of old age, and others had clearly died from egregious wounds — one of them had a hole in his belly that I could see straight through; another, her head lolling on a disturbingly angled neck, still wore the hangman's noose that must have done her in. I then noticed Tilia floating, or rather hovering, at the head of the group. Yet again, something about her features and dark hair struck me as familiar.

"Nigel. Who are these people?" I mean, if he'd called up the ghosts of professional soldiers, that'd be one thing, but these were clearly just ordinary people. Ordinary dead people, that is.

"My tour guests. I told you I was popular."

"That's great," I said, trying to sound appreciative. "But what exactly can they do? I mean, they can't hold weapons," I noted as a ghost in a pale grey, Edwardian-era top hat and morning coat tried to pick a flower, I assume for his buttonhole since he looked rather confused when his still-empty hand reached his lapel. "Because I doubt people who dub themselves as 'witch hunters' are going to be too put off by some spooky sounds or spectral apparitions. Also," I asked Mr Wood, "how in the world are you issuing commands to them?"

"Seems that all my time with the dead has given me a unique

ability to work with ghosts. Who knew, right?" Let me just say that I was not appreciating Mr Wood's jovial demeanor at that exact moment.

"Nigel, seriously, what's your plan here? I mean, your ghosts might be willing to help, but I know for a fact that they're just wispy bits of their former selves."

"On a day-to-day basis, yes, they are rather *wispy*, as you say. But believe me, as a former ghost myself, I know what we can accomplish when motivated. We, or rather *they*, can manifest themselves to hold solid objects. You've heard the tales of chairs flying across rooms, and that sort of nonsense. That's simply the end result of a ghostly temper tantrum. So, the first thing my more motivated troops can do, those still quite peeved about their deaths," Nigel gestured to Noose Lady, then snapped his fingers. About a third of the ghosts returned to Incognito Mode, "is to sneak in and steal as many of these fiends' weapons as possible."

"But the fiends will still have magic," I pointed out.

Nigel made a *pshaw* sound. "I don't know much about magic, but I do know it requires some training. So, the enemy does have power, but it's power they don't know how to use with any true skill. Some will be quick learners, sure, but most will resort to the regular smash-and-stab form of fighting using fists and weapons."

"Which they won't have," Mr Wood quipped, like he and Nigel were the Tower's newest comedy duo. "The weapons, that is. I suppose, unless they've had a nasty accident, they'll still have the fists."

"This is serious, Mr Wood," I told him. "You need to stay out of trouble."

"I'll do my best, but this certainly is far more fun than the brochure promised."

"Secondly," Nigel continued before I could comment that this was not one of the tour activities, "while you may think these witch hunters wouldn't be bothered by a little *boo!* here and there, you've really not experienced what a true ghost scare is like. Tilia, perhaps a demonstration?"

Tilia, looking thrilled at Nigel's attention, peered down at the battle scene. A witch hunter, apparently doing away with the subtlety of magic, had a battle axe in hand and was arcing it up, ready to bring it down on the head of one of the vampires. Tilia raced down so quickly I could feel the suck of the air. As she flew, she howled a haunting wail.

This caught the witch hunter so off guard he lost focus momentarily. Tilia took the chance to — and this did seem like it took a great deal of concentration — shove, without touching, the axe from the witch hunter's hands. The vampire immediately leapt for the axe and, well, let's just say, your basic blood clean-up kit wasn't going to make a dent in the mess left behind.

Tilia flew back to stand at the head of the spectral forces, and I don't think I've ever seen a happier ghost.

"*That* is what ghosts can do," said Nigel. "Nino and I will simply be up here, safely away from the worst of it, and directing our soldiers where to go." When I looked doubtful, he added. "I promise we'll be as safe as houses."

I didn't like any of it. I'd have preferred Mr Wood back at the funeral home, packing up the place for its future sale. But if this was his choice, I had to let him take it. Also, he seemed to be having a great deal of fun. Probably more so than going on his hiking trip, despite the lack of bacon sandwiches.

Still, my disapproval must have shown on my face, because Tilia sidled up to me, and said in her warm, eastern European accent, "I will be keeping eye on them. Making sure they don't get up to… What do you call them? Hijacks?"

"Hijinks," I corrected. "And, thank you. I'm sure you'll keep them in line."

Tilia remained behind as Mr Wood and Nigel turned to address their wispy troops.

"You're really only friend of Nigel?" she asked, looking rather despondent.

"Really. Besides, I've only got eyes for Alastair."

I pointed him out as he hurled a mini-hurricane down on a group of witch hunters, ripping off all their clothes and sending the garments flying off and into the Thames. Ashamed of their nakedness, the witch hunters were too busy trying to cover themselves with their hands and arms to fight off the swarm of elves who took them into custody.

"It was you, the one who brought Nigel back, yes?" Tilia asked.

"Well, a curse reversal brought him back, not me specifically. I can't make you—"

"No, no. I am not asking that. I like being ghost. You can," her eyes sparkled mischievously, "go places others can't. It is fun."

I wondered if I couldn't use Tilia as a spy in the future. She'd probably love it. Then, despite the seriousness of the situation, I grinned when Alastair turned to give me a thumbs up.

"He is very handsome," said Tilia. "Not vampire, though." Something I was acutely happy to hear. Her gaze then drifted back to Nigel, who, perhaps sensing her, looked back in our direction. "You will maybe put in a good word with me to Nigel?"

"I don't think I need to," I said as Nigel beamed a smile at Tilia. "You really like him, don't you?"

"He tells funny stories. I like that, yes."

And that's when I discovered that ghosts could blush.

"I'll see what I can do."

CHAPTER THIRTY-FIVE
GO TO YOUR ROOM!

As Nigel and Mr Wood led their troops off to do mischief, I scanned the oddest collection of fighters in the history of bizarre battles. Elves, trolls, Yeoman Warders, a dragon, vampires, and cricket bat wielding non-magic Magics. We needed every person who could fight. However, when I saw who was approaching, my brow furrowed.

"No, turn back right now and go to your room," I ordered.

"She's mad because we didn't bring pastries," my dad stage whispered to my mom.

"This is serious." Why was I having to say that so much lately? "You guys lost pretty much all of your magic, you haven't had enough time to recuperate, and don't take this the wrong way, but you both still look like the before picture for some sort of muscle-boosting protein powder. You're hardly fighting material."

"That's it. You're off our Christmas card list," my dad joked.

Before I could reiterate how serious this was, my mom cut in. "We'll be fine. Don't worry."

"Oh my stinking satyrs, that's all I do for you guys is worry. You're proving very irresponsible, you know."

"No, I mean, I'm glad you worry for us. That's very cute," my mom said with a delighted twinkle in her eye, "but we really are fine." She gave a familiar flick of her wrist, and three shields someone had left leaning against the wall went flying back.

"Was that a Shoving Spell?" I gaped.

"And I was holding back," she grinned.

"But how?"

"Runa was able to do a transfusion from Busby and Tobey."

"But you've been trying that for weeks with my magic, then Tobey's, then Busby's, and it never stuck."

My mom shrugged. "Runa's best guess is that we were bored in Rosaria, just bumbling around and snacking on Spellbound sweets. That boredom, that sort of drifting-through-life feeling must have robbed us of the self-assurance we needed for the magic to take hold."

"Despite all the scones and cinnamon rolls," my dad added.

This made some sense. Part of why my magic never showed through when I was a kid was because, thanks to a curse put on me, I'd been beaten down (both literally and figuratively) by nearly every foster parent I'd encountered. As an adult, things weren't much better until I'd settled into my work at Wood's Funeral Home. There, I gained some confidence in myself, my magic started kicking in, and then I ended up battling an evil wizard. Again, very relatable, right?

"And now?" I asked, still irrationally affronted that my magic alone hadn't instantly whipped them into magical shape.

"Now Runa thinks us returning to the field did the trick," said my dad. "The confidence boost of helping HQ and the vampires, of having a purpose, of facing this battle against the bad guys—" and no, I did not like the gleam in his eye when he rattled that last one off "—it finally made the transfused magic stick."

Which was great, but I couldn't be happy about it.

"I really don't want you guys in the fight."

"Cass, think about it," said my dad, in a tone that made it clear he was taking my worry seriously. "You've seen how Tobey and Busby are still at full power because they received your magic. We have now taken in *their* magic. Which means we have your magic in us. Which also means we won't be affected by this power-sucking malarkey the witch hunters have pulled. Those people down there need every bit of extra power we've got. We can't sit on the sidelines. It's too important."

"We promise to be careful," said my mom, like I was sending them out on their first solo trip on the city bus. Still, if being active was boosting their magic — not just boosting, but supercharging — when so many others had been weakened, then we needed them to charge into battle despite my misgivings.

I endured some super sappy hugs, we shared some words of encouragement and bravado, and then I watched them line up with the battalion Morelli was leading.

They don't recount this in most tales of adventure and derring-do, but even heroes need to pee. So, after watching my parents march off, I headed inside. Just as I reached my room's door, Alastair was stepping out.

"Hey, stranger," he said. After giving me a kiss, he explained that Morelli had insisted he take a quick break to refuel. "How's the battle going?"

"I don't really have much to compare it to, but I'm assuming that since we didn't all die in the first ten minutes, we should count that as a positive."

"There's that optimism I've—"

"Witch hunters!" gasped Rafi as he raced toward us, shoving

us both into my room and slamming the door behind us. "On their way. Moving fast."

My gut dropped so hard that I'm pretty sure it came out somewhere on the other side of the globe. So, if you happen to find some spare guts lying around, they might be mine.

"How?" I said, my throat so tight with fear, the question came out as a whispered croak.

"I don't know how, but they know you headed in here."

"She's not ready to fight them," insisted Alastair.

I would really love to have argued with him about assuming things about me, but he was right. I had no weapon. I had magic that wouldn't behave. I had a back-from-the-dead witch hunter armed with a deadly jewel who wanted to kill me. And, according to some stupid prophecy, even if I won against Hopkins, I might very well die anyway. I was not ready for this. Not yet. Maybe in about ten thousand years I would be, but right then, bravery had well and truly flown the coop. Plus, I was about to die of a burst bladder at any second, and that's simply no way to let the bad guys win.

Fists pounded on the door.

"Cassie Black, get thee out here now and face your fate."

Thee? Were these witch hunters taking their roles a bit too seriously?

"Thou knowest I, Matthew Hopkins, have the jewel. Your fate is sealed."

I froze. If I thought I wasn't ready to face Random Witch Hunters, I was really not ready to face Witch Hunter Numero Uno. And I know you're probably expecting more from the supposed hero of the story, but such is life. Sometimes nasty surprises smack you upside the head, and your brain just refuses to behave like you want it to. Especially when one of those nasty surprises is a witch hunter hell-bent on your death.

Matthew Hopkins called out his threat again. His voice was far reedier than I would have expected. I mean, not to judge or compare, but if you're going to attempt to blast thousands of people out of existence, you should at least have a big booming voice to stir fear and command respect. I know, nitpicking, but still, I've come to expect more from my villains. Even the Mauvais had a strong, deep voice that I still sometimes feel reverberating in my belly.

Loud grunts came from the hallway, then something that sounded very large and very heavy bashed into the door. The hinges loosened slightly.

"It's only going to take a couple more of those to do that door in," Alastair whispered.

"Yeah, if only we'd been cornered in Olivia's office," Rafi complained wryly. "That door can withstand a direct asteroid impact. We could try to Stun them when they get in."

"There might be too many of them," replied Alastair. "Did you get a count?" Rafi shook his head.

"Why are they not magicking the door open?" I asked critically. Not that I wanted to hurry up my demise, but if you're going to steal magic, why not make use of it?

"Battering rams do add a certain touch of drama," replied Rafi.

"Or they're saving themselves up for the attack," Alastair noted grimly just as a second bash splintered the center of the door.

"Out the window?" I suggested. "A Floating Charm on ourselves would do the trick."

"No, they're going to be in here any second," said Alastair. "We'd be easy targets if we're on the Green."

Hopkins shouted my name again. I cringed at the pure hatred in his tone. Pablo, meanwhile, merely let out a lazy mewling sound from within his carrier. He was likely basking in sunshine, high on catnip. Lucky bastar—

"Marshmallow Charm," Rafi and I said as one, both of us with our eyes fixed on Pablo's carrier.

Alastair hurriedly added, "And an Invisibility Charm on the carrier once we're in. I think I can do one of those."

I would have complained about conducting spells without being entirely certain they'd work, but Hopkins had just called out, "Three!" and from the hallway came the straining sound of determined men hefting something heavy.

The next thing I knew, my limbs went squishy. I've never been Marshmallowed before, but I expected to end up flopping about on the floor. Thankfully, I didn't. Instead, even though they felt far more limber than normal, I could control my legs enough to scramble into the carrier. Rafi and Alastair, their limbs as bendy as rubber bands, quickly followed.

From the patch of meadow he'd been stretched out in, Pablo gave a dazed look at the sudden intrusion to his kitty paradise.

Another sound of grunting. Alastair whispering, "Hidden." A thudding strike. The sound of wood blasting apart under sudden impact. Then the angry curses of a Head Witch Hunter not getting his way and accusing his goons of being morons in Shakespearean-style English.

Pablo purred and rubbed against me as we all breathed sighs of relief. I just hoped that Olivia wouldn't hold me accountable for the property damage to my room.

Not to sound like the biggest chickens on the planet, but we stayed in the carrier another fifteen minutes before daring to emerge. Five of those minutes were spent listening to Hopkins rail against his hunters. I kept hoping he'd reveal where he was camped out, since I'd prefer to gain the element of surprise, but he merely told them to get back outside, and that he'd soon be returning to the portal. Once the goon squad stomped out, I could hear Hopkins pacing the room, speaking to someone who gave only a toady's grunts to show he was listening.

"Shall I bringest the jewel together now, do you think?" Grunt of uncertainty. "Would that givest me the instant power to defeat her and clear the way, or is it better to err on the side of patience and wait until I have captured the wench?" *Wench?* Rafi mouthed amusedly. I elbowed him. "I wouldst revel in watching her face as the jewel joins into one, as she realizes her fate hath been sealed." Toady let out a you've-made-a-good-point grunt. "Exactly. I shall wait. God rewards the virtue of patience, as we all know."

Soon after, a pair of footsteps left the room, and the three of us showed our patience by waiting (and playing with Pablo) another few minutes.

"It's time to do this," I finally said. Guilt over my cowardice had been seeping in. My parents, Mr Wood, even de-magicked Magics were all out there fighting for the cause, and what was I doing? Hiding in a cat carrier. Hardly the stuff of legend.

"Do what exactly?" asked Alastair.

"Well, one, I still need to pee. Two, I don't really know what to do, but I do know sitting in here isn't how you go about saving the world."

CHAPTER THIRTY-SIX
TROOP COMMUNICATION

Rafi did his magical best to trace where Hopkins had gone after leaving my room, but whatever portal system Hopkins was using was both efficient and well concealed because there wasn't any sign of him in the hallway, stairwells, or beyond the White Tower.

"With all these hidden portals it might be pointless," said Rafi, "but I'll get Runa working on recent portal activity. See if she comes up with anything that could help." Looking uncomfortable, he added, "Olivia should be told as well. Either of you want to volunteer for that?"

"I was thinking we should let the— What are we calling them? Commanders?" I asked. Alastair and Rafi shrugged. "Well, whatever they are, they need to know what's going on. And I need to get out there," I said, then explained how I felt like a heel for hiding from Hopkins when so many others were outside facing down the enemy.

"You were caught unaware," said Rafi consolingly. "We all were. I mean, you didn't see Alastair or me challenging those thugs to a duel, did you? So don't you dare feel guilty. Hopkins isn't like those people outside. He's not some new recruit playing around with unwieldy magic. Unlike them, he's going to know exactly how to throw a killing hex, and if you're not fully prepared to strike back, or to at least put up a reliable Shield

Spell, you're toast. And trust me, you're crusty enough as it is."

"I agree," said Alastair, taking my hand. "Not about the crusty part, that is. I don't want you going against Hopkins at all, but especially not when he's got the jump on you."

I didn't so much as respond as swallow big, awkward lumps of emotion as we parted ways. Rafi dashed off to where he thought Runa might be, while Alastair and I headed back outside.

What I saw when we reached the ramparts was an all-out pitched battle with vampires fighting against the witch hunters; ghosts doing their best to wreak spectral havoc on the witch hunters; and my parents, Tobey, Busby, and a dozen elves exchanging attack spells with witch hunters. But despite our best attempts, the enemy gave no sign of weakening.

The only fighters of ours who seemed to be making any progress were the non-magic Magics who were hacking and whacking with whatever heavy, pointy, or sharpened implement they had gotten their hands on. And of course, there were plenty of cricket bats in the mix.

Wonky magic be damned, I couldn't just stand there. I got ready to hurl a Stunning Spell at a group of witch hunters. Maybe it's just hindsight and wishful thinking, but I could feel it was going to be a powerful hit, possibly one that would have taken down a fair number of witch hunters. But just as I was about to throw it, I forced the spell back. A jolt of pain zipped up my arms as the force of the blocked magic crashed into my fingertips.

"Cassie, what is it?" Alastair asked, likely concerned by the number of curses that had just spewed from my mouth. "Is it your magic? Is it something Hopkins is doing?"

I shook my head and looked out over the melee. At the spells being thrown. At the witch hunters showing no sign of slowing down. It all seemed too familiar. Granted, on a much larger scale, but too familiar by far.

"You know how you say I never seem to learn?" I asked.

"Too stubborn to learn is more like it."

"That may be, but when it comes to important things…" I tipped my chin up. "Watch."

A pair of elves and a trio of vampires threw coordinated spells at a band of witch hunters. Rather than the spells stopping them, the witch hunters only continued forward, grinning and egging our side on.

"Is the jewel affecting the vampires now, too?" asked Alastair as Morelli approached us. His t-shirt (featuring a sparkly unicorn) was a mess and his face was streaked with sweat, but otherwise he appeared uninjured.

"No, well, I don't know, maybe. Why are the vampires using magic instead of their teeth?" I asked Morelli.

"The gore was making a few of the ghosts sick. You wouldn't think they'd be bothered by that sort of thing, would you?"

"What's ticking around that head of yours, Cass?" asked Alastair.

"I think it's like when I was fighting the Mauvais. You told me to stop magically attacking him because every spell I was throwing at him was going straight into the watch and making him stronger, making him able to pull even more magic from me. The watch absorbed magic. Just like the absorbing capsules these witch hunters are carrying around."

"So every spell our side throws at them—" Morelli began.

"Only provides extra fighting power to the witch hunters." I thought for a moment. We had no way of communicating at a distance with our fighters. I mean, in the rush of prepping for this invasion, it's not like we stopped to set up a group text or anything. "How can we tell them to stop with the magic, to just fight the witch hunters like normal people? Or maybe just go back to ripping their throats out."

Alastair winced at this.

"Comm Spell," said Morelli. "Learned it in the M.A.G.E. It can send a message you hear in your head. Kind of creepy, but effective. It's been years since I've used it, though."

"Try it. If those absorbing capsules pull any more power from us, we're never going to get the upper hand."

Morelli concentrated hard, scrunching up his face like he'd eaten too much cabbage. Then his face softened and his lips moved as if talking to himself. And who knows, maybe he was. Some people just can't handle a crisis.

Below, several vampires began darting looks all around. Some shook their heads, others crouched down as if ducking from a particularly aggressive flock of geese. I don't know if Morelli added in some words along the lines of 'Don't worry. You're not going nuts,' but, slowly, the toothy troops began listening. They dropped their hands from any spell casting and instead opened their mouths, their canines snapping into place like dental switchblades. Morelli inhaled deeply through his nostrils, then muttered, "Go for it. And, Mattie, spread the word to the elves, then be ready with Caliban to force the enemy into retreat."

The vampires, like a band of raging barbarians going after some cocky Roman soldiers, surged forward. The witch hunters, who seemed to have gotten used to their opponents keeping their distance, were caught off guard by this. Some staggered back, scattering absorbing capsules across the battlefield as they tripped over their own feet and fell on their backsides.

While the front line of vampires swooped in and turned several of our foes into a bloody mess, the second line, made up of elves and non-magic Magics, barreled in with weapons at hand and took down quite a fair number of witch hunters. Behind the attack Magics, another line of troops, older Magics who weren't in top fighting form, stepped forward and scooped up as many of the abandoned absorbing capsules as possible. They then crammed the full capsules into the hand of any Magic they could find.

Their secret weapons now in the hands of people who knew how to use them, the witch hunters quickly lost the upper hand. Someone wrapped a Binding Hex around them, then hit the captured baddies with a Silencing Spell and a Slumber Charm. It's not to say taking down this one contingent was the end of the fighting, but we had won this battle, and we now knew how *not* to fight our enemy. Which turns out to be pretty important in a war.

"Holy dung balls, that worked," said Morelli, stupefied by his own power of telepathic communication. "I mean, not that I didn't think I couldn't do it. Magic's like riding a bike."

"And now I'm picturing you pedaling a tiny tricycle like a gorilla in a circus," I said wryly. Then, with genuine sincerity, told him, "Nice job."

Eugene Morelli got a little teary-eyed and very intent on staring at his boots.

"Come on," I told them. "Let's get down there before you wipe your nose on your t-shirt. That thing's dingy enough."

"You never change, Black."

"Like you'd ever want me to."

I was just about to cheer our success at doing away with this group of witch hunters, when I stepped back and everything went dark, twisty, and very squeeze-y.

CHAPTER THIRTY-SEVEN
IN THE GLOBE

I was in a theater. Not like a movie theater, but an actual theater with a stage. I was standing below this stage, near a set of wooden stairs in… I don't know, an audience mosh pit sort of thing? Several rows of seating scooped up and around from the mosh pit to form the walls of the theater in a near-perfect semi-circle, and there was no roof. No roof? In London? Where talking about the rain was a citywide sport? Were the actors simply the most optimistic people on the planet?

Just as it dawned on me that I was in the Globe Theater, built in the 1990s as close in style and location to the original Shakespearean acting palace as possible, movement on the stage caught my attention.

Hopkins and I locked eyes. The malevolence in his stare was so unnerving it made my interactions with the Mauvais seem like pleasant teatime chats. But at least the Mauvais hadn't wanted to kill me. He'd had a use for me, and even if it wouldn't have been the best life, he would have kept me alive. But Hopkins? No, that expression in his eyes spoke of deadly hatred and disgust for who and what I was. It truly made me understand how the saying *'If looks could kill'* might not be an exaggeration in certain cases.

Which is why every warm and fuzzy feeling fell out of me when I saw him turn to a very lanky man at his side. Although he had no camera with him, I recognized Gibson Todd. And when Hopkins told him to "*get to it*," he let out the same subservient grunt I'd heard when I'd been hiding in Pablo's carrier.

At Hopkins's command, Gibson dipped his hand into the zippered pouch he wore around his waist (and I thought those things went away in the 1980s). One by one, Gibson Todd pulled out five pieces of red jewel. And my heart sank when, one by one, he slipped those pieces into an intricate wire frame.

Meanwhile, from a pocket in his doublet (I think that's what you call those little jackets) Hopkins extracted four sample vials that looked exactly like the ones Runa used. They were filled with the glowing vapor of magic, and somehow I knew it was my magic. Oberlin, I cursed inwardly, had he taken my samples when he'd stolen Runa's saw? Why had we not thought to question him about that when we'd hauled him in?

"Accepting the devil's magic disgusts mine heart to its core," Hopkins began, "but oft times we must do what is deplorable to do what is right. God will forgive me when I defeat your evil kind."

There was a fair bit of cursing and scoffing from me at this point, but Hopkins ignored my salty tongue as he snapped the caps off the vials and pressed them to his palm.

"Your magic, Cassie Black, while a wicked thing, will allow me to control the jewel and rid the world of sin."

"God works in mysterious ways," mumbled Gibson as he fiddled with the small gemstones to puzzle them into place.

It was too late to stop Hopkins from absorbing my power, but I still had time to stop Gibson from securing that cage and locking the jewels together.

I raised my hands to throw a Shoving Spell. I didn't know if I was capable of much, but if I could just knock the jewels out of

Gibson's hands, I'd be happy. Shoving him off the stage and causing him a nasty head injury would be better, but that felt like asking for the moon right about then.

Gibson saw what I was about to do and, with the tiniest tip of his head, threw a Shield Spell around himself. At the same time, with barely a twist of his wrist, he cast a hex on me that created a powerful magnetic force between my feet and the ground, preventing me from moving as he finished slotting the jewel pieces into place. Don't you just hate multi-tasking show-offs?

At Gibson's handiwork, Hopkins grinned. And let me just say, he had some very seventeenth-century dental issues going on. Some teeth were blackened with rot, a couple were missing, and the rest sat at all the wrong angles. People might be afraid of dentists these days, but they should be more afraid of having a mouth full of chompers like that.

The tiny amount of hope I had that I might survive this faded when Gibson Todd closed the wire frame around the jewels and began to tighten some sort of spring-loaded thingamajig (sorry I should have had Alastair write this part so he could get the words for all the technical bits and bobs right). As soon as he gave the locking mechanism its first turn, however, Gibson slapped himself hard against the cheek.

With each turn of the cage's locking screw, Gibson slapped himself.

"Why's he hitting himself?" I asked. Sure, this wasn't the time for chitchat, but my curiosity tends to win out over my common sense sometimes.

"He is performing magic," stated Hopkins, his accent so strong, or perhaps his manner of speech so antiquated, I struggled to catch all of the words. "He must face the consequences."

"You all make no sense," I said as I fought to free my feet

from the flooring. I felt like Wile E Coyote when he's tried to catch Road Runner by spreading tar all over the road only to end up trapping himself instead. Some sort of Reversal Hex might undo the spell, but with my magic on the fritz, it also risked turning the skin and bones of my feet inside out, and I wasn't about to take that chance.

"How did you get me here?" I asked as Gibson continued to adjust the knob. The twist of his mouth showing his frustration.

Hopkins, however, continued to grin that grin only villains can manage. I imagine it's something they teach you in a free *So You Want to be a Villain* webinar. "John Dee may hath been one of your kind, but he was useful. He was also adept at creating portals and teaching others how to maketh them." And because villains just love demonstrating their handiwork, he pushed his hand through a point about a foot above the post for the railing of the steps that led from the stage to the mosh pit.

Before I could comment, Gibson turned the knob once more and the sound of something clicking into place echoed across the small space. There was a flash of red light, and Hopkins and I both watched with interest as the photographer turned the contraption-held jewel, examining it. "One more turn should do it, sir," he said.

The witch hunter muttered his surprise, as if he hadn't quite believed Gibson's efforts would work. Gibson, for his part, had picked up a chair leg and was hitting himself in the shins with it. Gotta say, the guy was nuts, but at least he was dedicated to his nuttiness. And what more can you expect from a murderous cult follower?

As Hopkins turned to take the jewel from Gibson's outstretched hand, I started shaking. Adrenaline and thoughts of my impending doom sent chills throughout my body despite the afternoon's heat. Seeking any warmth I could find, I crammed my hands into my skirt pockets. In one, I felt a small metal tube. The falcon whistle from Dr Torres's office.

Ridiculously, given the situation, my heart thudded with hope, and I couldn't fathom why.

Overhead, a crow cawed.

An idea fought for dominance over my fear as memories crackled like static through my mind. Nigel. The raven enclosure. Something about training. It was a long shot, but what other choice did I have? I put the whistle to my lips and blew as hard as I could.

Hopkins, meanwhile, seemed to be in no hurry to do me in. Which was both annoying and a relief. I mean, drawing out the inevitable versus a few more minutes of life? Tough call, right? He appeared to be inspecting the jewel while Gibson nodded. Hopkins questioned him further and, with Gibsons's mumbled grunts and Hopkins's thick accent, I couldn't make out the terse exchange.

Then Hopkins, with the shrug of someone satisfied but not thrilled with his subordinate's work, faced me. He gave the locking mechanism one last turn, and there was another flash of red light, brighter than the first. He raised the jewel, then chanted, "By the power of god, destroy mine enemy. Destroy the bringer of evil before me." He repeated this three times before muttering a bunch of phrases that sounded very curse-y. I'd probably have caught all the words, but I was doing my best not to wet my pants as my whole body tensed, waiting for the blow, waiting to be vaporized into a pile of Cassie dust, waiting to be racked with agonizing pain.

But it didn't come.

I hadn't realized I'd clenched my eyes shut until I opened them, thrilled to still have eyelids to open. Which, let me tell you, is just something you don't appreciate often enough.

Hopkins was still on the stage, glowering at the jewel. He thrust it forward again and said the same chant, this time invoking the power of God and Jesus and even a few saints for good measure.

Nothing happened. Unless you count my bladder growing less and less resistant to staying in control of itself.

A shadow briefly danced across my eyes as Hopkins shoved the jewel back at Gibson, whose shoulders were now hunched in shame. His fingers trembling, Gibson loosened the cage, shifted a few things around, then re-tightened the cage. Which I supposed was like the Control-Alt-Delete of magic jewel assembly.

The click of the cage locking the pieces together came again. Hopkins snatched the jewel from his colleague, secured the locking mechanism, then shouted his curses at me again, or rather another variation on it. As before, nothing happened.

The shadow cast over me once more. This time, I flicked my gaze upwards. The silhouette of a bird, of a raven against blue sky. My heart raced with possibility while I also bit back my hope. It could be any old bird, so there was no sense in getting all optimistic about things. After all, what could a damn bird do against a jewel-fueled witch hunter who'd come back from the dead just to kill me?

Then Winston swooped in.

CHAPTER THIRTY-EIGHT
S.P.A.M.

Six other ravens followed close on Winston's heels — or, rather, talons. The moment they were in the round theater, the group split. The other ravens swarmed Gibson, who was doubled over in pain, clutching his groin. Not because of anything the birds had done, but because, apparently, the shins hadn't been enough of a punishment for his spell-casting sins. Too overwhelmed with angry birds and self-induced agony to muster a defense spell, Gibson lumbered toward the back of the stage, where he disappeared into a portal just before reaching the backdrop.

With Gibson gone, the spell binding my feet to the ground broke, and... okay, I fell over at the sudden release. But, thanks to all the practice I'd gotten from my office chair from hell, I was back on my feet in record time.

Meanwhile, like some sort of avian stuntman, Winston had swooped past me and straight toward Hopkins, who tried to throw what looked like a Freezing Hex at Winston. To absolutely no effect. He tried again, a Shoving Spell this time, but again, the bird kept hurtling toward him.

And I know there was a lot going on, deadly jewel still in play, life in danger, avian rescue attempt, but I couldn't help but wonder why Hopkins, who Rafi said was quite handy with hexes and charms, couldn't magically protect himself from Winston. No one — except me, of course — who had my magic in them had shown any sign of their power weakening. But here was Hopkins, freshly supplied with Cassie Juice, and he couldn't perform even a basic spell. Dunno why, but it just struck me as odd. The things you notice when your life is on the line, right?

Momentary break for random brain farts over, Winston was still diving toward Hopkins, whose only remaining defense was to cringe away from "*the devil bird the witch hath conjured.*" Maneuvering with crazy skill between Hopkins's flailing arms, Winston stuck out his feet, talons extended, then clamped them shut as they gripped the caged jewel and tugged it out of Hopkins's hand.

As Winston flew up with his treasure, the other ravens dove toward Hopkins like osprey after a particularly fat trout. Two delivered the first hits, their talons raking against Hopkins's cheeks.

As soon as they soared up and out of the way, a third bird came in, beating his wings only a foot from Hopkins's face. I couldn't tell why the bird wasn't closing in, but then realized it was a diversion tactic. The witch hunter's hand flung out, trying to bat away his tormentor.

The instant he did so, another raven swept in, clutched his claws onto the guy's scalp, then bent forward and pecked hard. Just once, but that's all it took to aim its four-inch long beak into Hopkins's left eye. Hopkins dropped to his knees, his hands trying to catch the gloopy mess coming out of his face.

As if he hadn't wanted to be left out, Caliban appeared in the sky then rushed down through the open roof, landing in and taking up most of the mosh pit. I caught the smell of sulfur and felt a sudden swell of heat. I wouldn't mind seeing Hopkins roasted, but if the dragon unleashed his flame in the theater, after the heat of a dry summer, the resulting fire would spread across London's South Bank and I'd be caught in the middle of it.

"Caliban, no!" The dragon looked at me, disappointment in his green eyes. "Sorry, but just guard him." I didn't think it was possible, but the dragon's shoulders sagged. "You can do it menacingly, if you like."

"Devil woman! Vile woman who calls demons down from the sky!"

"That's me," I said, suddenly dizzy with elation. "Winston, to me."

Winston landed on my shoulder, the jewel firmly held in his beak. He then pressed the jewel into the side of my face. And it's not like he did this gently. He pressed hard, making my cheek squish up and partially close my eye.

"Winston, maybe a little less excitement at seeing me?"

He eased off so the pressure was more like a persistent nudge. And that's when I noticed a slight tingling trickling along my cheek. It wasn't powerful, but it had a familiar feel to it. And, to me, it smelled like donuts.

It was worth a shot.

"Get your friends to perch on Caliban," I told Winston, who then made a clacking noise with his beak. His feathered army landed on the dragon's head. Caliban didn't seem the least bit fazed by them, and I just knew I was going to have to find him a cow heart to reward him if I survived this.

I strode up the stage steps and positioned myself near the railing. If it only went from the Tower to the Globe, Hopkins's hidden portal wasn't a long-distance one. If just a smidge of my magic was working properly, I'd have no problem getting back. If not, I'd end up walking right off the edge of the stage. But it wouldn't be the first time that's happened in my life. A story for some other time.

The Unexpected Mr. Hopkins

"Caliban, place your tail on my foot. No man or reptile left behind, and all that."

The dragon's spiked tail looped loosely around my ankle. I stepped forward, toward the exact spot where Hopkins had shown off his portal.

Suddenly, I was back on the wall. This time with a raven on my shoulder and a very frightened dragon clinging to me. So much for Caliban's earlier bravery.

"Circe's sainted aunt!" yelled Tobey. "Where did you come from?"

"The Globe Theater."

"And they had a special running on dragons and ravens in the gift shop?"

"No, Hopkins. He had a portal. He tried to…" Before I could finish my sentence, my legs went wobbly, my head spun, and my stomach lurched. I whipped away from Tobey and threw up. Made a mess all over the stonework. But hey, I still hadn't wet my pants.

"Come on, let's get you inside," Tobey insisted.

"Are we winning?" I muttered, somewhat incoherently.

"We're doing pretty good. Caliban, they could use you over at the Green."

Once some of the uncontrollable shaking had subsided, I had a chance to look at what Winston had given me. For all the world, the Boncoeur Jewel looked whole, so why hadn't it worked? Had the vengeful magic leaked out, or mellowed as Dodding had said it might? Did it have an expiration date? Was I immune to cursed jewels?

Before I could contemplate further, Tobey grabbed my arm, touched something at his chest, and we were being squeezed and squished and swished through the fabric of the universe until we were spit out on the floor of Olivia's office. Climbing off my cousin, I saw the faces of Olivia, Rafi, Daisy, Fiona, Runa, and Alastair staring down at me. Not with surprise, but with that's-our-clumsy-Cassie looks on their faces. I got to my feet and held out the jewel to Alastair.

"I think they're going to want a refund. It doesn't work."

Alastair took the caged jewel and examined the locking mechanism. "No, it's how it should be. It really didn't work?" he asked, more disappointed with his creation not living up to snuff than relieved that he hadn't created something that might destroy the world. Again.

"Well, I'm not dead, so I'm guessing not." After visiting Olivia's ensuite loo, and after she'd called up a health- and mood-restoring amount of pastries and tea, I told them what had happened with Hopkins and Gibson and Winston.

"I always did like that bird," said Olivia.

"But how did I get this whistle?" I asked. "It was in my pocket this morning with a note from Dr Torres saying to keep it with me. Seriously, without this stupid little tube, I'd be dead."

"And you're sure you didn't take it from Dr Torres's office when you went there before visiting Professor Dodding?" Fiona asked.

"I've got a lot of faults, but being an amnesiac kleptomaniac isn't one of them. Wait," I said, considering the amnesia part, "maybe it is."

"Portals," blurted Tobey. And since he didn't elaborate, we all stared at him, which made him blush all the way from his chin to his perfectly coifed hairline. "Just a sec— Actually, is there a piece of scratch paper I can use?"

Olivia pushed a sheet forward, and Tobey grabbed the first pen at hand — one of Daisy's pink, puff-topped ones. He drew a box with an A inside it. Below the A he wrote *London, by 2 p.m.*

"This," he tapped the box with the pen, "is when Cassie was in the Globe and when she needs the whistle. But you first had the whistle…?"

"This morning," I responded to the question in his voice. "It was in my hoodie pocket when I got up, but I haven't worn that hoodie in months."

"When did you put on the hoodie?"

"Dunno, maybe a little after five."

Tobey drew another box a short distance from the A box. This one he labelled as B and added *London, before 5 a.m.* inside it. He then counted on his fingers and grinned.

"What are you smiling about?" I asked irritably, mainly because I hadn't a clue what he had already figured out.

"Time travel." Tobey then drew two more boxes, one labeled C: *Portland, this afternoon,* and another with *London* written below the letter D. "One of us needs to time travel," he declared with a self-satisfied grin.

"I'm not seeing it," Olivia admitted very slowly, and I was glad I wasn't the only one.

"If we use a time dilation portal to go from now— Sorry, I didn't do a box for that." Tobey hastily drew a box and wrote *NOW* in the center of it. "Okay, using a time dilation portal, we can go from NOW to Portland, specifically to Dr Torres's office this afternoon, and ask to borrow the whistle. He'll also have to add a note to it to make sure Cassie keeps it with her."

"Why not use a regular portal?" asked Runa, saving me from having to.

"Because it'd be too early in Portland. With the time difference, if we go back to Portland now using a regular portal, he's not going to be at work yet. Right?" Tobey looked to me.

I nodded. "Guy's dedicated, but I don't think he shows up at the crack of dawn."

"Exactly. So one of us takes a time dilation portal now to go to Portland. That puts our time traveler at C: Portland, this afternoon. The person gets the whistle and the note, then uses a regular portal to return to HQ, specifically to Cassie's room." A fuzzy memory of my dream of Tobey that morning tried to coalesce, but my cousin was on too much of a roll.

"Since regular portals don't adjust for the time difference," he continued, "that puts the person at B: London, before five in the morning. They sneak the whistle into Cassie's hoodie, then go back to Portland through the regular portal. That puts them there again at C: Portland, in the afternoon. From there they simply hop the time dilation portal back to—" Tobey tapped the corresponding box "—NOW in London."

"But what about D?" I asked, looking at the arrows Tobey had drawn to make his point.

Tobey glowered at me. "Okay, D should have been NOW. Give me a break. I think this is pretty good for only doing a two-hour seminar on Smart Portal Access for Magics."

"S.P.A.M.?" I asked incredulously.

"Cassie, now is not the time," said Olivia. "Tobey, as you seem to understand this, it should be you who collects and delivers the item. Cassie, you'll write a note requesting the whistle. Tobey can take it with him so Pascal understands what's happening."

Olivia, after sending an urgent message to the portal people in HQ, told Tobey where to go to arrange the portal permissions and locations in record time. To this very day, he gloats about his role in my not dying inside a Shakespearean-style theater.

"And Hopkins…?" Olivia asked once Tobey had left. The hope that I'd defeated my nemesis was clear in her voice.

I shook my head. "Alive. But he's got a lot of eye goop to see to, so we've got a bit of a reprieve before he comes after me again."

"But why didn't the jewel work?" Fiona asked. "Of course, I'm glad it didn't, but by all accounts, it should have."

"It doesn't even feel very powerful," I said. "Not really. There's some magic in it, but it's sort of muted, like an AM radio station fading before you enter a tunnel." I explained the return of enough of my magic to get myself back to the Tower through Hopkins's portal. Then, remembering him scrutinizing the jewel, I added, "Even Hopkins seemed perplexed by it."

While the others tried to sort out what had happened, I stepped over to one of the arrow slit windows and examined the jewel, turning it this way and that in the light provided. All the pieces joined up well. I could see my mom's pendant slotted into the gem from Winnifred's brooch, those two hugging Clive's marble, and the tiara's jewel nestled alongside that and what I assumed was the jewel from Runa's saw. But something wasn't quite as perfect as you'd expect an enchanted jewel to be.

"Does anyone have a magnifying glass?" I asked.

Olivia began rummaging through her desk drawers. And it sure sounded like there was a lot in there to rummage through, which surprised me since I would have thought Olivia's desk would be as minimalist and tidy as the rest of her office.

"I hardly use the damn thing," she explained as she shifted aside a tangle of cords, several tattered notepads, and a mountain of paperclips. "An Enlargement Charm usually does the trick on any small text. Unfortunately, some elf-enchanted documents refuse to be charmed," she said, glancing ruefully at Rafi, "and I have to resort to— Ah, there we have it."

She held out the magnifying glass, and Daisy, who'd been making notes in *An Enchanted History of the Portland Community*, rushed it over to me. I examined the space where the jewel from Runa's saw met the marble, the tiara, and the brooch. The joins at the marble and the tiara were perfect, but at the brooch, like a tricky piece of jigsaw puzzle that almost just fits, there was a sliver of a gap where it butted up against the saw's jewel.

"I don't think the saw's jewel was the right one," I stated. "That's why it didn't work. Not entirely."

"That's a relief," said Olivia.

"Is it?" I asked. "I mean, with or without the Boncoeur Jewel intact, I still have a back-from-the-dead witch hunter coming after me pretty soon and no way of getting rid of him without said jewel. Supposedly. I'm still not quite sure I buy that prophecy business." Especially as it foretold my death as being the only way to end our witch hunter problem.

"But if we assemble the jewel, he could take it back and use it to kill you," said Alastair worriedly. "We can take him down another way, can't we?" he asked Olivia. Olivia looked away.

I'm not quite sure what all was discussed, but the throng of people in the office started yammering away about what could be done to Matthew Hopkins without the jewel, how the witch hunters could be stopped with the forces we had at hand, and how Hopkins would *have* to surrender because look how good we were doing already. To which someone would throw out a doomsday counter-argument, and this would kick off a heated debate.

All of which was completely rude since I was trying to think. Not exactly easy to do in the midst of a crisis, but even more difficult when you've got a room full of Magics bickering over how to go about your upcoming demise.

CHAPTER THIRTY-NINE
HOLY BUNNY SLIPPERS!

After Olivia stashed the jewel pieces and Alastair's cage contraption into her desk drawer for safekeeping (I was a bit skeptical about this, but she promised me the drawer had on it a wide range of enchantments that only she knew about) most everyone dispersed. The non-human Magics and those with my power needed to get back outside and help where they could, so once we'd broken away from a lengthy and very I-don't-ever-want-to-let-you-go embrace, Alastair set off with Rafi, the two of them whispering conspiratorially about 'putting that project into play.'

Runa returned to the medical ward to tend to the wounded, and Fiona left to watch the portal networks to see if she could discern any unusual activity. I didn't think it would help. Hopkins was using hidden portals to pop into and out of the Tower of London. The official monitoring systems would show nothing, so it was anyone's guess as to when or where he'd return. The only thing we could know for certain was that he'd come for me as soon as he patched up his eye.

Since she'd already lugged *An Enchanted History of the Portland Community* to HQ, Busby assigned Daisy the task of recording the details of what was happening, figuring she might as well get the facts down while still fresh in her mind.

Other than trying to figure out where the missing piece of the Boncoeur Jewel might be, it was decided that my only job right then should be to get the tiny bit of magic in my cells buzzing as strongly as possible. Which is why, before she left, Olivia ordered up several types of cake, and Runa advised me to get as many wedges of it into my system. It had a sort of last-meal feel to it, and my gut was already queasy again, but I grabbed a plate and did my best to follow this most unusual of military and medical advice.

I was on my fifth slice when, from Olivia's desk, where Daisy had set up her secretarial station, Daisy began letting out grunts of annoyance. I tried to ignore her. Believe me, I really tried, but there's only so many peeved sighs that you can withstand before you finally ask, "Problem?"

"It's this stupid book." She thumped the massive collection of Rosaria's history. "It's the same as when I was trying to write in my and Tobey's engagement information and our wedding dates and our honeymoon plans. I write what's happened — or what will happen in the case of me and Tobey — but then I look later and there's nothing there."

"Perhaps try taking the cap off the pen?" I suggested.

Daisy actually examined her pen. And, really, am I supposed to not at least *think* that's a dumb blonde joke waiting to happen?

"Nope, cap's off." She scribbled on a piece of scrap paper. "And it's got plenty of ink. I paid twenty dollars for this pen. It should work on any paper, and the ad for it said the ink should last a lifetime."

"Keep trying?" I advised, mainly because it was keeping her busy with something other than asking me questions when I just wanted to rest, eat, and think about where the final jewel piece might be. I pulled out my phone and looked over the notes Dr Torres had sent about the courtiers and the jewels, but it got me nowhere. From the desk came the sound of a pen moving over paper as Daisy wrote in the book, but soon enough there again came the peeved sighing and she threw up her hands.

"See? Gone. This is so stupid. You try. Maybe it doesn't like me."

"I broke that book, remember? I doubt it has any feelings of friendship toward me."

"You're right. Maybe you're making it mad," she said with utter seriousness. "Go away."

"Olivia told me to stay here. You go away."

"Just for a minute," she pleaded. "Step outside and let me see."

"Am I actually paying you to journal?" Since I was pretty sure she was still on the clock.

"You're not paying me. HQ is."

"Fair point. Fine. I need some air anyway." I set aside my plate and figured it was a good time to stretch my legs, at least as far as the end of the hallway, that is. Despite all the cake, I had no energy for stair climbing.

Looking down through the window at the end of the hall, I could see groups of witch hunters under a Binding Hex who were being led away by Chester — the ghosts were delighting in swirling around and taunting them as they went. Elves and vampires were congratulating each other; and several Magics, cricket bats still in hand, were digging into a mountain of cookies the pixies had delivered. The crash, clamor, and uproar of fighting still rang out from across the grounds, and I still had a raving lunatic after me, but it was a relief to see we weren't going down without a good showing.

When I returned to the office ten minutes later, Daisy didn't look any happier.

"Not me, then?" I asked.

"Guess not. Sorry. You want to give it a try?"

"I don't know. There was a story about a book that hid what had been written in it, and that didn't turn out so well." I briefly wondered if Rafi had any basilisk fangs stashed amongst the mess in his office. "How about you show me?"

Daisy opened the book to one of the final pages, one that was blank, then picked up her pen and wrote, *Magics win fight against witch hunters,* along with the next day's date.

"Are you sure we'll win? And that soon?" I asked, the tiniest smidge of optimism trying to creep in.

"I can change it later," Daisy said, dismissively dashing my minuscule hopes. "Now watch." And so I watched. Nothing happened. The ink stayed put.

"Maybe the book is trying to give you a sign that you shouldn't marry Tobey. It seems to like what you've just written."

"I've never seen a prophesying book. Or heard of one, for that matter. You really think it could be…?"

I'd actually just made that up to goad her, but to play along I started to say it seemed possible. However, what came out was, "Holy cat guts! What was that?"

Because before I could torment my assistant, the sentence she had just written shifted away. It didn't disappear exactly, it just shifted as if moving somewhere else in the book. I asked Daisy to lift the page to see if the ink had soaked through to the other side, but the back of the page was clean.

I reached out to touch the paper, to verify it was real, but hesitated, recalling what happened at the British Library.

"Turn it to the middle," I said, recalling with a sense of cautious hope what Wordsworth had told me about book protections, as well as what I'd seen earlier in this very same book. Maybe it hadn't been a stress-induced hallucination.

Daisy flipped to a page about two-thirds of the way through

the book. At first it appeared to be what you'd expect to see in an account of a community's history: A scene of someone cutting a ribbon on what looked like the Spellbound building, although at the time it had been called The Enchanted Cheddar. Someone had written up a quick summary of when the cheese shop opened.

Beside this, in Gwendolyn's handwriting, was an addendum stating that a week after opening the shop, the owner spent four months recovering from hives. After six straight days of being surrounded by cheese for ten hours a day, he'd apparently developed a sudden-onset case of lactose intolerance. He then sold the building to Gwendolyn who, two months later, opened Spellbound Patisserie.

I'd barely reached the end of Gwendolyn's note when the whole page shifted. Again, that's the best way I can describe it. It was like all the text and photos on those pages slipped around a bit, then reformed. But they didn't reform into the text I'd just read.

"Holy bunny slippers," gasped Daisy. "Is that…?"

"I think so."

"But how?"

"A shifting book." When Daisy gave me a questioning look, I said, "Wordsworth told me about them."

"That's a spell," muttered Daisy, as if still not grasping what was in front of her.

I only had a moment to scan the spell. It looked like a basic potion for preventing fleas in werewolves, but just before the page shifted back to the article featuring the ribbon cutting, my eyes darted to the page's top margin. The lengthy title of Wordsworth's book stood out plain and clear. Well, until it disappeared, that is.

"It's been here all along," I said with a laugh.

"I don't understand. And don't make blonde jokes." Clearly she knew me better than I knew myself. "I really don't get what's going on."

I explained to her what Wordsworth had told me about how the contents of some books shifted between two, possibly more, subjects. I also mentioned his complaints about the nightmare of cataloging those books. I then told her what I'd seen at the top margin.

"So, you found Wordsworth a copy of his book. Does that mean you're going to complete his case and get your license?"

Honestly, I hadn't even considered that. Which goes to show I do have some priorities.

"No, it means we're going to be able to fight the bad guys."

Because this book — the shifted version, that is — should contain the spell that had brought Hopkins back from the dead. And if that spell were reversed, it might undo what had happened. It might be just the thing to send Hopkins back to the grave.

Daisy let out a yip of joy and clapped her hands with unbridled glee.

"But with our magic off, how do we get the page to stay put?" she asked.

"I have no clue," I admitted as the office's heavy oak door creaked open.

CHAPTER FORTY
WILLIAM CECIL'S WARD

"About time you admitted you ain't got a clue, Black," said Morelli as he marched into the office. His t-shirt was now torn, and he looked like he could use a weeklong nap, but otherwise he seemed okay.

"Why aren't you leading your troops?" I asked, although since I'd spent the past thirty minutes doing little more than eating cake, I made sure to keep any hint of criticism out of my voice. And really, I wasn't being critical. Morelli was proving to be a capable leader, and we needed him out there if we were going to have any chance of beating back the bad guys.

"Chester took over for a bit. He fixed a few souvenirs the witch hunters gave me—" Morelli held up his arm to show a series of already-healing gashes "—then Olivia told me there was cake up here and demanded I take a break. She'd have made a great general, that's for sure," he said as he picked up the platter that still held half a Victoria sponge. He didn't bother with a fork to eat it, licking jam filling from between his fingers as he devoured the dessert. Once done, he twirled his hands to clean them.

And that's when I did have a clue.

"You still have magic," I said.

"Yeah, duh," Morelli replied as he settled into a large slice of carrot cake.

"Can you do some sort of Pause Charm or Freezing Hex or something on a book?" I asked, pointing to *An Enchanted History of the Portland Community*.

"Why would I want to do that?"

"Because Cassie's discovered something really super duper," Daisy replied, then explained what we'd just seen.

Morelli abandoned his cake and strode over to the desk. "That's a shifting book? I never knew."

"I think that's the point," I noted.

"And if you have this spell you can take down Hopkins?"

"Well, I'd have to find him first, but since he seems to be good at finding me, I don't think that's going to be a problem. But yeah, this is my best hope right now. The jewel's incomplete, my magic's still not reliable, and I doubt Winston's going to come to my rescue every time Hopkins tries to kill me. With that, though," I pointed to the book, "I might have a fighting chance."

"So, why a Pause Charm?"

"Because it's a shifting book. If you don't halt the spell's page, it's going to shift back to Rosarian history before we can copy it."

"Nah, I mean, it'd be easier to Duplex the pages you need, wouldn't it? Actually," he said, his brow lifting with the idea he'd just had, "a Duplo-Reverso Charm would be better."

"Duplo-Reverso? Seriously? You just made that up."

"No," said Daisy, "he's right. It'll duplicate the page, but also put the words in reverse order. It'd make reading out the incantation so much easier when you have to fight that stupid poopy head witch hunter."

"Yeah, what she said," said Morelli, looking at Daisy with some skepticism. After all, you don't exactly expect someone who knows about the intricacies of spells to refer to one's mortal enemy as *poopy head*. "It was a precursor to some coded message charms we eventually crafted in M.A.G.E. Want me to do it?"

"Go for it," I said.

And to my surprise, now that he knew the book was a shifting book, Morelli had no trouble coaxing it to the version he wanted. I told him which page the spell was on. Using a sheet of paper Daisy had pulled from Olivia's desk drawer, he Duplo-Reversoed the entire spell, the words appearing on the new page in reverse order to how they were originally written.

To reward himself, Morelli ate most of a lemon gateau before saying he ought to get back out there.

"If I see her, I'll send Olivia up so you two can work out how to find Hopkins, okay?" he said gruffly. Then, in a tone of gentle concern, he added, "You keep that sheet with you at all times. Got it, kid?"

"Got it," I said, my eyes stinging. Before things could get sappy between us, we were both saved by the ringing of my phone. Morelli gave a sharp salute and marched down the hall to the stairwell as I took the call.

"Professor Dodding," I said with genuine delight. He may be a silly old flirt, but a chat with him would be a nice break from contemplating my impending demise.

"Miss Black," he said warmly, "I hope you won't think I'm being too forward in calling on you. Wouldn't want you to get the wrong impression."

"Professor, I think I've gotten a very precise impression of you." To which he gave a hearty, if raspy, chuckle.

"Indeed. Now, besides the lovely break in my day it is to chat with you, I have something I've discovered."

"How to turn lead into chocolate bars?"

"No, did that decades ago. The transformative magic does work, but the chocolate, well, it tastes like a cocoa-flavored lead bar. No, I'm actually calling about something that wonderful Dr

Torres sent me. He has all these courtier connections with the people in Rosaria. You got the draft of his research paper?"

Dr Torres had already written up his scraps of notes into a full research paper? The guy certainly did set out to impress.

"Not yet."

"Well, he's made some marvelous discoveries with those courtiers, and I can't wait to collaborate with such a brilliant mind, but there was one bit I helped correct him on, and that might be of special interest to you. Don't know why I didn't think of it before. Likely because I'd just gotten a shipment of chocolate malt balls in, and, well, you can imagine."

I could imagine. I could also barely contain my impatience over how he was teasing out his information. Was it going to be earth-shattering, or (and my pessimism said this was more likely) was it going to be another mildly interesting dead end?

"Anyway," continued Dodding, "it's all to do with Wiliam Cecil."

I perked up. "William Cecil, from Queen Elizabeth's court?"

"Yes, and through one of his descendants, he's connected with your jewel. It's a rather tricky path of descent as the line we're talking about stems from one of Cecil's wards. I'm sure you don't want the entire genealogical rundown today, but this ward ended up being a favorite of Cecil's. So much so that the ward eventually took the family name and even received a fair inheritance from Old Willy. The endowment included books, shares in some investments, and a 'jewel with ties royal and alchemical.' *Alchemical* here most likely meaning magical."

Although my heart was gyrating in my chest and my fingers were tingling with excitement, my brain remained skeptical about what Professor Dodding was telling me. Cautiously, I asked, "And this ward was…?"

"Charles Cecil."

"Cecil?" My pessimistic brain had been right to doubt the

usefulness of this piece of courtier trivia.

"Indeed," enthused Dodding, not one bit put off by my dismissive understatement. "See, the name changed in the early 1700s to Celle. Morphed to Cellar in the late 1700s when the family became wine merchants." Tainted teats of a harpy! My brain and body did a one-eighty back to hopeful excitement. "Finally, and here's where you'll be applauding me, in the late 1800s, the name switched again to—"

"Zeller?"

"Exactly. My, but you are clever. Have I been the biggest help? Should I reward myself with some Belgian chocolate truffles, do you think?"

I wanted to tell him he had been. But the part of me that doesn't get excited until I have clear reason to do so told me it could just be a coincidence. It could mean everything. But it could also mean nothing.

Then I recalled my magic. The wonkiness. It had begun before I'd gotten Clive's marble, my mom's pendant, or Winnifred's brooch. It had started before I'd even taken Matilda Marheart on as a client. Images of Pablo also sprang to mind. His hatred of the marbles. His strange behavior toward the tiara. His repeated break-ins to Alastair's workroom and making a mess of things. His attacking Alastair without any provocation.

"You should definitely reward yourself, Professor. I think you may have helped me find the final piece of the Boncoeur Jewel."

"Oh, how delightful. When you're done saving the world, would you mind if I treat you to a hot chocolate? There's a wonderful wizard in Switzerland whose brew will leave you swooning."

"If I survive saving the world, it's a date. Thank you so much, Professor."

"Anytime, my dear."

CHAPTER FORTY-ONE
RUMPELSTILTSKIN VIBES

"Daisy!" I hadn't meant to, but in my excitement after talking to Dodding, I'd shouted her name. She startled so hard she snapped her pen. After a quick apology, I asked, "Do you know where Alastair got to?"

"I think he and Rafi were working on something. Duplex Spells were mentioned," she replied doubtfully.

I went dashing down the hallway, then the stairway, then another hallway to find Rafi's office. But where I expected his office to be was a broom closet. I checked the inside thoroughly, thinking it might be a portal that led to his office, but the back was solid. Merlin's balls, I hated the White Tower!

I raced to backtrack my steps to my starting point and managed to find Olivia's office where it should be. Small favors, right? Walking backwards, I retraced the route my parents had taken after surprising me by showing up to Rafi's office upon their return from befriending vampires and hanging out with witch hunters.

It was as I turned the corner and saw a pair of familiar garden gnomes that I knew I'd found my destination.

"You can't seriously be on duty here as well, can you?" I asked Rosencrantz-possibly-Guildenstern.

"It were part of our contract, weren't it?"

"It were. I mean, it was. Sorry, what are you talking about?"

"We take orders from the half-troll," he replied in his broad Yorkshire accent. "The half-troll tells us to guard the door where Alastair Zeller were working. So, here we are."

"Sounds great," I said impatiently. "Now, let me through."

"Not until you show us a little respect," he demanded.

"Yeah, we keep places safe," asserted the second gnome. "We watch over things. We don't make noise or smelly messes. Unlike that cat of yours—"

"He peed on me once, you know," said the first.

"Couldn't get the smell out for weeks."

"You could have just moved out of his way," I said.

"Not when there were a human walking by outside," replied the second. "What do you think? That we can just go running about willy-nilly when faced with a problem? No, we have to stand our ground and bear the indignities."

"Which is why we're not moving until you tell us our names," insisted the first.

"Why? Don't you know your names?" I asked.

"That's not— Why—" the second one blustered. "Such insolence would be punishable most vigorously if you were amongst our ranks."

"Our names," huffed the first gnome. "Go on. One of us is Rosencrantz, and one of us is Guildenstern. Tell us who is who and we'll let you by."

"You do realize I could just pick you up and move you aside?"

"Go ahead and try," said the second gnome, putting up his fists while the other gripped menacingly tighter to the little shovel he always held.

While the sight was amusing, they were right; I should know their names. They'd been part of my daily life for months — No, *years*, since one had always been on guard duty somewhere outside Morelli's building since the day I'd moved in. To not know their names was indeed disrespectful and a bit hoity-toity for the likes of me who'd grown up being everyone else's punching bag.

And hey, I had a fifty-fifty chance of being right, which were far better odds than I'm used to when facing an opponent.

I looked back and forth between the two, their beards bristling, their eyes narrowing, their brows furrowing. Morelli had introduced them to me after cluing me in that they weren't just decorative kitsch in the weedy patch of dirt he used to call a garden. But even he had trouble telling them apart, and no wonder. I mean, it's not like they went out of their way to distinguish themselves. They all dressed alike in either a blue or red hat with blue or red trousers and slouchy brown boots. They all wore long white beards — even the lady ones, although they tended to go for pastels and flowers in their hair, so at least there was that.

But Busby had told me just a few days previous (which seemed like a few *months*) how to spot the difference: Every gnome had one accessory that set them apart. Glasses, a toadstool chair, a bit of patchwork on the hat. And in this case, a shovel. As the tiny scowls deepened, I fought to recall Mr T's mnemonic for telling the brothers apart. I swear, I was thinking so hard that my eyebrows started to ache. Suddenly, my brain spit out, *Guildenstern Shovel Earned*. Granted, it wasn't the most poetic memory aid, but it did the trick.

I pointed to Rosencrantz and said his name, feeling some serious Rumpelstiltskin vibes going on. I then pointed to the shovel-carrying twin and addressed him as Guildenstern.

For a moment, they both stared at me, the glowers turning to looks of annoyance that I'd been correct. They gave each other a look, then a pair of conciliatory shrugs.

Unfortunately, they still didn't budge.

"Come on. I need in there."

"And we need to be doing our duty," insisted Guildenstern.

"The fate of the magical world rests on me getting in there."

"Can't do, mum," said Rosencrantz.

"Look, if all Magics are dead or enslaved or whatever this Hopkins character is up to, you won't have anything to do but stand in people's overgrown gardens during heatwaves and snowstorms."

I honestly hadn't thought it possible, but the rosy patches at their cheeks paled.

"That's not a nice thing to say, mum," Rosencrantz said worriedly. "Only the lowliest of Guardin' Gnomes is made to do garden duty."

"Then please let me in," I said as calmly as possible, then coyly added, "I'll put in a good word for you with Daisy."

"You'll not tell anyone I failed in me duties?" he asked, shyly twisting his hands together.

"I'll tell them you both were part of the heroic team that helped save the magical world. Probably a medal in it for you."

The rosy patches had returned, and their eyes gleamed with possibility.

"That'd be... well, I—" began Guildenstern.

"Look, not the time for long speeches, okay?"

"Yes, mum!" they said as one. They clicked their heels, saluted me, then, for once, willingly stepped aside.

And I honestly don't know what I would have done if they'd switched shovel-carrying duties for the day.

I burst into the room to see Alastair and Rafi huddled over something on Rafi's desk.

"Alastair, Professor Dodding just told me— How did you not realize—? But then again, you were distracted, so..."

"Cassie," Rafi said, snapping me out of my rambling excitement, "have you lost the ability to form a complete sentence?"

Just then, the arm of a one-foot tall clockwork automaton on Rafi's desk shot out. And I do mean *shot out*. The arm extended with a snap that was so forceful it detached at the shoulder. The arm and whatever had been in its hand went flying across the workroom in my direction and crashed into the wall about four inches to the left of my head with such gusto it lodged itself into the plaster.

"What was that?" I shouted, sounding indignant but also shaking from the near miss. I mean, seriously, how many times can you almost die in one day?

"We thought if we could get it to work properly," Rafi said, "I could do a bunch of Duplex Spells on it and create an army."

"As you can see," said Alastair, "they're, um..."

"Effective?" Rafi volunteered.

"*Psychotic* might be more appropriate," I corrected.

The now-one-armed contraption stirred back to life, stepping forward with an eerily natural gait. At the edge of the desk it stopped walking and went down on one knee. The movement was smooth, and even non-sentimental me smiled at the romantic aspect of it.

"It's just something I was working on earlier," Alastair said, looking uncharacteristically bashful. "But Rafi suggested some modifications that might help."

"Modifications such as hurling weapons at passersby? Even ones who aren't the enemy?" Alastair shrugged at my criticism. "Anyway, not the point. Dodding just told me something you might find interesting. No time for details right now, but do you have any sort of red jewels you've been keeping from me? I'm thinking it might be a ring." I added, recalling Dr Torres's note about a painting of William Cecil in which he's wearing a red-gemmed ring.

Both Alastair's and Rafi's gazes went directly to the projectile now wedged into the wall. I turned, but before I could grab the loop of gold that was sticking out of the plaster, Alastair rushed over and cupped his hands over it.

"Alastair," I scolded, "are you hiding dangerous items from me again?"

"It's not what you think," Alastair said as he lowered his hands.

Given that the golden arc currently poking out of the wall had the exact curvature and size of a ring, I was pretty sure it was exactly what I was thinking. But if Alastair had a red jewel all this time, why had he not mentioned it? Obviously not every red gem in the world could be a part of the Boncoeur Jewel, but to not even offer it up for testing? It didn't stir up any warm and fuzzy feelings of trust and bonding, let me tell you.

With the tips of my fingers, I wiggled the small object to loosen it from the wall. I then pinched the exposed loop and gave a tug. Drywall dust crumbled to the floor and covered the ring's setting. I dusted it off. All questions suddenly answered, my shaking hand dropped the ring to the floor.

"Butterfingers," Rafi teased as Alastair bent down to pick up the ring, staying down on one knee as he held the ring aloft.

"Cassie, I—" he began in a very serious tone, but I cut him off, taking the ring from him and slumping against the wall in disappointment.

"An emerald," I grunted. "A green-as-troll's-snot emerald."

I suppose I should have been happy that Alastair hadn't been keeping secrets from me, but this had been my last chance.

Without the final piece, how would I have the magical strength to take down Hopkins when he came for me?

"Any red gems back at the apartment or in your pocket or up in the room?" I asked with dwindling hope as I fiddled anxiously with the ring.

"Down," Rafi corrected softly. "Your room is down."

"Not helping," I said flatly, having no energy to throw any bitter reproach into the words. Holding up the ring, I asked Alastair, "Yours?"

"My grandmother's," he said awkwardly. He remained on one knee a moment longer, then pulled a face and stood up.

Through all of this, I kept playing with the ring, hating it for not being a ruby or garnet or whatever. I'm not sure what fumbling move I made, but as I was about to hand it back to Alastair, the band caught on the tip of my thumb. The band being large and my fingers being bony, the ring slipped down to the base of my thumb.

And that's when I stopped hating the ring.

"What just happened?" I asked, backing away, even though it's rather impossible to back away from your own thumb.

"That's a world class example of a Concealment Charm," said Rafi in awe. He hurried over and took my hand in his, examining my thumb and the ring on it. The ring which now bore a gleaming red gem. "This is clever."

"What? How?"

"That is something I am going to be studying as soon as you save the world. Am I right in thinking this is your final piece of the Boncoeur Jewel?"

I nodded and briefly, in half a daze, explained what Dodding had just told me.

"My guess is the ring conceals itself until the person who needs it comes along," Rafi said. "Or perhaps it's a test of loyalty, only changing when the brave of heart puts it on. They used to love that sort of claptrap back in the day. Again, don't ask me how. Not just yet, anyway. Great Galadriel, that is a clever charm," he said again, fully impressed. "Of course, there's only one way to find out if this really is the final piece: You'll need to fit it with the others. Oh, and then you need to go track down the very guy who wants you deader than a plague victim. All in a day's work, right?"

"Again, not helpful," I said. "Look, Alastair, sorry about your ring, but I'm going to have to steal it for a bit. And sorry to dash off, but I've got to assemble this jewel and go kill an evil witch hunter."

"Well, you're not battling evil without me," Alastair insisted, and my heart thumped with affection for him. I mean, it may not be what most girls would consider a romantic statement, but it was the best thing he could have said at the moment. "Just, maybe, refrain from killing me this time."

"I make no guarantees."

CHAPTER FORTY-TWO
CRICKET BAT HOME RUNS

When I returned to Olivia's office, she was there with Morelli. He looked chastised, and she looked incredibly impatient.

"Morelli tells me you've found a way to defeat Hopkins," she said brusquely.

"Nope," I replied. "*Two* ways." As quickly as I could, I explained both the reversal of the book's spell and Dodding's information. I then showed her Alastair's ring. "This is the final piece. I think."

"Only one way to find out," Olivia said and removed the other jewel pieces from very deep inside what looked like a shallow desk drawer.

I set aside the saw's stone, pushing it toward Olivia and telling her to give it to Runa when she got the chance. I then carefully eased back the prongs holding the ring's gem. My heart thudded harder than that of a lifelong couch potato who's just jogged up eighteen flights of stairs, and my hands shook to the point I nearly dropped the delicate gems, but after a fortifying breath, I wiggled the ring's stone into the cage. The piece slotted in perfectly.

Without a single turn of the locking mechanism, I could feel the difference in the jewel pieces. Like a gaggle of school kids being told by their teacher to line up, the scattered and random power in the separate gems seemed to slide into order.

I glanced up. All eyes were on me. Most were encouraging me to get on with it, a few were fretful — whether for me or for what would happen if this didn't work, I can't say. Alastair's eyes, though, were begging me not to do this.

"I have to," I said, my throat tightening and the words barely getting out.

His voice shaky, Alastair said, "You don't, but I know you will anyway."

"Stubborn through and through," said Morelli, his own voice breaking. I made a note to tease him about that later, which gave me a very good reason to stay alive.

I turned the locking key once more.

The flash of light this time nearly blinded me, and the surge of power that rushed through me was about a gajillion times more intense than what I'd felt in the theater. Like the difference between touching your tongue to a 9-volt battery versus grabbing hold of a downed electrical wire that's still live. As with the gems' power feeling aligned, I felt my own magic juice flowing in a more orderly direction. A river of magic instead of a bunch of swirling eddies, stagnant pools, and churning rapids.

I aimed a gentle Shoving Spell at the tapestry on the wall. It fluttered, then rolled up a few feet, then unfurled once more. I couldn't repress my smile of satisfaction. Cassie Black was back. Well, her magic was. I hadn't gone anywhere. Except through a portal to my near-death. Sorry, that quip just got far too complicated.

"I think it's time for a certain witch hunter to fulfill a certain prophecy," I said, then realized a tiny flaw in my heroic plans. "Does anyone know where he is?"

***

After much discussion regarding whether it would be best for me to stumble into a hidden portal again or to bide our time until Hopkins found himself with a free spot in his calendar, it was decided I needed to take the upper hand. No giving Hopkins the element of surprise. This time, I'd be fighting on my own turf (well, HQ's own turf) at a time of my choosing.

"Why would he come when we ask him to, though?" I said. "I mean, he doesn't seem like the kind of guy who likes being told what to do."

"Because he thinks he has a higher power on his side," Olivia replied. "And I've no doubt he's pretty angry about losing an eye. He's going to want vengeance, and he's going to assume he's got every right to it. He'll want to come."

"There is one problem," Alastair noted. "We don't exactly have his number to invite him over for this play date."

"Wait a minute, though," I said. "You do. I mean, not directly, but the commission. You have Gibson Todd's number, don't you? You said you did everything through the *Herald's* offices, but their photographers mostly work freelance. They wouldn't have desk phones. Which, since I know you don't delete anything, means you probably still have his number in your call log."

"You really should delete things now and then to keep your phone clean," advised Morelli.

"I don't think now is the time to address Alastair's technology hygiene," snapped Olivia. "Alastair, do you have it?"

Alastair had already been scrolling through his phone. Given his fear for me, I half-expected him to say he no longer had it or to 'accidentally' delete it if he did find it. In fact, for the briefest moment I caught his finger hovering over a trash can icon before he swiped it away and said, "Got it."

The Unexpected Mr. Hopkins

Since we doubted the person who was helping the guy who wanted us all dead would take our call, Alastair opted to text what Olivia dictated to him.

We give up. Tell Hopkins that Cassie Black will be left near the Wellington Barracks in one hour.

It didn't take long before Gibson replied.

He will be there.

Olivia and the others, after many pieces of advice that I quickly forgot, gave Alastair and I some time alone together, which we spent wrapped in each other's arms and talking about anything and everything except what was about to happen. Forty-five minutes after Alastair had sent the text, we descended the stairs and exited the White Tower.

Rather than stand fully exposed in front of the Waterloo Barracks, Morelli advised me to wait at the corner of a small alley between the Royal Chapel and the barracks. The spot had excellent sight lines, and from there, I could watch for Hopkins's arrival without making myself an easy target when he appeared.

From my vantage point, I was also able to observe a walrus cowering behind a tree near a low pile of ruins at the corner of the White Tower, apparently refusing to step into the battle being waged in the greenspace near Beauchamp Tower (this greenspace being where the Tower's Great Hall once stood).

I couldn't believe Oberlin. First he gives the witch hunters the means to destroy us all, then he refuses to help us combat what he's done? The man knew no shame.

Even Winnifred, a woman who'd just staggered back from the brink of death, was out there on what's known as the Scaffold Site giving it her all. She'd gotten in on the cricket bat trend and was using her size to her advantage as she walloped a witch hunter in the gut. He bent over, the air clearly knocked out of him, then she gave her opponent an almost ladylike *thunk* on the back of the head with the bat. He crumpled like a beeswax candle in a hot oven.

Winnifred was looking around, an eager gleam in her eye for her next victim, when Gibson Todd materialized out of nowhere. Darting glances all around me, I checked the area for Hopkins, but there was no sign of him.

Before I could figure out why Gibson had shown up without Hopkins in tow, Gibson started closing in on Winnifred, working his hands in what I'd learned from Mr T during my mentorship was one of the killing hexes. I was just about to shout for her to watch herself, when suddenly a walrus was bounding onto the scene.

Honestly, I didn't think Oberlin could move that fast. He shoved aside another witch hunter who lost his balance and fell back on a pike one of the ghosts — the Edwardian-clad one with the still-empty buttonhole — had hurriedly shoved into place.

Unfortunately, the scream and gurgling cries of the dying witch hunter alerted Gibson Todd to Oberlin's presence. Both men threw their spells at the same time. Oberlin really should have listened to his own advice: You never go into a dangerous situation without first putting up a Shield Spell. I mean, it's Policing 101. But I suppose when you're trying to save your lady love from a deranged and traitorous photographer, you lose your sense of reason.

As such, Wesley went in unprotected. He threw his spell, a killing one Winnifred told me later. But with Oberlin's magic still weak, and his opponent already behind his own Shield Spell, it merely caused Gibson to stagger back a few paces rather than kill him. As such, Gibson was able to cast his own attack spell, and Oberlin took a direct hit of an Exploding Heart Charm to his chest. He howled in pain, then keeled over just as Winnifred ran up and hit a home run with her cricket bat.

And yes, I'm well aware that cricket doesn't have home runs, but I know absolutely nothing about cricket, and the hit to Gibson's skull looked very home-runny to me.

Regardless of what you call it, Gibson Todd dropped like a heap of dirty towels, his blood staining the grass beneath him.

Winnifred dashed over to Wesley and dropped to her knees beside him, but my attention was pulled away from her grief by a reedy voice shouting my name.

Throughout all of this, I'd kept hold of the caged jewel, not knowing when I might need it or even how to use it. At the sound of my name, my hand reflexively tightened on the cage, and I jerked around to face where the angry beckoning had come from. A clock chimed. It was exactly one hour since Alastair had sent his text. Hopkins might be a misguided, psychotic zealot, but at least he was punctual.

And I, having stepped out to watch Winnifred, was fully exposed to the attack spell he was throwing at me.

CHAPTER FORTY-THREE
FOOT-STOMPING FUN

As I ducked away from Hopkins's attack, Alastair, who'd been keeping an eye on things from one of the nearby walls, shouted, "Cassie! Run!" directly into my head via a Comm Spell.

I'm not exactly the kind of gal who wants the man in my life telling me what to do, but right then wasn't a moment to argue my independence. I ran, trying to get to a space where I could have a bit of cover while I did my best against Hopkins.

I tripped over a cobblestone as I narrowly dodged a bolt of red light. Its flash bore a frightening resemblance to the Exploding Heart Charm the Mauvais once used on Alastair. The attack missed me, but only because my clumsiness had sent me tumbling. I crashed down hard on my side. So, while I was thrilled to still have a beating heart, I had to pay for that survival with a throbbing hip.

I struggled to get up, knowing I had only seconds before another killing hex would be lobbed at me. Suddenly, as if everyone had shifted places, fighting was going on all around me. Martin, some elves, and Chester were forcing back a dozen witch hunters and had ended up between me and Hopkins.

Hopkins, taking advantage of a gap in the fighters, lifted his hands for another spell. I don't know what I'd done in my fall, but I couldn't get my leg under me. I threw up a Shield Spell, but it would do nothing if Hopkins could get close enough. Also, I worried that in my state of near panic, I might screw up, forget to drop the Shield, and end up bouncing my own attack spell back on myself. Terrific stuff for the magical comedies Alastair had introduced me to. Not so terrific in a fight to the death.

Chester stomped his way through as Martin took a hit to the shoulder with a dagger someone had lobbed at him. Hopkins marched toward me, and I readied myself to execute a Stunning Spell as soon as the path was clear. Drop the Shield, throw the spell. That's all I had to remember. Drop the Shield, throw the spell. That's all I had to do.

I then realized that's not all I had to do. Apparently, multi-tasking while fighting for my life is not one of my top skills.

I scrambled the sheet with the reversed spell from my pocket. I didn't need to worry about Stunning Hopkins if I could just call out a few lines of text. I cleared my throat, fully ready to annunciate every word on the page.

With Hopkins's path riddled with elves on the rampage, I turned my attention to the sheet.

Where I found not a single word.

I turned the sheet over, darting glances at Hopkins as he approached. Thankfully, he was unable to get a clear line of sight through the various fighters. I checked the sheet again. Still no words. *Why were there no words on the page!?* I mentally exclaimed.

Then it dawned on me: Morelli had not only copied the page, but also the book's shifting nature. I tried various revealing charms, but the spell refused to appear. Let me just say, I was getting really sick of disobedient reading material at this point.

Hopkins stepped around a trio of witch hunters who were facing off against Rafi. The distance between us was rapidly narrowing and would soon render the Shield Spell useless.

Chester's heavy stomping came again as I heard Rafi shout something that sounded very much like *Sticky Fingers*. I dared a glance over to see the three goons unable to stop their hands from joining, like the world's most bizarre round of Ring Around the Rosie. When they tried to pull their hands away from each other, thick strings of what looked like rubber cement held them together.

Rafi and his spells, I mused.

Rafi and his spells!

I would have let out a cry of joyful insight, but that was right when I noticed Hopkins now had a direct line of attack.

I threw down the sheet, kept hold of the jewel with one hand, and with my free hand, made a twisting motion near my nose as I hesitantly muttered the spell.

Nothing happened. I scrambled back as if I could hide under a stone bench and Hopkins would completely forget I was ever there. Was my magic on the fritz again? Had the jewel sucked all my power from me? Had I—

Had I suddenly become an idiot?

I'd forgotten to drop the Shield Spell. Thankfully, my uncertainty in delivering a spell I'd never used before meant it hadn't bounced back on me.

Again, the hand motions that resembled sign language, the Latin-esque words, the intention, the confidence, the visualization. And all that sounds simple, but keep in mind, I was in a lot of pain at this point and I had the president of the Kill Cassie Club closing in on me.

But only for another moment.

Because in the next moment, Matthew Hopkins dropped to the ground. He sprouted black fur, and a naked tail slithered out from his backside. His face lengthened, his body shrank, and his clothes did as well. And seriously? A rat gussied up in seventeenth-century garb? I have to admit it was pretty cute.

Hopkins's whiskers twitched, his senses probably on overload as he took in all the smells and sensations that would be unnoticeable to a human but would be blaring messages to a rodent.

"Chester! A rat!" I shouted.

Chester whipped around, spotted *Rattus hopkinsii,* and a very disturbing smile of delight spread over his face. (Personally, I think Rafi might need to address this rodent bloodlust of Chester's sooner rather than later.) Chester raised his heavily booted foot. Hopkins had time enough to utter one final ratty squeak before the boot came down.

I'd never been so satisfied by the sound of crunching bones.

The instant Hopkins was crushed, the jewel blazed with power. And now that I look back on it, it was one of those moments where I probably should have let my butterfingers take over and fumbled the jewel out of my hand. Or dropped it. Or done whatever it took to get as far from it as possible.

But damn it, I had worked really hard to find, retrieve, and assemble all those jewel pieces. The Boncoeur Jewel had restored my magic and given me the power I needed to defeat Hopkins. So, I held on, gripping it in my hands.

A rushing sensation crashed through me. You know when you stand up too fast and you feel like all your blood and sense of balance has fallen to your feet? It was like that, but rather than my blood dropping to my toes, my very being surged into the jewel which began glowing more brightly.

That's when I dropped it.

We call that a too-little-too-late moment.

The jewel clattered to the ground, rolling off and settling into a crack between two cobblestones.

Trepidation filled me. I'd had this feeling before. I wouldn't say I ever really notice my magic, just like you don't notice the hair on your head most of the time. But get a drastic haircut, and all the sudden all you feel is the difference in your scalp, the lack of something that was just there. That's how I felt then. The lack of something. The difference.

I tentatively pushed out my hand to perform a Shoving Spell, hoping to move the jewel just a bit. It remained still. The prophecy had been wrong. I didn't have to die to destroy Hopkins, but in killing him I had killed what I was: a Magic.

Which was really annoying because, I mean, seriously, I had the Boncoeur Jewel. Matilda was still alive, and she could sign off on a job done. I could get my license and become a magic detective. Only, as a person without magic, I wouldn't be allowed to have a life in MagicLand.

Irony is so annoying.

CHAPTER FORTY-FOUR
DRAGON DIGESTION

With Hopkins's death, many of the witch hunter army who'd witnessed it lost their zeal to fight. Still, there were plenty of others who had no qualms about carrying on the nutcase's work. I shouted to Rafi to use the Rat Charm, and the witch hunters around him soon fell under the heavy boot of a very pleased Chester.

Over the course of the next couple of hours, the vampires ravaged through a large number of the enemy; the ghosts sent dozens of our foes fleeing in trauma-inducing fear; and, when a cluster of witch hunters nearly gained the upper hand over one of our contingents, Caliban swooped in and aimed his flame with surprising precision, turning the bad guys into ash and dust that swirled about on the wind.

And now that I think of it, the fact that we were all breathing in witch hunter cremains as we regrouped and surveyed our losses is more than a little disturbing.

As the mayhem wrapped up, we gravitated (and I limped until Chester slapped his large hand on my hip and instantly healed the bruising) to the vantage point of the wall nearest to Wakefield Tower. From there we could observe both the inner grounds of the

Tower of London to one side and the Thames to the other. It also gave an unobstructed view of the ravens treating themselves to some scattered bits of witch hunter. Rather disgusting to observe, but also completely satisfying.

"At least the Ravenmaster won't have to prepare any meals for them today," said Nigel in his usual helpful tone. Tilia hovered by his side. "Will this be cleared up by opening time tomorrow, do you think?"

At this, Daisy, Runa, and a few others who had been weakened by whatever evil Hopkins had cast over the magic world, tested out their Shoving Spells to shift a few nearby body parts and broken weapons into a tidy pile. My parents followed this up with a Sparkling Clean Charm to wash away the blood left behind, and Rafi threw in a Guts Be-Gone Hex that I was pretty sure was just him making stuff up to lighten the mood.

"Perhaps if we get a few more hands on deck, we might be able to manage it," replied Olivia while scowling at the extent of the mess the battle had left behind.

Not far from us was Matilda Marheart. She stood before her vampire kin and looked very much the ruler as they listened to her intently and debated what rewards to give Caliban when they got home — an entire cow was bandied about.

Needing to take care of some business, I approached Matilda, but didn't interrupt her. When Martin saw me politely, and perhaps a bit impatiently, waiting, he cut his sister off and asked the other vampires to give us some space.

"I believe this is yours," I said, and held out the Boncoeur Jewel to the mayor.

Matilda took the caged gem and examined it, her face showing her delight as the stone's red sparkle reflected in her eyes. Which, I'll be honest, gave her a rather sinister look. I mean, come on, a vampire with glowing red eyes? The stuff of nightmares, right?

"This is my father's jewel," said Tilia, who had drifted away from Nigel's side, her eyes lighting up at the sight of the thing. "He cut this. I recognize it."

"Wait," said Matilda. "Your father? When were you born?"

Tilia shrugged. "Sometime in 1300s?"

"But every story has William Boncoeur cutting the original jewel, then making the box for it during Elizabethan times," I said.

"Yes, William Boncoeur," Tilia agreed, her face warm with pride. "He have similar name in my homeland, but my native language is difficult for English tongues to pronounce, especially names. So he change it to more Western version when we come to England.

"The king of my homeland hired my father to cut a rare stone, and my father did as requested. Did very beautiful work, no?" She gestured to the Boncoeur Jewel. "Jewel very special, so he put extra work into the commission. Extra facets for the— How you say?" She twinkled her fingers.

"Sparkle?" I suggested.

"Yes, this. But then the king—" her eyes darkened "—he not pay for the work and put my father in prison. So my father, very clever man, worked revenge magic into the jewel. Did not go as planned," she conceded, "but king eventually suffer. You do not tangle with my people."

This all struck me as eerily similar to the tale Dodding had told me in his office when I'd gone to visit him with Dr Torres, but I was still having trouble grappling with how Tilia was tied to William Boncoeur.

"So, was it a descendant of your father's who made the box and cut the jewel into pieces for Elizabeth?" I asked.

"No, William Boncoeur," Tilia said, with the impatience of a teacher speaking to a pupil who just doesn't get the difference between a noun and a verb. "My father. *He* is craftsman who make jewel for the king of my homeland. *He* is craftsman who cut jewel into five pieces for the queen of England. He also make box for it for first James of England."

"My brain hurts," I said, but Matilda had a certain knowing gleam in her eyes.

"Tilia, was your father a vampire?"

"Yes, of course," she replied, as if we should have known this all along.

"For the slower of us in the group," I said, "can we start again in your homeland." Tilia gave a curt nod of agreement. Recalling what Dodding had said about a servant girl possibly taking the jewel from an unjust, penny-pinching king who had lost his wife after a craftsman cursed a jewel the king had commissioned him to cut, I asked, "Were you a maid for the queen?"

"I was no maid," Tilia replied indignantly. "I was the Queen's Companion and Lady's Maid. Official title. Also, I was her cousin. Second cousin, I believe. Maybe third."

See, I'm not the only one who struggles with the degrees of cousinship.

"And you're a vampire, too?" I asked. Dodding had mentioned this queen had vampire blood in her, and how that was a highly sought-after trait in nobility back then.

"Of course. My father was full vampire. My mother was normal human, died soon after my birth. I am only half vampire, but the vampire side is very strong, and give me very long life until stupid English disease kill me. But yes, vampire. Now, do you want story or not?"

"Please, go on," I said, because some things were ticking into place but others just seemed to be bouncing off the surface of my skull. "Did you take the jewel? I mean, back a long time ago from the king of your homeland who imprisoned your father?"

"I had every right to. It was my father's jewel. The king never paid for it. So yes, one night, I slip the king a little sleeping draught. Okay, maybe a lot of sleeping draught. Then I take the jewel and free my father, and we flee. We end up going west and got good positions with a noble family. The wife was a strong Magic."

Dodding's story now clear in my mind, I asked, "Was this Jacquetta, by any chance?"

"Yes, exactly," Tilia said, brightening at the mention of her former mistress's name. "Vampires were losing former status as Magics took more power, but Jacquetta was welcoming. She recognize the power and beauty of my father's jewel and she pay very large sum for it. My father was glad to have someone who appreciated his work. The household eventually move to England, my father and I as well. He created fine pieces, the best the courts had ever seen. And I, as highly sought-after lady's maid, knew just how to make noble ladies look most fashionable and beautiful.

"Jacquetta's people accepted us for what we were, so my father and I stay in her family for generations. Passed down, I suppose you would say. Just like the jewel that was given to her daughter, and so on until we and the jewel end up in court of Queen Elizabeth — first one, not second. I friendly with her before she inherited crown, so it was difficult to call her *queen* for many months." Tilia smiled at the memory. "She found it funny. Nobles not so much. I even help her dress for her coronation. Very—" Again, she twinkled her fingers.

"So your father," I said, trying to clarify this wallop of information, "not a descendant of his, was both the original craftsman of the Boncoeur Jewel *and* the person who Elizabeth asked to cut the Boncoeur Jewel into these five pieces."

"That, as you say, about sums it up. I saw jewel pass from generation to generation until it get to Elizabeth. While I served her, I met a man, very nice fellow, high-ranking vampire, and we had two babies — twins are very common in my family. But personal happiness and status with queen are not enough to stop stupid English disease. I tell you," fire flashed in her dark eyes, "I was very angry when I die. I had so much to live for.

"My father, he survive stupid English disease, and he become part of King James court after Elizabeth die. My father did not like James, and James did not like any kind of Magics, so my father decide to return to our homeland. I still visit him on occasion. Of course, he always say not often enough," she added with a roll of her eyes.

We all stood there in dumb silence for several moments. Finally, Matilda spoke, "Tilia, I believe we're related. I'm a descendant of William Boncoeur. I'm a little lost on exactly how, something to look into later, but the Marhearts are a branch from the Boncoeur line."

"So, we are like cousins?"

"Of a sort, but that's not my point," said Matilda. "My point is that the jewel truly belongs to you. Since you're William's daughter, his direct descendant, not some random side shoot on the family tree like me, you should have it. It's only right."

"I do not want that thing." Tilia's nose wrinkled. "Firstly, I am ghost, clothes are nothing but illusion, so jewel fall right out of pocket if put there. Secondly, that jewel already cause so much pain in my life. Pain to my father, pain to my cousin the queen, and then this pain." She swept out her arm to indicate all the fallen fighters below us. "It is a bad thing. You do what you like with it, My Cousin the Mayor and Vampire Queen. Official title," she added with a wink.

Matilda grinned at this, thanked Tilia, then turned to me.

The Unexpected Mr. Hopkins

"I suppose I owe you a signed contract," she said. "And payment, of course."

"Whenever you can get to it," I replied with a shrug. It didn't seem like the time or place to go chasing down paperwork and IOUs.

Winston chose that moment to swoop down and land on my shoulder. His talons dug in and were probably ruining the only part of my shirt that wasn't already a mess. I reached up to scratch his head and asked Matilda as casually as I could, "So, what will you do with the jewel now? Have the box reset with it?"

Or use it to defeat your Magic enemies and claim your place as Queen of the Vampires? was what I was really thinking. But the contract hadn't been signed yet, and like I've said, I do know a couple things about basic customer service.

Matilda thought for a moment. Then she waved her hand over the jewel. The spell conjured an exact copy. Exact, except this one remained whole without any need of a wire cage.

"I think this," she indicated the copied gem, "will fit nicely into the jewel box. Could you hold that for a moment?"

I took the new jewel, then noticed another difference: it gave off no hum of magic.

Matilda, meanwhile, held tightly to the original jewel, muttering a few words while undoing the cage. With a flash of red light, the wire frame was off, and the true Boncoeur Jewel was in pieces once again. Matilda plucked out one, the one that had been in the ring, and offered it to Alastair. She gave him a wink and said, "I believe you had plans for this."

Alastair's cheeks turned redder than a Yeoman Warder's overcoat. He didn't make any move to take the gem — which had reverted back to green once out of the cage — but Matilda wasn't taking no for an answer. "I know you had plans for this, and I don't think it will cause any further problems." She then placed the piece into Alastair's hand and closed his fingers around it.

Matilda then passed the pendant's stone to my mom. After eyeing the gem a moment, my mom said, "I think it's best we keep these things as far from each other as possible, don't you?"

All of us readily agreed, and my mom hurled the pendant's gemstone into the Thames. I have to say I was surprised at how strong her throwing arm was. I reminded myself to suggest she sign up for the Rosaria softball team. If there was one.

Matilda then gave Clive's marble to Winston. "You get rid of that wherever you like, young man." Winston took the piece in his beak and flew off in a northerly direction. Two hours later, he returned empty-handed. Or empty-beaked, I suppose.

This left two remaining pieces of the jewel in Matilda's hand. The one from Winnifred's brooch and the one from the tiara.

"We can take this to Winnifred in a bit. As for the tiara's piece, should we give it to your contact to return it to the museum?"

Morelli shook his head. "My contact can just work a Replacement Charm on it. The art museum won't know the difference."

"As for the original piece…" began Matilda. She then called Caliban to her. The dragon hovered like a hummingbird beside the wall as she tossed the jewel to him. He caught it in his mouth like a dragon who's practiced that trick with plenty of treats. "Not for digestion," she said in a gently scolding tone.

"But won't he just poop it out?" I asked.

"If told not to digest, his firebox will incinerate the jewel before it ever reaches his gut. A handy feature of dragon anatomy, don't you agree?"

I did. I also agreed that I was now very curious to study dragon anatomy. Perhaps I could become a dragon veterinarian. You know, just in case the whole detective thing doesn't work out.

CHAPTER FORTY-FIVE
THE STOIC HERO

Although most of the jewels were now dispersed, hidden, and incinerated, I still worried. The truth of it was, no spell had been performed to render these gemstones powerless, and they'd already proven they wanted to be together. They had crossed time and distance to stay close to each other. They had found their way to me to be rejoined. Who's to say they wouldn't eventually wreak fresh havoc on some other unsuspecting victim of Banna's bad prognostication poetry?

Also, the jewel had absorbed my magic. That would make it more powerful than ever, giving the possessor unimaginable strength against his or her enemies. And there were world leaders these days that would do anything for that kind of power.

But I kept these thoughts to myself. You know, stoic hero and all that.

Still, I had questions. About ten million of them.

"Okay, so we're going under the assumption that my magic went wacky because I was near a piece of the jewel, right?" I asked Runa as we worked our way up to the medical ward where someone said Winnifred had gone — likely having dislocated her shoulder with as hard as she'd been swinging that cricket bat. I wasn't sure how badly she'd take seeing her mother-in-law's jewel while grieving the loss of Oberlin, but it wouldn't be the hardest thing I'd contended with that day.

Olivia had insisted on going with us to offer her condolences, Morelli had come along to check on his injured troops, and Alastair had come along as well because he said he never wanted to be apart from me again. I swear he says sentimental stuff like that just to see if I'll start blubbering with emotion.

"Right," Runa replied. "Your magic problem starting before you'd ever found Clive's marble never did make sense to me. But, Alastair, you had the ring in the workroom the whole time, didn't you?"

"Well, not the whole time," Alastair admitted. "I'd asked my grandmother for it a little bit before then. Remember how the electricity started being weird?" he asked me. "It was right after I'd picked up the ring."

"The ring's magic broke the electricity?"

"Yeah, so stop blaming my electric panel," said Morelli, whose t-shirt had been repaired, the unicorn on the front proudly glittering once again.

"That was likely the start of it," Runa said. "Magic can have an effect on Norm technology. We've mostly adapted to it with various types of Insulation Charms, but a powerful object can screw up all sorts of things like electric panels, cell phones, car batteries."

"That still doesn't explain why my magic was affected before anyone else's was."

"I don't know why, either. Maybe the pieces of the Boncoeur Jewel were sensing your part in the prophecy, or perhaps there was some power still within them to bring down an enemy."

"They couldn't have known I was an enemy," I scoffed.

"No, that's why your power would surge one minute, then

struggle the next. The jewel was confused as to your real intentions. And the more pieces you found, the more 'wonky', as you put it, your magic got. Until the Boncoeur Jewel was whole, it wouldn't be able to sort out what side you were on. Once whole, though, the prophecy would kick in and it would do whatever was needed against whichever worst enemy was at hand."

I shook my head scornfully. "You all really need to stop imbuing your inanimate objects with unlimited power like that. It's becoming a little problematic."

Runa stopped to catch her breath on one of the landings and said, "Well, we can't stop what Magics in the past have done to their belongings." A worrying thought if there ever was one. "There could be dozens of these problematically enchanted objects out there. We'll just have to deal with them as they crop up."

"Deal with them? Deal with them?!" I griped. "You do realize that this 'dealing with them' seems to put me smack in the middle of risking life and limb to save the fate of the world just a little too often, right?"

"Well, practice makes perfect," quipped Morelli. I glowered at him. "What? It all worked out in the end."

For some it had, I thought morosely, as Alastair took my hand and I felt no sensation of magic flowing between our palms.

"But what about those of us who had Cassie's magic in our systems?" asked Alastair. "Why were we not affected by the witch hunters robbing Magics of their power?"

Runa shrugged. "You expect me to have answers for everything?" We looked at her in a way that said, *Of course we do*. "Best guess? The witch hunters were meant to leave Cassie and her magic alone for Hopkins to deal with personally. That made you, Busby, Tobey, Simon, and Chloe, and your magic, the opposite of collateral damage. Trust me. I'll be doing a ton of research into this. It'll involve sample collection," she told me with a wicked grin.

I had to assume she'd be coming to Real Portland to get those samples, because without any magic in my system, my access to her clinic in MagicLand was now closed. I bit back the tears that tried to well up at the thought, and couldn't believe I was getting weepy over not having to give magic samples on a daily basis.

Also, I know I'm emotional and teary-eyed a lot in this book, but I mean, look at all this rushing around, nearly dying, and battling evil I've been doing. Don't tell me you wouldn't be physically and emotionally exhausted.

When we reached the medical ward, it didn't take long to spot Winnifred. Her back was turned to us as Jake the Nurse dressed a wound on her arm. We all stopped in our tracks, as if not wanting to be the first to approach the grieving widow.

Okay, I say 'we all stopped', but during all the stair climbing, my shoe had come untied, and I tripped over it as we entered, drawing everyone's attention, including Winnifred's.

She turned and, upon the sight of me, sneered.

CHAPTER FORTY-SIX
WINNIFRED'S GRIEF

"Hey, Winnifred," I said cautiously. "How are you doing?"

"This arm hurts worse than a hibernating ogre smells, but it's manageable."

Apparently, the sneer — more of a grimace, now that I think of it — was due pain, not me, because she was speaking brightly. Like someone who's just been part of a winning team, not like someone who's just lost their husband. Then again, if I'd been married to Oberlin, I might be feeling pretty peppy over his demise, too.

"I have the jewel from your brooch." I held it out like an offering. "The brooch itself… well, it was in my safe, and I don't know where it is now. But I thought you'd want this. Considering."

"The brooch is missing?" she said, dramatically exaggerating feigned disappointment. "Oh my, that is terrible news."

"You aren't upset?"

"Cassie, that was the most hideous piece of jewelry I ever had the misfortune to own. I only wore it when Wesley insisted. And from what I understand, part of it became a little troublesome?"

"Just a tad," I said.

"We'd prefer the jewel be destroyed," said Olivia, "but it's yours, so it's up to you what happens to it."

Winnifred thought a moment, then a devilish smile crept along her lips. "There's a volcano going off in Iceland that would be a perfect place for it. Too bad I can't send the rest of that gaudy peacock along for the ride. Just don't tell Wesley, okay?"

Now, I know I have a habit of chatting to ghosts and dead people, but this last comment struck me as odd. Also, considering she had Jake right there, it was a little weird the woman wasn't acting the least bit upset. Seems a little pretense of grief would be appropriate, don't you think?

"There you go, ma'am," said Jake. "The bandages are enchanted to release some pain-relieving charms that'll start taking effect any minute now. You can go see Mr Oberlin in room thirty-four, whenever you're ready."

"Yes, I suppose I should go pay him a visit," she said grudgingly, then her face softened. "He did save my life, after all. That's kind of sweet, isn't it?"

"A brave final deed," I said, wondering how the packed-to-the-rafters medical ward was able to dedicate a whole room to store a single corpse for viewing.

"Final?" Winnifred scoffed. "Hardly. As soon as he's recovered, I've got a list of chores for him that he's been neglecting."

"I'm sorry. What? Isn't he... Um... Well, *dead*?"

"Dead? No, just sleeping, I'd imagine. Although I'd like to kill him sometimes when he starts snoring."

"But he took a direct hit with an Exploding Heart Charm."

"His pacemaker..." Jake began, but then seemed unsure how to explain things. "I don't know quite how it worked, but it protected his heart, kept the cardiac muscle pumping despite the spell. You'd have to ask the medics if you want the exact mechanisms, but something about the Norm technology in the pacemaker canceled out the magic. Usually, it's the opposite way around, but you just never know with magic."

Something I didn't need to be told twice.

"Come on, let's go pop in and see him. He's got some apologies and amends to make," Winnifred said with a bitterness that was clearly for Old Walrus Face, not me. "That man. I swear, Cassie, sometimes you just do not know the person you're living with."

Given that Alastair had a bad habit of creating things that risked destroying the world, I understood exactly what she meant.

"Oh, hairy troll testicles," Oberlin groaned when I entered the room. "Am I not feeling awful enough?"

"Wesley," snapped Winnifred, "you will treat this young woman with more respect. Starting with some explanations for your behavior lately."

The Inspector crossed his arms belligerently over his chest and looked about as stubborn as a toddler staring down a plate of broccoli. Winnifred marched up to his bed, hovering over it like a hawk over a tasty piece of squirrel.

"You are doing this and anything else I ask of you, Wesley Seymour Oberlin, or Glinda help me, I will give the *Necromancer Enquirer* that interview they've been hounding me for. And you know how in-depth they can be with their *personal* questions."

"What do I have to do?" Oberlin asked without hesitation. Which was really unfortunate, because I'd have loved to find out exactly what he had to hide. Or, wait, maybe I didn't.

"Answer Cassie's questions," Winnifred told him. "Cassie, go on."

"Um..." I hesitated, unsure which of the Walrus's foibles to address first. "I guess you can start with what you have against me?"

"Well, you did call him Walrus Face," suggested Alastair.

"Oh, come on. I can't have been the first one. Even Chester noticed the resemblance," I said. Oberlin, to his credit, gave a self-deprecating shrug. "So, what's the deal? Did you have a crush on my mom, then my dad was mean to you when you guys were teenagers?"

"Cassie, this isn't a Harry Potter novel," complained Olivia.

"She's kind of right," muttered Oberlin. "But the other way around. I had a crush on your dad, but I worried everyone would make fun of me. I saw how Simon was with Alastair, and I thought there was a chance for me. But then I realized he was only being nice to Alastair because Chloe was nice to Alastair, and that Simon was over the moon only for Chloe. Holding in my disappointment over the matter may not have been the healthiest thing to do."

"And so you took it out on me? You kicked me out of the Academy for it? That's mental."

"No, I took it out on you because you were a smart ass and a powerful Magic who seemed to know her way around a legal matter and an enforcement spell better than me. Do you know how long it took me to master a Stunning Spell? A Freezing Charm? A Subduing Hex? Ages. But here you show up with hardly any training, and you're whipping up incantations like you've been doing them your whole life. I felt like that Salieri guy in the *Amadeus* movie. Work work work, and then along comes the protégée who runs circles around the melody he's striven so hard to compose."

"So, you were envious? Of me?" I asked, nearly floored with incredulity. "Did you think I wanted your job or something?"

"Yes. Basically. You had the backing of HQ. You had the support of Busby Tenpenny. You were Simon and Chloe Starling's daughter. You'd have been a shoo-in if it came to a vote."

"So you kicked me out to keep me from going anywhere in the Academy? And I walked right into it by calling you Walrus Face?"

"I may have provoked you by not moving the classes along a little more quickly. I'd heard you weren't good with patience."

"Can we just admit that neither of you were at your best?" said Winnifred. Oberlin and I shrugged half-heartedly. "Go on, say it's a truce."

"Truce," we reluctantly said together. Then, with a sigh of defeat, Oberlin said, "If you want to join the Academy's next cohort, I'd be glad to let you in. You are a good detective."

"Thanks, but I think I've got too many issues with authority to join the ranks. Still, if you need a consulting magic detective, you know where to find me."

"Yeah, like I'm going to do that. Now, if you don't mind, I'd like to spend some time with my wife."

"But I thought you liked—" I began.

"Stop being so binary, Black," Oberlin criticized.

"Wesley," Winnifred goaded, "wasn't there something else you had to say?"

After several moments of Oberlin clearly fighting with himself, he finally said the most grudging words I'd ever heard out of anyone's mouth. "You did pretty well out there, from what they tell me."

"I wasn't too shabby. And you'll probably be glad to know I'm going to have to leave Rosaria." I waggled my fingers. "Empty tank."

Oberlin quirked his lips, and I thought he was holding back a smug grin. He didn't say anything, though. Just sat there contemplating, debating something in his own mind. I was about to excuse myself from the awkward silence, when he let out a lengthy exhale through his nostrils that ruffled his bristly mustache.

"My jacket," he said, pointing to a dark blue policeman's jacket hanging over a chair. I grabbed it and handed it to him. He fished around in an inner pocket. Recalling the number of pain-inducing tools that could be stashed in a Magic policeman's coat, I started to back away just as Oberlin pulled his meaty hand out and said, "Here."

Nervously, I held out my own hand, palm up. He dropped six vials into it. Collection vials. Like the ones Runa used.

"What are these?" I asked, although I had a hopeful suspicion.

"I stole them from Runa's when I took the saw. I planned to give them to my contacts, but something in me just couldn't give them the type of weapon your damn magic could provide."

"Wait. My samples?" I asked, glaring at Oberlin. "Those weren't for you. They were for my parents."

"You purposely bungled the investigation into the break-ins at Runa's clinic, didn't you?" Winnifred accused. This was clearly the first time she was hearing about this, and I wondered what else she didn't know about her husband's recent behavior.

"A little."

"But Hopkins took my magic from the vials," I said. "I saw him do it."

Oberlin shook his head. "I also grabbed a few random samples. Pretty sure Tenpenny's was in there, but the others, they were probably just from some people's annual check-ups."

Cold realization crept all over me. In the Tower, Hopkins must have taken in Tobey's magic. That would explain why he was able to throw killing spells at me. Luckily, I'd been able to dodge them. But in the Globe, where I had stood exposed to every spell he aimed at me, Hopkins must have cracked open the vial from some random Magic whose power would have been drained by the witch hunters' meddling.

My gut went queasy again. Talk about your life hanging on a literal luck of the draw.

"But you did steal them. And you kept them. Were you going to take my magic for yourself?" I accused. Who knew walruses could be so duplicitous?

"Thought of keeping them for myself," Oberlin admitted. "Then I decided I'd give them to Tobey for a boost before his final stab at the Exams. But—" he seemed about to stop, but Winnifred gave him The Look "—you deserve them."

When I looked confusedly at the vials, the nurse on duty said, "You just pop that end bit off and hold the open edge against your palm. You'll want to space them about an hour apart, otherwise you'll get too strong of a hit, and I really don't need another patient to tend to."

I did as she said with one of the vials. The magic surged into me with a tingling sensation that went from my skull to my toes. I dared to try the gentlest of Shoving Spells on the clipboard at the foot of Oberlin's bed. The pages fluttered, and my unrestrained smile made my cheeks ache. It was good to be back. Again.

"And now, Wesley," began Olivia, "I believe you have a few things to tell Winnifred. And," she added when Oberlin balked at her advice, "I'd suggest you tell her everything before it comes out in the tribunal."

Once we'd left the room and pulled the door closed for privacy, Olivia said, "I suppose the Council on Magic Morality will have to decide a punishment for him. He may not have intended it, but he did betray us when he handed over those jewels to the witch hunters."

Just then, there came shouting from the direction of Oberlin's room. Shouting that sounded very similar to Winnifred's war cry.

"You gave the witch hunters what!?" Winnifred shrieked. "Of all the stupid—"

Olivia threw a Silencing Spell around the room, abruptly cutting off my entertainment. "Although," she continued, "Wesley will be enduring Winnifred's wrath over his poor judgement for the foreseeable future. That might be punishment enough."

"It wouldn't hurt to have the Council's sentence ready when she cools down, though, would it?" I suggested. "Winnifred might rain all the curses known to MagicLand down on Oberlin, but he nearly got me killed by a seventeenth-century zombie with bad teeth. That deserves some sort of official punishment, doesn't it?"

"It most certainly does," Olivia agreed, a broad and impish grin lighting her face.

As we left the medical ward, Alastair took my hand. The magic rushed between us like unrestrained electricity.

CHAPTER FORTY-SEVEN
CALENDAR COUNTDOWN

    Even with everyone's magic trickling back to its normal levels, Olivia couldn't hold to her promise to Nigel to get the Tower open by the morning after the battle. It ended up taking the rest of that day and well into the next to clean up the aftermath of the fighting. So, if you happened to be a tourist in London during that time, sorry about the Tower closure, but there were torn-up bits of battle victims all over the place. And, while visitors might love the torture exhibit, they probably don't want to see actual dead bodies scattered around the grounds.
    Then again, you just never know about people.
    Once the literal dust had settled, though, one of the first orders of business was to return Wordsworth's book to him. Mainly because he kept sending nasty emails to Olivia, complaining about my work ethic and how dare we all go 'gallivanting about' with vampires and ghosts when his collection still had such a gaping hole in it.
    With Rafi ready to work a form of Freezing Charm on the necessary pages of *An Enchanted History of the Portland Community* to keep them from shifting, I hesitated before opening the book. I mean, the thing had never caught on fire when I'd touched it before, but magic books, in my experience, seemed to have minds of their own.

"But do you think the pages *should* be copied?" I asked Olivia. "I mean, the words on them have caused quite the mess."

"You need your license," Olivia said, pointing to her calendar where the due date was flashing red. "With the Boncoeur Jewel broken apart, Matilda can't sign off on a job done, and neither can Winnifred nor your parents. The one item you can still make whole is the book, which, I hate to tell you, means Wordsworth is your only option."

"And," put in Mr T, "Fiona would never allow this book out of the Portland community for any length of time, so leaving the original with Wordsworth is not an option. Can you imagine us having to go to Wordsworth every time we need to add something to the Rosaria story?"

"I honestly can't think of anything worse," said Fiona. "However, these pages… I don't know if Matthew Hopkins could ever be raised again, but Cassie's right: the book remains a risk. Hopkins seems a determined bugger, and we've already seen— Cassie, you've got a look in your eye."

My cheeks flushed with heat as everyone turned to me. "I just had an idea: What if there was a little twist placed on the Duplex Spell?"

Rafi arched an eyebrow. "Spell crafting already? Took me until I was seventy-two years old before I started doing that."

"More like spell tinkering. You know how when you photocopy something, if you keep copying from a copy and then another copy from that copy, you'll eventually end up with something illegible?"

"Wordsworth won't take it if the book's not legible," said Olivia.

"No, we wouldn't do it to the whole thing. Just on these pages. You know, make a few words here and there a bit squidgy.

It would render the spell useless, and Wordsworth would be none the wiser."

"And even if he noticed, he'd never admit to his eyes going bad," Rafi said.

"Sounds like an excellent plan to me," Olivia agreed. When no one moved, she pointed to me. "Your idea, your magic."

I stepped forward, feeling the crush of performance anxiety. Rafi handed me a piece of top-quality paper that was a near match to that used in Wordsworth's book. I placed it over the first page in question, then conjured the Duplex Spell, picturing a hand-cranked mimeograph machine as I did so.

When Rafi lifted the copied page, he grinned approvingly.

"The third line of the spell, its letters are mushed together. I don't even know what that word is on the fifth line, and…" Rafi continued to critique my work until I snatched the sheet from him. I copied out the rest of what was missing from Wordsworth's book, and Rafi quickly scrutinized them. "It's good work. We'll make a spell crafter out of you yet."

"As long as it doesn't require licensing—" Rafi pulled a face. "It requires licensing, doesn't it?"

"Well, not to do it, but if you want to make the spell official, you have to register it and—"

"No, never mind. I've had enough with magic bureaucracy. Let's get these to Sebastian so he can do the repair, shall we?"

"With pleasure," Rafi said with a waggle of his dark eyebrows.

To get back to MagicLand while Bookman's Bookshop was still open, Olivia provided us with a time dilation portal — how she knew which of the beads at the end of her braids was the correct portal, I'll never figure out.

The flirting between Rafi and Sebastian started out cute. Unfortunately, there was no end to their coy banter, and my patience quickly grew as thin as the hair under a comb-over. If I was going to get my license in time, I needed to put a stop to their budding relationship faster than a conservative lawmaker from the Bible Belt.

"Oy! Book repair first. Flirting later. Or else just ask one another out and get it over with."

"Pushy pushy," teased Rafi.

Sebastian snorted a laugh. Then he caught sight of my scowl. "Right. Down to business."

It took Sebastian about twenty minutes to bind the pages securely into Wordsworth's book. Meanwhile, Rafi and I roamed the store, watching as books shifted from tattered paperbacks that should have been binned ages ago into hardbacks that looked as close to new as you could get.

"It's ready," Sebastian said after joining us in what looked like a newly renovated children's book section. When he showed us his work, there was no sign the pages were anything but the originals.

"Great, what do I owe you?" I asked. Then I caught the two of them looking knowingly at each other. "If either of you suggestively says something along the lines of *'I know how you can repay me,'* I will forever think of you as the two least witty people on the planet."

"Is she always like this?" asked Sebastian.

"Only ninety-five percent of the time," replied Rafi. Then, rather shyly, which surprised me, he said, "But if coffee could make up for all your help, I know of a place nearby. They have donuts," he added as if this was what was needed to seal the deal.

"Donuts would be great. We could go now. If that's okay with you, of course," Sebastian asked me.

"Fine with me." I pointed to Wordsworth's book. "I've got to get this back, anyway."

"Need help?" offered Rafi.

"I'm sure you'd rather stay here than go meet up with Wordsworth."

"I'd rather be trapped in a small enclosure with a rabid wolverine than meet up with Wordsworth." As if realizing his faux pas, he blushed and turned to Sebastian. "I didn't mean to imply you're a rabid wolverine or anything, it was just..." Sebastian was grinning at Rafi's discomfort. "Let me just say goodbye."

Rafi dashed over, swooping in and giving me a quick hug that I didn't even cringe away from. Then again, he'd done it very quickly, and, as an elf, he had that calming thing going on. He wished me luck, and I wished him the same. Although, I didn't think he was going to have any trouble hitting it off on his date.

With the book under a Lighten the Load Spell and the time dilation portal in hand. I zipped back to the Tower.

After examining the pages, Olivia was clearly impressed by Sebastian's work. "Then again," she admitted, "I'm not quite as *discerning* as Wordsworth. Should I call him in?"

"Yeah, let's get this over with," I urged, noticing that a sixty-minute countdown had just appeared by the due date on her calendar.

Wordsworth was not to be hurried, and nearly forty-five minutes ticked by before he waddled into the room. I was fine with that since most any wait in Olivia's office comes with, if not high tea, at least medium tea with scones, miniature tarts, and tiny sandwiches with various scrumptious fillings.

When he arrived, Wordsworth barely grumbled a greeting to

us before slithering over to the book. He inspected the binding and the pages, then stuck his face almost completely against the spine. When he stood up, his scrunchy face was made even scrunchier with the snarl on his lips.

"These aren't the original pages. I can smell elf magic on them."

"It will fade over time," Olivia said, appearing very calm and collected since her snacks had been accompanied by a gin and tonic, not an English Breakfast blend. "It's very good work Sebastian's done. And he is the best at repairs. I'm sure more than one tome in your collection has his signature on it."

"Yes, likely work undertaken before my time when the books were less well tended to. This is an embarrassment for me, a stain on my record of proper book care. If the other bookworms found out—"

"They'd probably all say they've used Sebastian at one point or other. And if they won't admit it," Olivia said conspiratorially, "I've got a complete record of Sebastian's work I could show you."

I didn't know if this was true, but if it was a bluff, it was a good one because Wordsworth relented, albeit very slowly and very reluctantly.

"I suppose it will do."

"Probably a bad time to bring this up," I said, "but I still don't understand why the copy at the British Library caught on fire."

"I had a feeling that was you," said Olivia. "Not at first, but I was beginning to suspect." To my sheepish look, she added, "We'll have Sebastian make a replacement copy when he gets time. As for the book itself, it had been protected with spells that sensed danger. It saw you as a threat."

"I only wanted to steal a few pages." Wordsworth gasped in

horror. "Not *steal* by ripping them out. We were just going to copy them, but I guess the spell on it protected it from damage?" I said doubtfully.

"It really wasn't protection from damage," clarified Olivia. "You had some of the pieces of jewel by then, didn't you?" I nodded. "The spell on the British Library's copy likely sensed the jewels on you. It would have been aware of any objects that could be used for ill purposes. Combine that with your intention to harm the book, and, well…"

I thought back, trying to recall that day. I'd gotten into the safe to get the rest of Lola's cookies. When I'd pulled the sack of sweets out, the marbles and the brooch had tumbled out as well.

"I'd handled a couple of the jewel pieces that day, but only briefly when I shoved them back into my safe. Could the spell be that sensitive?"

"Apparently. Books are wonderful things, but they're not always the best at sorting out the motives of their readers. It sensed the jewels, it sensed danger, and so it reacted."

"But then why didn't *An Enchanted History of the Portland Community* do the same thing?" I asked.

"Are you paying no attention?" snipped Wordsworth. "It was protected with a different sort of spell. The shifting was its protection. Do you truly think every book is under the same protective charms?"

"I think what Wordsworth is trying to say," said Olivia as she took a deep sip of her drink, "is that *An Enchanted History of the Portland Community* is a shifting book. *That* serves as its protection. Unlike Mr Wordsworth's copy, with its dangerous spells that can be read by anyone," she noted critically, "the Rosaria book only reveals its hidden side when it senses the person truly needs it for good reasons, honorable reasons." With a *beep*, the calendar began a five-minute countdown. Olivia barely gave it a glance, but my eyes locked on the declining numbers. "Now, Wordsworth, do you agree that Miss Black has found your book intact as per your agreement?"

"Well, close enough per our agreement. I wouldn't want to split hairs and say that this is not truly my original copy—" Olivia's eyes darkened, and even Wordsworth knew his limitations around a banshee. "It is fine."

"Then please sign off on a job complete." Olivia pushed the contract toward Wordsworth as the countdown ticked away.

His lips pinched with unspoken disapproval, Wordsworth took the pen Olivia offered him and signed the contract. I almost couldn't believe it and half expected the ink to disappear. For the paper to burst into flames. For tea to spill all over it and wash away the signature I'd so desperately needed.

But it didn't. The ink stayed put, and the paper didn't dissolve into ash. Even so, since I still hadn't officially submitted my application, the countdown — which had now reached the three-minute mark — continued.

Without a hint of gratitude, Wordsworth picked up his book and waddled out with it. Olivia breathed a sigh of relief. But I didn't. There was one more hurdle. Olivia dragged her finger along her glass to refill it as I sat perched on the edge of my seat. She took a long drink with a sigh of satisfaction, then caught me staring at her. Her eyes went wide.

"Oh yes. I nearly forgot." She glanced over the contract, then tapped her long finger on an empty line. "We still need a name for the agency on your application."

The due date hit the sixty-second mark, the numbers urgently flashing, but I didn't need any extra time to make my decision. It wasn't a name I would have chosen a few weeks ago, but now it seemed the obvious choice for my agency. The right choice.

"The Cassie Black Detective Agency," I said, knowing I'd grudgingly have to give Daisy credit for the idea.

"You rejected that name before," Olivia said.

"Yeah, but with the retraction in the *Herald* that Leo has promised, and the whole saving-the-world thing, I'm kind of hoping people won't hate me now. They might even want to work with me."

"So, are you saying you've found your place in Rosaria?"

"Let's hope so."

Olivia opened a drawer, pulled out a large rubber stamp, and, with fifteen seconds to spare, brought it down with a satisfying *thunk* on the contract. When she lifted it, it said *Denied*.

"What?" I complained, trying not to panic. "What did I not do?" I knew it had taken longer than it should have, but, still, I'd kind of saved all of Magic-kind, so what kind of bureaucratic B.S. was going on for her to deny my application?

"Oh, fairy farts! So sorry," Olivia blustered. "The damn pixies rearranged my desk drawers." She flicked her finger over the stamp, the ink shifted, and the mark changed to *Approved*. The countdown stopped with two seconds to spare.

Olivia held out her hand to shake.

"Cassie Black, you are now an official detective licensed by Magic HeadQuarters and sanctioned to work on any assignment, whether private or public sector, open or confidential. Congratulations and excellent work."

I waited a moment, then Olivia said, "What is it now, Miss Black?"

"Do I get a certificate to frame or a badge or something?"

"Oh yes, they should come in the mail within seven to ten business days."

"Of course they should," I groaned.

CHAPTER FORTY-EIGHT
CROCHET LESSONS

I'd been hoping for at least a few sandwiches and a platter full of cupcakes to appear on Olivia's desk to celebrate my officially becoming a licensed magic detective. But there was no time to celebrate as several other Magics arrived to barrage Olivia with questions. Olivia tipped her chin to indicate I could make my escape if I preferred.

I did prefer, and I left everyone to discuss things about... well, I don't exactly know because I wasn't in the room and this is a first-person narrative. On my way out, though, I caught sight of Morelli and Matilda huddled together just outside the Magics' door to the White Tower. Yes, I probably should have given them their privacy, but it's not like they were whispering, so the conversation was fair game for eavesdropping.

"So," I heard Morelli say awkwardly, "I was wondering if maybe you wanted to grab dinner sometime? Or, I was thinking of starting crochet lessons, if you wanted to be my first student."

"That sounds lovely, Genie, but I might be busy. Seems with the vampires having a stronger place in Magic society now, they want me to guide them on their way forward. The curse of being a queen, I suppose," she said with a self-deprecating shrug. "Once they get some direction, though, I should have more free time. But for now, for a few months, anyway, I'll be away from

Rosaria more often than not. I've already made arrangements to relinquish my mayoral duties."

"Right, I understand." Morelli scuffed the toe of his boot along the ground, then seemed to pull up a few pounds of bravado. "It was fun while it lasted, right?"

Matilda smiled at him, genuine warmth in her eyes for my lunkheaded landlord. There might also have been a bit of regret there as well. Which clearly proved she was out of her mind.

"You said something about crochet lessons?" she asked.

Morelli nodded. "Thought it would be a good way to share my passion."

Well, at least he wasn't sharing his passion for classic television reruns. Although, I could absolutely picture Morelli leading a book-club style meeting in which he set out cheap wine and savory treats and discussed the merits of *Laverne & Shirley*.

"Might these lessons be done online?" Matilda hinted, her porcelain pale cheeks warming. "Like as a video call type thing? I mean, it might not be the same, but if you wanted to try it... And, really, now that I think about it, after the first few weeks, I doubt my duties will take up *all* of my time. I could maybe bring my homework by now and then, and we could discuss it over dinner?"

Morelli lit up at this, and as I did not want to find out what Matilda's reward would be for getting an A+ on her granny squares, I left them behind to find Mr Wood.

I eventually spotted him chatting delightedly with Nigel, and was a little surprised to see my former boss dressed in hiking boots and knee-length khakis with a small rucksack slung over one shoulder. He was also clutching a highly polished walking stick that looked like it had been stolen straight from the Props for Gandalf Department.

"Ah, Cassie," said Mr Wood, beckoning me over. "Get over here and wish me well."

"Wish you well for what?" I scanned his outfit. "You going for a stroll?"

"No, well, yes, but not around here. I'm going to the Cotswolds. Bit delayed, but better late than never."

Something jolted in my stomach. It was a silly reaction, but Mr Wood had already gotten into trouble once trying to go on this walking expedition of his. Would he be pushing his luck if he tried again?

"Has Cotswolds Custom Tours sent someone to pick you up?" I asked, knowing I'd never feel comfortable with him setting off unless I saw him safely in the hands of the tour company. I would also be demanding the driver show me photo ID and at least seven other credentials.

"No, it's the most brilliant plan. Nigel, you tell her. It was your idea, after all."

Nigel stood up a little taller and said, "I'm going to be his tour guide."

"You?" I said, disbelief mixing with confusion and, well, all sorts of what-planet-have-I-landed-on sentiments.

"Of course. After all, I do have experience with that sort of thing. And Olivia says after my help with that little skirmish with those rather strange people, I've earned some time off. So, when I heard about the trip Nino had missed, I told him, why bother with all that tour bus flim-flam? Being carted here and there like a bunch of cattle? No, thank you. It'll be much more fun if I lead him on a guided walking tour of the Cotswolds. With a little help from my ghostly friends in Cirencester, of course."

"Nigel already knows all kinds of history about the place," said Mr Wood, his eyes gleaming with excitement. "It'll be perfect."

"What kind of history?" I asked dubiously. After all, before I'd set a few (okay, most) of his facts straight, Nigel had believed that the Tower of London had been built for London's Great Exhibition of 1851, much like the Eiffel Tower had been built for the Paris Exhibition of 1889.

"Like how the Cotswolds got its name by being the center of cot manufacturing during the Middle Ages," Nigel pronounced. "And how the town Slaughter was named because that's where Charles I slaughtered Oliver Cromwell."

Tilia materialized beside Nigel. She gave him a doting look, but there was also a large dose of skepticism in the arch of her dark eyebrows. A look that reminded me of exactly how Alastair looks at me when I tell him it was Pablo who got up on the counter and ate the last Spellbound scone.

"Pretty sure that's not right," I said.

"No?" queried Nigel.

"Makes for a good story, though," said Mr Wood enthusiastically. "You can find accuracy in any old history book. I like Nigel's versions of things. Creative."

"As do we," said another ghost — the prim and proper Edwardian-clad gentleman. He'd just appeared behind Nigel and Mr Wood with a dozen or so other ghosts who were all nodding their heads. "While we quite enjoy your Tower tours, Nigel, we'd be most delighted to hear these other clever tales of yours. And hearing them in a new location would be doubly splendid."

"Clever? Creative?" queried Nigel, blushing with shy pride while also seeming befuddled by the praise. "I'm just a chap telling a story in my own words. Now, if everyone's ready. The rest of you can meet us in Cirencester, where Maisy and Bernard are waiting for us outside of the bed-and-breakfast they're currently haunting. And," he added with a wink, "where they managed to sneak mine and Nino's names onto the registry."

"But how are you getting to this Chester-whatever-it-is-called?" asked Tilia, after struggling three times with the name of the Cotswold village.

"Olivia has set up a portal for us that, apparently, Nino can take us through. Isn't that marvelous?"

The ghosts all nodded while looking somewhat confused by this news. It was unlikely that any of them knew what a portal was or what it had to do with the round American in their midst. I, however, understood perfectly: Mr Wood was, and still is to this day, Magic, somehow regaining and holding onto his power unlike any Norm in recent memory. And yes, Dr Dunwiddle plans to study him as soon as she gets a chance.

"Nino, shall we?" suggested Nigel after Tilia had placed a quick peck on (and sort of *through*) Nigel's cheek before she and the ghostly group vanished.

"I suppose I'm off," said Mr Wood. I then caught a lily-scented whiff of his magic when he wrapped me in a warm hug.

A hug I didn't even try to resist. If you're the literary sort, you might call that character growth.

"Just make sure you come back in one piece. Both of you. Or, rather, all of you," I said, suddenly realizing that the tour would be ruined if the ghostly group crossed paths with an over-enthusiastic exorcist.

Which is not something I thought I'd ever have to worry about.

CHAPTER FORTY-NINE
THE FINAL UTTER FAILURE

If you've been keeping track, you might remember there's one more plot thread that needs tying off. Tobey's last stab at the Exams was scheduled not long after we returned from our Magical Battle Royale. And let me just say, Tobey would rather have faced another army of witch hunters, blindfolded with his hands bound and with zero magical abilities, than face another round of test taking.

"I can feel it," he said about two hours into the pre-Exam study session I'd agreed to. This, despite the three hours we'd done the previous day. His voice shook as he added, "I'm going to fail."

"Yes, you are," I told him. "Especially if you go in with that attitude."

"I don't have an attitude."

"Right. So, what do you want to tackle next?" I asked, even though I felt like we'd gone over every aspect of police rules and regulations at least a dozen times. And if Daisy had been quizzing him whenever I wasn't around, I don't know how Tobey wasn't repeating this stuff in his sleep.

"I don't know. How about the protocols for making an arrest, then crime scene procedures?"

I wanted to say we'd just done both of those fifteen minutes ago, that he'd answered every question I'd asked him with ease.

Instead, I asked, "Are those areas you screwed up during the last Exam?"

Tobey nodded. "And the most common statutes we needed to be aware of, the various civil liberties acts, the spells that were to only be used in an emergency, the—"

Basically, all the topics he'd aced in our previous practice sessions. When I gave him a you've-got-to-be-kidding look, he glanced away and muttered, "It would really help if you stopped asking me questions about my prior utter failures so we can get on to prepping me for my final utter failure. Arrest protocols. Quiz me."

I couldn't do it. I simply could not face hearing him answer the same questions over and over again. Promise or not, I would explode if any further quizzing took place. And no, I wasn't going to abandon my dear cousin. I had a better idea.

"Look," I said, darting a glance over my shoulder. No one was there, but I wanted Tobey to be aware that what I was about to say was very, *very* secret. "There is a way to get you through the test."

"I can't cheat, Cassie. I can't get kicked out like—"

"Like me?"

"Sorry, that was stupid of me."

"That's okay. I'm used to your stupidity. And it's not cheating. It's simply a type of memory charm that will make all this stuff stick. You'll be begging for a second test sheet just so you can share everything you've got stored in that pea brain of yours."

"I've only heard of spells that remove memories, not make them stick better. Besides, you keep saying I know this stuff, but when I get to the testing room, I don't."

"That's the way this works. It's one of Rafi's spells. He came up with it because of all that research Olivia was having him do. He was fine recalling stuff when he was in his office where the books served as a sort of memory catalyst, but once he got to Olivia's office or had to make a presentation to the Council, he'd forget half of what he'd found. Hence, he's named it the Memory Sticky Charm."

"One of Rafi's spells? Seriously?" he asked eagerly.

"Seriously," I confirmed, because everyone knew Rafi was the best spell crafter in recent magical memory.

"And he taught you how to do it?"

"Yeah. It's weirdly easy. And completely *not* cheating. You're not using anything but your own brain. Just a slightly enhanced version. Plus," I glanced around surreptitiously, then whispered, "I saved one of my sample vials from the ones Oberlin stole."

"You did?" Tobey exclaimed.

"Shhh, it's just a little boost. Runa told me students do it all the time."

"I don't know," he wavered, like he was in any position to back out of this obviously brilliant plan

"Come on, Tobey. It's too nice out to keep going over the same statutes and laws. You know this stuff, and this memory thing of Rafi's is perfect for your situation. That, plus my sample? You can't *not* pass. So," I goaded, "what do you say?"

"And it's not cheating?"

"It is *so* not cheating."

Tobey grinned, all trace of hesitancy gone.

"Alright, go for it. What do I have to do?"

"Sacrifice a goat, then eat the heads of three chickens that were slaughtered under the light of a full moon." Tobey's face went pale, but he still gave a weak nod as if he really were considering following my instructions. "Dude, I'm kidding. When's the last time anyone sacrificed a goat for a spell? Just sit there and don't move. I've got to aim this right at a certain spot in your brain for it to work."

His face full of relief at the lack of animal cruelty, Tobey straightened his back against the chair, sitting so rigidly he'd end up with a spinal injury if I didn't hurry.

I handed Tobey the vial and told him to hold it against his palm as I stood behind him, my fingers poised like I was about to clutch his skull. I racked my brain for the words to the spell, then cleared my throat and massaged his scalp as I said, "Stickum Cognitum."

Once I'd thoroughly messed up Tobey's perfect coif, I lowered my hands. Even so, he remained so still a meditation guru might take lessons from him.

"What are you doing?" I eventually asked.

"Letting the spell take hold," he said, speaking out of the side of his mouth as if making sure to move as little as possible.

"I think you're good," I said after another minute of waiting. "How do you feel?"

Tobey palpated his skull with his fingers. "Tingly."

"That's the spell." Or perhaps the peppermint pomade I could smell on his hair. "It's taken effect."

"How long does it last?"

"Six hours, at least. Plus, this is the first time you've had it done, so that means it will stick longer. Rafi said the first time he did it, it lasted twelve hours. So, you're good?"

"Really good. Do you think they'll let me take the test early? That way I can get to answering things while the spell is fresh?"

"Best to give it at least twenty minutes to seep all the way in," I said, feeling like I was talking about a new hair conditioner, not a powerful memory charm. "Then you can go test your little heart out."

I turned to leave, but Tobey stood, and before I could avoid it, he pulled me into a hug. "Thanks so much, Cassie."

I pushed out of the embrace. "Thank Rafi. Not me." I glanced at the clock. The Exam, Tobey's third and final try at it, was in thirty minutes. "We better get going. I'd wish you luck, but—" I tapped his head "—you're not going to need it."

It really was a gorgeous day. I suppose days seem sunnier and the weather more pleasant than ever before when you've just managed to save the world. Which is why Fiona, Alastair, Mr T, and I opted to wait outside the Academy while Tobey took his Exam. It was an hour since the test had begun, and we'd already seen seventeen of the twenty recruits file out. When the nineteenth test taker stepped out, shaking his head in defeat, Busby said, "It can't be a good sign that he's still in there."

"Poor Tobey. He's tried so hard," said Fiona. "Do you think HQ can find a spot for him? Maybe in records or as an administrative assistant or something?"

"I'm sure Olivia can find something for him," Alastair said encouragingly.

"I really thought it would work this time," I said.

"I'm sorry I was so hard on you," Busby told me. "You devoted quite a number of hours to helping Tobey, even amongst all this mess, and all I did was complain about you not helping enough."

"That's not exactly what I meant. I sort of did something to Tobey." I waggled my fingers. "I thought it would help."

"You aren't supposed to do magic on other people," Mr Tenpenny scolded. Which was true. With all the ups and downs of my power over the past six months, and especially the past few weeks, Dr Dunwiddle still wanted to make sure I was fully stable before I attempted anything on any living creatures. "You could have wiped his mind. Dear heavens," he groaned with sudden realization, "you *did* wipe his mind. That's why he's still in there—"

"Busby," said Fiona, putting a calming hand on her husband's forearm, even though she too was looking rather concerned for her step-grandson's mental state. Mr Tenpenny looked about to collapse with worry.

It was too much. I couldn't save the world only to kill off Busby Tenpenny.

"I didn't do any magic. I tricked him. Or thought I did. I made up that Rafi had invented some amazing memory spell that would last several hours. I also gave him one of Runa's control sample vials she fills with saline and told him it was my magic. I thought if Tobey believed he had some sort of boost, it would wipe away the test anxiety and give him the confidence to get through the Exams. The only magic I did was to shuffle my feet on the carpet so he felt some static electricity in his hair."

"That was very clever of you, Cassie," said Fiona. "And a creatively commendable effort on your part." She gave Busby a stern, don't-you-agree look.

"Yes, quite good," Mr T said without conviction. We then heard the door to the Academy *whoosh* open. Our attention immediately shifted from my questionably commendable trickery to Tobey slumping down the steps from the Academy's front entrance. His face was glum, and his hunched shoulders made him look five inches shorter and fifteen years older.

"Damn it," I muttered to myself.

"It's nothing to worry about," Mr T told Tobey, his voice shaky with emotion. "There are plenty of other options out there for you."

"I know," said Tobey morosely.

Mr T turned away and dabbed at his eyes, and as he did so I caught a slight twitch at the corner of Tobey's lips.

"You faker!" I shouted. Mr T and Fiona both started, Busby whipping around to scowl at me. But Tobey had lost all control over himself at that point and was grinning as broadly as four out of five dentists in a toothpaste ad. "You absolute faker! You passed, didn't you?"

"I did. I was the first one done, in fact," he said, putting on an air of faux haughtiness.

"Then why were you in there so long?" Alastair asked.

"I didn't want the others to feel bad. You always feel so stupid when someone finishes a test in half the time you do, so I waited around. I even wrote an essay on proper police procedure that the proctor said might be published in the Academy's newsletter next month."

"Well done, Tobey. Very well done," said Mr T, again wiping at his eyes, although this time he had a smile on his face.

"I think this calls for a trip to Spellbound, don't you?" suggested Alastair. "Daisy, Simon, and Chloe already have a table and a seven-layer Death by Chocolate cake reserved for us."

"Sounds perfect," said Fiona as she reached out for Tobey's hand. Alastair joined them, and as they headed off… well, they didn't exactly start skipping, but I think it was a near thing.

Busby Tenpenny remained back with me, a look of heartfelt gratitude softening his stern face.

"Thank you, Cassie. Sometimes you're cleverer than I could ever begin to imagine."

"Sometimes fooling yourself is the only path to success."

"I don't think that's going to replace *Keep Calm and Carry On* anytime soon."

"Give it time, Mr T. Give it time. Now, come on. There's cake waiting."

CHAPTER FIFTY
CHARACTER GROWTH

So that's how I saved the world and avoided getting killed by the bad guy, yet again. Not bad for a complete screw-up who can't control her magic, right?

According to the man himself (and the half a million photos he sent me), Mr Wood had a great time in the Cotswolds with Nigel and the ghosts. So much so, that once Mr Wood sold the funeral home (it's now an overpriced gastropub, go figure), he and Nigel decided to become roommates. They've also started a blog that somehow combines the silly side of bacon-based recipes and British history. As for Tilia and Nigel… well, it's a weird dynamic, but they seem to be hitting it off as well. Although, when he calls me each week, Mr Wood does comment on the disturbing sounds he sometimes hears at night.

The magic in my parents' cells seems to be sticking. It's also providing another area of study for Dr Dunwiddle's ever expanding to-research list. After an intervention with me, Busby, Runa, and Olivia, they've agreed to still do field work, but only field work that doesn't involve encounters with known killers. Still, their latest case, one involving a doping scandal at The Pacific Northwest Flying Cat Association, has me worried. I mean, have you seen a flying cat enthusiast when his kitty gets disqualified? It's not healthy, that's all I'll say.

And speaking of health, my parents are now doing sports. Namely, my dad coaching the Rosaria Rascals softball team, and my mom taking the mound as their star pitcher. Unfortunately, there aren't any other Magic softball teams yet, and the Norm teams the Rascals compete against just can't seem to outplay the physics of an enchanted softball. I can't complain too much, though, since every win means I get to attend a team party at Spellbound Patisserie.

Don't worry, my clumsy limbs aren't actually swinging bats or running bases, but since Pablo is the team mascot, as his owner, I get to join in the pastry-filled celebrations.

As for the missing Magics, all of whom are now no longer missing, the absorbing capsules that were found in the places they were being held have been tested to find out which capsule contained whose power. A drawn-out process, to be sure, but it means each Magic can be returned to full magical health with their own magic.

Runa and Olivia have now reinstated their plans for their Harry Potter Theme Park trips. This has included not only booking rooms and reserving rental cars, but has also involved selecting which animatronics in each park will be best to throw a little magic something-something at to wow the kids and scare the bejesus out of the park workers.

Sebastian and Rafi have also been spending more time together. Which is worrisome. Think about it... Sebastian's ancient guardian spirit power plus Rafi's mischievous elf magic and creative spell crafting? It's only a matter of time before they conjure up some trouble. And I just know who's going to get called in to fix it.

As for other couples, Tobey proposed to Daisy the very day he passed his Exams. Which was good since she'd already written that exact date for their engagement in *An Enchanted History of the Portland Community.* What was less good was her proclamation when she bubbled into the agency the following morning.

"We're going to be related!" she'd enthused as she bounded through the door with far too much cheerleader glee for eight o'clock in the morning. For any time of day, really.

"Only by marriage. And only just barely. I'm not even sure there's such a thing as a third-cousin-in-law."

"But there is, and *you* are going to be my favorite one."

"Lucky me," I had grumbled.

As for Morelli, as part of his budding relationship with Matilda, he's agreed to care for Caliban while she's away. To make room for what I'm told is only a mid-sized dragon, he's Expanded the front garden to its limit to accommodate the beast. And let me tell you, when dog walkers stride by, their pets get very nervous and they can't figure out why "Mocha, who always behaves like an angel on a leash" is suddenly tucking her tail and vigorously tugging to drag their owner up the block as quickly as possible. Caliban finds it amusing. Morelli finds it amusing. I just hope no one walks their pet cow past the building.

As a show of our new and very-weird-for-me friendship, the day the agency's window finally got my name added to it, Morelli came by with a crochet frame for my license. (Which is yet to arrive, by the way. Something about courier import tariffs. Damn bureaucracy.)

"Congratulations, Black," said Morelli. "You did good."

"I made a mess of things, then I bumbled around trying to clean up that mess."

"Yeah, but the mess wasn't entirely your fault. The prophecy."

"Merlin's balls, I hate prophecies. Are there any more about me?"

"Not my department."

"But I'm sure you know people in that department. People who owe you a favor, perhaps?"

"Yeah, owe *me* a favor, not you," Morelli had said as he looked over my desk. "Speaking of, that was only a loaner, but I'll let you keep it. Consider it a belated agency-warming gift."

"The desk?" I'd been pretty sure that had been my parents'.

"Nah, the chair."

"This is *your* chair?" Morelli looked at me, and I didn't like the impish glint in his eyes. "I should have known. Did you charm it against me?"

"Not saying yes, not saying no. Could be it's just got discerning tastes in backsides."

"I'm going to pretend I didn't hear that. And take it home with you. I can't work with something that prefers your backside to mine."

As for Alastair and I, we're also back on track, and he's agreed that from now on I will give the final nod for any and every commission he receives or project he comes up with. The world's likely a safer place already.

Penley Tremaine, possibly trying to cash in on our newfound fame, offered to stock Alastair's timers once again. Alastair politely refused since his online Elfsy shop has already proved a wild success. Oh, and that automaton he was working on in Rafi's office? That was what he'd been hiding in the workroom all those months. Both it and the cage had tricky tension issues, as evidenced by my death-by-flying-arm near miss a few chapters ago.

Also, I wasn't wrong about the thing's romantic gesture. Not long after we returned from London, I was having my morning tea when the automaton (arm now restored and far less deadly) walked up to me, went down on one knee, and held out a ring.

Not *the* ring, mind you. Without any goading from me, Alastair and his grandmother decided the best place for the Cecil ring was in the middle of the Pacific. To keep the *something old* aspect in play, she gave him another ring. Not an antique, but one she'd bought from the Sears catalog when Alastair was eighteen. I've had it on my ring finger for over a month, and so far it's showing no signs of sentience or evil, but I'm still not letting down my guard around the thing.

As Leo Flourish had promised, soon after the bad guy battle, the *Herald* ran a full retraction for everything that had been printed about me over the past several weeks, an explanation of why the pieces had been written (including his own blame in the matter), and then a glowing article about my role in taking down Matthew Hopkins.

Leo didn't specifically recommend my agency, but apparently my new celebrity status was tough for people to resist, and I've suddenly found myself with a gob of cases. Thankfully, none of them have involved missing jewels. A lot of missing pets, though. Which does have me concerned for Magics' ability to properly care for their cats, dogs, parrots, and iguanas.

About a week after the retraction article, the *Herald's* front page featured a sizable congratulatory note to "Dr Torres of the Oregon Historical Society for winning the grand prize in Magical Historical Research for his paper on the Boncoeur Jewel." Professor Dodding (who turned out to be the only judge of this prestigious award) was quoted as saying, "The discoveries were so interesting, the writing so engaging, I was so engrossed I completely forgot to drink my hot chocolate."

And while I was sure Dr Torres would enjoy his lifetime supply of chocolate bars, all this great news crumbled to dust when I saw the article right below the award announcement.

As she mentioned earlier, Mayor Matilda Marheart had to

temporarily relinquish her duties as mayor to go be Queen of the Vampires. Normally, this would mean the person who came in second in the mayoral race would take over. But since the Council had barred Oberlin from holding any official titles for the next decade, the mayoral title fell to the race's third runner-up.

Which was why, before I'd even had a chance to be horrified, my ears were nearly destroyed by a squeal of joy and Daisy exclaiming, "Oh, my golly! Can you believe it? I'm mayor! Mayor Daisy Honeysuckle!"

Even worse? I was too stunned to dodge the hug she threw around me. A hug I squirmed my way out of as soon as my senses returned.

Proving that character growth does have its limits.

* * *

Be sure to turn the page for a little behind-the-scenes peek at the story behind the story, as well as a couple bonus chapters that didn't quite fit to the book.... See you there!

BEHIND THE STORY
IT ALWAYS INVOLVES A PODCAST

Holy hexes! I've made it through the trilogy! *You've* made it through the trilogy! And I hope you enjoyed it. If you did, and if you're familiar with how I "roll" (as the cool kids say… they do still say that, right? I am so *not* cool…) this is where you'll be expecting some behind-the-scenes fun. Well, here we go…

As I mentioned in *The Unusual Mayor Marheart*, these books started out as a simple story about Wordsworth losing a book. But hey, why keep things simple when you can make them so complicated your brain might break at any moment? Actually, I think it did break a few times. That's what SuperGlue is for, right?

Sorry, wait, my doctor just said brain repair via ingesting SuperGlue is a no-no, and that I should get to the Emergency Room ASAP. I'm sure he meant as soon as I finish this little letter to my wonderful readers.

Anyway, the simple lost-book idea turned into the broken-apart-jewel idea, which then turned into the vampires-being-up-to-no-good idea. But the deeper I got into that notion, the more I felt that making vampires the bad guys was just too obvious.

But I couldn't think of another bad guy to throw in the mix. I mean, Werewolves vs. Vampires seemed so *Twilight*, and I couldn't bear to go down that sparkly road.

Then one day, I was listening to a podcast (actually, I have a slight podcast addiction… I wonder if that's tied to all the SuperGlue I've ingested?). The podcast was called *Scoundrel*, and it's unfortunately no longer putting out new episodes, but one of the last tales they told was all about Matthew Hopkins, Witch Hunter Extraordinaire.

Although I play with his timeline and his influence with the monarchy a tad bit, Matthew Hopkins really did exist from 1620 to 1647. A very short life, but one during which he was behind the executions of about 300 witches, most of them women. According to Professor Wikipedia, that's **more than the combined total** of people killed by witch hunters in the 150 years prior to Hopkins's career. Because, if you're going to be a misogynist psychopath, you should strive to be the very best misogynist psychopath out there.

Anyway, Hopkins's story is truly fascinating (and disturbing), so I highly recommend you look him up yourself. If you do, or if you're a big ol' historian smarty pants, you'll notice he would have only been five years old when King James I of England died. I know Hopkins was ambitious, but maybe not *that* ambitious. However, it worked better for connecting James's and Elizabeth's courts to the jewels to have Hopkins active while James I was alive. So, apologies to all the historians who were screaming at me for the past few hundred pages.

It also worked well to have Hopkins tied to James I because King James was… well, *confused* might be the right word. He not only feared and despised witches (seems he might have had issues with women, but I'll leave the psychoanalyzing to people who don't ingest SuperGlue to repair their brains), but he was also very curious about magic. He even wrote an entire book about magic and sorcery and necromancy and all that good stuff.

Of course, he made sure to hide his fascination with magic by endorsing the grand old sport of witch hunting. Which I think takes place after a bit of fox hunting... after all, if you're going to get dressed up to kill things, might as well make a day of it, right?

So that's how Matthew Hopkins came into play, how the witch hunters became the bad guys, and how the vampires ended up being the non-sparkly good guys.

As for the photographer, well, I have to admit I stole that story line straight out of *Sherlock* (the recent version with Martin Freeman and Benedict Cumberbatch). There's an episode where (spoiler alert) a wedding photographer ends up being the baddie and gets away with murderous things because "no one notices the photographer." I loved that idea. Plus, I really liked having someone capturing all of Cassie's pratfalls.

Is there more I could ramble on about regarding this second trilogy? Definitely, but I don't want to keep you too long past The End. Also, I really ought to get to that Emergency Room since I think the SuperGlue is starting to do some strange things. Unless it's normal for your eyelids to be permanently glued open?

Is there more for Cassie? I honestly don't know. These past three books of hers were written during some of the absolute worst times of my life (which is not a SuperGlue-induced exaggeration), making the complicated story lines even harder to suss out and the writing process like slogging through frozen mud.

There were several times when I thought I wouldn't be able to pull this off, there were several times when it took every ounce of effort to fight past the mental agony I was in to edit a page or two, and there were several times where I wanted to push Cassie off my version of the Reichenbach Falls so I wouldn't have to write another story with her in it ever again.

(If you don't get the Reichenbach Falls reference, Sir Arthur Conan Doyle used them as a way to kill off Sherlock Holmes because he was so sick of writing stories about the great detective. Fans got whiny, so he reluctantly brought Sherlock back. What a pushover!)

I'm slowly moving toward a better place (too slowly... the SuperGlue may be hindering my progress), but I'm still not sure about more Cassie books just yet. I have a ton of other stories I want to get to, including more from Duncan the Detecting Dragon (the bumbling, omelet-addicted star of **The Circus of Unusual Creatures** humorous cozy mysteries).

However, if you raise enough of a hullabaloo, I might be a pushover myself and reconsider Cassie's future. Or perhaps you'd like to see a spin-off series where one of the other characters is the center of attention. If so, don't be shy about contacting me and letting me know. Of course, you may also have to invent the seventy-five-hour day so I have time to write all these books, but you're amazing, so I'm sure you can manage that.

Anyway, I really should see about getting this SuperGlue out of my system. In the meantime, if you enjoyed this story (or any of my stories) it would mean the world to me if you could leave a review at the website of your favorite book retailer, Goodreads, or Bookbub.

Or, even better, tell a friend or two how much they'll like the Cassie Black Trilogies. Then, every time you see them, belligerently pester them until they cave in and start reading Cassie's snarky and silly misadventures. I would also be perfectly fine with you erecting a billboard emblazoned with "The Cassie Black Books Are THE BEST!" on a highly trafficked highway in your area. Just a suggestion.

Finally, more books are under construction as we speak (or

whatever this is), so if you want to keep up-to-date about when my next book is coming out, get a silly personal story every month, discover what books I'm enjoying, and see pictures of my cats, then please please please do sign up for my monthly newsletter at *www.subscribepage.com/mrsmorris* (all lower case).

Cheers and thanks for joining me on this wild ride! And to all of you who sent encouraging words along the way, a BIG THANKS to you… I honestly couldn't have done it without you.

—Tammie
February 2025

Freebie P.S. If you'd like to see a pair of chapters that didn't quite fit into the book, but that I couldn't bring myself to abandon, please visit
https://tammiepainter.com/a-cassie-black-bonus

Sales-y P.S. If you'd like to spend some more time with Sebastian at Bookman's Bookshop, please check out my novella **The Unwanted Inheritance of the Bookman Brothers.**

ALSO BY TAMMIE PAINTER

The Humorous stuff

THE CIRCUS OF UNUSUAL CREATURES

Hoard It All Before, Tipping the Scales, Fangs a Million, Beast or Famine

It's not every day you meet an amateur sleuth with fangs. If you like comic fantasy whodunits that mix in laughs in with murderous mayhem and mythical beasts, you'll love The Circus of Unusual Creatures.

THE CASSIE BLACK TRILOGY

The Undead Mr. Tenpenny, The Uncanny Raven Winston, The Untangled Cassie Black, The Unusual Mayor Marheart

Work at a funeral home can be mundane. Until you accidentally start bringing the dead to life.

THE UNWANTED INHERITANCE OF THE BOOKMAN BROTHERS

A novella celebrating the magic of books. Wills often come with unexpected surprises. This one especially so.

THE GREAT ESCAPE

Peculiar pet shops. Troublesome dream homes. And robot vacuums that just want to be free Looking for a captivating (and quick) escape from reality? These fifteen tales of humor, myth, magic provide just that.

The Serious Stuff

THE OSTERIA CHRONICLES

The Trials of Hercules, The Voyage of Heroes, The Maze of Minos, The Bonds of Osteria, The Battle of Ares, The Return of Odysseus

Myths and heroes may be reborn, but the whims of the gods never change. A six-book mythological fantasy adventure

DOMNA

The Sun God's Daughter, The Solon's Son, The Centaur's Gamble, The Regent's Edict, The Forgotten Heir, The Solon's Wife

Destiny isn't given. It's made by cunning, endurance, and, at times, bloodshed. A six-part historical fantasy tale filled with passion, political intrigue, rivalry, and betrayal.

THERE'S MORE...

To see all my currently available books and short stories, just scan the QR code or visit books.bookfunnel.com/tammiepainterbooks

MY NEXT BOOK
IS COMING SOON!

In fact, it might already be here by the time you read this, and there's probably been loads of exciting stuff you've missed out on. You know, like photos of my cats.

Anyway, I love staying in touch with my readers, so if you'd like to…

- Keep up-to-date with my writing news,
- Chat with me about books you love (and maybe those you hate),
- Receive the random free short story or exclusive discount now and then,
- And be among the first to learn about my new releases

…then please do sign up for my monthly newsletter.

As a thank you for signing up, you'll get my short story *Mrs. Morris Meets Death* — a humorously, death-defying tale of time management, mistaken identities, cruise ships…. and romance novels.

Join in on the fun today by heading to www.subscribepage.com/mrsmorris

ABOUT THE AUTHOR
THAT'S ME...TAMMIE PAINTER

Many moons ago I was a scientist in a neuroscience lab where I got to play with brains and illegal drugs.

Now, I take wickedly strong tea and turn it into comic fantasy whodunits full of mythical misfits and magical mishaps that I hope give you a giggle.

When I'm not creating worlds or killing off characters, I can be found gardening, planning my next travel adventure, concocting some sort of mess in the kitchen, or working as an unpaid servant to three cats and some very aggressive squirrels.

The quick-as-you-can story behind my books...

My fascination for myths, history, and how they interweave inspired my two historical fantasy series, The Osteria Chronicles and Domna.

But all those ancient myths and angst-ridden heroes got a bit too serious for someone with a strange sense of humor and odd way of looking at the world.

So, while sitting at my grandmother's funeral, my brain came up with an idea for a contemporary fantasy novel that's filled with magic, mystery, wry humor, and the dead who just won't stay dead. That idea turned into The Cassie Black Trilogy.

My latest humorous fantasy series, The Circus of Unusual Creatures, features cozy mysteries full of silly situations, confounding clues, oodles of omelets, and a detecting dragon.

You can learn more at *TammiePainter.com* or at that QR code, where you'll find probably more info than you could ever want or need.

Printed in Dunstable, United Kingdom